FIRE'S HAND FATE'S HEART

LINDSEY BROUNSTEIN

Cover design by MiblArt

Map by Cartographybird Maps

Editing by Between the Lines Editorial

First edition 2024

ISBN 978-1-964237-01-5 (paperback)

ISBN 978-1-964237-02-2 (hardcover)

ISBN 978-1-964237-00-8 (ebook)

www.lindseybrounstein.com

Content Warnings

Thank you for your interest in *Fire's Hand, Fate's Heart*, book one of the Five Fates series. This is a fantasy novel intended for readers 18 years and older. It contains strong language and violence. Specific content warnings are listed below. If you'd rather not see the content warnings, you can skip this page.

This story includes themes and descriptions of events that may not be suitable for everyone. These include:

- blood and physical violence

- murder of teens and adults

- mention of child abuse and neglect

- mention of amputation

- suicidal thoughts

- alcohol consumption

- death of a loved one

- grief

- panic attacks and anxiety

If at any point—including right now—you need to put the book down (whether for a little while or forever), please do so. Take care of yourself, friend.

THE KNOWN WORLD
MAPPED IN THE PRESENT AGE
CAPITAL CITIES
MINOR CITIES
NOTABLE TOWNS
SNOWFELD
THE WILDS
LOSTWARD
ARMATHAIN
WHITEHOLLOW
VALDA
CLOUD BAY
AETHERAN REACH
PORT MERRICK
THE CRESCENT MOUNTAINS
AETHIR
WESTHOLD
GOETH
THE MISTVALE MOUNTAINS
WERYN
FORDRYN
THE SOUTHERN ISLES
NEOMA

PYRRAH
EMBERCLIFF
KIREKWALL
THE MOONTIDE SEA
KYLERIA
BREMMARAN
RAVENSPORT
FALLWOOD
BROOKSHIRE
THE RED FOREST
DRAHKONIA
FINNEGAN'S FORDE
SOUTHREACH
TAERNFANE
SOUTHPORT

Pronunciation Guide

Aetherann: AY-ther-ahn
Aethir: AY-theer
Aethirian: ay-THEER-ee-an
Ainam: EYE-num
Bremmaran: BREM-mer-ahn
Corvin: COR-vin
Drahkon: DRAH-kon
Drahkonia: drah-KOHN-ee-ah
Drystan Serra: DRIS-ten SAIR-uh
Gregor Thalesen: GRE-ger THAL-eh-sen
Jaelyn Aleissandra: jay-LIN al-ay-SAHN-drah
Lanara: lah-NAH-rah
Lucien Longshadow: LOO-shin LONG-shad-oh
Pyrannis: pie-RAH-nis
Taerna: TARE-nah
Taernfane: TARE-in-fane
Tanithe: TAN-ith
Tykaras: ty-KAHR-us
Valda: VAHL-dah
Verity Corallan: VAIR-i-tee COR-uh-lahn
Vire: VY-er

For my griffins, Daniel and Dominic.
With all my love.

Prologue

I wake to you shaking me, whispering my name. Your strong hands on my shoulders rouse me, but it's the urgency in your voice that grips my attention. I have to follow you, you tell me. Something's happened and it's not safe. You're going to get me out. You promise that you'll protect me.

For a moment I wonder if you're playing a trick on me. Nothing ever happens here. Most of your fellow soldiers in the Aethirian army view being assigned to the College of Magi as a joke—guarding a bunch of spoiled, rich kids in the middle of the Mistvale Mountains. The only thing threatening our safety out here is our own hubris. And besides, I've made your life difficult for the last year, because I think I'm better than you. And I've worked hard to make sure you know that.

But something *has* happened. I follow you into the darkened corridor in my nightgown. I don't even grab my shoes. Your sword is out and your other hand extends toward me, shielding me and keeping me behind you as we move through the dormitory. Screams and clanging metal echo from other parts of the building. You duck into a room and pull me inside. I don't realize what you're doing. I wait by the door, idly wondering why the floor is wet. I turn to ask you, but before I can say anything, you are by my side again, ushering me from the room with a firm hand on my back. You don't let me look toward the bed. It's too late, you say. We have to move.

You lead me through the halls to another part of the school. I'm not even sure where we are. The screaming has all but stopped. I wonder what the odds are that the silence is a good sign. As we round a corner, you stop so suddenly that I run into you, but with my thin build, I don't think you notice. You curse under your breath, and when I look ahead of you, I see why. Five men block our path.

I have to stay behind you, you tell me. The men are wearing matching armor and tunics of red and gold. Soldiers. Why are there soldiers at the College? Are they here to help us? But no, their colors don't match the blue and silver of your Aethirian army tunic.

The men move forward together. You shove me around the corner and yell for me to run. I sprint the way we came, your boots echoing on the stone floor behind me. Knowing you're with me gives me the strength to keep running. There are more shouts. I burst through a doorway into a small training space. I skid to a stop, my bare feet scraping against the rough stone. Three soldiers stand around a fallen body—a young man in pants and no shirt, lying on his stomach. He's facing away from me. I don't know if I know him, but his blood is pooling on the floor, running in tiny rivers along the mortar between each slab of stone.

Faster than I can process what I'm seeing, you're behind me, your hand sliding around my waist. You pull me back, but the shouts from behind us are just on the other side of the door, so you step in front of me, your sword up to keep the men at bay. Your body presses me against the stone wall, shielding me, and the scent of your sweat fills my nose.

The soldiers crowd around us. There are eight of them, now that the five chasing us have caught up. The room is not that big, and they're blocking the exit. Some of them are grinning as I peer over your broad shoulders, one hand pressed against the taut muscles of your back.

There are too many of them. The fight is over before it starts. You hold them off for a moment, but your back is against the wall—against me—from the start. You slice one across the arm, even without much room to maneuver. The soldier cries out and falls back, but another takes his place. The mace he carries, heavy and spiked, knocks your sword out of the way, shattering it against the wall. The broken pieces clatter to the floor.

Another soldier lunges, driving his blade into your chest. There's a crack of bone, and I know it's the sound of your ribs breaking. You start to fall. I slide my hands under your arms to hold you up, but you're too heavy. We both fall to the ground. Your shoulders lay in my lap as I cradle your head in my pale arms.

The soldiers laugh. You look up at me, and I realize everything I've done wrong. My magic. I could have bent the light to make us disappear. I could have shielded you. But I didn't. I couldn't. Because I panicked, they found us. They hurt you. And now the one thing that's needed is the one thing magic can't do.

I can't heal you.

I can't staunch the bleeding or mend your broken bones. Only priests of Ainam can work those sorts of miracles and, even then, only some. I'm no priestess. I'm scarcely a mage, and so now you're dying in my lap. My vision blurs, tears streaming down my face to fall in your dark, disheveled hair.

What's your name? I beg you. All this time, all these months of seeing you every day, of tormenting you for no reason other than because you were there, and I realize in this moment, as I'm covered in your blood, that I don't know your name. *What's your name?*

But your dark eyes are staring somewhere past me. Your chest is no longer rising and falling with your breath.

You're gone.

The soldiers are still laughing as I push myself out from under you. My fingers find the hilt of your sword. Even with only half a blade, I can barely lift it. The sight of me, a scrawny teenage girl in my bloodied nightclothes, struggling to lift a broken sword, amuses them even more.

The leather of the hilt, warm from your grip, scratches against the palm of my hand. You died for *me*. Protecting *me*. There's a scalding pain in my chest, and I reach down through it, past it, into the reserve of power in the center of my being. I open myself wide to that power, letting it fill me more than I knew was possible. The serenity that fills me in that moment might scare me if I let myself think about it for too long. So instead I focus on the rote movements, the memorized words, the incantation to harden the air in front of me and force them back. But I change the calculation. I improvise one key piece of the movements, overriding my muscle memory. I will make them pay.

I will make them *burn* for what they've done.

A wall of fire erupts from my hand, exploding outward with a force beyond anything I could have imagined. The soldiers are incinerated where they stand,

and my own screams are drowned out by the grinding crash of stone as the whole building comes down on us all.

CHAPTER 1

WEAVING THROUGH ONE OF Valda's bustling market squares, Dare's boots were nearly silent against the cobblestones. The breeze off the bay scented everything vaguely of sea salt and was stronger in this part of the city, which overlooked the enormous expanse of the docks. The tall masts and huge sails in all the colors of the rainbow could be seen from the square, and the setting sun gilded everything as though it had been sprinkled with gold dust. Dare ignored it all as he made his way to the Raven and Hart.

He removed a small metal flask from his pocket, its finish stained and tarnished. To his left, a woman scolded her young child for running off into the crowded streets. To his right, a man in finely tailored clothing was eying a large necklace adorned with massive jewels at a merchant's stall. As Dare's fingers moved to the stopper of his flask, he stumbled over a loose cobblestone and jostled the man, who nearly dropped the necklace.

"Watch it!" the man shouted.

Dare righted himself and brushed some street dust off the man's spotless coat. "Sorry 'bout that, sir."

The man batted Dare's hand away, taking a step back as though worried he might catch something. Dare suspected that perhaps his travel-worn clothes and threadbare cloak might give the man a certain impression. Certainly the fact that he hadn't washed his hair in a while didn't help. And when had he shaved last?

"Drunkard," the man muttered, turning back to the merchant with a huff.

Dare sketched a quick bow and turned on his heels. "Ainam bless you, sir," he said cheerfully.

"Vire take you," the man cursed back.

Dare was around the corner and nearly to the Raven and Hart before he pocketed his flask— still unopened—and withdrew a small velvet coin pouch. It had a pleasant jingle as he weighed it in his palm. He transferred the contents to the pouch on his belt before letting the velvet purse slip from his fingers and onto the dirty street.

The Raven and Hart Tavern perched on a small hill that overlooked the market square and much of the bay below. It was one of many taverns and inns in the great city of Valda, but Dare liked this one in particular for its entertainment, ale, and discretion, though not necessarily in that order. He pushed open the wooden door at the front and was instantly greeted with warmth, raucous laughter, and the smell of roasting meat.

At a table on the other side of the tavern, Dare spotted three of the familiar wine-colored cloaks of the Crimson Brothers. Even from the door he recognized Caleb Tarneth. The solid wall of a man stood out in most situations. On one side of him was Finn Garrison, her golden blond hair and slight stature a stark contrast to Caleb. Dare couldn't tell who was with them, their back to the door.

As Dare made his way over, Caleb reached toward Finn's leg, though she stood at the same moment and took her presumably empty tankard to the bar for a refill. Caleb's hand stopped in midair and was withdrawn with the slightest hint of embarrassment.

As she reached the bar, Dare slid himself into the chair she had just vacated. He smiled across the table to the third member of their little company and realized too late that it was Almestra Dirigen.

Ah, shit.

Almestra shot him a look in return, her dark eyes nothing but embers of rage. She flipped her black curls over her shoulder. "What the fuck do you want?" she sneered.

Caleb leaned back in his chair, crossing his arms over his broad chest. Amusement played across the hardened lines of his face.

"Afternoon to you too, Almestra, dear," Dare cooed. She gave him a vulgar gesture, and he laughed outright. "What did I do to you this time?"

"She's mad at you," Caleb interjected, "for snaking the Tyrian job out from under her last week."

Dare threw his hands up, perfectly posed innocence. "It's not my fault the contract wasn't exclusive." A hint of a smile tugged at his mouth. "Or that I'm a better thief than you." He leaned his head to the side, avoiding the mug she threw at him. Thankfully it was empty. It would have been a terrible waste of ale otherwise.

"Stop tormenting her," said a cheerful voice beside him, accompanied by a playful punch in the shoulder.

Dare glanced up at Finn. "Me, tormenting *her*?" He tried to sound incredulous, but Finn simply rolled her eyes and slid into the empty chair between Dare and Almestra. "Fine, fine," Dare said. "I'm sorry, Almestra. Let me buy you a drink." After a pause, he couldn't help himself and added, "After all, I seem to have come into some coin recently."

"Go to hell," she spat.

"Which one?"

"Take your pick."

"Alright, that's enough," barked Caleb, dropping his hand down on the table.

Finn laughed into her mug, but Almestra pushed herself up from the table, knocking her chair over backward.

"Where are you going?" Caleb asked. "Don't let this asshole run you out."

At the same time, Finn piped up, "I thought you were hungry."

"I lost my appetite," Almestra growled over her shoulder. She stormed out of the tavern.

"Vire's demons, Dare, why do you always have to be such a shit?" Caleb grumbled. He ran a hand through his dark, short-cropped hair.

"It's just part of my natural charm," Dare said, flagging down a young serving girl and gesturing for an ale. "Besides, I can't help it if she doesn't have a sense of humor."

"She's going to slit your throat one of these days," Caleb muttered, "and I'm not going to stop her."

Finn set her mug down on the table and studied Dare for a moment before saying, "So what's all this about?"

Caleb snorted into his drink.

"What's all *what* about?" Dare asked, raising an eyebrow.

Finn waved her hand at him, encompassing everything from his greasy hair to his worn brown boots. "*This,*" she said emphatically. "This whole prince of paupers look. What is that?"

Dare leaned back in his chair. "I just got off a job," he said, trying to sound stern, but he knew his amusement was showing through. He let it. "Three days in the Downs. I'd like to see how *you'd* look after that."

Finn cringed, her slender nose crinkling as she shook her head. Little wisps of hair fell from where they'd been precariously set behind her ears. "Fine, that's fair," she said. "But what about the cloak?"

His hands ran along the thin fabric of the midnight blue cloak. "What about it?"

"Why don't I ever see you wearing the Crimson Brothers' cloak?"

The serving girl brought a mug of ale over for Dare, and he took it with a smile, handing the girl a coin. He took a long swig before answering. "With some jobs, it's helpful for the world to know you're a sword for hire." He gestured vaguely at Caleb. "So they know what they're dealing with. And other jobs, it's helpful for the world *not* to know what they're dealing with."

Finn angled her head, considering his words. "Do you ever take the first kind?"

"Not if he can help it," Caleb scoffed.

Dare ignored the implied insult and simply smiled. Caleb was a hammer and thought every job was a nail. "I've been commissioned with the Brothers long enough to have the luxury of that choice."

He marked the gleam of envy in Finn's amber eyes. She was still too junior to get to pick and choose the jobs she did for the Brothers. All new recruits had to work with a commander for at least a year, sometimes longer, while they learned the ropes and honed their skills. It was important to ensure they'd be assets to the Brothers rather than a hindrance. Finn had already been with the Crimson Brothers for almost two years, if Dare's memory held true.

"Don't start daydreaming," Caleb grumbled. He finished the ale in his mug and slammed it down hard on the table. "You'll get there when you're good an' ready."

"And when will that be?" Finn demanded.

"When I say so."

Finn's hands balled into fists. The girl looked barely older than twenty and was ready to start a fight with her commander, who was quite literally twice her size. It was bold, which Dare could appreciate, but it wasn't smart. He wondered, not for the first time, if Finn knew what she'd gotten herself into by joining the Brothers.

"Finn," Dare said, pulling her attention. Once he had it, he held it with an easy smile. "What're you drinking?" He turned his smile to Caleb. "Both of you. Next round's on me."

❁

Tempers eased as the ale flowed, which was later supplemented by food—the roasted meat Dare had smelled upon entering the tavern turned out to be wild boar—and a bit more ale. Once night had securely settled through the city, Finn pushed her chair back from the table.

"I better head home." A slight wobble as she stood was the only sign of how much alcohol she'd consumed over the last several hours. That, and the rosy tint to her cheeks.

Caleb stretched, arching his back with more than one audible pop, and rose. Dare stood quickly—maybe a little too quickly—and set a hand on the table to steady himself as the room swayed.

Finn giggled. "Too much to drink, Dare?" she teased. Standing beside him, the top of her head only came up to his shoulder.

Dare smirked down at her. "You're not one to talk right now, Fionna." His smile widened as her face shifted from amusement to outrage.

"Don't call me that." She slugged him in the shoulder, far less playful this time than when he first arrived. It sent an ache through the muscle, and Dare rubbed at the point of impact.

Good form . . .

"Let's go," Caleb said, far louder than he needed to. Half the tavern turned to look at the group, and Dare had to suppress a groan. Caleb reached a meaty hand out for Finn's elbow, aiming to lead her toward the door, but Finn started out before he could touch her.

"You're heading back to the House, right?" Dare asked, halting her. All the junior members who still worked with commanders were required to live at one of the chapter houses within the city until they became full-fledged members. When Finn nodded, Dare said, "I've gotta pick something up from there anyway." He turned to Caleb. "I'll make sure she gets back."

Caleb's eyes, glazed from drinking, wandered over Finn, lingering a little too long before he narrowed his gaze on Dare. The warmth of the alcohol Dare had drunk made everything just a little easier to tolerate, including Caleb, so he simply smiled.

With a grunt that Dare chose to interpret as begrudging acquiescence, Caleb left without so much as a wave over his shoulder.

When Dare turned back to Finn, she was glaring at him. "What?" He put his hands up, mildly worried she was thinking of punching him again.

"I don't need a babysitter," she said, and left.

Dare dropped a coin on the table for the server and followed her out. "I didn't say you did. I need to grab something I left at the House."

Outside the Raven and Hart, the shops and stalls nearby had closed for the night, tucking their wares safe inside. A few people still wandered along the streets, but the bustle of the afternoon had faded smoothly into the quiet of night. The wind coming up the bluffs from the sea was the only thing still moving at the same frenzied pace as earlier in the day. Dare pulled up the hood of his cloak as Finn headed northeast toward the guild district, not waiting for him.

"I'll make sure she gets back." She repeated his own words in a deep, awkward tone that he could only assume was a representation of how he sounded.

Dare fell into step beside her. "You would have preferred Caleb? I mean, I know he's quite the charmer . . ."

Finn snorted. "I don't need either of you. It's a quarter mile to the House."

While the independent city of Valda was massive, sprawling, and dangerous, a slightly tipsy nighttime stroll certainly wasn't beyond Finn's capabilities.

Dare gave her cloak a gentle tug. "Caleb likes to think of this as armor," he said quietly. "Someone sees you're a Brother, and they'll think twice before starting shit. And he's not wrong. But sometimes, people see a Brother walking alone at night, wavering a little in their steps, and they see an easy mark that'll improve their reputation with the right people. Sometimes, that cloak *is* armor. But sometimes, it's a target."

Finn was quiet for a long moment before she said, "You let Caleb walk home alone."

"Yeah, well, I don't like Caleb."

She laughed. "He tends to bring that out in people."

Before long, the wide, gray stone facade of the Crimson Brothers' chapter house came into view. "Thanks for the company," Finn said with a smile as they reached the door.

Dare bowed, though he swayed a little as he straightened. He caught Finn suppressing a chuckle. "I should say the same," he said.

As he turned to leave, Finn cleared her throat. "Didn't you say you needed to pick something up?"

Dare smiled tightly. The windows of the House were mostly dark with only a few lanterns lit inside for those who might be coming or going during these later hours. "It's late." With a gesture past the House in the same direction they'd been walking, he added, "I'm just going to head home."

Finn followed the wave of his hand. "You live that way?"

"Yeah, it's not far."

"Alright," she said, heading for the door. "Good night."

"Good night, Finn." Dare walked for two more blocks before he turned right down a narrow street and then right again, back the way they'd come.

CHAPTER 2

ALTHOUGH IT WAS LATE by the time Dare passed the Raven and Hart again on his way home, equal parts music and laughter floated from within the tavern and spilled into the quiet streets. He continued on to the flat he rented above a café a few blocks away, but he wasn't quite ready for his night to end. Not after three days stuck on the streets in the Downs. Some music, another pint, and, if he found himself in luck, someone to distract him for the rest of the evening might be just what he needed. *After* a quick wash and a change of clothes. Getting the grime off him sounded almost as enticing as the rest of the nightly activities he was now looking forward to.

As he reached the stairs that led up the side of the café to his flat, the sound of heavy boots behind him raised the hairs on the back of his neck.

"You're summoned to the Council," was all the man said.

Shit.

Dare turned, plastering a smile on his face. Pyris Helm, captain of the city guard and right hand to the Valdane Council, approached him, a guardsman on either side. He didn't look pleased as he closed the distance to Dare and crossed his arms over his immense chest, all sinew and corded muscle.

Dare tried to ignore the fact that this man's forearms were each roughly the size of his own thigh and kept the smile firmly in place. "Pyris," he crooned. "I'm surprised you don't have better things to do with your time than interrupt my evening." He cast a glance over his shoulder at the stairs. "It's late. Can't this wait until the morning?"

Pyris snorted his displeasure. "I *do* have better things to do. But it seems the Council deems it necessary to send me to wrangle your sorry ass. Apparently you have a habit of dodging their messengers. And my guards." His deep voice rumbled down the nearly empty street. "And no, it can't wait. You are summoned to the Council."

The nine members of the Valdane Council ruled the city-state of Valda and answered to no one. And they'd been making Dare's life hell lately. "Ainam's shining bollocks, Pyris—"

"Don't blaspheme at me," he bellowed. He hadn't moved his arms and yet each muscle seemed to threaten Dare with grievous bodily harm all at once. "You are summoned."

Dare gestured to the stairs. "Can I at least change my clothes first?"

"Now."

"Fuck's sake—"

"*Now!*"

"Alright, alright," Dare said, raising his arms in casual defensiveness. "Don't get all huffy."

Pyris Helm, arms still crossed in a most threatening manner, stepped to one side to allow Dare to pass. The two guardsmen led the way to a carriage, with Pyris falling into step just a little too close behind him.

After an hour, the carriage deposited Dare and Pyris at the Council Hall. Pyris marched him inside and down the wide corridor to the assembly chamber. The ostentatious, oversized doors, all carved and inlaid with gold, opened soundlessly, and Dare was prodded forward by a swift shove behind him. He knew better than to quip with Pyris when there were no witnesses, so he muttered a curse under his breath and entered.

The crisp and immaculate violet carpet led him to the center of the huge chamber with its vaulted ceilings and rows of exquisitely crafted chairs and benches—all of them empty—circling a raised dais. On the dais stood a long, gilded table with nine high-backed chairs along one side. A woman sat in the center chair. She stared silently at Dare, disdain rolling from her in waves, as he approached. The chamber doors closed behind him with a resounding thud. Dare took in the empty chamber and the sole council member before him. He waited.

After a painfully long silence, during which Dare contemplated how much trouble he would get into for making the snide comment that danced across his tongue, Head Councillor Myra Gartend spoke.

"Welcome, Dare." Peering down at him over the rim of her spectacles, she practically spat his name. "Thank you for joining us." She was an older woman, with gray hair that was still tinged with streaks of black and pulled back severely into a tight bun.

He bowed low so she wouldn't see how far he rolled his eyes into the back of his head. Nothing good ever came from these after-hours summonses. "Always a pleasure, Councillor." He straightened, setting a perfect smile in place, cordial and reverent. "What can I do for you at such an hour?"

Head Councillor Gartend did not return his smile. "The Council has a job for you," she said flatly. "We need you—"

"This couldn't have waited until the morning?" Dare asked reflexively.

"Interrupt me again," Gartend snapped, "and I'll have you whipped in the central square. How and when we conduct our business is no concern of yours."

Haggard shrew, Dare thought bitterly, but he bit his tongue. Silence filled the great hall. Heat rose in Dare's chest, but he maintained the cool exterior. It was all he had. Especially here.

The councillor stared him down for a full minute before she spoke again. "You'll be working with the Wardens. The Council has recently become aware that the Westholdens are preparing to declare war. And there are some troubling rumors that would be . . . unfortunate if proved true. Your job is to infiltrate Westhold, determine the veracity of these rumors, and report back."

Dare raised his hand, still biting his tongue so hard he could taste copper.

Councillor Gartend sighed deeply, not even trying to hide her irritation. "Speak."

"Wardens? As in Wardens of the Flame?"

Gartend arched one sharp eyebrow. "Is there another kind?"

"You want me to infiltrate the greatest military kingdom on the continent? With a *Warden*?"

"No," she said flatly. She waited just long enough for Dare's jaw to unclench before she added, "It will be two Wardens."

"Respectfully, Councillor, are you out of your fucking mind?"

From the shadows behind the head councillor, a form took shape. She was clad all in black—a bodice and pants that hugged her hourglass frame—and her fire-red hair cascaded over her shoulders.

Dare's stomach dropped as she moved to stand just behind Gartend.

"Must we remind you of the terms of your employment?" the woman asked, her voice low and playful.

Before he could answer, Gartend gestured to the woman. "Dare, you remember Tanithe Ash."

He lifted his chin. "Of course, Councillor." It was difficult to forget the Council's spymaster, especially when she was the reason he was chained to the Council in the first place. Not to mention the sinking feeling in his chest every time he saw her.

"Then there's no issue," Tanithe said, draping an arm over the back of the chair. Her lips parted in a slow smile as she gave Dare a wink.

"The issue," Dare said, matching Tanithe's friendly lilt, "is that what you're asking is impossible."

Gartend leaned forward to rest her elbows on the table, peering down at Dare as though he were nothing more than a spider she was about to squish with the heel of her shoe. "We are not *asking* anything. We are giving you a job to do. It is up to you to get it done."

"Don't you think a Warden of the Flame is going to have some reservations about working with someone like me?" he asked. "They're so . . ." He searched for a word that wouldn't get him lashed. "Virtuous."

"You're a mercenary, are you not? A member of the Crimson Brothers? Figure it out."

"Yes, but—"

"Figure. It. Out." Gartend paused for a moment, watching him. "Are we clear?"

Dare forced the smile back on his face. "Perfectly clear, Councillor. Thank you."

"Tanithe will provide you with further details." Gartend rose.

"Wait for me at my office," Tanithe said coolly. "Pyris will escort you."

Dare's stomach lurched again. "Lovely." The only thing less appealing than dealing with the spymaster was being alone with her.

The huge door slid open behind him, followed by heavy footsteps.

Dare bowed low. "Enjoy the rest of your evening, Councillor," he said.

He turned on his heels and strode past Pyris and out of the chamber. Pyris followed him, too closely yet again, and made sure that Dare was deposited in the bowels of the building, directly in front of Tanithe's office.

She made sure to make him wait for almost an hour before she returned, strolling down the hall like she didn't have a care in the world. "Dare, my dear," she said, brushing past him to the door. "Do come in, darling. Let's get started."

Dare snuck a sip from his flask behind her back and followed her inside.

❊

By the time Dare left the Council building, the beginnings of a hangover had his gut roiling and his head pounding. Outside, the sky glowed ahead of the dawn, but people already filled the streets. He watched them for a moment, reveling in the knowledge that they were all completely unaware of his attention. It was so nice, he marveled, not being noticed.

Dare glanced over his shoulder at the Council building. He could already feel Tanithe breathing down his neck and he hadn't even started.

"Vire's demons," he muttered.

He pulled up the hood of his cloak and made his way down the steps, disappearing into the growing crowd.

Chapter 3

Verity Corallan stood in the training yard, studying the new recruits. The five freshly minted Wardens of the Flame were wide-eyed and alternately staring at her and anywhere other than her as they gathered at one edge of the training circle. Verity stood in the center of the thirty-foot ring next to a wood-and-straw practice dummy. She was used to the reaction by now. Confused and curious stares were hardly the worst responses she'd ever received.

"Attention!" she shouted, her voice projecting easily across the yard. The recruits snapped their heads toward her, arms stiff at their sides. "You're here," Verity continued in a quieter but no less stern tone, "because Warden Sylus tells me that you lot are the only ones with any natural channeling ability. Is that correct?"

"Yes, Warden," the five recruits replied in unison.

"Warden Sylus also assures me that you've all been practicing your breathing exercises."

"Yes, Warden."

"Good. Today, you're going to learn how to cast a wall of force to act as a shield."

Nervous glances flitted through the recruits.

"Don't you want to show them how it's done first?" called a cheerful voice from behind her.

Verity turned, smiling only once her back was to the new Wardens. Drystan Serah jogged across the training yard toward the ring, his bow in his hand and a quiver of arrows on one hip.

"You're late, Warden," Verity snapped, keeping her voice from matching the amusement on her face.

"I was giving you a chance to scare the littles first," he said, stopping at the edge of the ring opposite the new recruits. In one smooth, deliberate motion, Drystan pulled an arrow from the quiver, nocked it, drew the bowstring back, took aim, and released.

No sooner had he drawn the arrow than Verity was moving. She uttered the familiar incantation in the same breath that stilled her mind and shifted her hands in the rote movement she had done more times than she could count. The arrow loosed, sailing for the training dummy.

And ricocheted harmlessly off the air a few inches in front of the dummy's head. The recruits gasped. Her back still to the group, Verity grinned. She always enjoyed the moment when new recruits saw combat magic for the first time. Magic was common enough across the continent—some places more than others—though it typically leaned toward more utility or luxury uses. It was rare to find magic used in battle outside of the Wardens.

"Nice shot," she said as Drystan stepped into the circle. "Would have had it right between the eyes."

Drystan covered the distance to the discarded arrow in a few long strides and slid it back into his quiver before stepping to Verity's side. He was nearly half a foot taller than she was, with broad shoulders and strong arms tanned from the sun. He slung his bow over his shoulder, watching the recruits carefully. He looked every part the soldier except for his bright green eyes, which were soft and kind.

"They're still staring at me, aren't they?" Verity whispered.

Drystan stifled a chuckle. "Oh yeah," he whispered back. "What'd you do to them?"

"Nothing."

He looked down at her, raising one eyebrow.

"*Nothing*," she repeated. "Don't look at me like that."

Drystan turned his back on the new recruits as well, leaning in toward Verity. He scratched at his short hair. The warm blond color of it always made Verity think of wildflower honey. "You know what they're staring at," he said, keeping his voice low.

"Yeah, I know."

"You're practically a legend around here, Vee."

"I know, I know," she said, though *legend* wasn't the word she would use. *Oddity*, maybe. She brought her hands up in front of her, the sunlight glinting off the metal plates of her fingers. "*The Warden with the metal arms.*"

Drystan slipped a hand around one of hers and squeezed it gently. The magic binding the steel plates and gears to her allowed her to feel the pressure of his grip, though nothing else. Not the warmth of his skin, nor the rough calluses on his fingers. She squeezed back, the tiny gears within her fingers whirring softly.

"You're more than that. They just don't know you yet." She looked up at him, that easy smile pulling at his lips. "Show them who you are, Vee."

She couldn't help but return his smile. "Alright," she said, raising her voice to carry to the other side of the ring as she faced the group. "At ease, Wardens. I can tell you're not going to be able to focus, so let's get this out of the way now."

She halved the distance to them, her thick braid of burnt umber hair bouncing between her shoulder blades as she walked. The *littles*, as Drystan always called them, were watching her every move. She knew they would never ask her. Not when nearly every Warden of the Flame, whether in their base in Whitehollow or the dozen other camps across the continent, had come from another life—usually one best left in the past. Almost all of them had been taken in, sheltered, and rehabilitated in one way or another. And so, no one would ever *ask*.

Verity raised her arms again, hands displayed. "Yes, these are really my hands," she said, opening and closing her fists a few times to demonstrate her motor control. The sleeves of her crisp, white shirt were already rolled up nearly to her elbows, but she pushed them up a little higher.

On the right side, steel met pale flesh just below her elbow. On the left, the metal continued up as far as the sleeve would reveal. She rapped on her left bicep, the clang of metal striking metal unmistakable.

"And yes, I really do have metal arms." She pulled her sleeves down and glanced behind her at Drystan, who was leaning against the practice dummy, a reassuring smile on his face.

Verity turned back to the recruits. "And now that *that's* out of the way, how many of you have actually cast any magic before?"

Even though these recruits were all natural Channels, any previous experience with magic would largely depend on their upbringing. No one moved.

"Can anyone tell me what magic *is*?"

Nothing but nervous glances.

Verity held back a sigh. "Magic is nothing more than energy that lives in the core of every single person. It can be used to alter other types of energy, like force or momentum." She gestured to the training dummy. "As I did a moment ago. We can also manifest that energy. Manifested magical energy can be used for Wards and Banishments, for example."

Verity surveyed the Wardens and was pleased to find their attention fixed on her words. Not her arms. "With enough time, practice, and patience, anyone can cast magic. But two things can make drawing on that energy much easier: knowing a predetermined incantation and being able to quiet your mind and open yourself up to the wellspring of energy at your center. Can anyone tell me the single most effective thing for making magic easier to cast and control?"

More cautious glances among her students. Verity was about to continue when the young woman at the end of the line spoke up, almost too quiet for Verity to hear. "Being a natural Channel?"

Verity nodded encouragingly. "Yes, exactly. Being a natural Channel gives you an advantage over everyone else. What would take most people years to learn, you can do by instinct. Almost all of the formally trained mages in the world are natural Channels." She gestured to the group of Wardens in front of her. "Just like you."

A little flicker seemed to ripple through the recruits, like a spark through underbrush, setting its path alight. Verity remembered that feeling well. She smiled as the wonder on their faces rekindled something inside her.

"As I said, Warden Sylus says you've all been practicing your breathing exercises. I'm going to teach you the incantation in High Aethirian for the force wall I used." She waved her hand toward where Drystan still leaned against the target dummy. "Then you're going to put those two things together and you're going to stop Warden Serah from hitting the target so we can wipe that smug look off his face."

Four hours and a few haphazard force walls later, Verity dismissed the recruits. Channeling one's inner power could take a lot out of someone who wasn't practiced at appropriately siphoning it, and by the end their heads were drooping with exhaustion.

There was some promise there, for sure, but they needed a lot more training before they'd be ready for much of anything. They were starting late in the game, at least by Verity's standards, but they were far from hopeless. Even if they'd never reach the level of a College-trained mage, she was confident she could get them to where they could use magic to protect others if they needed to.

"You did some good work today, Vee," Drystan said after the littles had stumbled away. He collected some of his arrows from the ground where the recruits had succeeded in deflecting them. The rest were bunched in a tight grouping in the target dummy's head. He gathered those too.

"Thanks for your help," Verity said. "I'm sure you had other things you'd rather be doing on your day off."

Drystan shrugged. "You asked me. I'm here."

"I asked you to send one of your archery students to help," she said, looking at him sidelong.

He laughed aloud, pleasant and infectious. "You told me you needed an archer to hit a target," he said. "*Hit* was the important part of that request. There was no way I was going to risk one of your recruits ending up with an arrow in the ass."

Verity couldn't help but chuckle. "Are they really that bad?"

"No, they're fine," he said, waving off his earlier gibe. "They need more practice, but they're learning. It's easy to forget what it was like when I was first learning to shoot."

"I know what you mean." Verity couldn't even remember learning to channel; her parents had started her so young. It was important in Aethir, where she grew up. Families prized mages for their power and their eventual political clout.

But the Wardens were healers and guardians, defenders and mediators sworn to protect the weakest and most forgotten people of the continent. Forsaking family titles and political standing alike. Broken individuals who started over and dedicated their lives to the Wardens of the Flame. Like her.

Verity's thoughts flicked back to her childhood in Aethir, her years spent training to be a mage as she looked out across the Wardens' compound, sprawling at the edge of the city of Whitehollow.

What a disappointment she'd turned out to be.

"Warden Corallan," a voice called out.

Three Wardens hurried toward her. She recalled them all taking their oaths about a year ago, if she remembered right. Verity smiled politely as they stepped into the training ring. "Yes?"

The Warden who had called out, a young man named Jonah, stopped a few feet away, a mischievous smile starting to sneak across his face. He was in his early twenties, probably only a few years younger than Verity, with short dark hair and handsome features, though the grin he was trying to hide made him look downright boyish.

He gave a quick salute to her and Drystan. "Sorry for interrupting. Are you interested in any training this morning, Warden Corallan?"

Verity cocked her head toward Drystan, who was watching the exchange with interest. "What did you have in mind, Jonah?" she asked cautiously.

Beaming, Jonah gestured to the two Wardens he had in tow, both of whom wore sheepish grins. "The lads here think I can't hold my own against you in a fight, Warden."

His co-conspirators elbowed each other, trying to stay quiet. She doubted that *hold his own in a fight* was the wording of whatever bet they'd made. He thought he could fight her and win.

Ainam save me from the male ego.

Drystan must have read it on their faces too, because he snorted a laugh.

Verity crossed her arms over her chest with a light *clink*. "Is that so?" she asked, her voice soft.

Jonah smiled a little wider. "Yes, Warden. I was hoping to have the opportunity to prove them wrong. That is, if you're up for a quick sparring match this morning."

Verity's mouth twitched with the beginnings of a grin, but she fought it back. "Sure, I could use the workout." She looked the three of them over. "Why don't your friends join in too? Make it interesting."

The young Wardens gaped. "At the same time?" Jonah glanced to his two friends.

Verity nodded as she grabbed a training sword from the rack and slid it through the open loop on her belt. "Why not?"

Confusion skittered across their faces. One of Jonah's friends gestured to Drystan. "D-do you two want to partner up?" he offered. "Two on three? You know, so it's more fair?"

Drystan laughed outright and sat on the bench at the edge of the ring, setting his bow down beside him. "Oh no, I'm good." He leaned back a little and crossed his ankle over his knee. "Please, carry on."

Warily, the three Wardens each grabbed a wooden training sword.

"What are we going to?" Verity asked, following them to the center of the ring. "First touch?"

The young men fanned out before her, swords in hand. Jonah was the thinnest of the group, though from how they'd jogged across the courtyard, he was also likely the fastest. She'd need to keep her eye on him.

Jonah nodded toward the wooden sword still hooked on Verity's belt. "On your count, Warden."

Verity let her full smile slide across her lips, her hands open at her sides. "Begin."

The three Wardens worked well together, coordinating the timing of their attacks—one striking high while another swung low, the third moving around behind her. Verity sidestepped the first two strikes, letting the lunge from the third pass by as she spun away from it. Jonah pivoted and swung in a downward arc toward her head. She stepped into it, blocking his arm at the elbow with her forearm as she moved past him, shoving him toward his friends.

Verity dodged more of their blows. She was aiming to let them tire themselves out, but Drystan called from the bench, "You should probably draw your sword, Vee. You don't want them to feel too bad about this."

Verity spared him a glance as she stepped around another strike. "Either you're in this fight or you're not!" she called. "No commentary from the sidelines." But she slid the sword from the loop on her belt as Drystan's warm laugh echoed across the ring.

She parried the next strike easily, swinging her sword around to slap one of the Wardens across the small of his back. He stepped out of the ring, breathing hard.

Jonah and his remaining friend circled Verity. They leveled their swords at her and charged as one. They were well-trained; Verity would have to compliment the master-at-arms the next time she saw him.

She parried Jonah's attack, spinning him into his friend. The two fell to the ground in a heap. Jonah's friend was the first on his feet, his sword arcing toward Verity. The man was built like an ox and swung the sword like a blacksmith striking iron.

Verity planted her feet and raised her sword. Her arms didn't buckle nor did her legs bow with the force of the blow. She simply met the strike full-on and stopped it dead.

The young man's sword clattered to the ground. He stepped back, shaking out his hands from the sting that was no doubt reverberating through his arms.

Verity flicked her sword out and tapped him lightly on the side of the knee. Then she looked at Jonah. The last man standing. His hair was matted down with sweat, and his chest heaved with every breath he forced into his lungs. His youthful face was bright red, though whether that was just from exertion or frustration, she wasn't sure. Either was fine. This would be over soon.

Jonah charged and Verity met each swing. His movements were slowing, becoming easier to read. When he pulled his arms back to swing across her abdomen, Verity saw her opening. She stepped into him, giving him no room to maneuver, and set the point of her wooden sword against the soft flesh beneath his chin.

"And that's match," Drystan called from the bench. "Well fought, Wardens, all of you." He grabbed his bow and started into the ring.

Verity collected the training swords and deposited them back on the rack, passing him on her way.

"Did you even break a sweat?" he whispered as they passed.

"A bit," she said with a grin.

Jonah stood in stunned silence, hands braced on his knees, while the other two Wardens were in various states of collapse in the dirt of the ring.

"And can you imagine," Drystan said to the group, "what it's like when she uses her magic too?"

"Thank you for the match!" Verity called. Drystan rejoined her at the edge of the ring. "We should do this again sometime."

Quiet groans were the only response as Verity and Drystan started the walk across the Wardens' compound in comfortable silence. Training rings and medic buildings took up much of the space, dotted here and there with storage buildings for supplies that could be handed out to people in need, and the barracks for the Wardens who called Whitehollow their home.

Crossing the central square, they passed the ever-burning brazier that marked the very center of the base. With a waist-high stone wall around it, the brazier served as a dedication to Pyrannis, the old god of fire and the original patron of the Wardens of the Flame.

The four elemental gods were hardly worshiped anywhere anymore. Most civilized lands worshiped Ainam, god of all things good and just, to the exclusion of all others. A scant few prayed to Vire, the demon god who lorded over the hells, though that was mostly in the hopes that he would turn his attention elsewhere. And while the Wardens had become purely secular long ago, they had always maintained the burning brazier as a symbol of the heritage of their order.

Walking by, Drystan touched his fingers to his lips and tapped the wall. An old superstition, he told her once. His mother had taught him a healthy fear of the old gods, even if no one had seen any sign of them in centuries. In the years they'd both spent in Whitehollow, Verity had never seen him pass by the brazier without touching his fingers to the low stone wall.

On the other side of the square, one of the teenagers who lived in the stronghold—a lanky, blond-haired boy, too old to go to an orphanage but too young to take the Warden's oath—waved at them, jogging over from one of the buildings.

"Good, you're both here," the boy said, breathing hard. "Commander Cairn wants to see you."

CHAPTER 4

"I DON'T LIKE THIS," Verity said as she and Drystan ate lunch in a small, walled-off park in the city-state of Valda. The garden seemed specifically designed to provide a little green space within the grimy streets of the city, the walls muffling the noise from the throngs of people going about their lives.

Drystan slung his arm around her, the familiar, comforting weight settling on her shoulders. "Cairn gave us our orders," he said. "I know you didn't want to leave the littles—"

"I *just* started their training. Any other team could have handled this."

Drystan squeezed, the pressure strong against the metal of her shoulder, before letting his arm fall to rest along the back of the bench. "First of all, you know that's not true. And secondly, the Wardens are spread thin right now. I'm not sure the commander had anyone to spare."

He was right on both counts. "We're not far from the Wilds here," she argued anyway. The area was due north of the city-state. "Surely one of the teams there could have made it to Valda just as quickly as we did."

Drystan took a bite of his lunch, which consisted of some sort of flat bread wrapped around meat and cheese. "Vee, those teams are dealing with their own problems. The monsters that go bump in the Wilds have been bumping a little harder than usual."

"I know," she muttered. The rumors coming down from the small towns along the southern edge of the Wilds suggested the shifters were causing a lot of trouble lately. Several teams of Wardens had been called in to help. Despite each and every shifter having once been human, they were the most violent and deadly creatures on the continent. The monsters claimed just two territories: the massive expanse of forest known as the Wilds to the north, and the Red Forest far away in the kingdom of Southreach.

Verity was beginning to wish for the frozen northern forests and the blood-thirsty monsters. She had never cared for Valda, though she'd only passed through a couple of times. It was far too big for her liking, too many people shoulder to shoulder trying to take up the same space. And it stretched on and on for miles in what felt like every direction. You could walk for two days and still not get from one side of Valda to the other on foot. It was its own little kingdom, ruled by a nine-member council rather than a monarch, all held within the walls and natural borders of the largest city on the continent.

She preferred Whitehollow's neatly ordered streets, quiet by comparison to the constant thrum of the city around them. But Whitehollow was a three-day ride behind them now. Forward was the only direction open to her. Backward was never an option.

"What did you think of the Council meeting yesterday?" Verity asked.

Drystan made a noncommittal sound around the food in his mouth. He swallowed before saying, "At least we know why we're here."

The meeting had been necessary to get the details of their mission but had left an oily taste in Verity's mouth. Not to mention the general sense of unease that had settled over her at the news that a mercenary would be joining their team. Verity had almost groaned right there in front of the Council.

Despite her assurances to the Council that she and Drystan could handle the situation alone, they hadn't been swayed. The talents of the two Wardens were truly impressive, the sharp-faced head councillor had said, but this particular mission would require an agent with loyalties to Valda who could, therefore, fully appreciate the sensitive nature of the situation. Verity had tried not to be irritated by their decision.

She had failed spectacularly.

Drystan glanced up at the sun as he finished the last bite of his lunch. "Almost time to meet our contact," he said. He didn't seem nearly as bothered by this whole mess as she was. But then again, he rarely seemed bothered by anything. He stood from the shaded bench, absently rubbing his knee as he rose.

Verity adjusted the cloak on her shoulders. "I'll take care of it," she said. "Why don't you head back to the inn?"

Drystan raised a brow at her. "Vee, I'm fine. It's just a little stiff from all the riding over the last few days."

"I know," she said. Still, there was no reason for him to have to push himself when he could get a little rest. They'd hardly stopped moving at all for the last four days. If she could give him this small break, she would. "I could use the walk to clear my head anyway." At his hesitation, she added, "I'll just go collect our contact and bring them back to the inn, alright? We'll go over everything together."

Drystan's mouth quirked as though he were thinking of arguing, but he nodded. "Alright," he said. "I'll meet you at the inn."

The heels of Verity's boots clicked against the cobblestones as she followed the directions to their meeting place. Ahead on the left, a wooden sign hung from a building, carved with the likeness of a large bird sitting on the shoulders of a great stag. *The Raven and Hart Tavern.*

The smell of food and ale greeted her as she walked inside, several conversations stopping as patrons turned to watch. She'd become accustomed to a certain amount of staring over the years, and so she ignored it, moving straight to the bar. Its position at the front of the establishment offered a full view of the open room.

She knew vaguely who she was looking for. He was a member of the Crimson Brothers, a mercenary guild based in Valda and with chapters stretching across the continent. The guild was known, generally, for their reliability and their discretion—two things that were of paramount importance when employing mercenaries.

Verity personally despised the idea, but the Crimson Brothers had a reputation for taking just about any job that came their way, including legitimate ones. Sellswords didn't *only* sell their swords for illegal causes, Verity reminded herself.

She scanned the room, searching for anyone who might stand out as her contact. She'd asked for a description, but the Council had been secretive. *Don't worry*, the head councillor had said flatly. *He'll find you.* Verity leaned her elbow on the edge of the bar, letting the metal joint smack into the smooth wood, and waited.

After her third time waving off the bartender, Verity spotted a man sitting alone in the middle of the tavern. Although everyone else had returned to their business minutes ago, he was still staring at her. He seemed remarkably average, with plain, nondescript clothing—a tan shirt open at the collar and dark pants tucked into darker knee-high boots—that might be suitable for a craftsman. His rich brown hair was tied back at his neck. There seemed nothing remarkable about him at all. But when their eyes met, one corner of his lips curved upward, and he stood. Had he just been waiting to see how long it took her to notice him?

Not seeing any weapons on him, Verity willed her hand to relax as the man crossed the room and took up a space at the bar. He ordered an ale before perching on a stool, angling himself toward Verity. His deep golden skin, though marked with a few small scars, was smooth with soft features, and his clothes, while simple, were clean and well-kept. He was far too neat and tidy to be a craftsman.

"Dare?" she asked. It was the only identifier she had been given for her contact.

The stranger nodded once and gave her a seated bow. "My lady."

"Warden," she corrected.

"As you wish, my lady Warden."

"Just *Warden*," she said, her voice growing sharper. "Or Verity, if you prefer."

Dare looked contrite and bowed his head. "Of course, Warden. My apologies."

Her shoulders relaxed, but only a little. She still wasn't sure what to expect from someone who sold his honor for coin. "My companion is back at our lodgings," she continued. "I can take you there so we can discuss the specifics of the mission."

The bartender set a mug in front of Dare, who took an appreciative swig before turning his attention back to Verity. His voice quieted so she could barely hear him over the low hum of the tavern. "As much as I would love to follow you back to your room, would you care to join me for a drink first?"

Verity balked. His eyes—greenish gray with flecks of brown and gold—sparkled with mischief as she stared, dumbfounded.

Maybe she should have let Drystan handle this, or at least let him come with her. No, that was foolish. She was a Warden of the Flame and had dealt with far worse than one arrogant mercenary.

Verity cleared her throat, schooling her expression back into careful neutrality. "I don't think we have time for that," she said, keeping her voice even.

Dare's mouth twisted into a wicked grin. "Shame." He turned to lean his back against the bar, surveying the tavern as she had done when she arrived. "Where are you staying?"

"The Magpie. Do you know it?"

The sellsword's face screwed up in complete disgust as he groaned. "The Magpie? I always assumed being a Warden came with some nice perks. I didn't expect you'd be slumming it in the Downs."

Verity crossed her arms over her chest. "The Wardens are concerned with function, not luxury. If there's a bed and a hot meal, that's enough."

"A hot meal at the Magpie might be pushing your luck," he said, all palpable arrogance. "I'm just saying, I wouldn't settle for being treated that way. What, they don't have any problems with you getting robbed in the middle of the night? It's disgraceful!"

Verity let a cold, stony calm wash over her face as she glared at him.

He took the hint, rubbing his hand along the back of his neck, the perfect picture of innocence. "But hey, what do I know about it, right?" He winked, breaking the illusion.

Verity resisted the urge to roll her eyes.

"I'll meet you there in two hours."

"Two hours? Why not now?"

He gestured to Verity. "Because I can't afford to be seen leaving here in the company of a Warden. It'll draw too much attention."

"Fine," she conceded. She couldn't fault him for that.

"Besides," he added, just as she'd decided to give him the benefit of the doubt, "I haven't finished my drink." Dare raised the mug to his lips and took a long swallow of ale, watching her over the rim.

"One hour," Verity snapped, letting the familiar, commanding tone slide into her voice.

Dare nodded, taking his mug and pushing off from the bar. "As you wish, my lady Warden."

CHAPTER 5

DARE MADE THE SHORT walk to the Downs and circled the inn once to make sure nothing was out of the ordinary before heading inside. It was a busy afternoon at the Magpie, where rooms were as likely to be rented by the hour as they were by the night. Yet even with the crowd, it wasn't difficult to spot the Wardens.

Verity sat at a table toward the back. Without the gray traveling cloak she'd been wearing earlier, the wide straps of her green bodice served only to highlight the metal plates of her arms. The steel encompassed her entire shoulder and clavicle on her left side and only up to her elbow on her right. Her Warden's mark was also clearly visible now—the literal brand of two swords crossed over a burning brazier that identified her as a Warden of the Flame—scarred into the right side of her chest. In case that hadn't been enough to draw attention to herself, she was also armed, a sword scabbard resting on her hip. While weapons weren't out of place in Valda, they did cause people to take notice, which was the main reason that Dare never carried any. Openly, at least.

With her was a broad-shouldered man who looked like he could pick Dare up and hurl him across the room if he had reason to. It would probably be best not to give him a reason, Dare decided.

Dare sidled into the open chair beside Verity, not bothering to remove his coat. "Afternoon, Wardens," he said as cheerfully as he could manage.

Verity eyed him tersely. Not so much as a nod of greeting.

Dare wasn't sure how long she'd had a stick lodged firmly up her ass, but it clearly must have been there for quite some time.

She indicated the blond man across the table from him. "Dare, let me introduce you to Warden Drystan Serah."

Drystan stood up just enough to reach across the table and offer him a solid handshake. "Nice to meet you," Drystan said, smiling. It was warm and genuine, not something Dare was used to seeing. Especially from a Warden.

He smiled back, keeping the surprise from his face. "Likewise," he said. Verity crossed her arms and glowered. When she didn't say anything else, Dare added, "Well, do you have a room, or should we discuss all of our clandestine plans right here in the open?"

Verity huffed and stood, pressing her hands against the tabletop with a solid *thunk*. Drystan stood as well, draining the last of whatever was in his mug. He led the way toward the stairs while Verity lagged behind, giving Dare no choice but to walk between them. Noting the reassuring weight of his daggers in the hidden sheaths in his coat and the one in his boot, Dare followed Drystan up the stairs.

The tiny room was cramped once Verity closed the door behind her. There was a narrow bed tucked in the corner, a cracked window, and a small table little bigger than a nightstand with a single chair. A longsword, a bow, and a quiver full of arrows—their white fletchings the only brightness in the room—leaned against the table.

As Drystan sat on the edge of the bed, the thin mattress flattened under his weight. Verity pulled the chair out from the table, so Dare propped himself against the wall near the window.

"Alright," Verity said, taking a seat. "Tell us what you know about the mission."

Dare suppressed a sigh at the command. He just needed to bite his tongue long enough to get through this job. "A couple of weeks ago, a body turned up in Whitehollow. As I understand it, the Wardens were called in to investigate. It soon became clear that the body belonged to a Valdane emissary, specifically the one who had been stationed in Westhold."

Verity stared at him, expressionless.

"Would you like the history lesson, too?" he asked. "Westhold's borders have been closed for at least a decade, save for select trade ships and a handful of emissaries who have extremely limited access to the kingdom. Rumors say Westhold has been preparing for war ever since they lost the last one . . . what, eight years ago?"

"Nine," Verity interjected.

He graced her with a tight-lipped smile. "*Nine* years ago. But no one knows what they're actually doing down there across the bay, so when the Valdane emissary to Westhold turns up dead in Whitehollow's port, it naturally raises some concerns. The Wardens ship the body back to Valda and offer to help investigate." Dare crossed his arms, leaning back against the wall. "Turns out, the emissary managed to hide some documents on his person before he was killed and tossed into the bay. The documents were waterlogged, obviously, but the legible bits seem to suggest that Westhold has some sort of magically imbued weapon. The rumor is this weapon is powerful enough to actually help them win this time."

Dare swept a hand across the room, taking in the two Wardens. "The Valdane Council has contracted with you, Wardens of the Flame, and"—he set his hand on his chest—"me, a Crimson Brother, to figure out if any of that is true. And if it is, we need to know exactly what this weapon is and just how fucked we all are now that Westhold has their warmongering hands on it." He slid his hands into the pockets of his wool coat. "Does that align with your understanding, my lady Warden?"

From his spot on the bed, Drystan choked on a laugh, which quickly turned into a conspicuous cough as Verity shot him a look.

"I assume the Brothers sent *you* for a reason," she said to Dare. "What skills do you have?"

Heat flashed across his face. The inflection she chose had been deliberate, and its implication was not lost on him. "You mean, what use will I be to you?"

She tapped her metal fingers on the small table. "Yes."

Drystan leaned forward, smiling warmly. "What Verity's asking is, what are you good at, Dare? Our plan should play to all our strengths."

Dare was obviously witnessing two of Drystan's strengths in action—putting up with Verity and smoothing out her edges around people. Dare could respect that.

He reached into an inner pocket of his coat and removed his flask, inclining his head toward Drystan. Maybe he could get through this more quickly if he simply ignored the other Warden for now. "My specialties are in getting into and out of places I shouldn't be with things I shouldn't have, whether it be an item or information."

"So you're a thief," Verity said.

It was Drystan's turn to send a look her way, but Dare just grinned as he opened the flask and brought it to his lips. "On occasion I've also convinced people to just give me the things I need." He took a drink.

"So you're a thief and a liar," she amended.

"Only professionally," he said. "As for this job, I can get into Westhold, gather the information we need on the weapon, and get out again."

Verity's fingers stopped tapping. "The whole mission," she said. "You can do the whole mission yourself?"

Dare gave up on ignoring her and cocked his head, meeting her gaze. "That is what I said, yes."

"You don't think you need us for anything?"

He took another sip from his flask, holding the alcohol in his mouth and savoring the burn. There was a seething ember in Verity's words, like a breath in the wrong direction might set her ablaze. Dare debated, just for a moment, in which direction to breathe.

The corners of his mouth curled upward as he inhaled, swallowed, and said, "Seems that way."

Verity opened her mouth—Dare could only assume it was to breathe fire at him, judging by her expression—but he pressed forward, cutting off whatever scathing comment she was about to make.

"Look, I work alone. Always have. But that's beside the point. We need a plan, and it just so happens that I have one." This back and forth was getting boring. Time to get on with it.

Dare slid the flask back into his pocket. "The dead emissary was stationed in Port Merrick on the south side of the bay. The documents on him had to have come from there, or near there. I can get us passage on a ship that can get us into Westhold just outside of Port Merrick tomorrow night."

"That's impossible," Verity said. "The coast is too rocky. The ports are the only way in."

"That's what Westhold thinks too," Dare said. "Once we're there, I'll gather some information and see what I can find out. Stay out of my way and let me do my job, and we'll be done with this whole unpleasantness in a few days. Maybe a week."

"No," Verity said. "Absolutely not." She turned to Drystan, her hand gesturing to encompass Dare where he leaned against the wall. "We can't just wait around while he runs through Westhold doing Vire knows what."

"Warden, you're going to need to trust me—"

"I don't," she snapped.

Tension rippled through Dare's shoulders. "You don't even know me."

"I know enough."

Drystan stood, stepping between the two of them. "The Valdane Council, the Wardens, and the Brothers put us together. Specifically *us*. It must be that they think we'll make a good team."

Dare added *idealist* to his mental list of Drystan's skills. "I don't need a team," he said. "If the Council had deigned to ask my opinion, I would have told them as much and saved you the trip."

Verity shot to her feet so she could see around Drystan. "You don't even know what we can do."

Dare smirked. "I know enough."

"Look, it doesn't matter what any of us think." Drystan's voice was as calm and level as it had been when they started. "We have our orders, and those orders are to work *together* on this." He looked from Verity to Dare. "Get us into Westhold. We'll give you some time to gather information, then we'll figure out what we need to do from there, and we'll take everyone's skills into account. Alright?"

"Fine," Verity bit out as Dare nodded.

"Good," Drystan said, returning to his seat on the bed. He gave Dare an upward nod. "Where should we meet you?"

"I'll pick you up here tomorrow, just before sunset." Dare pushed off the wall, aiming for the door. Another minute in this room was too much.

Besides, if he was going to be away from Valda for a week or so, he had a few things he needed to take care of first. And he was going to have to figure out how to tolerate Verity before she drove him mad.

Vire's hells.

As his hand touched the latch, Verity said, "I thought it would draw too much attention to be seen in the company of Wardens."

Fuck me.

It had been too much to hope that he could get out of there without another jab. "I have the distinct impression that my reputation isn't going to survive working with the two of you, so I may as well embrace it now," he said, tugging open the door. "At least this way I don't have to worry about you getting lost at the docks."

Before either of them could respond, Dare left.

A team. He was going to have to work with a team again. The last time that had happened, things hadn't gone well. At all. His reputation as someone not to fuck with was the only thing that had come out ahead on *that* little adventure.

And even worse than working with two complete strangers, they were Wardens.

Fuck.

He was going to need another drink to deal with this shit.

"Lanara, just drown me in the sea and be done with it," he whispered, though he doubted any of the gods, old or new, were listening.

CHAPTER 6

Verity's jaw clenched. She'd convinced Drystan to head downstairs a little early, but Dare was already waiting for them, enjoying a pint at the Magpie's bar.

"Give him a chance," Drystan whispered as they reached the bottom of the stairs.

Verity bristled, then whispered back, "I gave him a chance."

He let out a low chuckle. "When?"

"Yesterday."

"That was a hostile interrogation at best, Vee. We've got to work with him. I know this mission has you on edge, but just—"

"I'm not on edge," Verity shot back.

Drystan eyed her as they crossed the room. "Just try to be nice, alright?"

Thankfully, Dare was finishing his drink as they approached. He gave a courteous nod to them both and gestured to the door. "Shall we?"

Verity followed him outside without comment.

The sun dipped below the buildings. The walk to the harbor could have been pleasant enough had it not been for the sauntering pace Dare took. He truly irritated Verity's every nerve. Beside her, Drystan bumped her metal elbow.

"Hey," he said.

When he didn't say anything else, she nudged him back. "Hey, what?"

"You're so tense right now you look like you're about to take flight."

"How are you *not* tense right now?" she asked, not bothering to deny his observations. There was nothing about this mission she liked, and she was sick of pretending that it was fine. She'd been made to leave the new recruits behind in Whitehollow after only just starting their training, she and Drystan were stuck working with an arrogant mercenary, and they were heading into Westhold without any backup.

Drystan shrugged. "We have our orders."

He was always happier when they had a clear set of orders to follow. She appreciated that structure herself, if she was being honest, but Drystan thrived in it.

"I need to make a slight detour," Dare called over his shoulder. "I'll be right back." Without waiting for a response, he veered down an alleyway to his right.

"Is he serious?" Verity grumbled. She followed him, Drystan close behind.

After several random turns down other back alleys—why was it that mercenaries always conducted their business in back alleys?—he stopped at a large stone building.

Dare reached into his backpack and removed a sizable parcel. Approaching the building's back door, he set the parcel down on the stoop, knocked twice, and then jogged back across the alley to where Verity and Drystan had stopped.

"Now would be a good time to go," he said as he brushed past, disappearing into the shadows behind them.

She followed Dare toward the main streets, questions itching at her mind. What kind of illicit activity did she just witness? Verity wasn't sure she wanted to know the answer. It was clearly something illegal.

"Do I even want to know what that was?" she asked anyway. Drystan jogged to her side and gave her another nudge, but she ignored him.

Dare paused, studying her face for a moment. Verity kept her features hard and cold, her steel hands resting on her hips.

"Probably not," he said. A sly grin crept into place.

"How much farther to the docks?" Drystan asked before Verity could respond.

"Not far," Dare said. "This way."

They followed Dare down a cobblestone street toward the coast until they crested a small hill, and Verity got her first view of the Port of Valda from the city's perch on the bluffs. Nestled into the rocky coast of Cloud Bay, Valda's port was the trade hub for the western half of the continent. It was bustling, with at least twenty ships visible and space for dozens more. Hundreds of people hurried along the docks, some towing carts loaded down with crates and boxes, and some carrying bags slung over their shoulders, ready for a journey.

Overlooking the zig-zagging roads carved into the cliffs, the view was breathtaking. Verity stopped, looking past the rushing port and across the bay. A narrow strip of land was visible just along the southern horizon: the forested coast of Westhold. That was their destination, if all went according to plan.

"It's quite a view," Drystan breathed. His emerald eyes were wide as he took in the scene below. The setting sun glinted in golds and pinks across the crisp sails and the placid bay.

The amazement that sparkled in his eyes made her smile. "You look like you've never seen a port before," she said, jostling him in the ribs with her elbow. "You know there's one back home in Whitchollow, right?"

"I know," he said softly. "It's still beautiful every time."

Dare cleared his throat. "I don't mean to interrupt . . ." he said, clearly taking great care to interrupt as pointedly as possible. He was staring at them, hands in the pockets of his coat. "If you two stand there gawking much longer, you're going to get pick-pocketed for looking like tourists, and then we're going to miss our boat."

Verity hefted her knapsack higher up on her shoulders. "Waiting on you," she said sharply. "Lead the way."

He gave her half a bow before leading them down the steep, curving road to the docks. Once at sea level, they wove through the tangle of sailors, dock workers, and travelers. Verity was amazed anyone could find anything in this chaos, but she supposed working there all the time gave one the knowledge to navigate it. She thought back to Dare's parting jab the day before, about not losing them at the docks, and was silently grateful he was there to guide them.

Dare navigated the maze of sailors, wood, and rope until they approached a small ship with white sails and a worn, dark hull. A narrow plank led from the dock to the port side of the ship. A woman stood at the end of the plank, scanning the people walking past. Her hair was such a dark shade of black that it was almost blue, and her skin was a warm, rich brown. She spotted Dare, who tossed up his hand in greeting. The woman was nearly as tall as Drystan and was dressed in an assortment of muted blues, reds, and violets. Several silver coins glittered in her hair as they reflected the setting sun. Muscled arms were currently crossed over her chest.

"Evening, Captain," Dare called.

"Evening, indeed," the captain said without amusement. Her voice cut through the din of the crowd like a blade. "You're late."

Late? Verity stiffened and was about to inform this woman that they were in fact directly and promptly on time—early, even—when Dare laughed aloud.

"Oh, the fuck we're late, you ass," he said. "We're here a full ten minutes before you expected us to be, and you know it."

The captain stared down at the mercenary for a long moment while Verity wondered if she was going to have to stop the captain from pitching Dare into the water. Even if she did somewhat relish the idea of witnessing that, it would only delay them. Beside her, Drystan tensed almost imperceptibly.

The tall woman threw her head back in a raucous laugh and punched Dare in the shoulder so hard that it sent him stumbling back a couple of steps. "I'm just fuckin' with you," she cackled. "Come on, come on, let's get you folks on board."

Dare laughed and rubbed at his shoulder as he moved toward the plank. "Captain Gilmore, allow me to introduce you to Warden Verity Corallan and Warden Drystan Serah. Wardens, this is Captain Isabel Gilmore."

"Please, please," the captain said, holding out her hand to Verity. "Call me Gil."

Verity took Gil's hand and gave it a firm shake. To her credit, the captain gave Verity's metal hand only a moment's consideration. "Wardens, it's a pleasure to meet you both." She shook Drystan's hand in turn. "Let's get aboard the ship, then I'll give you all the details about how we'll get you folks where you need to go."

"Thank you, Captain," Verity said. She followed Dare up the narrow plank to the ship. The bold letters painted on the side of the prow read *The Second Chance.* She'd been on bigger ships before, but this one was clean and well maintained.

Gil boarded and motioned for the three of them to gather at the bow. "Alright, Wardens. And other guy," she said, adding a nod in Dare's direction.

Dare muttered something under his breath. Verity didn't hear what he said, but it earned him a jovial laugh from Gil.

"The goal is to get you three into Westhold, which ain't exactly as simple as taking a leisurely sail across the bay." She leaned back against the railing, her hands braced on either side of her wide hips. "But lucky for you, I'm the best smuggler on this half of the continent."

"Any chance we can get the best smuggler on the *other* half instead?" Dare quipped.

"I ain't opposed to chucking your sorry ass into the bay," Captain Gil said, clearly amused. "I'm certain these two Wardens don't actually need a glorified thug to do what needs doing."

Dare looked like he might have actually been insulted. "*Thug?*"

Verity cleared her throat. "Dare, can we focus, please?" she said before turning back to the captain. "Apologies Captain. Please, continue."

Gil gave a contrite cough, a hint of red coloring her cheeks. "Right, as I was saying, I'm the best there is, so I can get you across the bay and land you on the Westholden shore, right near the border of Aethir. That way, if anything goes wrong after the drop, you should be able to make a quick retreat across the border." She tapped the top of the railing. "The difficulty with traveling through Westhold is getting in. The borders and ports have the heaviest security, where they carefully check that each traveler has the proper documentation. But if you're already in, no one will look twice."

"As long as we don't draw too much attention to ourselves," Dare added.

Verity shifted uncomfortably. She didn't like the idea of being *smuggled* anywhere. "Is there no other way we can get in?"

Gil rubbed at the back of her neck while Dare tipped his head back. "My lady Warden," he said, and she did not appreciate the condescension in his tone. "Westhold's borders have been closed to all but the highest noble emissaries for years now. Even two glorious and upstanding Wardens such as yourselves wouldn't be allowed in. No, we're going to have to sneak in. But once we're in, we can easily fabricate a story about how we got there." After a moment, he added, "One that doesn't involve getting smuggled across Cloud Bay by Captain Gil here."

Verity chafed. "You mean lie."

Dare blinked at her. "Yes, I mean lie." He leaned in, as though closely examining her face. "You can actually lie, right? I mean, with a name like *Verity* I wouldn't be surprised—"

"I *can*," she interrupted, swatting him away. "Though I typically find I can get by quite well with being honest."

Dare snorted and waved a hand southward. "Then by all means, feel free to let the Westholden port authority know why you're there and see how well that works for you. But if that's your plan, let me know now because if that's the case, I'm going to stay in Valda."

Gil studied the railing of her ship, scratching at an invisible mark with her fingernail.

Why me? Verity wondered. And then, more accurately, *Why him? And why this mission?* The thought of having to skulk around Westhold was almost more than she could stomach.

Drystan must have sensed her mounting frustration because he set a casual but steadying hand on her shoulder as he said, "No, it's fine. We're quite capable of stealth and subterfuge."

"No one who is capable of stealth and subterfuge actually calls it stealth and subterfuge," Dare said flatly.

Drystan sighed.

See? she wanted to say. *It's not me. He's an ass.*

"I just mean we can follow the plan," Drystan said, as collected as ever. She always did appreciate that about him. He was the calm to her storm. As her temper could flare and burn, he was always even-keeled and steady.

"Great," Gil said a little too loudly, clapping her hands in an obvious effort to break the tension. "We'll set sail as soon as the sun dips below the horizon. Better to do these things under the cover of darkness, you know." The captain pressed up from the rail. "Well, I'll get to it then. Feel free to stay above deck, or you can head below to the mess if you prefer." And with that, she strode past the three of them toward the stern, shouting orders at a few of the sailors along the way.

Dare gave Verity an elaborate bow. "Anything else, my lady Warden?"

She swallowed a frustrated grumble and moved toward the port side of the ship, where the sailors raised the plank and untied the ropes that moored them at the dock.

The sky darkened, and before long, the wind rushed through Verity's hair as the ship slipped into the bay. She leaned her elbows on the railing, watching the dark water lap gently at the wooden hull.

The wind changed when they cleared the port. No, that wasn't it. Their direction changed despite the wind.

At the back of the ship, just beyond the till, Captain Gil stood with her long arms stretched out toward the sails, which billowed perpendicular to the way the wind was whipping her hair. Verity moved toward her, watching as she directed the breeze where she willed it, guiding the ship through the bay like a toy boat in a wash basin.

Gil noticed her staring and flashed a smile. "Impressed?" she asked, not stopping the motion of her hands that kept the sails aloft.

"That's how you're able to avoid the rocks. You're a mage," Verity said, unable to hide her surprise.

"I studied for a time," Gil said. "Didn't suit me."

"So you're a smuggler instead?"

Gil returned her focus to the sails. "Not everyone with a gift for channeling fits into the mold of the Mage's Guild, or the College, when it still stood. Some of us prefer other occupations."

In her time with the Wardens, Verity had met many people who were natural Channels but who had never received proper training. Rarely had she encountered anyone who'd had formal training and chosen not to pursue that calling.

She said as much, drawing a wry grin from the captain. "There are more of us than you might think," Gil said.

The idea of it was completely at odds with how Verity was raised. Mages were respected, in Aethir particularly but all across the continent. To be a mage was to help lead people and govern lands. It wasn't something many people just *stopped*. Her own journey not withstanding . . .

Verity watched Gil force wind into the sails of her ship. She was fascinated by how Gil shifted her weight, moving her hands to adjust the flow, as though seeing exactly where she needed it to go, how she needed it to change. And her focus had been darting back and forth between Verity and the sails as they were talking.

Verity took another step up the stairs toward the stern where Gil worked. "Are you a Perceptive?"

Gil's attention flicked to her. "Is it that obvious?" she asked.

"You're watching the sails and adjusting in the moment. You can see the magic, can't you?"

Gil smiled broadly. "Aye. That I can."

Verity's mind reeled. Perceptives were incredibly rare. They were among the most gifted Channels, and their ability to innately perceive magical energy through one of their five senses gave them a powerful advantage. Verity had only ever met one Perceptive before—Archmage Llewellan, the headmaster at the College of Magi. Sight was also his connected sense and was the most common. If one could call anything about this extraordinary ability *common*. Verity always wished to have been born with such an amazing gift.

"What does it look like?" she asked. She'd always been curious but had never been bold enough to ask the headmaster.

Gil glanced at her out of the corner of her eye, keeping most of her attention on her work. "Well, it looks different for everyone, I'm told," she said. "But for me, each type of energy has a color. The force I'm using to move the ship glows green."

Verity watched the billowing sails and tried to imagine what they would look like puffed up with a vibrant green glow. "That sounds beautiful," she said quietly.

"It can be," Gil replied. "It really can be."

"May I ask," Verity continued, "how do you keep it powered for so long?"

The captain flicked her wrist, around which hung a simple black corded bracelet with a red ruby in it. "This periapt stores enough power to keep me going for a while. I charge it slowly, over the days we're between jobs."

It was such a specialized use for magic—steering ships through Cloud Bay and the gods only knew where else—and yet Gil had used her abilities to become the best smuggler around, if her own boasting could be believed. Verity imagined it was true, though. What couldn't a captain do with a ship when she could control its movements to such a fine degree? When she could direct it exactly where she willed, avoiding hazards and other ships, regardless of where and how the wind blew? It was incredible to consider all Gil could have accomplished elsewhere, but she seemed happy here, on this ship, doing something she loved with the talent that was given to her.

Verity was still turning it all over in her mind as she bid the captain farewell and headed toward the bow of the ship. A thick band of stars and a bright half-moon shone overhead. The ship had only a small light tied to the center mast, with the lantern's glass tinted red. It was enough for the crew to avoid tripping on themselves or running into anything, but wasn't bright enough to call any attention to their position.

A dark shape sat huddled in the shadows behind a stack of crates on the starboard side of the ship. Verity paused in her walk to take a closer look. Against the thick woven netting that held the crates in place, Dare sat with his legs drawn up and his arms folded over his knees. His head rested on his forearms.

"Rough night?" Verity asked.

Dare lifted his head enough to glance at her sidelong before settling down against his arms again.

"Do you get seasick?"

Dare's muffled voice came from between his knees. "Why do you care?"

Verity shifted her weight, resting her hands on her hips. "I'm just being polite," she said.

"Don't bother."

She studied him, watching the slow rise and fall of his shoulders as he breathed deep. She dropped her arms to her sides. "Look, are you alright?" She needed to know if it was going to take him time to recover once they got to Westhold. She would need to plan for contingencies if they couldn't move quickly once they landed. Their lives could depend on it.

Dare lifted his head and leaned back against the cargo netting. Sweat gleamed on his forehead in the moonlight. "It's fine, Warden." He waved a hand at her dismissively, though his fingers trembled slightly. He spotted the tremor and pressed his hand flat against his leg.

"You look terrible."

"Thank you," he said, lips quirking.

Maybe it's been too long since he's had a drink, she considered. "Dare, look—"

"It's fine," he said again. "I'll be fine as soon as I'm off the ship. I promise."

Verity watched him for a moment, considering whether she had any reason to take him at his word. As Dare set his head down on his arms again, she realized she likely wouldn't get any more out of him, so she continued toward the front of the ship, leaving him on his own.

Drystan was at the bow, leaning on the rail.

"Can you check on the sellsword?" she whispered as she came up alongside him. He was always better at dealing with people.

Drystan looked back over his shoulder, quickly scanning the darkened deck of the ship. "Dare? Sure, why?"

"He's behind the crates on the starboard side. He doesn't look well," she said, keeping her voice hushed. "I think he's seasick, but I want to make sure he's not going to be a problem when we get to shore."

Drystan nodded. "Alright, I'll check in with him."

"Good," Verity said. "Thank you."

"And are *you* alright?" he asked.

"Of course," she said, a little too quickly. "Why wouldn't I be?"

Drystan turned to lean back against the rail and raised his brows.

"I mean, besides the fact that we're being transported illegally into a kingdom with closed borders, on an arguably vague mission with a minimal plan." Her fingers tightened their grip on the rail. "Why wouldn't I be alright?"

He chuckled. "Besides all of those things . . ." He lowered his voice, his easy smile fading. "It's *Westhold.*"

"I know," she said softly, staring down at her hands.

"If they really are preparing for war, that means soldiers."

"I know."

He watched her, his eyes twinkling in the soft light from the mast, looking a little like the stars overhead. "Vee," he began. But his voice was so gentle and so pained, she couldn't bear to let him finish.

"Drystan, it's fine. *I'm* fine." She looked out across the dark water, to the land that waited on the other side of the bay.

"Alright," he said, setting his hand over hers. "Just know that I'm always here if you need me."

Something eased in Verity's chest. "Thank you," she said. "But it was a long time ago. It'll be fine."

Drystan squeezed her hand and straightened. "I'd better go check on our seasick mercenary."

As the sound of Drystan's footfalls faded behind her, Verity watched the water part before the prow. How long would it be before she was back in Whitehollow? A week? If Dare was half as good as he thought he was, and everything about this mission went as smoothly as she'd been assured it would, then it was possible.

Verity sighed. When had anything ever gone as smoothly as she was promised?

CHAPTER 7

Verity stayed on the deck for the few hours it took to cross Cloud Bay. Captain Gilmore brought the ship to a silent stop as close to the Westholden shore as she could. There were no lights along the lonely stretch of beach on the northeastern edge of the kingdom. The ship dropped anchor, and Gil ordered a small dinghy lowered into the water.

"The border with Aethir is an hour's walk east," Gil said. "Port Merrick is three hours west. I recommend you find a safe place to spend the night before heading into the port. Travelers at this hour will be looked on with more scrutiny than someone passing through in the daylight."

Dare gave the captain a broad smile. "Thanks for the lift, Gil."

"Do you have an exit strategy?" the captain asked.

Dare shrugged. The gesture made Verity's blood simmer with the carelessness of it, as though it didn't matter. "It'll depend on what we find and how long we're stuck here," he said.

Gil nodded. "Well, I pass by here at least once every couple of nights. I'll keep an eye out on the beach. If you need a lift, you just shine a light out this way."

"Gil! Are you going sentimental on me?" Dare teased.

"Don't be an ass just 'cause I'm offering to save yours!" The captain shoved Dare toward the edge of the ship, nearly sending him toppling overboard. Dare laughed as he caught himself on the rail.

Well, Verity thought, *it seems he's recovered.* True to his word, Dare had started to look much better almost as soon as the ship had stopped moving. "Thank you, Captain," she said before Dare could say anything else to insult the woman offering to pull them out of enemy territory. "We really appreciate your help."

"May Lanara bless you while you're within sight of her waters or under the light of her moon," Gil said as she shook each of their hands in farewell.

Dare's face softened. "Lanara's blessings to you as well, my friend."

Drystan, Verity, and Dare climbed down the rope ladder, silent and swift, into the waiting rowboat. A member of the crew rowed the three of them ashore, depositing them and their gear on the empty beach.

Even Dare agreed that Gil's advice was sound, so they found a place to camp just inside the tree line. They didn't bother with a fire. The risk of getting caught sneaking into Westhold was a far greater threat than the chill night. The next morning, Verity donned a black shirt with long sleeves to hide the shining steel of her arms.

As she tugged on a pair of black leather gloves, Dare mumbled something under his breath that sounded like, "Thank the gods."

Verity opened her mouth, but Drystan caught her eye. He shook his head, and she could hear his words as clearly as if he'd spoken them aloud. *Not worth it.*

Biting her tongue, she silently finished packing her gear before they set off toward Port Merrick.

As Gil had suggested, the guards at the gate paid them little mind as they entered the city along the main road. With their heavy travel packs and their weapons bundled in canvas under Drystan's arm, resembling a large tent or stall awning, they looked just like every other market-goer passing through the gates that morning.

Port Merrick was a darker, grimier reflection of Whitehollow. Where Whitehollow's streets were wide thoroughfares of well-maintained cobblestones, Port Merrick's were narrow roads of dirt and mud that curved through the buildings with little discernible pattern or order. The same salt air was as pervasive here as it was in Whitehollow and Valda, though there was an unpleasant tinge to it, as though a dark fog hung just above the city, darkening the sky and thickening the air.

Dare led the way, his gait swift despite the heavy pack he carried.

"Do you know where you're going?" Verity asked as she matched his purposeful strides.

Dare smirked. "Absolutely."

It was the smirk that made her ask, "So . . . you've been here before?"

"Taerna's stone tits, of course not," he said, chuckling quietly.

Her jaw tightened. "You just said—"

"I know what I said." At the next intersection, he glanced in both directions before making a left. "Cities are all the same. The details change, but the heart of it never does, no matter where you are." He waved a hand at the buildings they passed. "Cities are arranged into districts—like with like. There are only so many variations. And there's a flow to the streets and the way people move through them. It's easy to find your way if you know how to read it."

Verity tried to see what Dare must be seeing, but she couldn't find a pattern in any of it. Yet soon, the buildings they passed were getting larger, with more shops and specialty craftsmen the further they walked.

But the deeper into the city they traveled, the more Westholden soldiers filled the streets. A weight settled in Verity's stomach as more and more of them appeared around each corner, dressed in their tunics of crimson trimmed with gold. She couldn't stop her fists from clenching, so she pulled her cloak around herself to give her hands something to do.

The next turn had the street opening up to a large market square where shopkeepers and stall owners were setting up for the day. A fountain built of plain dark gray stone sat in the center of the square. It had no shape or design other than what it needed to perform its function as a fountain. A man stood on the edge of the stone, arms upraised to the crowd. Deep lines surrounded his eyes and mouth. His face was framed by shaggy, graying hair, and he wore stained robes that perhaps once were white.

His voice bellowed across the square. "Do not forsake the old gods!" he cried. "For they have not forsaken you! Ainam is the false prophet who seeks to lead your souls astray. Do not forget the gods who breathed life into the world!"

Dare let out a low whistle, then muttered, "That's not going to end well."

"Remember Taerna of the earth, mother to all, who nurtures us and nourishes our harvests!" the man continued.

Verity followed Dare's gaze. A small group of soldiers stood nearby, their attention fixed on the preacher. Even from this distance she could spot the hunger on their faces, like wolves on the hunt.

"Remember Lanara of the waters, whose flowing rivers, seas, and lakes provide endless bounties and give all things life!"

"Why do they care?" Verity whispered to Dare. "He's just a follower of the old gods. He's not hurting anyone."

"Remember Aetherann of the air, whose very element is the breath in our lungs, with which we uncover the mysteries of the world in his honor!"

Dare winced as the soldiers stalked toward the preacher. "I might be wrong," he said, "but I'm pretty sure proselytizing about the old gods is illegal in Westhold."

"So they'll arrest him . . ." Verity said as the soldiers closed in. The laughter on their faces sent her heartbeat skittering. She swallowed, willing her pulse to steady.

"Remember Pyrannis of the flame," the man continued, "who tempers us to withstand hardship and prosecution as fire tempers steel." He was watching the soldiers now. He knew what was coming. "Who burns away impurities with his holy fire."

The soldiers formed a ring around the preacher, jostling each other as though vying for who should be the one to pull him off the edge of the fountain.

One of the soldiers grabbed the preacher by the robes and pulled him forward. The old man fell prostrate at their feet. They laughed as he lay there sputtering, trying to catch his breath.

"Verity, where are you going?" Drystan called, but she barely heard him. She had already thrown her pack at his feet and was sprinting across the square, her heart pounding in her ears. What was she doing? Their mission demanded secrecy. She knew that—somewhere behind the memories of laughing soldiers and blood, beyond the rising fear, she knew. She needed to play it safe. But she couldn't just do nothing.

She would never *do nothing* ever again.

One of the soldiers issued a kick to the fallen man's ribs.

"Hey!" Verity shouted.

They looked up, indignant at the interruption of their sport.

"Move along," one of them said, making a point to rest his hand on his sword.

"*You* move along," Verity barked. "You're harassing this man." She planted her feet in the dirt near where the man had fallen, her years of training taking over, all thoughts of her volatile mission gone. The preacher hadn't dared stand, but the soldiers gathered together on his other side, opposite Verity.

The soldier with his hand on his sword stepped toward her over the fallen preacher. "Who the fuck are you?" he scoffed. "This ain't any of your fucking business."

Verity lifted her chin. He wouldn't make her feel powerless. Not her, and not the man at her feet. She wouldn't let him. "I'm making it my business."

The soldier scoffed and lunged forward, grabbing her by the collar. She pivoted as his thick fingers gripped the fabric of her shirt, pulling him forward a single, unexpected step. She placed her hand on top of his, her fingers wrapping around his palm and her thumb pressing firmly against the bones on the top of his hand. And when she stepped forward again, his arm contorted at an awkward angle. His fingers lost their grip as she peeled his hand away, but she didn't release him.

It happened as quickly as he'd grabbed her, and now the other soldiers all gripped their swords. "Stand down," she commanded.

The soldiers took a collective step forward, rage twisting their features. She only had one more moment before they set on her. One more breath. Verity pulled the collar of her shirt to the side, revealing the symbol of two swords crossed over a brazier branded into her skin. "I said, stand *down*."

They froze. "What in the hells is a Warden of the Flame doing here?" one of them asked, her eyes widening.

"That's not any of your business." Verity released the man's hand, letting him straighten. He stepped back toward the others, glaring at her. "Now let's start again. Why is a group of upstanding soldiers in the honorable Westholden army harassing this man?"

A couple of the soldiers tensed, but the one who'd lunged at her didn't hesitate as he answered, "Worship of the old gods is illegal, Warden."

Verity set her hands on her hips. "And what is the punishment?"

The soldiers in the back were starting to look uncomfortable, but the one in front just sneered. "A fine. Failure to pay the fine results in an arrest and time in the city jail," he said, practically gritting his teeth.

She let a smile play across her lips. "What's the fine?"

The man's face screwed up in disgust as he waved derisively toward the preacher at his feet. "He can't pay! He doesn't have any—"

"What. Is. The. Fine," Verity repeated, biting off each word.

He squared his shoulders. "Twenty gold."

A muscle twitched beneath her eye. That was easily a week's lodging and an exorbitant amount for such a mundane crime. She opened the small pouch on her belt and counted out twenty gold coins. Verity held them out toward the soldier. "Consider his fine paid."

The soldier snatched the coins and stuffed them into his pocket.

"Be on your way." When none of the soldiers moved to leave, she added, "Now."

They left the square in a huff, the one who'd grabbed her casting a withering glare over his shoulder.

Verity crouched beside the preacher. "Are you alright, sir?" she asked, lowering her voice. "Can I help you up?"

"No, no, thank you, Warden," the man said, pushing himself onto his knees. "I'm alright. I thought it best to stay out of the way . . . Yours and theirs."

He stood slowly, and Verity rose with him. At least half the people in the square were still watching her and the preacher.

"Thank you," he said, taking her gloved hand between both of his. "I owe you a great debt."

She smiled but pulled her hand away quickly, clasping her hands behind her back. "Perhaps just find a safer city to preach in."

The man straightened the pendant that hung around his neck, a circular emblem with the symbols of the four elemental gods. "Where better to remind people of the Four than in the places where they have been most forgotten, most forsaken? Than in the lands where Ainam and Vire hold the hearts and souls of men?"

Most of the crowd had gone back about their business, the excitement for the morning extinguished. Verity leaned toward the preacher and said, "But the old gods are gone. They have been for hundreds of years. Why risk your life for gods who no longer exist?"

He smiled at her, all crooked, stained teeth and sad eyes. "They're not gone," he said softly. "Lost, maybe. But not gone. Perhaps it is up to us to find them." He looked up at the sky. "And what is my life if not in the service of those who created the world? What purpose does my life serve if not as a beacon to guide them home?" The man bowed his head. "Thank you, Warden. I think Pyrannis would be proud to count you among his sacred order." He turned and walked away from the fountain that had been his pulpit and the busy square that had been his congregation.

Verity turned his words over in her mind, watching until he was out of sight. When she headed back to where she had left Drystan and Dare, both men stood with their arms crossed, though one of them was smiling.

At her approach, Drystan bent to scoop up her pack and held it out to her. She snatched it, hefting the weight onto one shoulder.

"Are you done?" Dare asked flatly.

Verity faced him. "What?"

"She can't help herself, can she?" he said to Drystan.

"Don't talk to him like I'm not here," she said. "What's your problem?"

"My problem," Dare said, rounding on her, "is you flashing the first soldiers we came across because they were doing something you didn't like."

The newfound intensity in his hazel eyes only served to stoke her own rising frustration.

Dare lowered his voice to a seething hiss. "We've been here less than a fucking hour, and you've already announced to the army that there's a godsdamned *Warden* in their city. If that news gets around, don't you think they're going to start to wonder how you got here? And *why*?"

Verity stepped toward him so they were face to face, only a few inches apart. He wasn't wrong, but . . . "So when he grabbed me and I defended myself, should I have killed them all instead? Or would you rather I'd have let them beat that man—maybe kill him—for nothing?"

Dare held his ground, searching her eyes. After a moment he stepped back with an exasperated growl, dragging his fingers through his hair. "No," he conceded, the sharpness fading. "But you just made our job here immensely more difficult." He looked between the two Wardens before gesturing down the street. "Let's find an inn. We're going to need to lay low today."

As Dare led the way, Verity spun to face Drystan, who flinched under the weight of her ire. He'd certainly seen it often enough, though it was rarely, if ever, aimed at him.

"What?" he asked, taking half a step back.

"You could have helped me."

"With the soldiers?"

"Or with him," she said, nodding toward where Dare already had a good lead on them.

The concern on Drystan's face dissipated. "Vee, I have your back. I always will. I know that being here—"

"Don't say it," she snapped. The tightness in her chest and the knot in her stomach was from the damned mission and being stuck with a mercenary. It had nothing to do with those soldiers.

Drystan's voice softened. "You're one of the best Wardens in the order. I'm not about to stick myself into the middle of something you can handle. I was watching every move those soldiers made. If you needed backup, you know I would have been there in a heartbeat." He started to walk, keeping Dare in sight ahead. "And as for him . . ." Drystan chuckled. "You definitely don't need me defending you with him."

"He's a condescending asshole," Verity muttered.

Drystan smiled. "That may be," he said, "but you haven't exactly been all cheer and compassion. I'm going to keep saying it until you actually do it. Give him a chance, Vee. And look at it this way." He paused at a market stall and bought a couple of apples, tossing one to Verity. "This still isn't the roughest mission we've ever been on." He nudged her elbow. "Remember Embercliff?"

Verity grimaced. She absolutely did.

They followed Dare, maintaining a comfortable distance, until he stopped at an inn several blocks from the busy square.

"We're going to stay here today," Dare said. "And tonight. And probably tomorrow." He led them inside and purchased three rooms from the elderly innkeeper, who thanked him kindly and toddled off into the kitchen.

The main room of the inn was empty at this early hour, so Dare pulled them to a table at the far side of the space, dropping his pack on a chair. He surveyed the two Wardens.

"Vire's hells, you two stand out," he muttered, rubbing at his eyes with his forefinger and thumb. "Just try to keep your heads down, please. Maybe we'll have a little luck and those soldiers will be too embarrassed to report what happened." He turned toward the front door of the inn.

"Where are you going?" Verity asked.

Dare slid his hands into the pockets of his long coat. "I'm going to do what I do best. I'm going to talk to people and get them to tell me things."

CHAPTER 8

DARE WAS GONE THE whole day. It wasn't until after Verity finished dinner with Drystan in the main room of the inn that he returned. It was a busy night, which made Verity profoundly uncomfortable.

"Shouldn't we find somewhere less crowded?" Verity muttered to Dare as he joined their table, a plate of food and a mug in his hands.

"Hello, it's nice to see you," he said, taking his seat with a wry smile. "Yes, I had a productive day. Yes, I stayed safe. Thank you so much for asking." She narrowed her eyes at him as he took a bite of bread, but then he paused and surveyed the busy room. "No, crowded is good. No one will notice three more travelers."

"Did you find out anything?" Drystan asked as Dare shoveled more food into his face, as though he hadn't eaten all day. Perhaps he hadn't.

Dare shrugged, taking a long swig of whatever was in his mug. "Some," he said around the last of the food in his mouth. He swallowed and shook his hair back out of his eyes. "The rumors are true, for one. Westhold *is* preparing for war. What we've seen here with the number of soldiers in the streets—it's like that everywhere. They've been marshaling forces since they lost the war ten years ago."

"Nine," Verity corrected, her voice sharp. If he was going to keep bringing up the war, the least he could do was get the facts right.

He ignored her. "I'll see what else I can dig up tonight."

"You're going out again?" Drystan asked.

Dare nodded. "Daytime underworld is entirely different than nighttime underworld."

"But when do you sleep?"

He chuckled, still hunched over his plate. "I'll stay out most of tonight, get a couple hours of sleep, and go back out again tomorrow. Then I'll stay in tomorrow night and just catch up. It's fine, mother hen." He winked at Drystan. "I've done this hundreds of times."

Verity and Drystan were left to lay low in the inn for the rest of that night and the entire next day. Drystan didn't seem to mind. He had managed to bring a couple of books with him and spent most of the day reclined on Verity's bed with a small volume, its green leather cover cracked and worn. Verity attempted training to keep herself occupied, trying desperately to ignore the fact that they were just sitting around and waiting for their mercenary to tell them what to do. But the small room didn't allow for more than basic calisthenics, and Verity's frustration only increased with being cooped up inside. By the afternoon, it was suffocating.

"How can you just lay there and read all day?" she asked Drystan.

He didn't look up from his book. "Easily. Besides, this one's my favorite."

"How did you even find room in your pack for those?"

The corner of his lips curled as he turned the page. "There's always room for what's important, Vee."

❋

Verity and Drystan were in the common room late that night when Dare returned. It was well past dinner when he skulked in and plopped down into the chair across from Drystan. There were dark circles under his eyes, and his disheveled hair hung loose around his face.

"How'd it go?" Verity asked, eager for any news of the city beyond the inn.

Dare rubbed at his eyes with the palms of his hands. "Nothing new to report, I'm afraid. But I've set the stage. I just need to let a few things develop over the next couple of days." At her frown, he added, "The good news is that I haven't heard anyone talking about a Warden in Port Merrick, so it should be safe for the two of you to venture out tomorrow." He smiled sweetly. "So long as you keep out of trouble."

She ignored his patronizing comment, returning her attention to the crowd. It was busy again tonight, with more people still coming in and gathering around the bar. Dare leaned back in his chair, keeping a trained eye on the tavern's patrons and the general flow of the room.

Verity was about ready to feign exhaustion and head up to her room to avoid any painful small talk when Dare's back stiffened. He set his feet back on the floor from where he had just propped them up on the table.

"Well now, who are *you*?" Dare mumbled under his breath.

Verity followed his gaze and spotted the source of his interest. A group of soldiers had entered the tavern, the one in front claiming the attention of everyone in the immediate vicinity. The light seemed to almost be absorbed by his raven black hair, which was short and somewhat matted, like it had been beneath a helm not long ago. He wore the Westholden colors of red and gold with officer's stripes on his shoulders. The soldiers behind him—ten or so—funneled into the room. People at tables near the door stood quickly, allowing the soldiers to fill in the newly vacated seats.

Dare leaned his elbows on the table as he watched. "Interesting," he muttered to no one in particular.

Drystan's back was to the door, but he kept a close eye on Verity. He was trusting her to tell him anything he needed to know, including if and when he might need to be on his feet.

"Soldiers," she whispered.

Drystan watched her, brows rising in a silent question. He was worried about her. She shook her head to reassure him that there wasn't a problem, but his arms tensed at the gesture. He wasn't buying it.

I'm fine, she mouthed. She focused on the soldiers before he could give her another one of his looks. A few filtered into different parts of the room, but the officer slid onto an open stool at the bar, talking with one of his men.

Maybe if she got closer, she could at least overhear a name or, if she was lucky, something about whatever orders they might have. After nearly two days being uselessly stuck in her tiny inn room, the idea was thrilling. It was certainly better than waiting for Dare to order her around. Verity stood and grabbed her empty tankard.

"Where are you going?" Dare hissed.

Drystan looked about to push up from the table, ready to follow her lead, but Verity stopped him with a firm hand on his shoulder.

"I just need another drink," Verity said, a little too innocently.

"Verity." Dare's eyes were wide, though he didn't move to stand. It was the first time he had used her name, and something about the way he said it made her pause. "He isn't some enlisted pawn. He's an officer. And a high-ranking one on top of it. If he makes you, we're fucked."

Even if Dare was afraid of these soldiers, Verity wasn't about to let them stop her from completing the mission. They needed information, and this was finally something she could do to help.

"I'm just getting a drink," she said before making her way through the crowd to the bar and sliding onto the stool beside the officer. He was surprisingly tall, but lean for a soldier, and peeking out from the collar of his uniform was a thick scar. It started below his ear and ran across his throat. A rope scar. She waved to the bartender for a drink, ignoring the pounding of her heart.

The dark-haired man with the scar around his neck marked her presence and gave her a brief but polite smile, which she returned, before another soldier came up on his other side, joining the first.

"Good work today," the officer said. His voice was deep, but pleasant and not unkind.

"Thank you, Captain."

"If all goes well, Ainam willing," the captain continued, "we'll head south within the week."

"Very good, sir."

The bartender brought Verity a mug of ale, which she clasped in both hands. Who was this dark-haired Westholden captain? What had they been doing? Where were they going in a week and why? Verity glanced at him out of the corner of her eye. *Who are you?*

As the enlisted men took their leave, the captain turned toward Verity and paused, as though seeing her for the first time. "Good evening," he said, shifting on the barstool to face her.

"Evening," Verity said quietly, giving him another faint smile.

"I'm Corvin." He held out his hand.

Verity tensed. Her eyes darted to his hand and then back to his face. His olive skin was smooth and unblemished, and his steel gray eyes flicked to her mouth and back up again. The line of his lips curled faintly. She kept both hands on her drink as she said, "Nice to meet you."

He waited a moment, hand still outstretched, before he said, "And you are?"

Shit.

She needed to think of something to say. Anything to say. He wasn't supposed to *talk* to her. She hadn't thought of a fake name to use, and now she was drawing a blank. If she didn't give a name soon, he was going to suspect something, if he didn't already given how she was avoiding shaking his hand. But even through the leather gloves, she was sure he'd be able to feel the metal of her hands beneath.

Say something!

"Verity," she said, opting to stick with the truth as much as possible. It was a much safer area for her anyway.

The captain finally put his hand down. "Verity," he repeated, as though committing it to memory. Just what she needed. He leaned against the bar, settling in for a conversation. "Are you new in town? I don't recall seeing you before."

This was rapidly dissolving into a disaster. "Just got in," she said. She glanced past him to the other side of the room where Dare and Drystan still sat, both now facing her direction and watching intently. Maybe she could duck out of this mess she stumbled into and make it back to the table.

"Well then, welcome to Port Merrick, Verity." He offered a charming smile.

She set her mug down as though she were finished, even though it was still full. "Thank you," she murmured as she stood. "Have a good night."

As Verity stepped away from the bar, another soldier stumbled by, jostling her into Corvin. She felt the pressure of Corvin's arm bump against the steel of her forearm. She tensed.

And the Westholden captain tensed.

Something flickered in Corvin's eyes as they snapped to her, like a flash of light that spiraled inward across his irises. Verity moved to go, but he caught her by the elbow. His grip was so strong it startled her.

"What are you, Verity?"

She instantly regretted giving him her real name. She tried to pull herself free from his grip and failed. "Let go," she commanded.

Corvin pulled her closer. "What is it you're doing here?"

"Leaving." Verity pivoted and yanked her elbow toward the gap between his fingers and thumb. Her arm slipped through, and she started toward the door. She couldn't go back to the table with Drystan and Dare, not now that she'd managed to get the captain's full attention. She would have to try to meet up with them somewhere outside.

As she pushed through the crowd, Verity wished for her sword, or a dagger—anything that could help give her a degree of authority besides her Warden's brand. She'd already gotten away with using that once; she didn't think she'd get so lucky when it came to a captain of the Westholden army. But their weapons were still wrapped and stowed upstairs with the rest of their gear.

Why had he even noticed her? Was her luck just that bad? Verity muttered a curse under her breath. So much for avoiding attention. Again. It felt like half the bar was watching her.

She reached the door, but Corvin's tall form slid into it, barring her exit. "*Verity.*" Her name on his lips was like a caress. His eyes flashed again as he caught her by the shoulder. "Verity, what are you looking for?"

A weapon, she thought. *I'm looking for a weapon. Something to get me out of here. To get you to back off. I need a weapon.*

Something pulled in her throat, and the words tumbled. "The weapon," she said, though she clamped her mouth shut as she heard the words that came out, and the unintended emphasis. Not *a* weapon. *The* weapon. Her heart raced. How could she be so careless?

The light that had spiraled through Corvin's eyes flickered again and a grin danced across his face. "Interesting," he murmured, inching toward her.

Chairs scraped across the floor as shouts rose up from the other side of the room. Corvin glanced up at the commotion. That was her chance.

As soon as he looked away, Verity grabbed him by his shoulders and drove her knee upward. He doubled over, all the air knocked out of him in a groan as her knee struck solidly between his legs. Then she ducked through the door and into the darkened streets of Port Merrick.

CHAPTER 9

DRYSTAN WAS ON HIS feet the moment the officer grabbed Verity's arm. He nearly reached them when she kneed the officer in the balls and slipped through the front door. The man dropped instantly to his knees, and Drystan, pausing in his rush to Verity, resisted the urge to let out a triumphant laugh.

A crowd of soldiers gathered around their leader, hoisting him to his feet. The officer pointed at several of them. "You three!" he shouted, sputtering, still half bent over. "Go after her. Now!" He coughed, barking out the rest of his orders in ragged gasps. "The rest of you . . . fan out. No one . . . leaves this tavern until . . . I've questioned every person here!"

Drystan had to act fast before they could go after Verity while he'd be trapped in the building. He charged forward, closing the rest of the distance to the soldiers. He lowered his head and drove his shoulder into the gut of the nearest one, who'd just turned to sweep the room. The man flailed and stumbled into the three heading toward the door. They all fell to the floor in a heap.

Careful to keep his back toward the officer, Drystan grabbed another patron by the front of his shirt. "Sorry about this, friend," he said softly, then shoved the man into the table behind him, spilling their round of drinks. The table erupted in outrage. Drystan scooped up one of the flagons as it slid off the table, spun on his back foot, and hurled it across the tavern. Angry shouts chorused from the far side of the room.

Drystan didn't stop. He took two more steps before he kicked the edge of another table, its contents scattering as it toppled. He ducked into the crowd, hoping to sneak out before any fingers could point his way. But a burly man caught him by the shoulder, spinning him around.

"Hey!" the man shouted. "What the f—"

Drystan snapped out his fist in a sharp jab. The man released him instantly, both hands flying to his bloodied nose.

Fights were breaking out across the tavern, and the soldiers were trying to contain the rapidly unfolding chaos. Drystan ducked a wild punch, returning it with a right hook that sent a familiar sting through his hand as his attacker went sprawling. On his way toward the kitchen—and a quick exit—he glanced toward the table he'd been sharing with Verity and Dare. It was empty.

Drystan grabbed the door to the kitchen, but the crimson and gold of a soldier's uniform gripped his arm from behind.

"No one leaves," the man barked.

Drystan shot his elbow up and back. A crunch preceded a yowl of pain, and the hand on his arm released. Drystan ducked into the kitchen without turning back.

He sprinted through the side door and into the streets, searching for Verity. There was no sign of her. He shook out his hand, which still stung.

Dammit.

The streets were mostly empty at this time of night, with just a few folks heading home after a long day. Drystan hooked right up the main road, toward the part of town they'd passed through the previous morning, praying he'd find Verity before the soldiers did.

Drystan had known the Westhold mission was a bad idea from the start, but they had their orders. And with so many teams diverted elsewhere, there hadn't been much room for negotiating on which Wardens should be sent.

It felt like he'd been searching for an hour, although reasonably it had only been a few long minutes before he spotted Verity dart around the edge of a building. He breathed out a sigh. The tension that had been building in his chest loosened. It looked like she was heading back toward the tavern. He quickened his pace into a run and caught up with her before she had the chance to move into another alleyway.

"Verity," he whispered as loudly as he dared.

She wheeled around at the sound of his voice, relief washing over her. "Gods," she breathed, stooping a little to rest her hands on her knees. "Drystan. What happened after I left?"

"I caused a distraction, but they're looking for you," he said, hurrying to her side. "I ducked out right after."

She nodded, still breathing hard. "And Dare?"

"I didn't see where he went." He took in her pale skin, which was even paler than usual, and the way she shifted from foot to foot. She was shaken, almost panicked. Drystan had never seen her so rattled. Or so reckless, if he was being honest. Verity was always careful, methodical. Being here—in Westhold, with soldiers everywhere they turned—was affecting her, even if she didn't realize it.

"Are you alright?" he asked. "What happened?"

Verity tucked a few strands of loose hair behind her ears. "I don't know." She leaned back against the wall of the alley. "Drystan, I don't know what happened."

He took her by the shoulders and pulled her into an embrace. "It's alright," he said against the top of her head. "We'll figure it out. We always do."

"Fantastic," Verity muttered, pulling away from him gently. "Our first few days in Westhold and we've already alerted a military leader to our presence and lost our mercenary."

"Don't worry," a voice crooned from around the corner behind him. Dare stepped out from the shadows and leaned against the corner of the building, crossing his arms. "You haven't lost your mercenary. And *we* didn't do anything." He stared daggers at Verity. "*You* decided to flirt with someone *I* told you to stay away from, and then *you* were made."

Tensing, Verity straightened. "I wasn't *flirting*," she bit out.

"Well not successfully," Dare sniped. "And now the only thing *we* are is fucked."

Squaring his shoulders, Drystan faced Dare. "That's enough," he said sharply. "It's not her fault. It's nobody's fault," he added before Verity could issue a retort. He'd spent every moment since they'd met up in Valda trying to get these two to work together, and Mother Taerna, they did not make it easy. They got along about as well as a spark and dried grass. And Drystan needed to make sure they didn't burn the whole damn city down with them. "Now is not the time," he continued, still focused on Dare. "We'll deal with it, but let's fix this first."

"That was a hell of a brawl you started back there," Dare said, grinning.

"You started a *brawl*?" The revelation pulled Verity out of her panic. He expected anger, or at least disappointment, but worry creased her brow.

"I . . ." Drystan flexed his right hand, glancing at the small cuts along his first two knuckles. He'd worked hard to leave that life behind, but . . . "I needed to do something . . ."

"Look, if you'll listen to me this time," Dare interrupted, "we need to move to another part of the city. Now."

Verity stepped past Drystan, approaching Dare with a threat building in the tightness of her muscles. Her fists clenched at her side, and Drystan shifted his weight to the balls of his feet in case he needed to stop her from striking him. He didn't like it, but they needed Dare.

"We need to get our gear," Verity said, her jaw set.

Without even a blink at her approach, Dare twisted around the corner he'd been leaning against and tossed Verity's knapsack at her feet, her cloak tucked neatly into the shoulder straps. "Now let's go," he said.

Moving around the corner beyond Dare, Drystan spotted his own knapsack, as well as Dare's gear and their wrapped bundle of weapons all leaning against the wall. Despite his frustration with him, Drystan had to give him some credit for that. "Thanks," he said.

Dare gave half a shrug, picking up his pack as Drystan grabbed his things and the bundle of weapons.

Verity wrapped her cloak around herself and hefted her bag onto her shoulders, still glaring at Dare.

"Come on," Drystan said to her quietly. "Let's go."

Chapter 10

Dare led his wayward Wardens through the darkened streets for an hour before they stepped into another inn in a different part of the city. It was closer to the docks, which wasn't ideal, but people in this part of town were more likely to look the other way, especially with a few liberally applied bribes. He'd spent the better part of two days learning his way around this side of Port Merrick. He could use that to his advantage.

As they entered the small inn, Dare waved Drystan and Verity off to a table and went to work securing them some rooms for the night. And, more importantly, ensuring their presence wouldn't attract any unwanted attention. A few people were lounging about in the common room, but most of them had the look of wanting to be left alone. Perfect.

It cost him more than he wanted—and certainly more than he would admit to the Wardens—to make sure there wouldn't be any trouble. But Verity's little stunt turned his timetable on its head. Sleep would have to wait. He had more work to do.

Keys in hand and coin purse a good deal lighter, Dare returned to his two companions. Drystan was leaning forward, elbows resting on the table, while Verity had her forehead in her hands.

"That was shit," she muttered toward the table as Dare approached.

"What happened?" Drystan asked.

She let out a sigh and rubbed at her face with her gloved hands. "I'm not sure. I was trying to learn something about who that was."

"And?" Dare slid into the chair beside her, dropping his pack onto the floor. "What did we learn?"

Drystan shot him a warning look that Dare chose to interpret as *if you upset her, I will hurt you*. He also chose to ignore it.

Verity dropped her hands to the table with a dull thud. "Only that they're planning to head south within the week, but they didn't say why. And the man with the scar said his name was Corvin."

Dare's stomach twisted into a knot. "Corvin Crosse?" he asked, his voice lowering. The name had caught his ear earlier in the day, and he'd flagged it as someone to dig more into tomorrow.

She shook her head, her brow furrowing slightly. "I don't know. He didn't say. But another soldier called him Captain."

Shit.

"Who's Corvin Crosse?" Drystan asked.

"I'm not entirely sure. Captain Crosse," Dare said quietly, "showed up in Port Merrick three weeks ago with an entire company of soldiers, and for some reason, his arrival has the city in a figurative uproar."

"That's it?" Verity asked. "That's all you've found out?"

Dare raised a brow at her. He liked it better when she was stunned into a self-pitying silence. "We've been here two days, my lady Warden," he said. "These things take time to unravel."

"Maybe if you let us do something instead of insisting we stay cooped up inside—"

"I'd say you've done quite enough."

Drystan's fist slammed into the table. Both Verity and Dare jumped. "Knock it off!" he snapped, shooting a damning look at both of them.

Dare thought of another comment or two but bit his tongue. He was in no mood for this shit tonight anyway.

Drystan blew out a breath, the tension flowing out of his shoulders as he leaned back in his chair. "Did you hear or see anything else, Vee?"

"There was something strange about his eyes," Verity said. "It was like they flashed when he looked at me. When he grabbed my arm."

Drystan leaned in closer. "His eyes *flashed*?"

"Yes. Like with an inner light. It was . . . odd. I've never seen anything like it."

"You ever hear of anything like that?" The table was silent for a moment before Dare realized that Drystan was talking to him.

Dare shook his head. "No," he said. "Never."

Verity pushed her hair back behind her ears. "So what do we do now?"

"We stick to the plan," Dare said quickly. "No more going off script. We're here to gather information, and that's what we're going to do. Port Merrick is a big place. Maybe we can simply avoid our new friend Captain Corvin Crosse. If we get lucky, we might be able to stay out of his way and maintain what's left of our low profile."

Dare sighed. He wasn't feeling particularly optimistic about their luck, if recent events were any indication.

But maybe this could still work. Maybe he could stick to his original plan of catching up on sleep tonight and going out tomorrow to ask more questions, grease more palms. And now he had a face to go with the name he needed more information on. It might work . . .

"Unless," Dare added after a moment. Something about the way Verity was sitting, her shoulders forward slightly, her arms tucked around her middle, set Dare on edge. "Unless there's anything else that we should know about your exchange with the friendly Westholden captain?"

Verity stiffened, her brown eyes darting to Drystan.

"Verity?" Drystan asked quietly. "What else happened?"

She swallowed. "When he grabbed my arm, he asked me what I was looking for . . ."

Gods, she's scared, Dare realized. He leaned closer, planting his elbows on his knees. "What did you tell him?" He spoke slowly, gently.

Verity didn't look at him. "I needed to get past him," she said, explaining it to Drystan alone, like they were the only two people in the tavern. "I wanted my sword or a dagger or . . . any weapon, so I could get past him."

Dare's mouth went dry as Drystan leaned in and set a hand on her knee. "You told him you were looking for a weapon?" he asked.

Verity shook her head. "I said I was looking for *the* weapon."

There was a growing chill in the pit of Dare's stomach.

"Why'd you tell him anything at all?" Drystan all but whispered.

"I don't know," she said, the words rushing out of her now. "He was grabbing my arm, and it was like the answer to his question just slipped out of my mouth as soon as the thought crossed my mind."

"Could he have compelled you somehow?" Drystan asked. "With magic?"

"That's impossible," Dare said. "Magic can't affect the mind like *that*." He paused, swallowing the lump in his throat as he added, "Can it?"

Verity gave a helpless shrug. "Not with any mind magic I've ever seen. Not that quickly. But . . . he must have. Somehow."

If Dare thought they were fucked before, he knew now they were well and truly fucked. He was on his feet in the next moment.

"Where are you going?" Verity asked, finally deigning to look at him.

Dare fished into his pocket and tossed two iron keys on the table. "Your rooms for the night," he said. "I'll be back in the morning."

"Where are you going?" she repeated.

Dare sighed toward the ceiling. "You literally told him exactly why we're here," he said tightly. "We are now, officially, running out of time. If we have any hope at all of salvaging this job *and* making it out of here, I need to get to work." He looked between the two of them. "Stay here. Keep your heads down. And in the name of Vire's unholy fucking ass, don't talk to anyone."

Before either of them could argue, he slipped out of the inn.

✳

Dare stuffed his hands into the pockets of his coat as he walked through the city streets. With a little luck, the Wardens would just sit quietly. It was getting late, after all. How much more trouble could they get into tonight?

He quickened his pace as he headed back to the inn where they'd started, trying to track down this captain that Verity had stumbled into and all over with her attempts at eavesdropping. The place had cleared out, but Dare asked around and discovered that Verity's dear captain was indeed Captain Corvin Crosse, and he was in charge of some pretty secretive stuff in the Westholden military. Unfortunately, none of the lackeys Dare spoke to knew anything about it. Though one helpful and very drunk corporal did provide the location of the military barracks where the captain and his men were being housed while in town. He said Crosse had rushed off in quite a hurry after his run-in with a woman in the tavern a couple of hours ago. Dare bought the man another drink and hurried back out into the night.

In a narrow alleyway, Dare wove around stacked crates and discarded boxes on his way toward the barracks. Where the alley met the main road, he pressed himself against the wall and checked around the corner. Heading his way was a group of soldiers. Dare immediately recognized the leader.

Just my fucking luck. Dare slid into the shadows behind a stack of boxes and crouched out of sight to watch the soldiers pass by.

Only they didn't pass by.

The captain stopped and angled his head toward the alley, as though he heard a noise. Dare knew he hadn't made a sound, but he ducked his head down further and slowed his breathing. The shadows and his dark coat would keep him hidden from a casual glance.

Crosse's footsteps crunched on the dirt road as he took a single step into the alley. "Who's there?" he called.

Dare held his breath. Crosse couldn't have heard him. There wasn't a chance. Dare had been tailing people since he was a kid, and he'd never been caught except once or twice when he'd gotten cocky during his first years in Valda. There was no way—

The heavy boots moved closer. Maybe he could pass for a drunkard, passed out from too much ale. But a tightness took hold of his heart, and a voice in the back of his mind said to run. Dare waited another moment, another footstep, until he was certain the sudden thundering of his heart was going to give him away.

"I know someone's here . . ." Crosse called again. He couldn't have been more than fifteen feet away now.

Run, the voice said again. *Run!*

Dare took off at a sprint. Crosse shouted, and boots pounded the gravel as the soldiers gave chase. They might be fast, but Dare was faster. He'd been outrunning trouble all his life. He ran as fast as he could, turning down a winding street. He used the wall of a shop to slow his momentum and swung into another alley. The shouts were a short distance away, around the corner. He was out of their line of sight. Now was his chance.

Using an upturned crate as a vault, Dare launched himself up the wall of the building to his left. His foot met the top of the door frame as his hand grabbed the bottom of a windowsill, and he hurled himself up, rolling onto the roof as the running footsteps entered the alley below. They slowed.

"Where is he?" one of the soldiers shouted. "Where'd he go?"

"Spread out," Crosse ordered. The soldiers fanned out across multiple streets. "Sergeant," the captain continued, though he lowered his voice. Dare barely made out the words as he said, "Tell the general we need to move the weapon immediately. And tell him I'm dealing with a couple of spies."

"Yes, sir," came the sharp reply as one set of boots ran off.

Yet the other set remained far closer than Dare would have liked. "I can feel you here," Crosse said. His voice was soft, encouraging.

Silence fell everywhere except for the pulsing of his blood in his ears. Dare held his breath as he lay on his back at the edge of the roof, not daring to move another inch away from the eaves.

Then the voice came again. It was directly beneath him. "I wonder . . ." Crosse said, and it felt as though he was whispering in Dare's ear, claustrophobic in its closeness. "Can you feel me too?"

Dare pushed away from the ledge and onto his feet. He sprinted again, this time across the top of the building. Willing his legs to carry him as fast as they would move, he threw himself off the edge toward the next building. Dare couldn't maintain his footing as he hit the hard, flat roof. He stumbled and fell, slamming his shoulder as he tried to roll with the momentum. He scrambled to his feet and kept running, leaping again to the next building, and the next. When he felt like he'd put enough distance between him and Crosse, Dare dropped onto his side and slid to a stop flat against the edge of the roof.

His chest heaved as he lay there for a moment and simply listened. An occasional shout reached him, but they were far away. The soldiers were still looking for him, but that was probably about as good as he could hope for. Without waiting to catch his breath—there would be time for things like *breathing* once he was certain he was out of this mess—Dare rolled off the roof. He gripped the building's edge and lowered himself down in a fluid, controlled motion, though his shoulder raged as he silently descended. He found the ledge of a window with his foot and scaled down the side of the building, jumping the last six feet. He tucked into another roll as he landed.

What in Vire's hells was that? But he didn't wait for an answer to come to him before he broke into a run, back toward the tavern where he'd left the Wardens.

He took the long way back to the inn. Twice he had to double back and find another route because of soldiers moving through the streets. They were rounding up the drunkards and anyone else unfortunate enough to still be out at this late hour. In the gray light just before dawn, Dare slipped through the back door of the inn and up the stairs. He wasn't sure how the Wardens had split the rooms between the two of them, so he took a chance on which of the two he was about to awaken *very* early.

Only a few seconds after he knocked gently on the door, it swung open. Verity stood on the other side of the threshold.

Dammit.

She was wearing her green top with the wide straps and her black pants, but no belt or boots, like she was still in the middle of dressing for the day.

"Dare?"

He braced himself for her ire, but her face softened as her eyes swept over him from head to toe.

She stepped to the side and motioned for him to enter, closing the door behind him. "What's going on?"

As the door latched shut, the adrenaline of his escape finally began to wear off. As did the dulling effect it had on the pain in his shoulder . . . and apparently his knee, Dare discovered. It throbbed as he moved into the center of the small room. He peeled off his coat and inhaled sharply through his teeth as his shoulder twisted.

"Are you alright?" she asked. "What happened?"

"I'm fine," he said, dropping his coat on the table against the wall. "I just had a run-in with your dear Captain Corvin."

Verity's whole body stiffened. He expected her to chide him for the unfortunate encounter. "Sit here. Take your weight off that knee," she said instead. He hadn't realized his discomfort was so noticeable. She guided him with a firm hand to the single chair that was angled in the corner of the room. "I'll get Drystan."

Dare listened to the padding of her bare feet in the hallway, then the quiet knocking of metal against wood. The creak of a door. Hushed voices, a door latching firmly closed, and then two sets of footsteps walking the short distance back to the room where Dare now sat, rotating his shoulder to test his range of motion. It twinged at the apex of the circle, and Dare was pretty sure he'd be sporting a colorful bruise by this time tomorrow.

The door swung open again and Verity entered, followed closely by Drystan. He leaned back against the door while Verity perched on the edge of the bed. With the two Wardens present and focused on him, Dare relayed everything that had happened once he left the inn.

When Dare reached the end of his tale, Drystan crossed his arms over his chest. "So they do have a weapon and now they're getting ready to move it. Did they say what it is?"

Dare shook his head. "No, just that it's here. In the city."

Drystan looked to Verity. "You've got to get a message back to the Council."

Verity nodded and retrieved a small roll of parchment with a quill and ink from her knapsack. She laid everything on the little table and scribbled a brief message. When she was done, she held the parchment in the air between her fingers, and it disappeared into a wisp of silvery smoke. Dare shuddered.

"It's not even dawn," Verity said quietly. "I don't know how long it'll be before we get an answer."

It wouldn't be long, Dare was certain. Not for something like this.

"What do we do in the meantime?" Drystan asked.

"Lay low," Dare said, rubbing at his knee, which had transitioned from throbbing insistently to a dull ache. "I don't think any of us should risk going out again. Not until it's time to get the hell out of here."

A moment later, another strip of paper appeared on the table beside Verity. She picked it up and read the text aloud. "*Find the weapon and destroy it.*"

"What?" Drystan pushed off from the door to look at the note himself. "Destroy it? Why? *How?*"

"I don't know," Verity said.

"The fuck," muttered Dare. "We don't even know anything about it!" This was supposed to be an information-gathering job. He was supposed to be gone a few days, maybe a week, and then back to Valda. Back to his life. Finding and destroying some kind of military weapon was not part of the agreement.

"We know it's magical," Verity mumbled, still staring at the worthless note the Council sent. "And we know roughly where it is now," she added after a moment.

Dare leaned back, resting his head on the wall. "Yeah, but we're not going to be able to get it while it's here," he said. "They're going to be on alert for anyone out of place, and that's definitely us."

Drystan studied the note, turning it over as though that would reveal more of the message, or maybe would elucidate whatever the hell the Council was thinking. But when Drystan flipped the paper, Dare caught a glimpse of the note's graceful, flowing script. *Tanithe Ash.* Of course she was calling the shots. He should have seen this coming.

"What about taking it while it's en route to wherever it's going?" Drystan asked.

"Same issue," Dare said, refocusing on the immediate problem. "They'll have the thing well-guarded while they move it. They won't risk the possibility of losing it in transit."

Verity took up Drystan's vacated spot propping up the door. "So we follow them and take it once it gets to wherever they're going," she said. "We get it when they think the danger's passed."

A ghost of a smile danced across Dare's lips. "My lady Warden, I do believe I'm becoming a bad influence on you." His smile widened as she rolled her eyes.

"That could work. But we'll have to play it smart. And careful. But . . ." He gazed appraisingly at Drystan. "But I think I might actually have a plan."

CHAPTER 11

Securing a soldier's uniform in Drystan's size turned out to be even easier than Dare had expected. With so many soldiers currently stationed in Port Merrick, many of the local tailors and launderers had a fairly constant supply of uniforms. Dare was able to pilfer a corporal's uniform with no trouble at all. And the paperwork from the recruiter's office that Drystan requested had been just as easily acquired.

'Bout time something goes well.

Verity complained, of course, but Drystan was the only one who would fit in with the other soldiers. Neither Dare nor Verity would pass even a cursory glance. Drystan, who had been hunched over parchments on the small table for the better part of the morning, had looked momentarily offended but didn't comment.

Now, Drystan definitely looked the part. His broad shoulders, close-cropped blond hair and new crimson and gold uniform would help him fit in perfectly. He strapped the belt with standard-issue Westholden sword and dagger around his waist. Dare took a step back to admire the picture he presented, though Verity hardly looked at him.

"Be careful," Drystan said to them both.

"You too," Verity replied, staring out the window. Her arms were wrapped around her middle again.

Drystan lingered, watching her. "I will," he said. When she still didn't look at him, he hesitated only a moment longer before he was out the door.

"And what do *we* do?" Verity asked after Drystan was gone.

"We follow. From a distance."

"Where do you think they're taking it? The weapon."

Dare considered Crosse's options. "I doubt they'd bother moving it if they were planning to just keep it in the same city. I'm betting they'll take it to another city or to a stronghold somewhere." He eyed Drystan's pack where he'd left it by the table, near Verity's and Dare's. "And given that we'll likely be needing to extricate ourselves pretty quickly once we destroy this thing, I don't think we'll be coming back this way. Best make sure we have everything we need before we leave."

Verity nodded and didn't argue. Good. Dare had hardly slept for the last two and a half days and wasn't in the mood to bicker. He dragged his fingers through his hair. He'd better get some coffee before they headed out again.

Verity gestured toward the bed. "Why don't you get a little bit of sleep," she said. "I'm sure we can spare an hour or two before we need to move, right?"

He was going to say that they should be ready to go at any moment, but realistically Drystan would need some time to ingratiate himself with the other soldiers. Not to mention that something of this level of importance would be moved either under the cover of darkness or at first light tomorrow. Since it was now just after noon, they likely had some time.

With a resigned nod, Dare crossed to the bed, a very slight hitch in his step from where his knee didn't quite want to straighten all the way.

"How's your knee?" Verity asked.

"It'll be fine," he said. "I twisted it once when I was a kid, and sometimes it just acts up a little."

Her brow furrowed, her gaze going distant for a moment before she shook off whatever thought she had.

"Are you sure about this?" Dare asked, sitting on the edge of the bed. When she cocked her head, he added, "I mean, this is your room. I can go to mine."

Verity waved him off. "It's fine; you're already here. And we should probably stick together."

Dare couldn't argue with that. He kicked off his boots and unfastened his belt, dropping it at the foot of the bed. He fully intended to make some sort of witty remark as he laid on top of the perfectly made bed with its perfectly tucked in blanket, but he was asleep as soon as his head hit the pillow.

"Dare."

His eyes snapped open and he took in his surroundings with one quick sweep. He was still in Verity's room, lying on the bed. The Warden was crouching next to him, her hand on his forearm to wake him. Nothing out of place. No danger. His shoulders relaxed back against the blanket.

"It's been a couple of hours," she said. If Dare didn't know any better, he might think she sounded apologetic.

He held in a groan. "Right." He blinked slowly to clear his head of sleep before sitting up and swinging his legs over the side of the bed. He rubbed at his shoulder, which started throbbing again as he moved.

Verity sat beside him. "This is going to work, right?"

He was caught off guard by the question, by the vulnerability in it, and so he paused and looked at her—*really* looked. She was worried. It was clear in the lines of her face, the tightness of her jaw. She was worried for her friend, who they'd just sent deeper into enemy territory with only the two of them as backup. And they hadn't exactly proven themselves capable of working together.

"It's a decent plan, and Drystan seems like a really smart guy." Dare tried to sound as confident as he could. "I believe it'll work."

He couldn't tell if she was satisfied with his answer, but she stood and turned back to the table, where she had laid out the contents of Drystan's pack. She began sorting them into different bags that lay open on the floor.

Dare rose and stretched a little, testing his knee and his shoulder. Good enough, he figured. Then he helped Verity finish sorting their gear into what they needed to take and what they could afford to leave.

Verity took a stack of three books and moved them to the pile of things they were leaving behind, but she stopped before she set them down. Dare glanced at the stack but couldn't make out any of the worn titles along the spines.

"What are those?"

"Drystan's books," she said. The metal of her fingers brushed along the cover of the topmost book. It was bound in green leather and looked as though it had been read more than the other two, although all were well-loved. She separated the green one from the others and crammed it into her knapsack, relegating the two to the *leave behind* pile.

With their gear sorted and a last look at one another, Verity and Dare left the inn and headed across town. Toward Drystan and, hopefully, the weapon they had been ordered to destroy.

Walking through the streets of Port Merrick, Dare realized he had spent so much time and effort working on his part of the plan—the part they were currently engaged in—that he hadn't thought too hard about Verity's part of the plan. The part that involved actually destroying this incredibly powerful weapon, whatever it was.

Dare's curiosity got the better of him and he broke the silence. "So," he said quietly. "You're able to use your abilities to destroy magical items?" The intelligence from the Council mentioned she was a mage, but she hadn't done any magic other than the Sending spell that morning, and that could have easily been enchanted parchment rather than her doing anything.

"I thought you knew enough about what I could do." Verity eyed him sidelong. "That's what you said in Valda, right?"

Dare shrugged and then bit back the wince at the twinge of pain. "I did when the job was just *finding* the damn thing," he said. "The job's changed."

She rolled her eyes but said, "Yes. It takes a lot of energy, but I can do it."

"You've done it before?"

"Mm-hmm."

"How much energy does it take?"

"It depends," she said. "Most magical objects have their own sort of shield to prevent them from being destroyed with something simple like a Banishment. Instead, you need to pour your own magic into it first, letting your power mingle with the object's magic. Once the magic's balanced, or close to it, then you can manipulate it, and manipulating magic has always been one of my areas of expertise. I'm one of the best there is." She wasn't boasting or bragging, just stating a fact.

"So you have to add magic to destroy magic," Dare muttered.

Verity nodded. "Even if it's as powerful as the rumors suggest," she continued, lowering her voice, "I should be able to destroy it, though I might be pretty tapped out." They walked a few more steps in silence before she added, "Worst case scenario, Drystan will let me channel from him to fuel the last bit of the spell. That way I can still function, and we can get out of there in one piece. Me at twenty-five percent and Drystan at seventy-five percent is better than me at zero and needing to be carried out of there," she said. Her tone was neutral, as if they were talking about the weather.

Dare blinked. Channel *from* . . . ? "You can pull energy from others to power your magic?" He tried to keep the concern out of his voice.

"I can," she said, glancing at him as they walked. "Not all mages can, though. It takes a powerful Channel to be able to use another person as a source in addition to themselves."

"Does it have to be given willingly?" Dare wasn't quite sure he wanted to know the answer.

Verity shook her head. "No." A shadow fell over her face. "It's harder to do when the person is unwilling, but it's also morally objectionable. I don't do that."

Despite the tension on her face, Dare couldn't stop himself from asking, "Never?"

A muscle fluttered in her jaw. "Once," she said. "Only once. It was a dire situation. But even so . . ." She hesitated a heartbeat before saying, "I wouldn't do it again."

So many questions ran through Dare's head. But he saw the tightness rippling through her body, the fisted hand at her side, and he dropped the subject. He needed her focused, not wound up so tight that she would explode at the first person who looked at her the wrong way. Especially because that would very likely be him, and now was really not a great time for that.

Dare let the silence settle around them again until they reached the barracks. Groups of soldiers were milling about the training yard behind the building, and Dare easily spotted Drystan among them. He found a spot where they could keep an eye on things without calling attention to themselves for loitering. "And now," he said. "We wait."

✸

As the sun dipped behind the buildings, the soldiers gathered outside the barracks, including Drystan, who blended in with the soldiers better than even Dare had expected. Dare watched with amusement as Drystan chatted and joked with several of them, their body language telling him that they were relaxed and comfortable, open to anything Drystan had to say. And when the soldiers formed ranks and moved out, Drystan went with them, as though he belonged. No one gave him a second glance.

"He's good," Dare said quietly.

Verity only smiled.

Dare and Verity followed a safe distance behind, sticking to the lengthening shadows. Their next stop was some sort of warehouse on the outskirts of the city. By the time they arrived, it was fully dark out, and torches lit the front of the building. A handful of the soldiers peeled off from the group and went inside.

"If you want to get closer," Verity whispered, "I can shield us from sight."

Dare shook his head. "No, this is good. I don't want to risk getting too close." He kept checking behind them, as well as down every street he could see from their vantage point. He needed to make sure that Crosse wasn't around somewhere to get the drop on them.

After about an hour, as a misty rain began to fall, three wagons came around the building. The soldiers repositioned themselves to surround the wagons, which were each drawn by two horses. Another figure stepped out from the building then and moved around to the side of the group, addressing them all in a line. Every muscle in Dare's body tensed at his presence.

"Is that . . ." Verity whispered beside him.

"Yes." Dare didn't need to have a good view of the officer to know it was Crosse.

They couldn't hear what was said, but soon a cheer rippled through the line. Crosse mounted a horse and rode to the front. The soldiers and wagons followed.

"Where to next, do you think?" Verity asked.

"Out of town," he said. "South, possibly, if we can assume the information you overheard from the captain was about this. And if they're getting out of the city and into the open, we'll need to hang back. Especially with our dear Captain leading the way. We'll have to stay out of their line of sight. Entirely."

Verity watched the soldiers—and Drystan—move down the street, toward the edge of Port Merrick.

"If we're out of their line of sight," Verity said, taking a slow breath, "then they'll be out of ours too."

"We'll be able to track them," Dare said gently. He turned the collar of his coat up against the rain. "There's what, forty men there, plus the wagons and horses? Their tracks will be hard to miss."

"Alright." Verity pulled up the hood of her cloak. "Lead the way."

CHAPTER 12

THE CARAVAN TRAVELED THROUGH much of the night, making it easy to follow the distant glow of their torches. Much of the land on the eastern side of Westhold was rolling plains and prairies, with very little in the way of cover. Dare kept the caravan as a speck on the unmarred horizon.

Around noon the next day, Dare called a brief break. They ate some of the dried food they'd packed, but Verity's attention kept drifting up, toward the caravan in the distance.

"Stop worrying so much," Dare said, his exasperation seeping through. It had to have been the fifth time she looked up in as many minutes. "We're not going to lose them."

"I'm not worried," she retorted, not very convincingly. She glanced up again not a minute later.

"Vire's fucking hells, could you—"

"Someone's coming."

Dare snapped his head up, following her gaze. A cloud of dust billowed against the skyline in the distance. "Ah, fuck," he muttered. And there was nowhere to hide on the wide expanse of the plains.

He shrugged out of his wool coat and tossed it to Verity. Once they'd left the city, she'd done away with the long sleeves and gloves, the steel of her arms clearly visible now. "Put this on," he said. "And take off your sword."

"What? Why?"

"Because, while I doubt anyone in Westhold has heard of *the Warden with the metal arms,* you'll likely attract more attention than we want."

Verity grimaced, her brow furrowing. "Do you think those are soldiers from the caravan?"

"I don't know," he said. The dust cloud was getting larger as whoever it was approached at speed. "But regardless, it'll be best if we can make them think we're travelers so they pass us by."

Verity clutched his coat, making no move to put it on.

"I know doing things my way goes against your very being, my lady Warden. But . . ." He could just make out the shape of horses now. "But for fuck's sake, could you listen to me just once and put on the damn coat?"

Her eyes narrowed on him, but she stood without another word and slipped her cloak from her shoulders. She tossed it to Dare.

"And the sword," he said.

"I hope you know what you're doing," Verity grumbled as she unhooked the scabbard from her belt. Dare reached for it, but her grip tightened. "What do you need me to do with it?"

He held in a sigh. "Wrap it in the blanket and tuck it in with the rest of the gear," he said. He fastened her cloak around his shoulders and laid back in the grass, clasping his hands behind his head and staring up at the sky. Just a traveler enjoying a break.

Verity hid her sword as Dare instructed and then tugged on his coat. She barely finished pulling on her gloves when hoof beats thundered close, three men approaching on horseback. They slowed as they neared Verity and Dare, the gold edging of their crimson uniforms glinting in the sun.

Dare sat up and gave them a warm smile in greeting. "Afternoon, sirs," he drawled, draping his arm casually over his upraised knee. "Ainam's blessings to you."

The soldiers drew their mounts to a halt. "On your feet," one of them barked. "State your business."

Dare squinted up at them, shielding his eyes from the sun as he stood. "My wife and I are just heading south to visit my sister." The lie rolled off his tongue as easily as the Westholden accent he'd heard around the city.

"Your sister?" The soldier eyed him, bringing his horse closer.

"Yes, sir," Dare said. He set an exuberant smile on his lips and laughed. "She's about to have a baby. I'm going to be an uncle—can you believe it?"

"Where's your sister live?" the soldier demanded.

Dare pulled a name from the Westholden maps he'd studied before they left Valda. "Smith's Run."

The other two soldiers moved around behind Dare, circling him. Tension fluttered through his shoulders. His fingers twitched toward the dagger in his coat an instant before he remembered he wasn't wearing it.

The soldier directly in front of him cocked his head. "Smith's Run, eh?"

Dare kept the smile firmly in place. "Yes, sir."

"Seems strange no one would've told you," he said, sneering. "Smith's Run burned to the ground more than a year ago."

Shit. "You don't say?"

There was the scrape of blades being drawn, the stamp of hooves behind him.

Dare held his palms out, open, unarmed. "Sir, we're just travelers—" he began, but the rest of the words choked off, pain shooting through his bruised shoulder as one of the mounted soldiers kicked him. He stumbled into the lead soldier, whose waiting fist crashed down like an avalanche.

Dare's vision went white. For a moment, there was only the throbbing in his shoulder and a sharp, stinging pain in his temple, but soon the taste of dirt mixed with blood clued him in that he was prostrate on the ground.

A deafening crash of thunder boomed, sending a ringing through his ears that drowned out the cries of the frightened horses. Dare looked up in time to see them rearing, one of them throwing its rider.

Verity. The soldiers had disregarded the Warden entirely. Beyond the ring of startled horses that surrounded Dare, Verity was moving toward the man who'd fallen. To his credit, the soldier was on his feet, sword in hand, by the time she reached him. The other two worked to pull their spooked mounts under control. There were muffled shouts, but Dare couldn't make out the words over the bells reverberating in his ears.

Dare's head swam. The Warden and the soldier circled each other. It lasted only a moment before the soldier lunged. Verity stepped into him, angling her body to face the sword that had been aimed for her gut. Dare couldn't see what she did, but the soldier dropped, hitting the ground hard, and Verity held his sword in a reverse grip. She pivoted and drove the blade down into his chest.

The other two soldiers regained control of their horses and rounded on the Warden. Verity made a motion with her open hand and both soldiers were launched from their saddles in opposite directions, as though some great force exploded out from between them. One of the soldiers stood, but Verity had already crossed to him, her strides determined, purposeful. She slashed the blade across his throat before he could raise his sword.

Dare could only watch, awestruck, from his position in the dirt. It all happened faster than his dazed mind could follow—maybe ten seconds from when Dare hit the ground to when the second soldier did. The last soldier, the one who had struck Dare in the face, dropped his sword and threw his arms up in the universal sign of *Ainam's mercy, please don't kill me*. Verity wheeled to face him but stopped when she saw his upraised hands.

"Verity," Dare said. He could barely hear himself, though he wasn't sure if it was his ears or his voice that failed. He pushed himself up, pausing in a crouch to make sure his balance would hold. The ground still swayed gently as he steadied himself. He could make out only some of the Warden's words as she crossed the distance to the soldier.

"Do . . . yield? Why . . . believe . . ."

"Please . . ." the soldier was saying. ". . . mercy . . . Don't . . ."

She couldn't be considering letting him live, could she? They were less than a day out of Port Merrick on foot. The soldier could easily get back to the city and muster some backup to overtake them. And with nowhere on these blasted plains to hide . . .

The Warden's face was set in a glower. The soldier's hands were still raised, pleading. Dare shook his head as he stood. His ears popped and the sound rushed back in all at once: the wind through the grass, the horses stamping their hooves, Verity's voice.

"On foot," she said. She pointed northward with the sword she held—the sword from the first soldier she'd killed. "Get out of here."

She was letting him go. "You can't," Dare blurted out. "He'll send more." It was all he could manage to articulate with his wits still scattered. But Verity turned away from the soldier, glaring at Dare. The conflict on her face was clear. She hardly liked it any more than he did.

"He surrendered!" she shouted. "I'm not just going to—"

But the soldier was moving toward the Warden, sunlight glinting off a small blade in his hand.

Her back was to him. And Dare was too far away, with his own blade still tucked neatly in his boot. The soldier would be on her before he could crouch again to draw it. All he could do was shout. And hope it was enough.

"*Verity!*"

The Warden spun as the soldier leapt. And *froze*. He was held in midair, suspended as though caught in some invisible net mere inches from Verity. The man's eyes wide in terror and confusion. How had she . . . ?

Without hesitation, Verity drove her blade through his throat. She closed her left hand into a fist—Dare hadn't noticed the splayed fingers until she let it relax—and the soldier's body fell to the ground.

Verity tossed the sword in the grass like it was some worthless trinket and stormed to Dare. She slid his coat from her shoulders and flung it at him. "What were you saying about doing things your way?" she spat.

Dare swallowed hard. He'd known the moment he met her that he'd never want to find himself on the wrong side of her blade, but seeing her in action . . . Aetherann's breath, that was something else entirely.

But he'd let Vire's demons drag him to hell before he'd admit it. And so he set a lazy smile floating across his lips. "A slight miscalculation," he said.

"Slight?"

"You fared just fine, my lady Warden."

Verity seethed. "If you ever try to convince me to leave my sword behind again, I will run you through with it. Is that clear?"

The words flowed from his mouth before he could stop them, though he wasn't sure he would have cared to anyway. "What if I surrender first?"

Her eyes narrowed, and the heat of her flaring temper threatened to scald him as she brushed past, not bothering to avoid checking her shoulder into his bruised one. He drew in a sharp breath between his teeth. He was grateful in that moment that only one of her shoulders was made of metal.

"We've wasted enough time here," she said, snatching her sword from their gear. "We need to move."

※

The caravan continued south, stopping for the night just after dark. They started moving again at dawn and traveled all through the next two days. By the time the sun was setting on the third day, the landscape had transformed into sloping foothills.

"We must be nearing the borders of Aethir and Weryn," Verity said as they climbed a rocky outcropping. "I think these are the foothills of the Mistvale Mountains."

Dare nodded, although he had no idea without having a map to consult. He could navigate city streets in his sleep, but this—the untamed terrain beyond the walls? He was grateful Verity seemed to have at least some sense of where they were.

Climbing the next hill, Dare spotted the army wagons outside the entrance to a cave. Only two soldiers were left outside to stand guard.

He crouched so he wouldn't be spotted as he crested the hill. "What in Vire's hells," he muttered. "Is this where they're stopping?"

"The Mistvale range has tons of tunnels carved throughout the mountains," Verity said, lying flat on her stomach to peer over the top of the hill. "But I didn't think they extended all the way into Westhold."

"What are the odds of there being another entrance we can use to get in there?" Dare asked.

Verity shrugged. "Without a map? I have no idea."

Dare angled his head back the way they'd come. "We need to find someplace to set up camp where we won't be spotted."

Deeper into the foothills where there was more cover, they found some large rocks jutting from the ground. The ground sloped to meet the stone, creating an overhang with a narrow opening where they could remain hidden from view and get some shelter from the weather. Dare took off his pack and slid on his stomach to get under the rocks. Once inside, he could crouch without hitting his head, and there was room for them both to lie side by side, with their packs at one end or the other. From the outside, there was no way anyone would see the entrance unless they knew where to look.

"It might be a bit cozy, but there's room," Dare called to Verity. He moved to the far side to allow her space to shimmy through the opening. As he leaned against the wall, his shoulder immediately reminded him that it hadn't healed yet. He rotated it slowly, as much as he could in the small space, and peaked under the collar of his shirt. Even in the low light, the dark purple bruise was visible, coloring a swath across his shoulder.

"That looks terrible," Verity said, crouching beside him.

"Just what every man longs to hear when curled up in the dark with a woman."

The Warden rolled her eyes and dug some trail food out of her pack. She thrust it against Dare's chest. "Here, eat something."

"Is this your way of telling me that you don't want to talk?"

"Yes."

Grinning, Dare ate.

As the darkness settled in around them, Dare stretched out on the ground. "So that cave the soldiers were guarding is part of a tunnel system that extends all the way into Aethir?" he asked.

Verity lay on her back beside him, body heat radiating from her. "Most likely."

"Even now? After the war? Why didn't Aethir block them off? Why give their enemy hidden access to their lands?"

"I don't know," Verity said. "I didn't even know they extended this far west."

Dare stared up at the blank stone, trying to see shapes or patterns in the rock against the near complete darkness. "Why even have tunnels like that in the first place?"

Verity let out a long sigh, making sure he didn't need to see her expression to know she was annoyed. "The mountains are expansive, so Aethirians use the tunnels to travel through and across them more quickly, and it makes it easier to get to some of the more treacherous areas."

He tilted his head, though he couldn't make out more than her silhouette. "You're Aethirian, aren't you?"

She shifted, and there was a long pause. Longer than such a simple question warranted. "Yes," she said finally.

Dare laughed. "That explains a lot."

"What's that supposed to mean?"

"I just mean it makes sense. You have a certain . . . way about you that aligns with most of the other Aethirians I've met." *Arrogant assholes, the lot of them.* He stared up at the featureless black of the rock. "Tell me more about the tunnels."

"Why?"

"Because I'm *bored*, Warden." And he was. Pyrannis's fiery bollocks, he really was.

She sighed again, though more quietly this time. "There's nothing more to tell."

Silence filled the space between them and around them, taking root. Outside their little outcropping, the nearly full moon shone down, illuminating the landscape, but under here, among the dirt and rocks, it was only the darkness that surrounded them.

"Do you have a way to reach Drystan?" Dare asked after a time. He had expected them to be moving the weapon to another city, not the middle of nowhere.

"We have a sign that we leave for each other," she said. "If he can get outside at all, I'll be able to signal him and tell him where we are. Maybe he'll be able to find another entrance we can use to get in there."

Dare breathed deep. Despite starting out as a complete disaster, it was starting to look like they just might pull this off.

The following day had them nearly biting each other's heads off by lunch, even with Verity venturing out to leave the secret markings to signal her fellow Warden. Desperate to be anywhere other than that damned hole in the ground, Dare spent the afternoon scouting more of the foothills to the south. He found a small mountain stream, eliminating one concern that had been building. The water was perfectly clear and ice cold, which was wonderful for drinking but would not be as pleasant when it came to bathing.

By the evening of the second day, Dare was bored out of his mind. He'd perfected rolling a coin over his knuckles while reclining and sadly got no further amusement from the trick once he mastered it. And he'd given up trying to have any sort of conversation with the Warden, as they only bickered any time they spoke. He was ready to ask her whether she knew any interesting jokes or dirty limericks when a whistled trill that sounded like a bird call floated into their little space. Verity nearly launched herself over Dare to get outside. He followed as quickly as he could, pulling himself through their hideout's narrow entrance. Verity had Drystan by the arm and was tugging him against the outside wall of the outcropping, keeping the rocks between them and the direction of the soldiers.

Drystan seemed no worse for wear for his time spent in the army. His eyes lit up when he saw Verity, relief washing across his handsome face. Dare sidled up alongside them as they crouched in the dry grass.

Drystan leaned his head back against the rocks, his shoulders sagging. "I was worried I wasn't going to be able to find you," he said.

Verity looked similarly relieved, but Dare spoke first, still keeping his voice low. "What have you learned while you've been in there?"

"Not as much as I would like," Drystan replied. "I think I know where they're keeping the weapon, but they're only letting a few of the higher ranked enlisted anywhere near it. There's a whole stronghold carved into the mountain, and most of the men aren't allowed on the lower levels."

"What is it?" Verity asked. "What's the weapon?"

Drystan shrugged. "I have no idea. They sent almost everyone ahead to ensure the tunnels were clear when they brought it in. I didn't even see them unload it from the wagon."

"The tunnels . . ." Dare said, thinking. "Anything there? Are there other entrances?"

The Warden smiled, his green eyes twinkling in the setting sun. "There are. And guess who's been assigned to the guard rotation for one of them."

Finally, a stroke of good fortune! "Brilliant. When?"

"In two nights."

Fuck. Still, it was better than nothing. "That's fine," Dare said, trying to convince himself that waiting around for another two days with Verity wasn't just about the last thing he wanted to do. "Where?"

Drystan drew a map in the dirt, showing the foothills from the perspective of their little outcropping, and marking the spot on the southern side where another entrance lay. "Here, the night after tomorrow," Drystan said, tapping the mark. "At sundown. I'll try to learn more about where they're keeping the weapon and maybe even what it actually *is* by then."

Verity was studying the drawn map. "Alright. Two days."

Drystan glanced quickly at the surrounding area. "I'd better get back before anyone notices I'm gone." He set out the way he'd come at a jog, leaving Dare and Verity to wait.

Chapter 13

"Kellan!"

Drystan turned easily at the fake name he'd been using for the last week.

Ian Mathieu, a private on his third assignment with the Westholden forces and one of the soldiers Drystan had befriended, came up alongside him. "The captain wants to see you," Ian said. "I'm to escort you."

Drystan scratched the back of his head, pushing down the sinking feeling in his stomach. "I'm just about to start my shift," he said—he was due to meet Verity and Dare at the tunnel offshoot—but Ian shook his head.

"I'm sorry, I have my orders. The captain said to bring you to him now."

Drystan smiled and let the young soldier lead him up a level to where Captain Corvin Crosse had established his offices.

The tunnels within the mountain were decently lit thanks to the torches fastened to the wall every twenty feet. They burned an odorless oil Drystan had never seen before. It produced a smokeless flame, important for being stuck underground with limited ventilation.

The main tunnel bore straight into the mountain and was easily large enough to accommodate six men walking shoulder to shoulder. Smaller tunnels branched off to either side. Every fifty or sixty feet, a hole opened in the floor or the ceiling along one of the walls, with an iron ladder attached to the stone, leading to the other levels of the stronghold.

On their first night, some of the soldiers said the tunnels had been carved by great machines. Drystan believed it. Westhold was known for two things: its military and its engineering, so Drystan wasn't surprised that they had used one to create a stronghold for the other.

Crosse sat at a wooden table, studying some paperwork as Ian led Drystan into the room.

"Corporal Kellan Pyre to see you, Captain," Ian announced with a formal salute.

Crosse glanced up and waved a hand. "Thank you, Private. Dismissed."

Drawing himself up to his full height, Drystan stood at attention. "You wanted to see me, sir?"

The captain peered at him over the top of his paperwork. "It seems so." He leaned back in his chair, discarding the papers on the desk. "Three of ours were killed on the road half a day south of Port Merrick."

Drystan waited, silent. What was this about?

"They were the messengers we'd sent back north from the caravan our first full day on the road. Killed in cold blood, Ainam bless their souls. Cut down with their own blades." He stared at Drystan, his stern face unreadable.

Crosse couldn't be much older than Drystan was himself, he guessed. And being just shy of three decades seemed awfully young for him to be in such a position of power, with so many under his command.

When the captain didn't say anything further, Drystan cleared his throat. "I'm sorry to hear that, sir."

"What are you doing here, Corporal?"

Drystan blinked. "You . . . asked Ian—Private Mathieu—to bring me here. Sir."

Corvin Crosse rose and rounded the table, moving to circle Drystan. "Not *here* as in right now, Corporal. *Here* as in stationed here. At this stronghold." He stopped directly in front of him.

"Sir?" There had been so many soldiers gathering in Port Merrick for the last few weeks that no one questioned an extra one claiming to have been assigned to transport detail. Drystan hesitated for only a moment. "I was assigned here."

"Only you weren't, were you?" Corvin gestured to the pile of papers on his desk. "The documents weren't matching up. A name added to the approved list that I provided in Port Merrick. And when I inquired as to how this additional soldier ended up with us here, do you know what I was told?"

Drystan swallowed. He had a pretty good idea. "No, sir."

"I was told," Corvin said, stepping closer, "that *I* had personally requested that Corporal Kellan Pyre be added to the transportation detail's roster. Seeing as how I remember the name of every soldier who's ever served under my command, I can say with certainty that I did no such thing. And considering I had spies in my city a week ago, and three dead soldiers on the road, I will ask you again, Corporal: why are you here?"

Drystan's heart thundered in his chest. If he was found out here, he'd likely be locked up or killed, and another soldier would be reassigned his post at the tunnel entrance. If they hadn't been already. He didn't have much time. "Permission to speak freely, sir?"

"Granted."

"All due respect, Captain, if you didn't send for me, I have no idea who did. I have my orders right here." He reached into the pocket of his crimson uniform and withdrew a folded piece of parchment, which he offered up for Crosse's inspection.

Drystan held his breath as Crosse opened it, eyes flitting across the page. They landed on the sigil of the Westholden army, the signature of a staff sergeant stationed in Port Merrick, and the very clear instructions that Corporal Kellan Pyre was to report to the west barracks for transportation detail at the personal request of Captain Corvin Crosse—all parts of the forgery Drystan had spent hours creating in Verity's room the day he joined the army. It had been a long time since he'd plied that craft. He prayed his work would pass Crosse's scrutiny.

The captain's dark brows drew together as he refolded the letter and placed it in the breast pocket of his officer's coat. "It seems I will have some issues to straighten out when I return to Port Merrick," he said, his jaw tight.

"Yes, sir," Drystan said. "I apologize for my part in the confusion." He paused a moment before adding, "Will that be all, sir?" It was getting late, and he needed to be back at his post to meet Verity. If he wasn't there . . .

"Just one more thing, Corporal." Corvin's gray eyes flashed with an inner light as he set his hand on Drystan's shoulder. "*Why are you here?*"

It was an easy thing, to lie. To lie *well* was harder. But to make someone believe a falsehood while staying within the technical bounds of the truth . . . That was a skill Drystan had mastered long ago, in his life before the Wardens. And although the memories of the lies he'd fed people under the guise of truths sometimes kept him awake at night, it was a skill he kept polished, like a blade in a display case. No longer used, but just as sharp when wielded by a practiced hand.

As Corvin's grip tightened on his shoulder, Drystan felt the pull of the truth. The words were trying to claw their way up his throat. He tried to fight them back, but he couldn't stop them. The truth was coming forward whether he wanted it to or not. And so he found that skill, tucked away, and twisted the words as they emerged against his will.

"I'm here because I believe in the mission." Drystan swallowed hard, and a bead of sweat ran down the side of his neck. He hoped that Corvin wouldn't ask him *which* mission.

Corvin studied him, and Drystan held his breath. "That'll be all," he said sharply, turning back to the desk. "Dismissed."

It was all Drystan could do to keep himself from sprinting back into the tunnels.

✸

It was nearly dark outside when Drystan spotted Verity and Dare searching along the sheer rock wall for the entrance. Thank Pyrannis he'd made it back in time.

The opening—little more than a crevice in the rock—was narrow for about ten feet before opening up into a wider tunnel that almost immediately sloped downward toward the main tunnels.

He wanted to breathe a deep sigh of relief at seeing Verity again, and at being one step closer to completing their mission, but there was no time for that. Not yet.

Drystan ushered Verity and Dare into the crack in the mountain, the last of the dying twilight filtering in past them and providing just enough light to see their faces as they spoke.

"Did you find it?" Dare asked, keeping his voice low. "Do you know what it is?"

Drystan shook his head. "No, but I have it narrowed down to a couple of lengths of tunnel, two levels down."

"How do you know?" Verity asked.

"Because I got threatened with a court-martial when I started asking questions about what was down there."

Dare smiled in the dim light. "Fine work," he said. Then he angled his head toward Verity. "Does that meet with your approval, my lady Warden?"

"Don't start," Drystan warned. He ran them through everything he'd learned about the layout of the tunnels, directions to where he believed the weapon was being kept, and the paths and timings of the guard rotations. After he let this information sink in, he also told them about his encounter with Crosse.

"I saw it too, Vee," he said when he reached the end of his explanation. "His eyes flashed, and it was like I *had* to answer him."

"So he really can compel the truth," Dare muttered. "That could be problematic." He rubbed at the back of his neck, focusing on some thought that seemed to vex him.

"You should be able to keep out of his way," Drystan continued. "He's buried in paperwork in his office. You'll be four levels away from him nearly the whole time. But . . ." He drew a breath as he watched his two companions. "He said three soldiers had been killed on the road. Was that you two?"

"Unfortunately yes," Verity said, though she cast a derisive look at Dare as she added, "It couldn't be helped."

"It's fine," Drystan said before Dare could snipe a retort. "But they're going to be on alert."

"What's our exit strategy?" Dare asked, squinting down the darkened tunnel to where a torch clung to the wall ahead.

"If you can find the weapon and destroy it without raising the alarm, you just need to get back here. Then we all leave through this entrance together," he said. "These mountains form the border with Weryn to the south. We can cross there and make our way back home. It'll be taking the long way around, but it'll keep us out of Westhold."

Verity nodded, but Drystan knew the question she'd ask next. She didn't disappoint. "And if we raise the alarm?"

He flashed her a warm smile. "Then I'll do what I can to distract them, and you just do your best to get back here."

Verity huffed at what she no doubt took as a flippant answer. Drystan swore he saw Dare's jaw clench at the sound, but he didn't say anything.

Drystan pressed on. "I'll go first and make sure your path is clear, at least as far as getting you to the lower levels. The patrols down there happen twice an hour. Wait here about five minutes, then go."

Verity studied the tunnel ahead of them, the darkness punctuated by torch-light. "Once we get close, I can bend the light around us," she said, not looking at Dare. "If we run into any patrols, they won't see us. But we'll have to stick together."

Dare jerked his head sharply to the side. "No." He left no room for argument, and Verity immediately set her arms across her chest, ready for the challenge. Drystan could only imagine how the last week had gone for these two. He was a little surprised they were both still in one piece. Or, more accurately, that Dare was.

"I need to be able to move freely," Dare continued. "I can't be tethered to you." He surveyed the shadows. "Do what you like, but I'll keep myself out of sight."

"And if someone sees you?" she asked.

"They won't."

"Crosse spotted you in Port Merrick," Verity said, the corner of her mouth twisting.

Dare straightened and squared his shoulders, facing Verity head-on. "He didn't *spot* me," he bit out. "Not at first. And if we run into him down here, and he somehow senses us like he did then, how much good do you think it's going to do for us to be side-by-fucking-side, my lady Warden?"

Verity threw her hands up. "Fine."

Drystan suppressed a sigh. "Remember, five minutes, then go."

He started down the tunnel, but Verity grabbed his hand, stopping him before he'd taken more than a step. Back in Port Merrick, she'd hardly been able to look at him when he'd donned the uniform Dare had procured. He couldn't blame her.

He knew what it meant for her. He was the only family she had—she'd chosen him for that role in her life, just as he had chosen her for the same—and having to stand in front of her wearing it made him sick to his stomach. But now her eyes were focused on his face, her jaw set.

"Be careful," she said.

"When am I not?" he said with a wink.

"Drystan, I'm serious."

"So am I." He squeezed her hand. "I'll be careful, Vee. I promise."

"We'll meet back here," she said, grim determination on her face. It sounded closer to an order than anything else.

"Yes," he said, matching her determination with his own. "*We* will."

Verity released his hand, and Drystan moved farther into the tunnel.

It was surprisingly easy to distract the soldiers and make sure Verity and Dare had a clear path to the ladder they needed. It was a maze once you got deeper underground, but Drystan had mapped as many areas as he had access to. All he could do now was keep the way clear as much as possible. He hoped it would be enough.

The rest was up to Verity and Dare.

Chapter 14

Dare stuck to the shadows between torches, but thankfully Drystan had done his job well. No soldiers blocked their path as he and Verity followed the tunnels deeper into the mountain. In the four days he'd been in the underground stronghold, Drystan had mapped tunnels and offshoots, tracked guard shifts, and narrowed down the location of the weapon to only a few possible areas. Dare had to hand it to him, it was solid work. It was a shame he'd gone and joined the Wardens. He'd have made an excellent Crimson Brother.

Dare didn't need to look back to know that Verity was fifteen feet behind him. He had told her to stay twenty feet back with the hopes that she'd keep to at least ten. Even if he did turn around, he wouldn't see her. When they descended the second ladder, she used her magic to shield her presence. Visually, at least. Her boots still echoed down the empty corridor. Dare focused on the tunnels ahead, alert to any change in lighting or flicker of movement in the shadows.

The lower levels were largely the same as above, with torches lining the walls at regular intervals. Archways carved into the stone, some with heavy wooden doors and others left open, led to rough-hewn rooms of various sizes. There was a dampness and a chill to this level, however, that wasn't present on the others.

Getting to the first of the possible locations for the weapon took longer than Dare wanted, though they managed to skirt the first patrol. Barely. And of course, they found nothing. Dare knew he'd been too optimistic in hoping their first guess would be the right one.

There were only a few places they could be holding the weapon, according to Drystan, but every minute they spent within these tunnels increased their chances of getting caught. Dare didn't want to rely on their luck holding out. They had to be quick. And smart.

The next two corridors turned up only machinery and storage rooms. There was one tunnel left where it could be, and they were rapidly running out of time before the next patrol. Dare silently cursed with every soft thud of the Warden's boots on the stone.

When they reached the last possible tunnel, Dare tried to reassure himself that it would be only a few more paces before Verity could destroy the weapon, and the three of them would be out—out of these damned tunnels and out of Westhold. Then he would be blessedly done with this job and with the Wardens.

He tried not to think about what remained unspoken, once it was apparent that Drystan would have to play distraction instead of coming with them. *Worst case scenario*, Verity had told Dare before they left Port Merrick, *Drystan will let me channel from him to fuel the last bit of the spell.*

But if Drystan wasn't there . . .

Dare wouldn't be able to get her out if she drained herself too far and collapsed, and surely she realized that too. Could he let her siphon *his* energy?

Verity said she wouldn't channel power from someone who wasn't willing, but if the situation were dire enough . . . if the enchantments on the weapon were too strong . . .

Would she do it anyway?

There was a door of iron or steel up ahead on the left. It was the only door in this dismal stretch of tunnel—the only metal one he'd seen anywhere down here. This was the place. It had to be. A soft glow illuminated the wall at the far end of the corridor, and voices echoed faintly. They only had a few more minutes before the next patrol.

Dare slid up to the door, kneeling so he was at eye level with the lock. *Locks*, he realized, as he spotted the massive padlock bolted above the lock built into the door. He carefully slipped his knapsack from his shoulders and pulled out his set of worn tools. The cold damp soon soaked through the knees of his trousers. The scrape of Verity's boots on the stone signaled she had moved in alongside him as he studied first the padlock, and then the locking mechanism of the door. Not to mention the whole thing was bound to be magically warded.

"I assume you can banish Wards?" he whispered.

Verity reappeared as she dropped the magical effect she'd been using to stay hidden. "Yes," she whispered back, crouching at his side, "but I need time to do a Sight ritual."

Dare bristled a little, wishing he'd thought to bring a Sight Stone. The trinkets were hard to come by, but Dare had won a few in a card game a couple months back. All the benefits of a Sight ritual—seeing all magic in one's field of vision—without the frustratingly long time it took a mage to cast it. It also eliminated the need for a mage at all in most instances, which was always a perk as far as Dare was concerned.

"We don't have time for that," he said, still staring at the locks, the door, the unknown weapon of unknown power that lay behind it.

The Warden hissed, "I can't banish a Ward if I don't know what I'm banishing or from where."

He fiddled with his lock picks, twirling them over in his fingers before setting them down on the stone floor. She was right. Of course she was right. Banishing a Ward had to be directed. And precise. Otherwise, you were more likely to trip the Wards than dispel them.

Fuck. He knew the answer, but he didn't like it. At all. But what choice did he have? "If I could tell you exactly what was here," he said, "could you do it then?" He tapped his fingers against his knee.

"It would need to be *exact.*"

"It will be."

She scoffed lightly. Just enough to let him know he was full of shit. "How would you manage that?" Her obvious disbelief set his teeth on edge.

Dare took a deep breath and raised his hands until his palms hovered about an inch from the reinforced metal door. "Very. Carefully." He closed his eyes and let his focus shift away from the darkened corridor, the sounds at the far end, the breathing of the woman beside him. He let all of that fade from his consciousness until he was focused solely on the door and the energized thrumming that tickled his palms and the tips of his fingers. The hair on his arms stood on end as he shifted his hands.

Most magic was overt, impossible to miss. But Wards were subtle by design, intended as alarms or, in rare cases, deadly traps for the unsuspecting. He slid his hands along the fine web of energy until—*there!* He pinched his thumb and forefinger together as if grabbing a stray thread on a tapestry, but by doing so, he interjected himself into the circuit, completing the connection with his body.

The subdued magic of the Wards rushed through him like a million tiny needles prickling every part of his being from the inside. Dare followed the strand to its terminus, sliding his fingers with practiced deftness along the invisible thread, feeling the connections of the Wards that were blocking their path.

"Here," he said, the word scarcely emerging from his throat. With his eyes still closed, Dare held the strand of magic with his right hand and extended his left toward Verity. "Give me your hand." His voice sounded strange to his own ears, like trying to speak underwater. "There are three Wards. They merge here. If you can cast a strong enough Banishment right here . . ."

"You're a Perceptive . . ." A note of incredulity wove through her whispered voice. "Ainam above, do you know how rare that is? Why didn't you tell me you were a mage?"

Dare forced his jaw to unclench. "I'm not," he said tightly.

"Yes, but you—"

"I never learned to cast magic. Verity, give me your hand."

He swore he heard her chin hit the floor. "You never learned? How is that possible? It would have been so easy for you. Why would you throw away such an amazing gift? You could have done anything."

Everything she was saying, Dare had heard more times than he cared to recall. Through the prickling of magic coursing through him—which was growing harder to ignore with each passing moment—Dare could hear each of her words echoed in his father's voice. His father's insistence. His father's disappointment. Dare focused on the thread of magic pinched between his fingers, holding it steady despite his body screaming to let it go. He took a calming breath. If he broke his concentration now, he would trip the Wards.

"Verity," he said through his teeth. "If it pleases you, perhaps we could discuss the nuances of my profligacy at a later time?"

"Of course," she mumbled as her fingers brushed his open palm. The cold steel added a new layer to his mounting discomfort, though there was something else there too. A slight needling sensation, barely noticeable given the Wards, and yet it was distinct. Magic.

Inhaling deeply, Dare placed Verity's hand over his, pressing her palm against the back of his hand where he held the strand of magic, careful not to disturb the Wards.

"Again, if you can cast a powerful Banishment here," he said, pushing her palm harder against his hand, "that should dissipate all three Wards."

He braced himself for a jolt, but nothing happened.

"It's a harmless spell," he said, guessing at the reason for her hesitation.

"To a *normal* person," she countered. "With your sensitivity to magic, what would it even do to—"

"It's nothing. It'll be fine." He wasn't entirely sure which of the two of them he was trying to convince. "Do it before I change my mind."

"Have you ever done this before?"

Vire's fucking hells, of course he hadn't; he wasn't insane. And at this point he wanted nothing more than to shake off her hand and drop this fucking thread of magic. The incessant prickling was wearing away at his patience. And his focus. The magic shifted between his fingers, but he tightened his grip. They were out of time.

"Now, Verity."

"Dare . . ."

His eyes snapped open as he barked in a hoarse whisper, "*Now!*"

Verity's hand tensed against his. She muttered the requisite incantation under her breath and channeled the Banishment straight into Dare.

His vision flashed a brilliant, blinding white as the spell surged through him like a lightning bolt. The tingling running through his entire body amplified in that instant a hundredfold. But the little thread he'd been holding fizzled.

As the shock began to fade, other sensations slowly made their way back into his awareness. Something hard lay across the middle of his back. Dare's vision resolved into the dark of the tunnel, and he realized it was Verity. She was still grasping his hand, but her other arm had moved to stop him from pitching over backward.

Verity hoisted him up onto his knees again. "Did it work?" she asked, releasing his hand when he remained upright.

"It worked," he whispered, a bit breathless. There was a ringing in his ears and a general slow spin to the room, and his entire body felt as though every nerve was sounding off to ensure it still functioned. It took a not insignificant amount of concentration to remain on his knees.

"Is your hand alright?"

Dare looked down at his right hand, the epicenter of Verity's casting. It was trembling. Despite shaking it out and flexing his fingers, everything from his fingertips to his elbow was entirely numb.

"I'm fine," he said, shaking out his hand again. When he reached for his tools, he caught the Warden watching him, brow creased with worry. He considered whether to make some snide comment so she would roll her eyes.

Look at me like I'm an idiot, just don't look worried about me.

But he had a job to finish here. He settled his hand on the tools laid out on the ground.

Verity kept her voice low. "Are you able to—"

"The guards will be starting their rounds soon," he said.

Dare grabbed one of the picks and was pleased to find that his fingers closed around it. That was good. He didn't need to feel it. He just needed to hold it steady. He slipped the picks into the lock and began to maneuver them agilely left and right, feeling with his left hand for the subtle movement of the pins within. The satisfying click and release of first one lock, followed by the other, coincided with a quiet sigh of relief from the Warden.

Dare shoved his tools back into his pack. He remained on his knees as he silently turned the latch and pulled the door open enough to peer inside. The small room was empty save for a bundle of dirty rags and crumpled blankets in the corner.

There was no weapon, no artifact of power, no sign of what they had been sent to Westhold to find. And destroy.

Wait . . .

"There's nothing," Verity said, peering over his shoulder. "How can there be nothing? Where is it?"

Dare ignored her. Keeping low to the ground, he carefully pulled the door open a little wider and slipped inside. He heard Verity stand up, but he held his hand out to stop her from following. "Keep an eye out for the patrol," he whispered, urgency tightening his voice.

The stone walls and floor of the room were cold and slick. Dare moved forward, still crouched low, and drew a dagger from one of the hidden sheaths in his coat. Movement flickered at the edge of his vision, and he whirled to face it.

The blankets in the corner shifted.

Chapter 15

VERITY STOPPED AT DARE'S upraised hand as he moved into the room. The empty room. She stood in the tunnel outside the door, shifting her weight from foot to foot. At the end of the hall, the stomping of boots and echo of voices grew louder. The guards were beginning their rounds and would be heading this way any moment.

They had come all this way, risked so much. And for what?

She was about to tell Dare to hurry up when the door swung fully open. A stranger stood in the doorway, head bowed, one shoulder leaning against the stone arch. His other arm braced against the opposite side of the door. Verity stepped back, her hand instinctively falling to the hilt of her sword.

She didn't draw it. In the dim light, he was scarcely more than a shadow, all grays and grimy browns. But his clothes were ragged and torn, and his hair fell knotted and wild over his face. He was no Westholden soldier.

Dare appeared beside him, ducking under the man's shoulder and sliding an arm around his waist. The man was larger and more solidly built than Dare. When he stopped bracing his arm against the doorway and let it fall over Dare's shoulder, they both nearly collapsed, but Dare managed to keep him upright as he ushered the stranger into the tunnel.

"There was nothing else in there," Dare whispered. "Just him."

At least a dozen questions raced through Verity's mind, but she slid herself under the stranger's other arm, taking some of his weight across her own strong shoulders. She wouldn't leave a prisoner down here to rot. He was heavy, but she wouldn't let that slow them down.

"We have to move," she said.

"My thoughts exactly, my lady Warden."

The stranger said nothing as Verity and Dare carried him toward the ladder. Behind them, the soldiers were starting their patrol. Their time was up, and somehow the weapon hadn't been in any of the places it was supposed to be. They needed to get back to the entrance and regroup with Drystan.

Dare gripped the ladder with one hand, still supporting the stranger with the other. "Verity . . ." He was breathing hard.

"I know," she muttered. Trying to get this man up the ladder was going to be a challenge. One she wasn't convinced they had time for. She tapped her fingers gently against the stranger's back. "Hey," she said to him. "Can you climb at all?"

The stranger lifted his head to regard the ladder. "I can try," he rasped. His voice was quiet and hoarse, as though he hadn't spoken in a very long time.

Dare ducked out from under the stranger's arm, setting the man's hand on one of the rungs. "I'll keep them off your back," he said. He started toward the cell where the weapon should have been, toward the patrolling guards.

"Dare—"

"Just get him up the ladder," Dare said. He stepped into the shadows. "I'll catch up."

The stranger drew a deep breath as though preparing for the challenge ahead of him. Verity focused on him, on the task they had to do. "It's alright," she said, setting his other hand on the ladder as well. She still supported his weight with one arm around his waist. "I'm going to help you."

The man's knuckles whitened as he gripped the rungs, the muscles in his arms shaking with the effort of pulling himself up. He made it two steps before he started to sag with the weight of his own body.

Verity muttered a few words in High Aethirian, the language of ancient history and magic, and let her mind go blank as she opened herself up to the wellspring of power in her core with practiced ease. She set her hands against the back of his legs and released the magic, letting it amplify the force exerted by his muscles. The shaking in his arms lessened as it became easier for him to pull himself up the ladder.

Something as simple as modifying the amount of force generated by movement took very little effort or power on her part. She had plenty of reserves left, even after holding the Light Shell around herself earlier and channeling the Banishment to dispel the Wards. The Banishment she'd channeled *into* Dare.

Who was a Perceptive.

Why hadn't he told her earlier? But if he had, would she have believed that he could *feel* magic and yet had never studied it? She scarcely believed it now, even after seeing it with her own eyes. What he'd done should have been impossible. Verity had never seen or heard of anyone literally grabbing a strand of magic. But then again, Verity had done impossible things herself once. More than once, if she was being honest.

What a waste.

She forced her attention back to the present. When the stranger neared the top of the ladder, Verity checked down the tunnel where Dare had gone. She couldn't see him through the dim light, but she couldn't hear the heavy, booted footsteps of the guards anymore either.

Had Dare killed them? She hadn't heard a fight or a struggle. These men might be her enemies, but they weren't the ones pulling the strings. They weren't the ones giving the orders. She would have given them a chance, as she did with the men they'd encountered on the plains. Would Dare do the same? He'd argued against it then . . . Left on his own, would he skulk through the darkness and stab them in the back?

The grinding of her teeth echoed in her ears. She would deal with it later. Deal with *him* later, if need be. The iron rungs of the ladder clanged softly as she raced to join the stranger on the level above.

Thankfully no one was in the tunnel, and Verity practically launched herself out of the hole in the floor. The stranger huddled against the wall, knees drawn up to his chest, breathing hard.

"Come on," she whispered, gripping his elbow.

She lifted, and he obeyed. His legs were sturdier than they had been thanks to the lingering effects of her magic. Verity slid under his shoulder again as soon as she got him to his feet. The stranger was a similar height and build to Drystan—tall with broad shoulders and dense muscles—and with the weight of her gear strapped to her back as well, Verity's thighs burned as she propelled them both forward.

A cacophony of bells echoed through the stone halls. Someone had raised the alarm. *One more ladder*, she told herself. *Nearly there.*

Shouts traveled through the tunnel as the bells continued their angry clanging. The way they needed to go was swarming with soldiers. She reached down into her wellspring again, then threw another shell of magic around the two of them, bending the light to keep them out of sight. Yet even with the boon of being invisible, she spun them both around and took the stranger the other way. The magic would keep them hidden but wouldn't stop them from bumping into someone if they couldn't stay out from underfoot. They'd be better off trying their luck down one of the other tunnels. If she could find another ladder up one more level, they could double back toward Drystan and the exit.

The tunnel forked ahead, and Verity hooked right for no reason other than because it was easier to pivot that way with the man on her left side. The shouting behind her grew louder and Verity willed herself to move faster. The stranger's legs started to buckle, her other spell wearing off. Another fork in the tunnel lay just ahead. If they turned right again, it would lead them back the way she wanted them to go in the first place. Her legs ached, begging for her to stop. Verity spared a quick glance behind them, where flickering lights danced on the wall at the far end—the bobbing of torches being carried. They had to keep going.

Verity whipped around the corner and collided with someone tall and solid, the flash of crimson and gold against the darkened stone launching a spike of panic through her chest. She staggered back a step, the extra weight she carried on her back threatening to topple her and the stranger both. The impact knocked her focus from the spell, and the Light Shell dissipated.

She didn't have time to think. She planted her feet and released the stranger's arm to grip the hilt of her sword. He dropped to a knee. Verity drew her blade. But the steel of her forearm collided with one of flesh and bone.

"Vee," Drystan said as he blocked her draw.

Verity blew out a breath, reining in her frenzied heartbeat.

Concern and confusion warred on Drystan's face as he eyed the stranger. "Who's this?" he asked, his tone hushed but urgent as he shook out his arm. "Where's Dare?"

"I don't know," Verity said, answering both questions at once. She heaved the stranger back to his feet and slid beneath his arm.

Drystan did the same on the man's other side. "Is it done?"

Verity shook her head. "We couldn't find it."

"What? What happened?"

"Later," Verity said. The three of them pushed forward until they reached another split in the tunnel. "Which way out?"

Drystan gestured toward the tunnel to the left. "Our exit was compromised," he said. "But I have another way."

Where was Dare? Was he headed toward their planned exit and the soldiers waiting there? She forced her thoughts back to Drystan and the stranger now draped between them. They couldn't complete their mission if they got captured, no matter what had happened to Dare.

Drystan easily took more of the stranger's weight across his shoulders, allowing them to move swiftly through the tunnels.

Soon the tunnel split to the left and right again. Drystan swung them left, but a shout came from the other way. Verity looked over her shoulder as a soldier broke into a sprint toward them.

Drystan cursed under his breath.

"Go," she told Drystan, spinning out from under the stranger's arm. Her fingers wrapped around the worn leather hilt of her sword. It was the hilt of a longsword, but as it slid free of the scabbard, the blade that emerged was only half the proper length, the edge of it forming a jagged point just off from the blade's center. The weight of the broken sword was comfortable in her hand, an extension of her arm. She leveled it toward the soldier.

The young man skidded to a stop, his own sword drawn. His eyes were wide, but he tightened his jaw. Verity had seen that look on many new Wardens their first time in the field. It was the look of a young man wanting desperately to be brave. *Don't make me do this,* she pleaded silently. She might have said it aloud.

The soldier regarded her for a moment, weighing his options.

"Ian . . ." Drystan said gently.

Verity gripped her sword tighter, the leather straining against the strength of her fingers. She wanted Drystan to keep moving, but if he could somehow talk the soldier out of trying to stop them . . .

She didn't want to have to kill him.

"Ian," he said again. "You don't need to do this." His voice was calm and steady. "Just turn around. No one needs to know you saw us. Just walk away."

"But . . . Kellan?" the young man asked. His voice trembled. "Who *are* you?"

"Just walk away," Drystan urged again.

Ian fixed his attention on Verity. He took a step forward.

Only a single step.

A hand slid over Ian's mouth, and his eyes widened with fear and pain. He tried to cry out, but the hand over his mouth held firm, muffling his scream.

Dare dropped slowly to one knee and lowered the young man to the ground. When he stood, his dagger glinted in the torchlight, the blade coated with the boy's blood.

Verity's hand flexed around the hilt of her sword, fury sparking in her chest. "Why did you do that?" she demanded.

Dare stooped to wipe the blade on the young man's uniform, the blood disappearing against the crimson. "We have to go," he said quietly.

He started past her, toward Drystan and the stranger, but she caught his arm. "Why did you do that?" she asked again. They had just needed another moment. They could have convinced him. He hadn't needed to die.

"You can dissect my actions later, along with all the rest of my life choices if it suits you." Dare's eyes were hard and cold as he stared at her. "Now is not the time."

She didn't let go of his arm, her grip like a vise on the bend in his elbow. "You killed him. For nothing."

"And are you going to kill me?" Dare watched her, his face expressionless, but he didn't try to pull away.

"Verity," Drystan said.

She didn't turn. She didn't move.

Dare's brows rose. "No? Then we need to leave. Now."

"Verity," Drystan said again, as gently as when he'd spoken to the young man who now lay dead on the stone floor. "We can sort it out later."

Verity released Dare's arm and sheathed her sword. Drystan led the way, still helping the stranger along. He was having no trouble, so Verity stayed a few paces behind, guarding their rear. Dare kept his distance.

"This way," Drystan commanded. He nodded to a narrow opening in the wall, little more than a crack split into the rock, barely wide enough for someone to pass through sideways.

Before she could ask any questions, Dare slid off his knapsack, shoved it into the narrow passageway, and slipped into the complete darkness inside. Drystan started forward, but Verity grabbed the stranger's other arm to help guide him through the tight space between the rocks.

"Where does it lead?" she asked. "Out?"

Drystan shook his head. Sweat beaded on his brow. "They're looking for us, so they'll have all the exits blocked. This cuts through to another tunnel deeper in the mountain."

"Deeper?"

"Vee, please, just trust me."

She did trust him. There wasn't anyone she trusted more. With her free hand, she removed her pack and pushed it into the opening, pulling the stranger behind. Drystan followed.

Verity's chest tightened. The darkness was all-encompassing. She couldn't see her hand holding her pack in front of her, nor the stranger behind her. Her back pressed against the stone, the other side only a breath away. Her pulse quickened as she expected the passage to constrict further, crushing her, or for the ceiling to crash down. She moved as quickly as she dared, each sidestep testing the ground for holes or loose stones. The sounds of running boots and shouting soldiers faded away.

"A little farther," Drystan said. "It'll open up to a tunnel."

Something clattered to the ground ahead, followed by a hurried scuffing and a quiet grind of metal. Soon there was a soft *click click click*, each strike accompanied by a spark of light. A flame took hold where the spark had been, and Verity had to shield her eyes as Dare lifted a torch, its end ablaze with yellow, smokeless flame.

He'd made it through, and with the way lit, Verity could make out the edges of the passage a few feet away.

Her pack cleared the opening first, and she tossed it to the ground. She nearly hit the ground after it, grateful to be out from between those oppressive walls. As the stranger emerged, she took his weight across her shoulders so Drystan could pull himself through. The opening was barely wide enough for him. He breathed deeply once he was out, as though he'd been unable to take a full breath until then.

A few feet to the left of the crack, an empty torch bracket was mounted to the wall. The lit torch in hand, Dare moved twenty feet or so one way before doubling back and going the same distance in the other direction.

"Which way?" he whispered.

"I'm not sure," Drystan said. "I haven't come much farther than this." He closed his eyes, fingers moving subtly in the air, as though tracing a path in his mind, orienting himself to their new location. "Left here should head north," he said after a moment. "We can start there."

Dare muttered a curse.

They continued on for another quarter of an hour before Drystan called them to a halt. "Let's rest a bit here," he said. "I don't think anyone else found that passage we took, so if they're sticking to the tunnels to search for us, it'll be a long while before they make it out this way."

Verity nodded, helping the stranger to sit against the wall.

Dare set the torch in a holder bracketed to the stone and began rummaging through his knapsack. He produced some dried meat from what was left of his travel rations and moved to the stranger, a surprisingly gentle smile on his face. He crouched, offering him the food. The man hesitated a moment before taking it, gnawing on it hungrily.

Drystan leaned against the wall beside Verity. "Vee, what happened down there?" he asked, his voice low. His eyes were fixed on the stranger.

"We searched everywhere you told us. There was nothing there," she said. "Just him. They had him locked up and warded. Had you heard anything about a prisoner?"

"No, nothing," Drystan said. "He looks terrible . . . What do you think they did to him?"

"I don't know." Her heart ached at the way he curled in on himself, arms wrapped tightly around his knees, like he was trying to make himself smaller.

As she watched, Dare returned to the man with a waterskin and a bundle of clothes. "Hey," he said softly. "My name's Dare."

The stranger lifted his face as Dare spoke.

Dare set the bundle on the ground and took a step back. He turned and gestured toward where Verity stood with Drystan. "I know he looks like one of those soldiers," Dare said, "but he's not. He's with us." He smiled, his face open and compassionate. "His name is Drystan. And that's Verity."

Dare had killed a man—likely more than one—not more than thirty minutes ago. And yet, this gentleness was a side of the mercenary she hadn't seen.

"What's your name?" Dare asked the stranger.

He didn't answer.

Dare kept his distance but crouched to be eye to eye. "Is there something they called you?"

The man shook his head.

"What about your family?" Dare asked. "What did they call you?"

He shrugged, a subtle raise of his shoulders.

Verity drifted closer to the two of them. "You don't remember?" she asked.

He shook his head again.

Verity took another step. "Do you remember anything? How did you come to be here?"

The man tensed and shrugged again. Dare held up a hand, trying to catch her eye, but she ignored him.

"While you were here," she continued, "did you hear the soldiers talk about anything? A weapon?"

The man pushed himself further back as though he wanted to meld into the stone wall. He buried his face against his knees and—gods, he was trembling.

"Ainam's armored ass, Verity," Dare grumbled over his shoulder. "It's not a fucking interrogation."

She stiffened, but Drystan's hand on her shoulder stopped her from stepping toward him. "I wasn't—"

"Just give it a rest," Dare said before turning back to the stranger. "Hey . . ." His voice softened, like he was trying to soothe a frightened animal. "Hey, it's alright." He nudged the waterskin closer to him. "Here, have some water."

After a long moment, the man finally lifted his head again, though he didn't move to take the water.

"Is it alright if I ask you one more question?" Dare asked. When the stranger nodded, he said, "Do you know why you were locked up?"

The two men watched each other for a long moment until the stranger finally spoke, his voice small and pained.

"Because I'm dangerous."

Chapter 16

Eventually the prisoner uncurled himself enough to drink from the waterskin and change into the fresh clothes Dare had set out for him. They were Drystan's, which Dare had been carrying in his pack. They fit the man rather well, and Verity suspected Drystan didn't mind at all.

Though the tunnels had their own oppressive silence, another kind of silence—one of exhaustion—wove itself through the group. They ate, Drystan, Dare, and Verity each taking a half portion since they had no idea how long they might be stuck underground, and then traveled for another hour to put more space between them and the stronghold. The stranger was steadier on his feet for having some food in him, but when they stopped to rest for what remained of the night, he silently took the blanket Dare handed him and was asleep almost as soon as he set his head on the ground.

Verity was sure Drystan had more questions, and she certainly had questions for Dare, but none of them spoke about any of it that night. She was grateful for the silence, heavy as it was, and for the time to think about this stranger and their current predicament.

They hadn't found the weapon. In its place—or what they'd expected to be its place—had been a prisoner, sealed away behind locks and powerful Wards. And when she asked him if he'd heard anything about a weapon . . .

Could it be a coincidence?

The mercenary and the Wardens took turns keeping watch. The soldiers were no doubt still scouring the stronghold's tunnels looking for them. Drystan was optimistic that they wouldn't make it out this far, and Verity hoped he was right.

In the morning, or whenever it was that they woke, Drystan crouched beside Verity as she packed up her blanket. "So what do we do?" he asked.

"About him, or the mission?" she said, keeping her voice low.

Drystan gave a wry smile. "Both."

Verity sighed. "There's nothing else we can do about the mission," she said. "We failed, and we'll have to deal with that when we get back to Valda. For now, we need to get somewhere safe and regroup." She nodded toward the stranger. "And we take him with us."

"He said he's dangerous," Drystan whispered.

Verity pulled the tie out of her hair and rebraided it. "Do you believe him?"

Drystan's brows furrowed. "I think *he* believes it, and it terrifies him." He tapped Verity's knee. "What do you think?"

"I don't know what to think," she admitted. "But right now he hardly seems capable of hurting anyone."

"True. Want me to get Dare so we can confer?" He nodded to where the mercenary was checking on the stranger. "Make sure he's good with the plan?"

She waved her hand, dismissing the idea and Dare both. "Just tell him what we decided," she said. "We don't have any other options, and if he doesn't like it, he's going to have to deal with it."

When they set out again, Dare lit a second torch and scouted the paths ahead, leaving markings on the wall as he noted their twists and turns. Using Dare's information and all he'd learned while being undercover in the stronghold, Drystan was able to identify the most likely path out of the tunnels.

After a little more food and water, and a decent night's sleep, the stranger seemed to be faring much better. He was walking on his own now, though he needed to stop often to rest.

Verity walked beside him, holding the other torch. She was painfully aware of how much she had frightened him the day before, and so did her best to tread gently. "We should think of something to call you," she said. "We may be traveling together for a time. Until we can get you somewhere safe, I mean."

His head tilted toward her, but he didn't speak, and his hair blocked most of his face from view.

She'd been turning the thought over in her mind since yesterday, among the larger questions of who this man was and why he was locked away. She didn't have many answers, but the question of what to call him seemed like one she could do something about now.

"I grew up in Aethir," she said. "It's a tradition there that people are named after virtues it's hoped they'll possess. Charity, Temperance, Verity . . ."

The stranger paused to catch his breath, bracing his arm against the tunnel wall.

She studied his face, the way his dark, grimy hair fell to frame the strong line of his jaw. There was a softness to his cheeks and around his eyes that, despite his height and broad shoulders, made him look so young. He lifted his gaze to meet hers, looking her in the eyes for the first time since they'd found him. And his eyes . . . They looked as though they were marbled through with stars set against a canvas of steel blue. The colors almost seemed to shift along with the flickering torchlight. They were extraordinary. But the pain and fear in them were as clear as if they were scripted there.

"Solace," she said, finding her voice again. "I'd like to call you Solace. Would that be alright with you?"

"Solace . . ." he repeated, letting the name hang in the air between them for a moment. He watched the space where it floated, as if taking measure of it. "Yes. I'd like that."

Some hours later, Dare returned from one of his scouting excursions with the welcome news that he'd found a path out of the tunnels. They pressed forward, all of them eager to be back in the open air. At last, pale gray light pierced the darkness ahead, and a gust of wind blew cold against Verity's skin. She couldn't help but breathe a sigh of relief as the fresh air filled her lungs.

They emerged at a wide entrance high up on the side of a rocky slope. It looked to be late afternoon, although the sun was obscured by the cloud cover. The foothills continued westward, while the peaks of the Mistvale Mountains rose higher, stretching east into Aethir. And a little further east, nestled into those high, snow-covered peaks . . .

"We should wait here," Dare said, snapping Verity back to herself. He was surveying the wide expanse of the plains to the north. "Leave under the cover of night. With all the twisting underground, I don't know how far we are from where we started, and I don't want to risk being spotted."

Drystan peered down the length of the foothills. "That's probably for the best," he said.

Verity watched the stranger—Solace. He stood at the very edge of the tunnel, his face tilted to the sky. He closed his eyes, and the faintest trace of a smile curved his cracked lips. In the daylight, his hair was a sandy brown and his skin was pale, though it was likely not the same fair complexion she had herself, but rather a paleness that came from being kept too long from the sun. How long had it been since he had seen the sky? Or felt the wind on his face?

"Vee?"

She turned to Drystan. "Hmm?"

His face was smeared with dirt, but his emerald eyes were shining in the waning sunlight. "I said, what do you think? Should we wait until nightfall and then head east into Aethir before turning north? We can decide on the way where to go, but whether it's Whitehollow or Valda, they're the same direction from here."

"They'll expect us to cross the border," Dare said, sliding his hands into his pockets. "We should stay in Westhold and head north."

"Back toward Port Merrick?" Verity asked. "Are you insane?"

Dare flashed an infuriating smirk. "They won't be expecting it."

"Sure," Verity said, every muscle tensing, "because they wouldn't expect anyone to be that stupid."

Dare kept grinning, but Drystan cleared his throat. "He's not wrong, Vee."

A frustrated groan rumbled from her throat, but she was too tired to argue. "Fine," she snapped, rubbing at her temples. "But at the first sign of soldiers on our tail, we're cutting east."

Dare sketched a half bow, hands still in his pockets. "As you wish, my lady Warden."

Drystan surveyed the entrance of the cave. "This is pretty exposed," he said, summoning Verity's attention. "You think you could put up a shield for us? Keep us hidden until dark?"

Verity grimaced. It was one thing to shield one or two people for thirty minutes. It was another to hold something like that across a twenty-foot span for the next five hours or more. It was too much. At least, it was too much for her to do alone and be as alert as she needed to be.

"I can, but"—she caught Drystan's eye—"I'll need an assist."

Drystan didn't hesitate. "Anything." They'd done it a number of times before, and he knew what was needed. More importantly, he trusted her. He knelt on the stone near the mouth of the cave and rolled up the sleeve of his corporal's uniform.

Dare muttered something about scouting a couple more tunnels and hurried off, out of sight.

"What was that about?" Drystan asked.

"Who knows with him," Verity scoffed as she crouched at Drystan's side, though a part of her wondered if it had anything to do with her magic.

Drystan handed her the small dagger from his belt. She immediately slid the blade across his forearm, just enough to cause some blood to well to the surface.

"Ready?" she asked.

"You're supposed to ask that *before* you cut me," he said with a quiet chuckle.

Her brows drew together in mock annoyance as she fought back a grin.

"I'm ready," he added with a wink.

Verity set her hand over the blood on his arm. Blood always made the smoothest conduit for channeling magic from another person. Closing her eyes, she opened herself up to her own wellspring. Then she began the incantation that allowed her to siphon magic through Drystan's blood.

Behind her eyelids, Verity felt reality stretch gently out in all directions, sloping down and away for what felt like miles. She knew how long to let it go before she cast the barrier across the tunnel's entrance and prepared herself to hold it in the back of her mind for the next several hours.

"There," she said, releasing his arm. "It's done."

Drystan inhaled deeply and pushed himself back to settle against the stone wall. His blinks were slower, heavier, like he was just waking up through the last tendrils of sleep.

Verity pulled a roll of bandages out of her pack and wrapped the shallow cut on his arm. "Don't waste the linen," Drystan protested as she worked. "It's hardly more than a cat scratch."

She narrowed her eyes, her lips tightening. "Don't start," she warned.

Drystan leaned his head back and shut his mouth, knowing when he wouldn't win an argument with her. He smiled warmly at Solace, who watched everything.

"Are you . . . alright?" Solace asked, barely louder than a whisper.

"It's nothing," Drystan said. "Don't worry."

Solace nodded to the bandage as Verity finished tying it off. "You did that so they won't find you here?"

"So they won't find any of us," Drystan said. "It's to protect us all. Together."

"Together," Solace repeated, like he was testing the feel of the word in his mouth.

Drystan gave a soft, tired laugh. "That's right. We're in this together. But now, we finally have a little time to relax while we wait for nightfall."

Verity couldn't help but smile. How long had it been since they could take a breath? Though it was strange to see Drystan relaxing without a book in his hands.

"Gods, I almost forgot!" Verity rummaged through her knapsack, ignoring Drystan's quiet grunt of curiosity. Finally her fingers closed around the small, worn book she'd managed to fit into her pack before she and Dare had left the inn in Port Merrick. She handed it to Drystan. "I'm sorry I only have the one."

He leaned forward, his face brightening as he spied the familiar dark green cover. "Vee . . ." He took the book and drew his fingers across the pages. "You found room for this? I was sure you'd had to leave them all behind. Thank you."

Verity's smile widened. The sight of her friend, her brother, happily thumbing through the worn pages of his favorite book soothed something deep within her. "There's always room for what's important," she said. Then she rose and left him to read while there was still enough light.

CHAPTER 17

Once they left the cave, they traveled several hours through the night, stopping once they hit a thin forest of birch trees, their leaves already yellowing with the first signs of autumn. Verity set up camp, and Drystan built a small fire to keep away the chill. The three men each found a spot to curl up for what remained of the night, and when she heard their breathing slow into the steady rhythm of sleep, Verity stepped away from the ring of firelight. Her mind was still racing. It had been ever since Dare brought Solace through that darkened doorway in the mountain stronghold.

Her body was exhausted, but sleep would not come easily in these last few hours before dawn. She wandered through the trees, dragging her fingers along the paper-thin bark of each one she passed, careful to keep the low fire in sight. Eventually, when her legs felt close to giving out, she returned to the edge of their little camp and sat beneath one of the larger trees. She leaned against it, her legs drawn up and her hands clasped around her knees. Her mind was still on Solace and the dozens of questions to which she had no answers.

"Do you think it's him?" Dare's voice cut through her thoughts, startling her. It was barely a whisper, but it carried in the dark. He sat against another tree only a few feet away.

"I thought you were asleep," she said.

"Do you think Solace is the weapon?"

Verity sighed and set her head back against the tree. "He was behind an iron door, locked and warded, exactly where the weapon should have been, and he said himself that he's dangerous. So it's looking that way, isn't it?" But then there was the question she'd been too afraid to ask. She tilted her head to look up at the stars. "Do you think the Council knew? If it really is him, do you think they knew that it was a person they sent us after?"

There was a quiet rustle of fabric as Dare pulled his coat more tightly around himself. "I would bet a fair sum of coin the Council knew it was at least a possibility. Their spymaster is the best I've ever seen."

"You speak from experience?"

"Their reputation speaks for itself."

Verity tried to recall anything she knew or had heard about the Valdane Council. "Who's their spymaster?" she asked. "I don't think I've ever heard of them."

"Exactly."

"If they knew, then why bother sending us in to gather information they already had?"

Dare chuckled softly. "That's the question, isn't it? What would be your guess, my lady Warden?"

"I don't know," she said, watching the stars, searching them for an answer. "Because . . ." Her breath caught in her throat as the thought struck her.

She could practically hear his grin as he said, "So you've got it then?"

"Because it was never about gathering information," she whispered slowly. "They already knew Westhold had the weapon. It was always about destroying it. But the Wardens would never have agreed if they knew the truth."

There was a long, tense silence, pulled between them like a rope. Then Dare said, "So they sent us here with the expectation that he would die."

The quiet frustration that had been building in Verity's chest since Valda ignited, though she kept her voice hushed. "The Council knew! This whole time, they knew, and they . . . How could they have expected us to do this?" she demanded.

"They didn't," Dare said, his voice flat and somber. "They expected *me* to do it. Because they knew you wouldn't, and they wouldn't be able to force you to."

She couldn't look at him. She just kept staring at the same group of twinkling stars. "You knew?"

"Of course not."

"Then why would they expect you to kill him? Clearly they thought you would do it. They were counting on it."

"Clearly."

"Why?" Verity asked.

"Because they assume I care more about myself than someone else."

She sighed, still watching the stars. "And do you?"

"Do I . . . ?"

"Care more about yourself?"

"Often."

Her next sigh was nearly a groan, her irritation sparking at his deflection.

A breath passed between them in silence before he said, "Ask the question you want to ask me, Verity."

She could ask, but could she trust him to answer honestly? "You've killed people before," she said. "Been paid to kill them?"

There was the slightest hesitation before he said, "Yes."

"Are you going to kill him?"

"No."

Dare had been in that room with Solace for less than a minute. He had found this young man in the space where they expected to find the object of power they were ordered to destroy. Dare could have killed him in the time it had taken Verity to decide to follow. He had killed that Westholden soldier in less time and with less reason. Why take the risk to rescue a stranger?

"Why is this different?" she asked.

When he didn't respond, she finally pulled her gaze away from the stars. Dare's focus was on the camp, toward where Solace was curled up under the blanket Dare had given him. The faint glow of the firelight reflected against the lines of Dare's face. In the two weeks she'd known him, she'd seen many expressions cross that face—he'd been aloof, frustrated, annoyed, and dismissive, among a handful of other things. But there was something different painted across it now: sorrow.

"Because," he said at last, "I'm fairly certain he hasn't done anything to deserve it. Or if he has, it was in another life that he doesn't seem to know anything about. I refuse to hold that against him."

"You would bet on that?" she asked. "You would risk everything on the gut feeling that this man doesn't deserve to die?"

Dare dragged his fingers through his hair, which was loose and falling in a wave of bronze to his shoulders. "Apparently." A long moment passed before he added, "I suppose I did the moment I brought him out of that cell."

It was a nice sentiment, but it didn't add up. Not with everything else. "And what about that soldier in the tunnel?"

"What about him?"

Verity looked away from Dare and the camp, toward Aethir to the east. "Did he deserve to die?"

"He was going to attack you," Dare said, bitterness coating his words. "We couldn't afford the noise or the delay."

"We had it under control."

"You didn't," he said. "I was in the alcove when you and Drystan rounded the corner with Solace. I saw everything."

"And what do you think you saw?"

"More than you. Unless you saw the blade he was drawing with his other hand."

Verity's fingers tightened around her knees. Was it possible? Could— "I don't believe you."

"You don't have to."

A dagger landed in the grass at Verity's feet. A standard-issue Westholden army dagger. They had procured one for Drystan just like it. "That doesn't prove anything," she spat. "All this proves is that you killed him with his own blade."

"For fuck's sake, Verity," he muttered. He sounded tired, all the fight leaving him. "Believe what you want. But I'm not going to apologize for stopping him from trying to hurt you or Drystan. Or Solace."

Verity inhaled deeply. She didn't have the energy left to argue either. "You were contracted for this mission through the Crimson Brothers," she said, shifting the topic to where she had more footing. She'd heard rumors of what happened to anyone—the mercenaries or those who hired them—who reneged on a contract. "What'll happen to you if you don't follow through?"

Movement in the corner of her eye pulled her attention. Dare stood and moved to Verity's tree. The sorrow on his face seemed to slide from his features, replaced by an easy indifference as he peered down at her. "Are you worried for my safety, my lady Warden?"

She scoffed, refusing to even acknowledge the question.

Dare sat beside her so they were nearly shoulder to shoulder. He leaned back, extending his legs out and crossing them at the ankles. "There's magic around him," he said softly.

Verity stiffened. "What? Around Solace?"

"It's why I could barely help carry him. There's magic clinging to him. And it's *not* a small amount."

"Clinging to him?" Verity repeated. "What does that mean?"

"You're the mage," Dare quipped. "You tell me." But he huffed quietly before Verity could respond and said, "There's something around him, pushing inward. Almost like it's . . ." He hesitated, searching for the right word.

"Binding him," Verity suggested.

Dare nodded. "Exactly." He shifted his gaze back to where the young man lay sleeping. "But what do you think it's binding?"

"Something Westhold thinks will win them a war." Verity swallowed hard. "And something the Valdane Council would kill to take out of play."

Silence surrounded them, though after a few minutes, Dare loosed a sigh. "You may as well ask me the other question you want to ask."

"What do you mean?"

"Warden," he said, tilting his head back to look at the sky. "You were not graced with the blessing of subtlety. And that goes for your emotions as well as your actions. You're as easy to read as one of Drystan's books."

Verity's jaw tightened, and she was grateful the shadows and flickering firelight might keep him from noticing. She had many questions she wanted to ask him, but there was only a little time before dawn. She could still get a few hours of sleep if she turned in now. And yet . . .

"Does the Council know you're a Perceptive?" she asked. "Is that why they sent you?"

"Fuck no," he blurted out. "Only two people in this world know I'm . . ." He swallowed around the words. "Know about me. And that was years ago. I doubt they even remember."

Hardly anyone knew about his ability? Verity couldn't imagine keeping such a critical part of herself—her magic—secret from anyone. It was who she was. "I guess there's three now," she said. She ventured a small smile, though he didn't turn to see it.

"I suppose you're right."

The morning sun rising over Aethir was a welcome change after so much time traveling in darkness. Every so often, Verity caught Solace staring up at the sky in a moment of quiet, private joy.

A twisting stream paralleled their path north. They made their camp alongside it that evening, just on the north side of a gently sloping hill. As frigid as the stream was, finally washing the dirt from her hair and face felt exquisite. Drystan snared a few rabbits, which they shared for their dinner. If they followed Dare's suggestion and kept their course heading north, they still had a few more days of travel before they'd be safely out of Westhold.

Even though they caught glimpses of darkened shapes against the horizon—the Westholden army was still hunting them—and even though they would all be killed without hesitation if they were found, their spirits were higher that night than they had been since Verity and Drystan had set out from Whitehollow.

Gathered around the fire, Drystan and Dare took turns swapping stories of their wilder days that had Verity laughing in disbelief and second-hand embarrassment. Even Solace was smiling.

"It was supposed to be a harmless dare," Drystan said. "Run through the temple of Ainam from one end to the other, naked as the day I was born."

He laughed as Verity clapped her hands over her eyes, though she peeked through her fingers when the deep rumble of Solace's laugh washed over them. He sat beside Drystan, legs crossed and back hunched, elbows resting on his thighs.

The more distance they put between Solace and the underground strong-hold, the more he seemed to open up.

"But I swear," Drystan continued, "my brothers must have known when the temple services were set to start, because I was just rounding the altar when the first worshipers started filing in. I ducked behind it faster than I could think, but then I was stuck!"

Dare took a swig from his flask before holding it out to Drystan. "Ainam's mercy, what did you do?"

Drystan shook his head at the offered drink. "Nothing," he said.

Verity groaned. She'd heard this story before, and she knew precisely what he was about to say.

"The priest never showed up, and everyone just left before long. I gathered up my clothes and went home."

"What?" Dare gaped at Drystan. "That's it?"

"That's it," Drystan said, a smile lighting up his face.

Dare leaned forward, sputtering. "That *cannot* be the end."

Verity thrust a finger at Drystan, shaking her head. "Don't you say it," she muttered.

Drystan winked at her before saying to Dare, "All stories end."

Verity flopped back onto her blanket, another groan escaping her lips.

"But not like *that*, surely!" Dare turned to Verity as though begging for her intercession. "Tell me he's joking."

How many times had she had the same reaction to one of Drystan's stories, and how many times had he told her the same thing? *All stories end, Vee.* It drove her mad. Sure, all stories ended, but they could at least end well.

At the silent shake of her head, Dare laughed and tossed another handful of sticks on their campfire, keeping it just large enough to drive away the night's chill. "Regardless," he said, "I'll do you one better."

Curiosity getting the better of her, Verity propped herself up on her elbow. These two had been at it for a while, and Verity wondered what insanity the next tale would hold.

"Will it have a better ending?"

All three of them turned to Solace as he spoke, this stranger who had barely said a handful of words since they had found him two days ago. His youthful face flushed a deep shade of red at the sudden attention.

"Sorry," he mumbled, probably worried he had offended Drystan. Drystan was trying, and failing, to look mortally wounded by Solace's words, but he and Dare were already laughing.

"I will have you know," Dare said with a devilish curl of his lips, "that I *always* provide a satisfying ending."

They traveled all the next day, narrowly avoiding a Westholden patrol that would have easily spotted them in the open prairies had it not been for a well-timed shell of magic to hide the group from view until the soldiers passed. Solace had looked about to panic, but Drystan's hand on his shoulder had steadied him. Dare had stood as still as a statue, but Verity swore a shudder ran through him once she let the spell fade.

By early afternoon the following day, they finally approached Cloud Bay. Verity intended to turn east into Aethir and follow the coast around, but Dare dropped his pack at the edge of the tree line where it met the rocky shore.

Verity stared at him, a breath away from demanding what the hells he thought he was doing, when she followed his gaze through the thinning trees to the bay.

"Captain Gil," she said suddenly.

Dare grinned like a cat who just caught a mouse.

As much as Verity loved the idea of getting a ride, the notion of an army still hunting for them was disconcerting to say the least. "Can we afford to just wait here?"

"Random patrols notwithstanding," Dare said, "we still have at least a half day head start. I say we try our luck tonight. If Gil's not here, we'll head out in the morning and take the long way around."

"We're only a few hours outside of Port Merrick. What if they're looking for us?"

"I doubt word's gotten back here much faster than we did. And besides, they won't expect us to bring Solace all the way back to where he started." The feline grin returned, his hazel eyes glittering like the bay. "As someone very wise once said, they wouldn't expect anyone to be that stupid."

"You'd better be right about this."

That night, Dare set the torch to burn at the shore, waiting for a returning light that would signal Gil was nearby. Verity had thought him foolish for taking one of the smokeless torches from the tunnels, but he'd insisted. He must have been planning on Gil from the start.

She joined Solace where he sat at the edge of the trees, listening to the gentle waves lapping against the rocks.

"It's beautiful," he said. The bay was calm, reflecting the moon and stars like glass.

Verity sat beside him. "Is this your first time seeing the bay?"

Solace shrugged. "I don't know," he said wistfully. "I wish I could remember."

Her chest tightened. He truly didn't remember anything from his life.

She sat with him, listening to the waves, until Dare appeared to collect them a few hours later.

"Our ride is here," he said with a bow, like a steward announcing an honored guest.

Finally, Verity thought. *Finally, something is going right.*

A small rowboat came ashore and bore them out to where *The Second Chance* waited for them.

Gil greeted them warmly, extending Solace the same welcome as the others, as though they were all old friends. "Where to?"

"Under the circumstances," Dare said, leaning against the railing, "I don't think we should go back to Valda."

There was only one place where Solace would be safe. And only one place where there was anyone who might be able to help unravel this mystery. "We should take him back to the Wardens in Whitehollow," Verity said.

Dare tensed, his lips twisting as he considered the suggestion. Verity braced herself for an argument, but he nodded. "It's the best we've got."

"Alright then," Gil said. "We'll have you folks in Whitehollow by morning."

At the captain's invitation, Drystan took Solace below deck to find some food. On her way to the till, Gil stopped beside Verity. "I feel obliged to tell you, Warden," she said, dropping her voice, "that new friend of yours is lit up like a damn bonfire."

Verity suppressed a wince as she remembered that Gil was a Perceptive, that she could see magic. At least it lined up with what Dare felt. "Yes, thank you, Gil," she said, trying desperately to sound unconcerned. "We have the situation in hand."

"Aye, Warden," she said. "Of course." She didn't sound completely convinced, but she continued toward the till.

"I trust that information won't leave this ship," Verity added hastily before she made it more than a couple steps.

Gil set a hand over her heart. "You have my word."

"Thank you, Captain." Verity headed toward the hatch that led below deck. Just a few more hours and they would all be back in Whitehollow, and she'd have the time and space to sort through the mire of questions still circling in her mind.

Behind a stack of cargo, Dare hunkered down and pulled his coat tight around himself.

Verity abandoned her plan to join Drystan and Solace below and crossed to the corner of the netting that held the crates in place. "You don't get seasick, do you?"

Dare looked up at her, a ghost of a smile on his lips. "No, I don't."

She considered asking him what it felt like, but the ship lurched into motion, Gil sending wind into the sails to turn the ship eastward, and Dare closed his eyes. He leaned his head back against the crates.

She turned to leave him in peace, but something stopped her. "Do you need anything?" she asked.

The mercenary smirked wickedly. "What are you offering, my lady Warden?"

Verity rolled her eyes. "Forget it," she muttered and headed below deck.

CHAPTER 18

CAPTAIN GIL DOCKED THE ship in Whitehollow as the sky lightened into shades of pink and orange. As grateful as Dare was to be off the ship, he would have preferred to walk the city for a while and get his bearings, rather than heading straight to the Wardens' compound. It had been years since he'd traveled through Whitehollow, but Verity insisted she and Drystan report to their commanding officer immediately.

"I know it's early," Dare said as Verity led them across the open courtyard of the compound, "but I always thought that the base of the fabled Wardens of the Flame would have more . . . Wardens." He expected people would be around at all hours, doing whatever Wardens did when they weren't out in the world, but the paths and training rings were silent and empty.

Verity and Drystan exchanged a look, but didn't say anything. Dare glanced over at Solace. He walked with his head bowed, watching only a short distance ahead of his feet.

Solace had no idea what to expect from the Wardens. How could he? For all he knew, they were leading him headfirst into another cell. Dare didn't know what was going to happen either, but he knew Solace was innocent, only having been locked up for who—or *what*—he was and not for anything he'd done. A weight settled in the pit of Dare's stomach.

He could empathize.

He wiped his palms on his coat and checked for the reassuring weight of his hidden daggers. Dare had risked everything to get Solace safely out of Westhold. *I'll be damned if I let anyone lock him up again.*

The four of them cleaned up and stowed their gear at the barracks before heading to another building close to the central square. Drystan led them inside to a large set of oak doors, and a chill ran through Dare. It was amazing the things that could trigger a memory, even after so many years, though he reminded himself that these were different doors, that he was in a different building, in a different city.

When Drystan rapped his knuckles on the solid wood, a gruff voice beckoned them to enter. It was sharp, as though the person it belonged to was very busy and would rather not be disturbed. Dare stuffed his hands into his pockets to keep from fidgeting.

Verity gestured to a bench along the wall. "Dare, can you and Solace wait here?"

Dare raised a brow. Why had she insisted they all come to the damned compound if she was just going to make him and Solace wait in the hall? "Is that an order or a request, my lady Warden?"

She didn't look amused. "Wait here," she repeated, omitting the niceties this time.

Order, it is.

He was about to remind Verity that he did not, in fact, have to listen to her, when Solace sat at one end of the bench, resting his elbows on his knees and bowing his head. As much as Dare wanted to tell the Warden where she could shove her orders, he also didn't want to leave Solace alone. Dare had been the one to make the call, bringing him out of that underground cell; he was Dare's responsibility. So he bit his tongue as he crossed to the bench and sat beside him.

Whatever magic surrounded Solace, it was focused so tightly inward that Dare could barely feel it unless he touched him. But it was there, like a film of oil clinging to the surface . . . If touching that oil felt like slamming your hand against a porcupine.

Dare leaned back against the wall as the doors swung open and shut, the Wardens disappearing within.

"So, they're Wardens of the Flame," Solace said when they were alone.

It didn't sound like a question, but Dare answered anyway. "They are. You're familiar with Wardens?"

Solace nodded. "Are you a Warden too?"

A laugh burst from Dare before he could stop it. "No," he chuckled. "No, I'm commissioned with the Crimson Brothers."

"The mercenaries?"

"Mm-hmm."

He studied Dare through the strands of hair falling over his face. "Why were you there?" Solace asked. "In my cell?"

Dare took a slow breath. "Westhold supposedly has a powerful weapon they plan to use to bring war to the entire continent," he said. "We had reason to believe it was there, in that underground stronghold where we found you."

Solace shifted, his fingers tracing over the lines on his palm.

"How long were you down there?"

"A few days," Solace said. "We traveled more before that." His brows drew together, as though he were having trouble finding the thought. "Though I don't know from where."

"And you don't remember anything?" Dare tried. "About how you came to be with the soldiers? Or from before the soldiers?"

"Nothing," Solace said, his voice going small.

Maybe . . . maybe if he asked around it . . . "How long have you been with them?"

The young man shrugged, then hunched his shoulders.

"Weeks?" Dare asked gently.

Solace shook his head, voice cracking as he said, "Longer."

"It's alright. The Wardens aren't going to send you back there." Dare swallowed before asking, "Were you there for months?"

He nodded. "I think so. It was . . . more than a few, but less than a year." Solace turned on the bench to face him, lifting his head. "But what if they come looking for me?" There was a tremor in his voice. "What if they try to take me back there?"

Dare hesitated as he got his first clear view of Solace's eyes. Bright blue and deep green, amber and silver, all swirled together unlike anything he'd ever seen. But he shook his head, focusing on Solace's words and the worry and fear in the young man's voice.

"Verity and Drystan won't let that happen," Dare said. He believed it to be true—they had certainly worked hard enough to free him—though if he were wrong . . . "And neither will I," he said, adding a truth he was more certain of.

The massive doors swung open. Drystan exited, and a shorter, stockier man followed. He was middle-aged, and his dark hair was cut short, nearly to the scalp, with a neatly trimmed beard that covered his chin and upper lip.

"So," the man said, his tone just this side of irritated, though there was a warmth in his eyes as he looked down at Solace. "You must be the young man my Wardens were telling me about." When his gaze shifted to Dare, the kindness evaporated. "And you must be the mercenary."

There was a weight to the man's stare, to his presence. Here was a man who was used to being in charge and getting his way. As it happened, Dare was used to dealing with people like that. And pissing them off. He plastered a smirk on his face as he stood.

The man ignored him. He said to Solace, "Son, my name is Joseph Cairn. I'm the High Commander of the Wardens of the Flame here in Whitehollow. I would like to talk to you a bit about your experiences, if that's alright with you."

Solace looked up at the commander and stood, though his eyes flicked between Drystan and Dare, uncertain. Nervous.

Cairn turned toward the doors, Solace trailing obediently behind. Dare started to follow, but the commander's voice stopped him. "Drystan, escort our *friend* to the guest quarters."

Dare's jaw clenched. "What's the matter, High Commander? Worried you can't trust me?"

"Not at all," Cairn said, his voice bereft of emotion. "I know I can't trust you."

A wave of heat flashed across Dare's face, there and gone in an instant, settling into a gentle burning in his ears. "Don't trouble yourself," he purred. "I'll find a place in the city."

"Just as well," Cairn said, holding the door open for Solace. "Though as a Crimson Brother I do trust your discretion in this matter."

Dare widened his smile, throwing in a flash of teeth for good measure. "Would you like me to swear an oath on it while I'm here?"

Many claimed oaths sworn in the presence of a Warden of the Flame were magically binding—or at least they used to be—but most clung to it only as a superstition. It was all horse shit, but magical or not, they were legally binding in every kingdom on the continent.

"No need, I'm sure," the commander said. "I know what the Brothers do to those among them who say too much."

Dare shrugged, his frustration sliding from his shoulders. "Suit yourself. Am I free to go?"

"Yes," Commander Cairn said, dismissing him with a wave of his hand, "but Warden Serah will still escort you."

"Wonderful."

Cairn shut the door firmly behind him.

"Come on," Drystan said, gesturing with his head in the relative direction of the building's main foyer. "We'll gather up your things, and I can show you to an inn not far from here."

"An armed escort," Dare quipped. "Lucky me."

The Warden stifled a groan. "I'm just following orders."

Dare crossed to the large doors Solace and the commander had disappeared behind and leaned against the wall beside them. Commander Cairn's stern voice was muffled but audible. "I'm sorry you've had to deal with that mercenary."

Verity's voice came through next, a little clearer. "All due respect, sir, but Dare was crucial to us finding Solace. He's been nothing but helpful."

There was a grumble of a response Dare couldn't make out before the sounds faded as they moved further into the room. He'd anticipated Cairn's reaction, but Verity's was . . . unexpected.

"Dare," Drystan said, pulling his attention away from the voices on the other side of the door. "Come on."

Dare took out a coin, rolling it over his knuckles. "Do you do that a lot?"

"Do what?"

"Follow orders."

Drystan let out a surprised huff. "Well, yes," he said, palms open at his sides. "It's kind of part of the job. Let's go."

Dare didn't move. "And you always do what you're told?" he asked. "You never question it?"

"I believe in the work we do," Drystan said. He crossed his arms over his broad chest. "Why are you asking?"

Dare pushed off the wall, pocketing the coin. He moved down the hall past Drystan. "So your commander says to take me somewhere, and you do? He says Solace is safe here, and he is?"

Drystan's long strides caught up to Dare without any trouble. "Yes," he said. "I'm sure it's different than what you're used to. We can't just choose the jobs that we fancy, or that pay well, but for some of us the structure of a chain of command is . . ." He paused, searching for the right word. "Reassuring."

Reassuring? That was an interesting idea. Until recently, Dare never had to follow orders. He'd had jobs with specific guidance or instruction, but at the end of the day, the decisions—and the consequences—were his, and his alone. But things were different now, and not in a way that was sitting well with him. Tanithe Ash may not keep a short leash, but it was a leash all the same. And it was barbed.

What was it like to have such blind faith in an organization that you could follow their orders without hesitation? Without question?

"What if he ordered you to kill Solace?" Dare asked as they started across the courtyard. "Or me? You would do it?"

Drystan laughed. "He wouldn't do that."

"But what if he did? Humor me, Warden. What if he ordered you to kill me?"

"I trust Commander Cairn completely. He's a good man. I wouldn't follow someone that would do something so horrible." They walked past a large brazier, burning bright in the morning sun, and Drystan pressed his fingers to his lips and touched the wall surrounding it. "Part of taking orders is knowing who to take orders *from*."

Drystan's words settled somewhere in a corner of Dare's mind where he could turn them over later. The problem was, Dare knew exactly who he was taking orders from.

And she terrified him.

CHAPTER 19

"I TRUST YOU CAN find your way back to the base if you need us," Drystan said, depositing Dare in front of the Snapdragon Inn. "And we'll know where to find you."

Dare eyed the exterior which, like many of the buildings in this city, was painted obnoxiously white.

"Why don't you come in and have a drink?" he said before Drystan could start the walk back to the Wardens' headquarters.

Drystan glanced up at the morning sky. "It's not even *close* to midday."

"Why are you assuming I mean alcohol?" Dare asked, feigning insult, a hand over his heart. "I mean, I did, but that's beside the point. Regardless, we haven't slept, so the difference between evening and morning is simply a matter of daylight."

Drystan raised one eyebrow at him, but Dare caught a flicker of amusement.

"Come in for breakfast then," Dare said, abandoning all hope of having a drinking companion. At least maybe he wouldn't have to eat alone. "You do eat, don't you? Or do you Wardens just subsist on duty and honor?"

A soft chuckle snuck out of Drystan. "I think I can spare a few minutes," he said, and followed Dare inside.

The inn was quiet this early in the morning. Dare rented a room from the innkeeper before sliding into a chair at an empty table toward the far wall. Drystan sat across from him, and a young serving boy came over to the table.

They each ordered a hot breakfast and a coffee, though Dare requested a shot of whiskey on the side. He promptly dumped it into his coffee when it arrived ahead of their food. He leaned back in his chair, letting the front legs lift off the ground as he stretched and clasped his hands behind his head.

"Tell me about yourself," he said. "Distract me from my boredom."

Drystan curled his hands around his mug. "Where should I start?"

Dare's mouth twitched into a grin. "You weren't always an honorable Warden of the Flame," he said, adding an unnecessary emphasis on the title and causing Drystan to sigh quietly. "I assume," he added. "Tell me about what you did before joining their noble ranks."

Drystan stared into the black depths of his coffee, steam drifting and curling upward. "That," he said slowly, "is a long and complicated story." He winced a little at whatever thought struck him. "A story for another time, I think."

Dare leaned forward to grab his own mug. "Or tell me about you and Verity," he said. He tilted his chair back again. He had to admit, he was curious. "You two seem close. Are you . . . ?" He let the question hang in the air.

The corner of Drystan's mouth quirked up. "No," he said, bringing the mug to his lips. "It's never been like that."

"Oh." He aimed for noncommittal, but he was tired enough that some of his surprise came through. They had such a strong connection, it was hard to believe.

Drystan must have caught it because he smiled as his gaze drifted down to his coffee again. "I don't think a relationship has ever been much on Verity's mind," he said. "But regardless, her interests lie elsewhere."

"She does seem rather dedicated to the mission," Dare mused into his mug. He took a sip.

"No, I mean, I'm not the right kind of partner for her in that regard."

"*Oh*." Dare mentally scratched the idea of bedding a Warden of the Flame off his bucket list. As irritating as she was, he'd be lying if he said the thought hadn't crossed his mind. "In that case, when did you two start working together?"

"Gods, I've known Verity for . . . nine years. We met while I was recovering in the Wardens' care."

Dare set the front legs of his chair back on the floor. "Recovering?"

"In addition to providing mediation or protection, the Wardens also provide a place for people to convalesce or rehabilitate. Wardens will sometimes pass through war-torn areas or places that have witnessed a disaster, and they'll find survivors. Help them pick up the pieces of their lives. Or sometimes, when the damage is too great, they'll take the wounded with them and let them recover under their direct care."

Tension was building in Dare's throat, but he swallowed. "And that's what happened to you?"

Drystan nodded. "Though mine was a disaster of my own making." One hand rubbed absently at his leg beneath the table. "I was lucky the Warden who found me was so kindhearted. Others may not have given me the second chance."

He hadn't known the Warden very long, but Dare considered himself a good judge of character. What could someone like Drystan possibly have done to not deserve a second chance? The question dashed across his tongue, but he bit it back, opting instead to ask, "And Verity? Was she already a Warden?"

"Verity came to the Wardens around the same time. After the Westholden attack on the College of Magi in Aethir."

Dare leaned forward, resting his elbows on the edge of the table, the mug of coffee nestled between his hands. "I remember hearing about that."

He'd only been living in Valda for a short time when news came that Westhold had attacked a school. Westhold had been skirmishing all along its borders for years, but this . . . The upper tiers of Aethirian society were built around highly educated mages who spent years studying everything from magic to politics, art, science, and philosophy. Westhold knew it, and they had sent their army to attack the largest, most prestigious college in all of Aethir, where it would hurt the very bedrock of their culture.

And Verity was a mage. An Aethirian mage. "Verity was at the College when it fell?"

Drystan only nodded.

"Was she an instructor?"

"A student," Drystan said. "She was only seventeen." A shadow fluttered across his face. He took another sip of coffee before he said, "But that's a story for her to tell."

Shit . . . Seventeen? That actually made her a couple years younger than Dare. "I . . . thought she was older."

Drystan gave a wistful smile. "She does give that impression."

Their food arrived—eggs, bacon, dark bread with butter and honey—and Drystan exhaled a quiet breath, no doubt grateful for the distraction.

Dare picked up a piece of bacon and took a bite. "So you met while you were being tended by the Wardens. And then, what, you joined the ranks when you were better?"

Drystan stifled a chuckle. "Basically." As Dare's brows rose, he added, "There was a bit more to it than that, but yes. I joined first, as my recovery was . . . well . . . I joined up first. A few months later, when she was ready, Verity took her oath." He stared at the table for a long moment, a shimmer of silver rimming his eyes, but he blinked quickly and took a long swallow from his mug now that it had cooled.

"And you've traveled together ever since?"

"More or less. There were a few times when our missions sent us separate ways. But we work well together. Our skills complement each other. Cairn realized that early on and tried to keep us together as often as he could."

Dare smiled around a pang of jealousy. Trust was not something he'd been fortunate enough to find in Valda. Maybe before, but . . . Dare reined his thoughts in before they wandered too far down that path. He finished the rest of his coffee, the whiskey in it still warming his throat.

"It must be nice to work with someone you can rely on. To know there's someone with you who always has your back," Dare said. "The fact that you complement each other in the field is an added bonus." He turned his full attention to the plate in front of him, grateful for a meal that didn't involve dried meat, stale bread, or having to skin his own food first.

They finished their meals in a warm, pleasant silence. But between yesterday's travel, waiting to signal Gil for a lift, and then dealing with the Wardens this morning, exhaustion was pressing down on him. He could use a few hours of sleep. In a bed. *Oh gods, a fucking* bed! Dare rose from his chair and dropped a few coins on the table to cover both of their meals and a handsome tip for the server.

Drystan swirled what was left in his mug before downing the rest. "Hey, what about your story?"

Dare grabbed his coat from the back of the chair. "My story?" He was about to deflect the question, as he usually did, but Drystan leaned forward, curious. He wasn't asking because he wanted something, but because he was genuinely interested. Dare picked up his pack from where he'd dropped it beside the table. "My story's not exciting at all, I'm afraid." He glanced toward the ceiling, searching for the right words among the rafters. He gave a dry chuckle. "I was a horrible disappointment to my parents, of course. I left home when I was eighteen. I make my living by stealing things or convincing people to give me things." He gave Drystan a crooked smile and a halfhearted shrug. "That's about it. I'm going to get some sleep." He turned toward the stairs.

"Where are you from?" Drystan called after him.

Dare stopped and swiveled his head, looking back over his shoulder. "I grew up in Bremmaran. Born and raised in Brookshire." The image of the city rolled into his mind unbidden, nestled in the cradle of where three rivers met. The roar of the falls was such a constant, Dare had had trouble sleeping those first few weeks after he'd left. It had been a while since he'd had occasion to even think about the city, and now he found himself wishing he still hadn't.

"That's in Duchy Wilhaven, right? I've passed through there. Spent a week or so in Brookshire," Drystan said. "It's a beautiful city."

One corner of Dare's mouth curved, though the gesture didn't reach his eyes. "It is."

Drystan leaned back in his chair, sliding his hands into his pockets. "You have anyone still there?" he asked. "Disappointed parents notwithstanding."

Dare turned fully back to him, unsure whether to be annoyed or amused by the sudden questions. "I'm not getting to sleep, am I? You know your orders were fulfilled when we made it to the front door, right?"

Drystan shrugged. "Yes, and you said we should have breakfast. This is what you get."

Shoulders sagging, Dare sat back down and stared pointedly at Drystan.

"So, anyone special back home?" Drystan prompted again.

Dare rubbed a hand along the back of his neck. "That's a complicated question."

"Not complicated," Drystan said with a warm smile. "The answer is either yes or no."

"Alright, Warden. Yes."

"Who?"

"See, now it's complicated."

Drystan raised his hands in innocence. "It's still a very simple question."

The memories of home wandered through his mind. Memories of the two people closest to him, of laughter and tears and heartfelt goodbyes—the one he'd said, and the one he hadn't. "My friends." At the encouraging look from Drystan, Dare added, "Jaelyn and Gregor. We were really close when we were kids."

Drystan smiled. "See, that wasn't so hard."

Dare ran his hands through his hair, unable to stop himself now from picturing their faces. "Yes," he muttered. "It was."

"What were they like?"

Dare loosed a sigh as he slouched a little in the chair. "I wouldn't even know where to start. Jaelyn was brilliant, and brave, and stunning. She was like a storm at sea—beautiful, but she'd drown you if you weren't careful. And Gregor, he was—" He shook his head, fixing his eyes on the Warden across the table. "Aetherann's ass, why am I telling you this?"

Drystan grinned, looking a little too smug. "I have a friendly face. It inspires confidence and trust."

Vire's hells, I really do need sleep if I fell for that. Dare pushed himself up from the table again. "Shit, you should do my job," he said. "You'd probably make a hell of a living."

"I did."

Dare blinked and studied Drystan, but the Warden's green eyes were steady and cold. "What?"

"I told you," Drystan said, his voice flat, unreadable. "My story's complicated."

"Apparently," Dare said slowly, tucking that piece of information away for another time. "Well, good night. Or . . . morning . . ." Dare hefted his knapsack onto his shoulder again. How he'd been lugging this heavy thing around for almost two weeks was beyond him. Ever since Port Merrick—

"Oh, shit!" Dare set his pack down on the chair and started digging through it. He couldn't believe he'd almost forgotten. There they were, crammed at the bottom beneath everything else. He slid the two books up and out, careful not to spill the rest of the pack's contents. He set them on the table.

Drystan's eyes widened. "Wha—" He reached across the table and grabbed the small stack. "My books . . . How?"

Dare shrugged, keeping his face neutral. "Verity gave the impression they were important."

"She didn't tell me you had them."

"She didn't know."

Drystan grinned, full and heartfelt. "Dare, I . . . You don't know what these mean to me. Thank you."

The joy and surprise on the Warden's face was so pure, so genuine, Dare could barely keep himself from beaming. If he started to smile at all, he wouldn't be able to keep it under control, so he tightened his jaw. He would keep his delight to himself. "It was nothing," he said, closing his pack again. "Good night, Drystan." The bed was calling his name.

"I'm sorry about what happened," Drystan said before Dare had gotten far.

Those were not words Dare expected to hear and they stopped him in mid-step. "What?"

"With Commander Cairn. I wanted you to know I'm sorry Cairn said he didn't trust you. He just doesn't know you yet."

Dare waved him off. "He's right; he shouldn't trust me. Even if he knew me—*especially* if he knew me. Honestly, if the High Commander of the Wardens let a sellsword into his office, he'd be an idiot."

"All the same," Drystan said gently. "I wanted you to know that I trust you."

Dare pushed the thought away, but the echo of those words followed him up the stairs and into his room at the end of the hall.

CHAPTER 20

DARE EMERGED FROM HIS room in the midafternoon. He'd bathed and slept
and was feeling much more like his usual self. He'd almost been able to put the
events of the last few weeks out of his mind.

But as he descended the stairs, he spotted Verity sitting at the bar. Just like that,
he was back in Valda, back at the Raven and Hart, watching her scan the room
for him at their first meeting. He should have walked away then—walked right
past her and out the tavern door—but he'd had his orders, and he'd been afraid
of what he'd lose if he disobeyed.

And now it was too late for him to walk away.

The afternoon sun slanted through the window and splashed across the bar,
glinting off the metal of Verity's hands and arms and highlighting the red tint
of her hair. Dare considered making some comment to amuse himself, to try to
make her roll her eyes, but the look on her face—eyes narrowed and jaw set—told
him she was in no mood for it. Neither was he, he decided.

"What are you doing here?" she asked, raising her voice to be heard halfway
across the main room. A few of the inn's patrons turned to look.

Always making a scene . . .

Dare crossed the distance and slid onto a stool beside her. "I should ask you
the same question, my lady Warden."

"Stop calling me that," she growled.

Dare flashed a smile, though it lacked warmth. "To what do I owe the pleasure?"

"What are you doing here?" Verity repeated.

Dare looked down at himself. He had changed his clothes from the travel-stained things he'd arrived in that morning and pulled his hair back out of his face. "Sitting here?"

She glowered at him. "Dare." A warning.

He leaned against the bar, setting his chin in his palm. "Being interrogated?"

Her hands flexed. "Ainam's glory, are you always so irritating?"

"Depends on the day." Though when she made it so easy . . .

Verity inhaled deeply through her nose. "Why are you wasting your coin here instead of just staying at the base?"

A harsh laugh erupted from him before he could stifle it. "How many reasons would you like?" When she simply stared at him, he said, "I am *not* a Warden of the Flame, Verity. I'm a mercenary." He lowered his voice. "A thief and a liar, as you so aptly put it once before." He ignored the flicker of irritation in her eyes. "I've known plenty of men like Commander Cairn. Trust me. It's better if I stay elsewhere."

"Better for *you*, you mean."

If that was how the Warden wanted to play this, then fine, he could play along. "Yes, it's better for me." He let a lazy smile slide across his face. "Besides, I've been a couple weeks away from a friendly city. I mean to get drunk this evening, and I'm not going to feel like stumbling my way back to your compound in the middle of the night."

Verity's mouth twisted as though she'd tasted something truly foul. She crossed her arms over her chest. "Not going to feel like, or not going to be capable of?"

The smile didn't falter, even as tension wove through his shoulders. "Both, if I'm lucky."

She scoffed loudly and stepped down from the stool. "We're meeting with Commander Cairn and Lorekeeper Harrow tomorrow at midday to discuss Solace," she said, all business and arrogance. "Don't be late."

"Oh, am I invited to the conversation this time?"

Verity rolled her eyes so hard Dare thought she might pull a muscle. Turns out he didn't have to try after all. "And don't show up drunk," she added.

Dare gave a seated bow with a little flourish. "As you wish, my lady Warden."

Verity muttered something under her breath and left the Snapdragon Inn.

Truly, Dare had planned on drinking that night. What he hadn't planned on was starting so early, or getting so drunk he'd have trouble getting anywhere. But he couldn't help but view Verity's blatant disgust and irritation as a challenge.

✺

After a full meal, some luck playing cards, and several rounds of drinks—despite himself, he'd lost count—Dare barely felt like making it to his room. He made it, though, sometime in the wee hours of the morning, if he could be any judge by that point. He even managed to get his boots and belt off before he collapsed into bed, welcoming the blissful abyss of drunken sleep.

The world roiled, stuttered, and heaved. Dare's stomach lurched, and his vision flashed white behind his eyelids. This wasn't the dizzying spin of too much liquor, and that realization brought at least some of his wits back to him. This was forceful, like something had hurled him through the air and now he was in free fall.

A wave of pain crashed into the back of his skull and sent a sharp tingling straight down his spine. He could barely keep to his feet.

Feet? He was standing? Dare hazarded taking a look.

Pulses of white light swam in his vision, but beyond them a vast chamber resolved into focus and Dare knew, with another lurch of his stomach, precisely where he was. The perfect violet carpet beneath his feet led away through rows and rows of empty benches to a raised dais in the center of it all. The massive, ornate table, long enough to seat nine comfortably along one side, was also empty. Dare wavered on his feet as he took in the vaulted ceiling and the dome in the center of it, streaming in daylight.

The assembly hall of the Valdane Council.

But . . . how?

He'd been asleep in a tavern in Whitehollow; even the Council didn't have the power to bring him back to Valda in the blink of an eye. Dare drew in a long, steadying breath and tried to focus. Flecks of dust drifted through the fingers of

151

light. No, they weren't drifting. They were suspended. Each fleck of dust held perfectly still, catching the sunlight.

Dare blinked his eyes slowly, trying his damnedest to clear the spots from his vision. Everything was static, like an image trapped in time.

Like a memory.

The nauseating pain radiating from the base of his skull and prickling down his spine only served to reinforce his theory. It wasn't real. Someone had used magic to yank his consciousness from where he slept in Whitehollow and bring him into their memory of the assembly hall.

That explains the headache.

"Are you alright there, Dare?" The silken voice of a woman floated to him, undulating the air in time with the roiling of his stomach. It had no particular point of origin. It was all around him, above and below, and directly inside the pounding in his head. "You look a little unsteady on your feet."

Dare knew the voice, knew it all too well as it haunted him through Valda over the last few months. A chill chased the pain that danced through his nerves. He had no idea how she was accomplishing this, but he let a mask of calm indifference slide over his face and through his mind.

"I was drinking last night," he said into the open space. There was no echo. "Why don't you come out so we can talk?"

"What makes you think I want to *talk*?" A wisp of breath fluttered against his ear, though her voice still came from everywhere at once.

He forced a playful grin. "I assume you dragged me from my bed for one reason or another. Generally those reasons, talking or otherwise, are best done face to face, wouldn't you agree?"

A shadow shifted on the dais. Dare's stomach lurched again as reality warbled and Tanithe Ash appeared, sitting on the edge of the table. She wore black leathers with bands and straps and blackened steel buckles that held more weapons than Dare truly felt like counting. Her flame-red hair was pulled back into a neat braid, and a cowl of black fabric hung loose around her neck. She reclined against the table, one long, slender leg braced against the floor, while the other dangled from the table's edge, her delicate fingers resting against the gilded tabletop.

As the spymaster for the Valdane Council stared down at him with cunning, piercing eyes, her lips curved into a wicked grin. "Face to face?" she purred. "Do you really lack such imagination?"

"Evening, Tanithe," Dare said, dropping his voice to match her playful lilt. He fell into the character she liked for him to play, even though the very thought of it made his insides churn. "And my imagination works just fine." He let his eyes wander over her as she perched on the Council table. "A pleasure to see you again, as always." Dare leaned forward into a bow, though the motion sent another swell of dizziness washing over him, even if it was only in his mind. He kept the discomfort from his face, but if this was in his mind, he'd have to steady his thoughts as much as his expressions. He couldn't have her seeing—

"Seeing what, my dear?"

He suppressed a grimace and said, "I can't have you seeing what you do to me in here." He tapped his temple with one finger, his eyes glinting with mischievous intent. He could let her infer the meaning he intended. "It's unbecoming."

Tanithe arched her back a little as she took a long, slow breath, expelling it with a soft moan. "Oh, I have missed our little banter."

Her eyes on him were blades of ice. She shifted to sit fully upon the table, accentuating her curves as she leaned back and crossed her ankles. "Why are you in Whitehollow, my pet?" she asked. "Was I not clear in conveying your orders?" The amusement was still there, though there was another reason for it now. She was toying with him.

"We needed to go back to the Wardens," he said, letting the truth be a shield against Tanithe prying into his thoughts. "There were unexpected complications in Westhold."

"You failed to destroy the weapon?"

"We couldn't. It was . . ." He fumbled for the words. The throbbing in the back of his skull was making it hard to think. "We needed clarification on what we're dealing with."

Tanithe's gaze roamed over Dare, like she was appraising a horse, already planning on how to break him. She either wasn't surprised by this new information, or she wasn't letting Dare see it. Both were possible, though his money was on the former.

"You're to bring the weapon directly back to me in Valda," she said, her voice lowering.

"What if the Wardens know a way we can destroy it?" He already knew the answer, but he needed to ask the question. She couldn't know that he'd already figured out her plan.

"Bring it to Valda," she repeated. Any sign of playfulness dissipated. Her silken voice turned to acid. "Need I remind you that you work for me?"

"You mean the Council?" As the spymaster, it was Tanithe's information that had forced Dare into the Valdane Council's service, but to say that he worked *for her* belied the ruse she'd so carefully cultivated. It was foolish of him to point out the slip. He doubted she would ever be so careless with her words again. It was a sloppy execution on his part, but if it could throw her off balance, maybe she would tip her hand. Maybe there was more he could glean.

"Of course," she said, her eyes narrowing on him. "The Council."

Between one blink and the next, Tanithe was standing in front of him. She hadn't hopped down from the table, nor crossed the expansive room to where he stood, and yet now she was there, so close they were sharing the same air.

Magic rippled from her, rolling through him like a pulse, flicking every nerve in his body on its way by. Yet there was something else with it, something entwined with the familiar, disturbing thrum of magic that Dare couldn't place. There was an oppressiveness to it, as though something heavy was pulling him down into a spiral, like a spun top about to hit that first wobble before it falls.

The shock of her sudden appearance was real enough, and he desperately hoped it proved a sufficient mask as he fought the dizzying, nearly overwhelming nausea that forced him back a step. Dare struggled to maintain his footing. The whole damned hall was spinning like that top.

Dare clenched his jaw as Tanithe watched him with predatory interest. "We own you. *I* own you." She prowled closer. Her pale hand closed around the front of Dare's collar, holding him in place as she pressed herself against him.

"You think you've built something for yourself, Dare. And yet a single word from me—a single *name*—will shred your pathetic existence before you can even beg for mercy." Tanithe leaned past his face, her lips grazing his ear as she whispered, "Bring me the weapon and I'll allow your little charade to continue. You can keep playing the thief and the mercenary as long as you like."

The room was gyrating, the angles all wrong. Dare had to close his eyes as she whispered in his ear, the hand on his chest both the only thing anchoring him and also causing the dangerous spiral he found himself in.

"Keep pretending that any of it matters in the least." Her tongue drew a line up his jaw before she shoved him back.

As Tanithe released his shirt, he was falling. Falling and spinning and reeling. The concepts of up and down were indiscernible from one another as Dare toppled through a darkness punctuated only with blinding flashes of light.

Dare jerked awake. The bed might as well have been the deck of Gil's ship in a hurricane. He got one glimpse of dawn breaking outside his window before he rolled to the edge of the bed and was violently sick on the floor. Dare lay motionless and shut his eyes tight against the room that refused to stop spinning.

The vertigo abated slowly, though when the smell of fresh bread and coffee from downstairs wafted into his room, it resumed full force, his insides threatening to riot. By the time Dare was able to move again, it was approaching midday. His stomach rumbled angrily, but even the thought of food still made it want to turn inside-out. At least he could ride out the rest of his magic-induced hangover without having to deal with Verity and her—

Meeting.

The meeting with the Wardens. And Solace. He was late.

Fuck.

CHAPTER 21

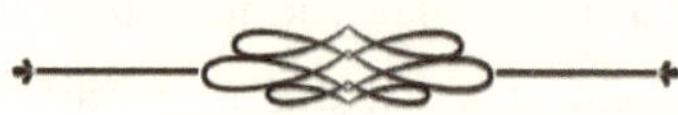

VERITY'S BOOTS CLICKED UP the stairs, muscle memory guiding her as she walked through the familiar halls. She didn't need to think about where she was going. How many times had she climbed these stairs? Even if the person she would find in the visitors' chambers was different, this place, these people, always felt like home.

Two Wardens were stationed upstairs, each placing their right hand in a closed fist over their heart in a quick salute as she approached. She returned it in kind.

Verity stopped at the room on the left. "Solace," she called, giving the door a quick knock. "It's Verity. Can I come in?"

The door opened and she hardly recognized the man that stood before her. Solace was wearing some of the standard dark grays and blacks of the Wardens' training clothes. Now that his hair was washed and combed, it was a light, ashy brown. He'd pulled it back at the sides, leaving the rest to hang to his broad shoulders. And his face, no longer obscured by his tangle of hair, was softer than she had expected, making him look even younger than he had in the tunnels. He couldn't be much past twenty years old, if she had to guess.

The bright swirls in his eyes were so much more pronounced than they had been before—cerulean, amber, and a deep, mossy green, all flecked with silver and spiraling toward the center. Verity stared up at him until a shy, boyish smile crept across his lips.

"I imagine I must look different than when you found me," he said softly.

Verity blinked away her surprise. "You look *well*," she said, "which is much better than before, I'll admit."

A slight flush colored Solace's cheeks. "Is it time to go?" he asked, staring at the floor.

"Yes, if you're ready."

He nodded, and Verity led him back toward the stairs. "I don't think I thanked you," he said, tucking a strand of hair behind his ear. "For helping me. For taking me with you."

"You don't need to thank me."

"I know I . . . wasn't what you were expecting to find."

They descended the stairs and stepped into the midday sun. "We didn't know what to expect," Verity said truthfully. She led him through the courtyard, past the burning brazier in the center, though he stopped to stare at the dancing flames.

"Verity." It was the first time he'd spoken her name, and it drew her over to stand beside him. "I don't want to hurt anyone."

Her heart sank at the pain in his words. "Why do you think you would?" she asked.

He swallowed as he watched the ever-burning flames. "I was locked away because I'm dangerous. And yesterday, you told your commander that you thought they meant to use me to start a war. To *end* a war."

She flinched. He'd been standing right there as she conveyed the story of their infiltration of the Westholden stronghold to Commander Cairn. She hadn't considered how that must have sounded to him, how it must have felt to be talked about in that manner, like he was a thing to be wielded. A weapon.

"I'm sorry I said those things," she said, and she meant it.

"It's true though," he said. "I really am just a weapon. I'm dangerous." Sorrow was etched in the soft lines of his face.

"Why do you think you're dangerous?" she asked carefully.

Solace didn't turn away from the flames as he touched his open palm to the center of his chest. "There's power here that I shouldn't have."

She needed to tread lightly. "Have you always had that power?"

He shook his head, the slightest movement. "No," he whispered. He turned to face her, and his eyes were rimmed with tears that glinted silver in the sunlight. "I think I stole it."

Verity's mouth went dry. "Stole it from who?" she managed.

Solace closed his eyes, a tear slipping down his cheek. "I don't know."

"Can you tell me what happened?"

He didn't answer.

"If you can tell me anything about what happened," she pressed, "it could help us figure this out."

"I don't remember." The words rasped out of him, like they clawed at his throat on the way out.

Verity stepped closer, setting her hand gently on his arm. "Solace—" But he shrank back from her, pulling away.

"I don't . . ." he choked. "I *can't* . . ."

Too hard. She'd pressed too hard, and now he was scared because of her. She wished Drystan were there. He was always better at talking to people, at navigating their emotions.

"I'm sorry," she said. "We don't have to talk about it." She turned to face the brazier and rested her hands on the low stone wall. They were going to be late for their meeting with Lorekeeper Harrow if they didn't start moving again soon, but she could afford to give him a few minutes.

Ever since they'd found him, he'd been so quiet and closed off, but also gentle. She wondered, not for the first time, what was going on inside his mind. "Just know," she said after a moment, "that I don't think you're dangerous."

Though Solace didn't respond, his shoulders unwound themselves slightly at her words. Over the next few minutes of silence, he slowly unfurled until he was standing much as she was, hands resting on the wall, watching the fire.

"I'm sorry, Verity," he said.

It broke her heart. "Solace, you have *nothing* to apologize for. Whatever happened to you in Westhold . . . whatever was done to you, it's not your fault."

He searched her gaze, and Verity hoped he saw the truth in her heart. "How can you know that?" he asked.

It was a fair question. If Solace couldn't even remember what had happened to him, how this power—whatever it was—came to be in his possession, how could she be so certain of his innocence?

"Because I believe you're a good person," she said. "You said you don't want to hurt anyone, and I believe you."

Solace watched her, the faintest curve of a smile crossing his lips as he exhaled the tension he'd wrapped around himself. "Thank you." He took one last look at the burning brazier before he gestured past Verity and across the courtyard. "We'd better get going," he said. "Lead the way."

The lorekeeper's office was nestled in the back corner of the compound, away from most other important buildings. Verity had long suspected this was partly because Lorekeeper Ardyn Harrow didn't like to be bothered when she was working, and partly because Commander Cairn was convinced she was going to mix the wrong reagents together and blow herself up. Part library, part workshop, part laboratory, the space held a unique combination of bookshelves, alchemical equipment, and workbenches strewn with papers and open books.

As she pushed open the heavy door, Verity was greeted by the vaguely sour, acrid smell that always seemed to permeate the lorekeeper's workshop.

"Right on time!" The voice of Lorekeeper Harrow sliced through the room. She was standing at one of her worktables, at least a dozen instruments, crystals, small bowls, and bottles of colorful liquids spread before her. Her half-moon glasses perched on the end of her hawk-like nose, and despite being pulled back into a bun, her dark, wavy hair fell to frame her face. A quill seemed to be all that was holding it in place.

Lorekeeper Harrow was several years younger than Commander Cairn, who stood beside her, arms crossed over his chest as he studied some papers at the edge of the table. At the time of her appointment to the honored position of lorekeeper, she was the youngest in history. And she still was, almost fifteen years later.

By the door, Drystan leaned against the wall beside one of the bookshelves, hands stiffly in his pockets. It was the look of a man who'd been told too many times not to touch anything and had made the mistake of disregarding that instruction at least once.

Cairn looked up, a scowl set on his face. "Where's the mercenary?" he asked.

"I'm not his keeper," Verity blurted out, tacking on an abrupt "sir" as Cairn arched an eyebrow.

Drystan cleared his throat. "He's staying at the Snapdragon," he offered. "I can go see if he's—"

"No," Cairn interrupted. "It doesn't matter."

Harrow smiled at Solace where he stood behind Verity. "Hello, child," she said, her tone gentle and sweet, like trying to coax a stray dog inside. Bright eyes peered out of golden skin that was marked with stray ink smudges and charcoal dust. The silver chain wrapped around the waist of her simple, gray robe clinked gently as she stepped around the worktable toward Solace. "I'm Ardyn." She gestured to a nearby stool. "Would you please have a seat? What would you like me to call you, child?"

The young man stepped around Verity slowly. His shoulders were stooped as he crossed the room to perch on the stool beside the lorekeeper. "Solace," he said, his eyes flicking to Verity. "Please, call me Solace."

Lorekeeper Harrow smiled, welcoming him like an old friend. "Very well. Let's begin."

❈

While Harrow guided Solace through a series of questions, Verity paced near the bookcase where Drystan stood uncomfortably still. She watched the closed door on each small loop she made.

"I'm sure he'll be here," Drystan said quietly from his spot as far from any of the lorekeeper's trinkets and poultices as he could manage. In the center of the room, Harrow and Cairn were focused on Solace.

Verity paused in her circuit. "Who?"

"Dare."

He was late. Why should she have expected differently? "What makes you think I'm worried about that?"

Drystan snorted. "You're going to wear a rut in the floor."

"What does it matter if he's here anyway," she muttered, crossing her arms and leaning against the bookshelf. Her fingers began to rhythmically tap against the steel of her arm.

Drystan inched closer, nudging her shoulder with his. "Because even though he has a contract between the Valdane Council and the Crimson Brothers to work with us, you feel responsible for his presence here, and you worry his behavior will reflect poorly on you."

Dammit, how did he do that? "You know me too well," she conceded.

"I know."

A few minutes later, as Harrow moved on to running assorted tests with Solace, the door swung open. Dare trudged into the room, looking like he'd rolled straight out of bed. His hair was loose and tousled like he'd barely managed to drag his fingers through it.

"You look like hell," Drystan said.

Dare acknowledged him with a silent, halfhearted wave before he slunk into the corner where the wall met the bookshelf. He crossed his arms and set his head back against the wall without a word, closing his eyes. A few stray strands of hair fell across his face.

"What happened to you?" Verity asked, keeping her voice low so as not to interrupt Harrow and Solace. Although she already knew the answer, she wanted the satisfaction of him admitting it.

Dare opened one eye to peer at her through his bronze hair. "What does it look like?"

She scoffed. "It looks like you're so hungover you can barely move."

"Astute observation," he drawled, closing his eye again. "Then why did you ask?"

Verity resumed her pacing, though Drystan gave her the *it's not your responsibility* look. He gave her that look often. She blew out a sigh, her irritation deflating a little. It was true. Dare wasn't her responsibility. Whatever he chose to do in his free time wasn't her concern. Unless it interfered with the discussion of what to do about Solace. In which case it might not be her responsibility, but it would be her problem.

The tests went on for a long while, though Lorekeeper Harrow was always careful with Solace, checking with him between each test as she scribbled notes into a book that lay open to her left. Did he need a break? Did he want to stop? Harrow was used to dealing with people on the verge of breaking, Verity realized. Or people who were already broken. Even Verity had found the lorekeeper's gentle manner to be a balm when she'd first met her.

Eventually, Harrow closed the book with a resounding thud. Dare startled from where he still leaned against the wall. Had he fallen asleep? He ran his hands through his hair, pulling it away from his face.

"Thank you very much, my child," Harrow said to Solace, taking the young man's calloused hand in her own. Then she gestured for the Wardens and Dare to gather around the table. "To begin, Commander Cairn told me what you discussed yesterday, and I believe your guess is entirely accurate, Warden Corallan. There *is* a Binding spell around him, holding the power within him at bay. Tell me, how did you intuit there was a Binding spell?"

Verity straightened as everyone's attention fell on her. It had been Dare's Perceptive abilities that had revealed the spell, but that was not her secret to share. And yet, could she tell an outright lie to Harrow and Cairn? Drystan always said that you could be truthful without telling the *whole* truth, that sometimes it was alright to simply leave certain things out. She'd done that initially when relaying the story to Cairn—she hadn't mentioned Dare was a Perceptive then either—though omitting that detail had made her stomach clench. But now she was being asked a direct question. Everyone was still looking at her. She needed to say something.

"I, um . . . well, Dare . . ." She swallowed, buying herself another second to think.

But the mercenary slid into the moment. "It was a hunch," he lied. "It made sense. If Solace really is some sort of all-powerful weapon, how else do you keep him prisoner? A few Wards and a locked door would hardly be enough to keep him in if he didn't want to be there."

Harrow adjusted her glasses. "Yes, yes, precisely," she said.

Verity glanced at Dare out of the corner of her eye. He still looked terrible, but at least he was more focused than when he'd first arrived. He met her gaze and flashed a brief smile.

"What magic is it binding?" Drystan asked. If he noticed any of the exchange between Verity and Dare, he didn't let on.

"Ah, that's the thing of it," Harrow said, tapping one of her pages of notes. "It's not."

"What do you mean, *it's not*?" Drystan asked.

Cairn watched the lorekeeper carefully. Dare crossed his arms as Verity stiffened.

"I mean, it is, but not in the way any of you are thinking about it." Harrow waved a hand toward Solace where he still sat on a stool, hands clasped between his knees. "The Binding spell is holding in power, but not *magic* as we're used to. I believe the power within this young man is divine in nature."

The room went completely silent. Even Dare didn't say a word, didn't breathe.

"Divine? Ardyn, are you saying this boy has the power of Ainam?" Commander Cairn asked. "Or Vire?" he added as an unfortunate afterthought. "How is that even possible?"

Solace tensed, drawing his arms tightly around himself. Drystan stepped beside him and set a hand on his shoulder.

Verity's mind raced. *The power of a* god?

"It is not unheard of, Joseph," Harrow said to the commander. She crossed to one of the massive bookshelves. "Surely you must remember the story of how the Wardens of the Flame were founded."

Solace shifted on his stool. "The Wardens?" he asked in a small voice.

Drystan squeezed his shoulder. "Lyran Corovar founded the Wardens of the Flame nearly six hundred years ago," he explained. "The story is that he had been blessed by Pyrannis, the god of fire."

"More than blessed," Harrow said, taking a heavy tome from the shelf. She dropped it unceremoniously over the papers sprawled across the table. She thumbed through the pages. "Lyran Corovar was chosen by Pyrannis to be the god's hands in the mortal world. He was granted some of Pyrannis's power to use at will, without needing to pray for intercession as a priest would."

Verity inched closer to the table and saw the page Harrow flipped to. It was a drawing she had seen a thousand times growing up. Four symbols—one for each of the elemental gods—sat within a closed circle, outside of which were the two symbols for Ainam and Vire, the gods of good and evil.

Harrow tapped the image. "Now I'm not saying that's necessarily what happened here. Lyran is but an example of how the gods have been known to grant some of their power to mortals."

But if the power had been granted to Solace, why did he feel like he'd stolen it? "If we're right and he is the weapon the Westholdens uncovered," Verity said, trying not to notice the way Solace flinched when she called him that, "where does the *weapon* part come in?"

"I have heard," Harrow said, "of artifacts of arcane magic that require attunement to a human to be sufficiently powered and wielded. It is *possible* there exists something similar, but for the divine. And perhaps our young friend, Solace, has found himself in possession of one. I cannot be certain, and I have no answer to the questions of *what kind* or *why*, but I believe this young man has the power of one of the gods."

"Attunement?" Dare's voice chimed in, less weary than before. "You mean that it's bound to him?"

Harrow angled her head, considering. "Yes, that's one way to look at it. If that is the type of weapon we are dealing with, it would likely be bound to him on a spiritual level."

"He wasn't carrying anything when we found him," Verity said, half to herself. "Solace, do you remember picking anything up before you were captured by Westhold? Or maybe there would have been a ritual of some kind?"

Solace shook his head, lowering his gaze to the floor. "I don't. I don't remember anything."

"Unfortunately," said Lorekeeper Harrow gently, "the absence of a positive does not prove a negative."

Verity pressed her hands against the table. "But if the weapon isn't with him, where is it?"

"There are too many variables to be certain, Warden," Harrow said, her voice grave. "It could still be in Westhold's possession, awaiting a reunion with its power source, or it could conceivably be a part of the young man's being now."

"What in the hells does that mean?" Dare asked.

"It's theoretically possible that it could be bound to him physically as well as spiritually," Harrow replied.

Dare's jaw went slack. "Literally? It could *literally* be part of him?"

The lorekeeper nodded slowly, as though her head were heavy with the weight of all the implications.

Verity ran through every theory on magical artifacts she'd learned in school, but she'd never even heard of there being anything similar for divine magic. She was out of her depth. "How is that possible?"

Harrow cleared her throat, furtively glancing toward Solace. "Perhaps that would be a discussion best left for another time."

"No," Solace said. He sat up straighter, wiping his palms on his thighs. "I want to know. Please."

"There's a theory," Harrow began slowly, "that a potent enough magical artifact could find a simple dermal power transfer to be inadequate and require full fusion with a host in order to obtain a sufficient energy transfer. Such a connection would be stronger than anything previously known by an order of magnitude. Not to mention the efficiency of such a transfer would be astronomical."

"Ardyn, in layman's terms," Cairn said, scratching at his beard.

"If the artifact is strong enough," Verity translated, "simply holding it might not be enough to power it. It's possible it could have merged with Solace to draw directly from his wellspring of power."

"But it's only a theory," Harrow supplied. "It's never been proven."

Solace's hands shook as he rubbed them over his face.

Drystan squeezed Solace's shoulder. "So we're dealing with something created by either Ainam or Vire?" he asked.

"Or one of the elemental gods," Harrow said, tapping the image in the book again. "There are six gods, don't forget."

Verity couldn't look at Solace, so she studied the book laid open on the table. "We see the miracles that signal the presence of Ainam, and we see the corruption Vire sends into the world . . . But Lorekeeper, there's been no sign of the old gods for hundreds of years."

"Because they're dead," muttered Dare, crossing his arms. "Or maybe they never existed at all."

Harrow locked eyes with Dare, and the mercenary took half a step back, arms falling to his sides again. "Or maybe, they are simply lost."

Lost . . . That was the word the preacher in Port Merrick had used. *They're not gone,* he had said. *Lost, maybe. But not gone. Perhaps it is up to us to find them.*

"Is there any way to know which god?" Drystan asked. His voice sounded hoarse, like it had been stuck in his throat. "Or what the extent of the power is?"

Harrow held Dare's gaze for a moment longer before turning to Drystan. "Not without removing the Binding spell. And since I don't know a single mage alive who would know how to bind divine magic, we wouldn't be able to reinstate the spell. I'm afraid that without having more information, it's far too dangerous to attempt to remove it." Her face softened as she turned to Solace. "I'm sorry, child."

No one spoke. No one could. Drystan hadn't moved his hand from Solace's shoulder. Verity recognized the grip, having been on the receiving end of it many times. That firm and constant squeeze of his hand that said *you're not alone.*

Dare was the first to break the silence. "If it is an artifact, like what you spoke of," he said. His voice was strained. "A weapon attuned to a human, is it possible to *un*attune it? Or to . . . separate them somehow, if it's bound to him as you suggest?"

Ardyn Harrow drew a long breath. "I don't know."

Dare opened his mouth to say something else but promptly shut it again.

"More research may need to be conducted to discern the reality of what we are dealing with here. Joseph, I'd like to send word to my colleague in the Reach for his thoughts. He's far more an expert in the realm of the divine than I."

Cairn nodded. "I fear time may not be on our side here," he said gravely. "Westhold certainly is aware that the man is missing. They'll be looking for him.

And assuming any of what you've said here is true, it's unlikely they'll simply chalk his disappearance up to a bad day and carry on."

"And there's Valda to consider," Verity added. "They contracted with the Wardens and instructed us to"—her throat closed around the word, but she forced it out—"destroy the weapon, if we found it . . ." She glanced quickly at Solace. His jaw clenched so tightly, she thought it might snap in half. "Since that's obviously out of the question," she continued, "what do we do about the Council?"

"If they knew what we know," Dare said with an upward nod toward Solace, "they'd want us to bring him to Valda. Three guesses as to why."

Lorekeeper Harrow considered this for a moment before shaking her head, her soft features crinkling in consternation. "The fact that we're talking about a *person* notwithstanding, I do not think a theoretical artifact of such power should be in the hands of anyone, be they an individual or government body."

"I can't say I disagree," Dare said quietly. Was that slightly deeper exhale a sigh of relief?

Verity stepped toward Solace and set her hand on his other shoulder. "Lorekeeper, let me take him to your colleague in the Reach," she said. A wave of heat flickered across her face as she looked down at Solace, at this human being sitting right in front of her. She was talking about him like he wasn't even in the room, like he wasn't a part of this decision. But this was his life they were talking about in theories and hypotheses. "That is, if you're up for a trip to Aethir."

Her heart ached as he said, "If you think it will help, I'll do it."

"It'll be dangerous," Cairn said, his brow creasing. "While Westhold is looking for him, he'll be a target."

Harrow closed the book. "I'm sorry to say it, but it will be dangerous no matter where he is. The only hope he has is for us to figure out exactly what has happened to this boy and how to undo it."

"Alright," Cairn said to Verity. "You and Drystan take him to the Reach. See what you can learn. And Verity?"

She stood a little straighter. "Yes, Commander?"

"In the name of all the gods, be careful."

CHAPTER 22

THE GROUP FILED OUT of Lorekeeper Harrow's office in a heavy, stunned silence. Verity and Drystan had their orders. They were taking Solace to the Reach with the hope of finding some answers. It was the only thing they could do until they had more information. Verity was glad of the direction, but the uncertainty still weighed on her. Her thoughts were spinning in circles after everything Harrow had said.

Drystan offered to walk Solace back to his room, and Dare had disappeared to Vire only knew where. The thought that he was unsupervised somewhere on the base worried Verity somewhat, but she didn't have it in her to care.

It was late afternoon, and the training yard was empty. She draped her cloak over a bench before moving into the center of the ring. Verity took a deep, steadying breath. She drew her sword, sliding into the first position of the memorized form. Then she was moving through the steps with fluid, practiced ease. Step, thrust, step, parry, spin, slash. The broken blade had a reassuring weight in her hands as she moved. Her mind stilled, and the tension running through her body eased as she focused on the movements, the position of her feet, her hands, her sword.

She finished the form once and began again, not bothering to stop in between, but a voice called from too close behind her, "Remind me never to get on your bad side."

Verity spun to find Dare just beyond the reach of her blade, hands on his hips and that obnoxious smirk on his face. He'd lost his coat somewhere along the way, and the sleeves of his beige shirt were rolled up to his elbows despite the cool breeze.

"What makes you think you're not already?" she said, restarting the form. "Even you should know it's a bad idea to sneak up on someone swinging a sword." The thought brought with it a memory of a young soldier with a hand over his mouth and Dare's dagger glinting red in the torchlight.

Step, thrust, step, parry, spin, slash.

"I heard what you said yesterday," Dare said. "You stood up for me to your commander. And you kept my secret. If you wanted to be rid of me, I'd say you missed two perfect opportunities."

Verity continued her movements. "You were eavesdropping?"

"Not intentionally."

"I wasn't trying to keep you around." Spin, slash, block, thrust. "It just wasn't fair of him to say those things. And you asked me to keep your secret, so I did." Step, parry, step, slash.

"I never actually asked you to keep it a secret." He chuckled. "Though I'm incredibly appreciative that you did."

Verity tried to ignore him, to regain the focus she had before he'd arrived.

"Wouldn't that be easier with a sword that was in one piece?" He was still smirking.

Verity stopped the form, sliding her sword into her scabbard. "Broken things can still serve their purpose." She faced him, crossing her arms over her chest. "What is it that you want, Dare?"

"I want to know when we're leaving for the Reach."

Why could he possibly want to come with them? It was crazy. What they were doing was very likely crazy. "You don't have to come," she said.

His brows furrowed as he titled his head. "What do you mean?"

"I mean that your contract is fulfilled," she said. "You were hired to help us find the weapon . . ."

"And *destroy* it," Dare added. "Which we haven't done. In case you've forgotten, it's still walking and talking, apparently wearing Solace like a cloak."

"Dare . . ."

He ran his hands through his hair, leaving them clasped behind his neck as he bit the inside of his cheek.

Verity wasn't sure she'd ever seen him think so hard before opening his mouth.

"I'm coming with you," he said.

She stepped closer to Dare, lowering her voice despite the still-empty training yard. "After we found Solace, that night in the trees, you never told me what will happen to you for not completing the job from the Brothers. For walking out of there with Solace."

Dare's hands fell to his sides. "I'm not here working for the Crimson Brothers," he said. "I'm working for the Valdane Council."

"Don't argue semantics," she snapped.

"I'm not."

Verity's jaw tightened. *I swear, if he's been lying this whole time . . .* "You work for the Crimson Brothers," she said flatly.

"I do. But I also work directly for the Council."

"For how long?" Her face grew hot. If he could see the rage beginning to simmer within her, he didn't show it.

"Off and on," he said. "Whenever they need something done."

"Something illegal."

"Well . . ." He gestured vaguely to himself, inviting her to think of another reason they'd need him for anything. "Yes."

Verity closed her eyes, rubbing at them with her forefinger and thumb. "Why are you working for them?" she asked. "And why wouldn't you tell us?"

"Why do you think?"

She opened her eyes and narrowed them on him. "Money?"

Dare snorted. "That's really what you think of me, huh?"

Verity only glared.

"My lady Warden, you think I would work for the most corrupt government body on the continent for coin?"

She had thought that, but now she hesitated. She knew the Valdane Council wasn't the most benevolent group in power, but *corrupt*?

Dare clicked his tongue. "Come now, even you can't be so naive as to think—"

She silenced him with a sharp wave of her hand. Regardless of the Council's lack of civic duty, if Dare wasn't doing it for the money . . .

"They're blackmailing you."

Dare grinned wryly.

"What do they have on you?"

"Now you're asking the right questions. I'll just say that it was enough of a threat that I didn't think I could survive it getting out. So I took every bad job they handed me. To protect myself. *That's* why they expected me to kill Solace when we found him. And since I didn't, they'll expect me to bring Solace to them." He held his arms out to the side. "As you can see, I'm doing neither."

Verity's head was reeling. She thought she had understood Dare from the very beginning, but now that she knew the truth of it . . . Was he really saying he was willing to throw his life away for a stranger they pulled out of a tunnel in Westhold?

"You should get out of this while you can," she said. "Westhold is going to be looking for Solace. You can tell the Council the Wardens forced you to give him over into our custody. I'm sure the Council will understand that we can't just kill him." As the words passed her lips, she knew how ridiculous they sounded, how truly naive.

Dare took another step toward her, closing the distance. "Warden, the Council expected me to *kill him*. I didn't. Which means they will kill *me* if I go back to Valda without him. They will not care about the how or why of any story I spin for them. They are cold-blooded, calculating, and heartless. And now that Solace is outside of Westhold's borders, I would bet that they want him just as badly as Westhold does. And if that's true, I can promise you, they will come looking for him. But I can help if you take me with you."

"I can't pay—"

"Vire's hells, Verity," he snapped, "I don't want your money. I want to *help*. I can help you in the Reach."

Verity studied his face. The lazy smile was gone, replaced by a set jaw and the tight line of his lips. "You? Want to help with research?"

And it was back. Despite the tension, the corner of his mouth tugged upward in that same smirk that had been irritating her ever since she'd met him. "You'd be surprised what I'm good at."

She stepped closer, taking up the last of the space between them. He wasn't much taller than her, so they were nearly eye to eye. "You told me yourself, your skills are in getting into places you shouldn't be and leaving with things you shouldn't have. Are you going to be able to help keep him safe if Westhold finds us? Or Valda?"

To his credit, Dare didn't back away. "Not in the same way you or Drystan can, but I won't be a burden if that's what you're worried about."

Verity gestured to the rack of practice weapons at the edge of the ring. "Why don't we grab a couple of swords and you can show me what you can do."

Dare threw his head back and laughed, long and loud. "Oh, my lady Warden." He wiped a tear from the corner of his eye. "You would kick my ass faster than I could blink."

"You don't know how to handle a sword?"

His brows rose mischievously. "Would you care to rephrase that?"

"Dare." She was rapidly losing what little patience she had.

"You're no fun," he grumbled. When she continued glaring at him, he said, "Of course I do. But my strengths lie elsewhere."

She set a hand on her hip. "Show me."

With a wink, Dare squared his shoulders with the training dummies at the edge of the ring. His arm shot out, and a dagger struck one of the targets directly where its heart would have been. She hadn't seen him draw it, hadn't even known he was armed.

Verity raised an eyebrow as the hilt of the dagger still thrummed from the impact. She hated to admit it, but it was a hell of a throw. "Nice shot. Especially with a hangover."

Dare sketched a quick bow.

"And here I thought your fighting skills were limited to stabbing soldiers in the back." The words tumbled out of her before she could catch them.

When he straightened, his face was grave. "Is there a question you would like to ask me?" All mirth, all hint of friendly banter was gone.

They'd already discussed it. She already knew the answers, even if she still wasn't sure whether she believed him.

"Why did you kill that soldier when we met back up in the tunnels?"

Dare held her gaze, unflinching, steady. "I told you. He was going to attack you," he said without hesitation.

"How do you know?"

Dare tipped his head back, looking up at the overcast sky. "Verity, my livelihood—my *life*—depends on being able to read people. If they're going to make a move, I need to be a step ahead." He pointed across the training ring to the dagger embedded in the target. "That right there is the one shot I get. If I miss, I'm dead. If I'm too slow, I'm dead. I don't get second chances."

It was true. It had to be. He wasn't strong, but he was fast. In his line of . . . work . . . he would need to be able to calculate the odds in an instant. And given his mouth, a skill like that was likely the only reason he was still alive. The only question remaining was if he was lying.

Verity's ears began to burn. Was she being foolish? If he was going to travel with them, she would need to feel confident she could trust him, trust his judgment.

She'd said it herself inside Cairn's office just yesterday, hadn't she? *He's been nothing but helpful.* Had he given her any real reason to doubt him?

Drystan's voice echoed in her head, chiding. *Give him a chance, Vee.*

"Alright," she said, inhaling deeply through her nose. She blew the breath out quickly, trying to send all her doubts about Dare along with it. "I believe you."

Dare took half a step back, brows rising. "Good." He crossed to the target dummy and snatched his dagger from its chest. "So"—he replaced the blade in some hidden sheath behind his back—"when do we leave?"

CHAPTER 23

VERITY MET DRYSTAN AND Solace at the stables at dawn. A young woman was fitting a saddle onto one horse, while Drystan strapped a saddlebag onto another, securing his sword in its scabbard and his bow along with it. His quiver of arrows, their fletchings an assortment of white and mottled gray, was just visible on the other side. He wore his usual black pants tucked into black boots and a pale green shirt beneath his mossy gray-green cloak.

Solace stood nearby, wearing the borrowed Wardens' clothes in shades of gray. He held the reins of a third horse with one hand while he absently stroked its mane with the other.

Three horses, and three of them. There was a distinct lack of irritating mercenary—a minor blessing at this early hour.

"Where's Dare?" she asked. Maybe he'd changed his mind and decided to stay behind. Or maybe he'd gotten drunk and overslept again. She couldn't tell if the twinge in her chest was relief or disappointment. Although she wasn't exactly looking forward to spending several more days—possibly weeks—in his company, Verity thought they had reached something of an understanding yesterday.

"Good morning, my lady Warden." Dare appeared from the other side of the stables, leading a mare that was saddled and ready. He was surprisingly chipper this morning. His bronze hair was pulled back and tied at the nape of his neck, and his navy wool coat was unbuttoned, revealing a cream shirt tucked into sable-colored pants.

Verity forced a smile of greeting and set about securing her pack and sword to the horse the stable hand was preparing. It was about a three-day trip from Whitehollow, situated toward the southeastern edge of the kingdom of Armathain, to the city of Aetherann's Reach nestled high in the snowy peaks of the Crescent Mountains in Aethir.

Three days before they might hopefully have some answers and a path forward, if luck was on their side.

⬢

When they stopped for the night, Drystan and Dare kept them all entertained with more stories. As one of Dare's raucous tales drew to a close, Drystan nudged Solace.

"Are you alright?" he asked. "Do you want us to stop?"

Verity hadn't noticed until Drystan pointed it out, but Solace's shoulders were hunched, as he sat and stared at the fire, his young face clouded by sorrow.

"No, I'm sorry," he said softly.

"You have nothing to apologize for," Drystan said. "You seem sad is all."

Leave it to Drystan to spot another's discomfort.

"No . . . well, I . . ." Solace pushed his sandy brown hair out of his face. "You all have these wonderful stories of your lives. But I . . . I don't have anything like that."

"I'm sorry," Drystan said gently. "I can't imagine how hard it must be to have lost all memories of anything beyond a few months ago."

What must it feel like to have no memory of one's past, good or bad? Verity's own past had made her who she was now. Who would she be if she remembered none of it?

Dare leaned back. "Well, he remembers plenty."

Verity shot him a look. "Dare!"

"No, no," he said, raising his hands. He gestured to Solace. "I mean, you remember how to speak, how to dress yourself. You remembered who the Wardens and the Crimson Brothers are. So you haven't lost all your memories. A few of them are just . . . missing."

Missing? He had a point. And a surprisingly empathetic one.

175

Drystan scratched his ear. "That's an interesting theory." He set a hand on Solace's shoulder, as he'd done in Lorekeeper Harrow's office. "Has there been anything, like a sight or a sound, a smell, that felt familiar to you? Even if you weren't sure why?"

Solace drew a slow, shuddering breath as he thought. "Well . . ."

All three of them leaned in a little closer.

His face flushed as he said, "Sometimes, I . . . hear music. When I close my eyes."

Drystan smiled. "What does it sound like?"

Solace closed his eyes. And then he began to sing, soft and low. There were no words, only a slow, sad tune, and his voice was beautiful as it carried with it love and longing. He sang the music he heard in his mind, a memory, perhaps, of his life before he had found himself a prisoner of Westhold.

Verity forgot to breathe while he sang, his deep voice encircling their little camp. When he reached the end, the blush on his cheeks deepened. "I'm sorry," he said again, lowering his face. "I don't remember the words."

"That's alright," Dare replied softly from across the fire. "It didn't need any."

Drystan's smile broadened. "You know, that reminds me of a song my mother used to sing. I haven't thought about it in ages." It was not as gracefully sung as Solace's, but it was sincere. Verity stretched out on her blanket and grinned as he sang. By the second verse, Solace was humming along, harmonizing with Drystan's tenor notes.

"You two are far too sentimental," Dare said, leaning back again.

Verity pushed herself up on her elbow. "Don't you—"

But it was too late. He was already singing, and it was far from the heartfelt tunes of the others. It was a drinking song, by the sound of it, and a raunchy one at that. Drystan nearly fell over laughing, though Verity groaned and pulled her blanket over her head.

"That was filthy," she lamented from under her blanket.

Dare chuckled and said, "Then let's see you do better."

"Not a chance," she called.

"You're going to let him get away with that challenge, Vee?"

Verity sat up, pulling the blanket down onto her lap. She eyed Drystan, who was doing a poor job of keeping a straight face. He was baiting her, but with Dare pretending to ignore her completely, and Solace's whole face lighting up with curiosity, she couldn't resist.

"Alright then." There was an Aethirian mountain song she had learned as a child, the type that seemed catchy and fun at first, until the words were considered as an adult. She sang, stunning all three men into silence.

"That was disturbingly twisted, my lady Warden. Truly," Dare said, taking a long drink from his flask.

Solace was laughing, though whether it was at the song or at Dare's horrified expression, Verity wasn't sure. "You have to teach me that one!" he begged.

Verity laughed and promised that she would.

Another day and a half of travel brought them into the foothills of the southern arm of the Crescent Mountains. The higher they climbed, the more they were forced to slow their pace, but by noon on their third day, they arrived at the gates of the Reach.

The capital city of Aethir, Aetherann's Reach stretched and curved along the side of the range's largest mountain. Stairways and walls were carved into the very rock, with buildings of white and gray stone built along the spiraling tiers. The city was named after the god of air, though local legends held that Aetherann himself had built the uppermost tier of the city, leaving the humans who worshiped him to figure out their own way up the steep and treacherous mountainside. Only when they reached the peak did they earn the right to call themselves Aethirians, claiming the city as their capital.

Several inns, stables, and supply stores cluttered the bottom tier, catering to those traveling into and out of the city. Complex systems of pulleys were enchanted to effortlessly transport people and cargo on moving platforms from one level of the spiral to another.

They boarded their horses at one of the stables, as the narrow streets and dizzying views of the Reach were not conducive to anything beyond small, foot-powered carts. Verity led the way into the city, stepping onto one of the moving platforms that would carry them up the side of the mountain.

Dare groaned and looked back along the road, probably considering whether the spiraling path carved up the mountain would be better than the platforms.

"How far up are we going?" he asked.

"The top tier," Verity said. "The library is an annex off the Aerie, where the Cabinet meets. It's the highest building in the Reach."

"Of course it is." He shoved his hands in his pockets as he stared at the long track up the mountain. "I have a bad feeling about this."

Verity watched the city slide past them as the platform carried them higher up the mountain. The frigid wind whipped her braided hair over her shoulder, and she appreciated feeling the wind's cold bite on her face and her right arm, down to where the metal of her forearm began. Her left arm felt nothing except a slight pressure from where she leaned against the railing.

The fact that she could feel anything at all was incredible. But as she ran her fingertips along the wood, a lump formed in her throat. The railing should feel smooth and well-worn. She tried to remember what it had felt like when she was a girl, the last time she had ridden a lift like this one and had let her real fingers, made of flesh and bone, glide over the wooden rail.

No, these were her real fingers, she reminded herself. These were all she had, and they were a part of her. They were real, and the pressure of her fingers touching the wood, whether she could feel its smoothness, its chill or not . . . *that* was real.

Verity pushed away from the railing. Dare was leaning back against one corner of the lift, his eyes closed and his hands tucked firmly in his pockets. It looked as though he were trembling from the cold.

But it was from the magic. He would be able to feel the magic powering the lifts up the side of the mountain. She hadn't yet worked up the nerve to ask Dare what magic felt like to him, but she was starting to get a picture of it.

Solace stood nearby, his charcoal gray cloak wrapped tightly around himself, the hood pulled up. "Do you not like heights?" he asked Dare.

The corner of Dare's mouth crooked up. "Are *you* worried about *me*, Solace?" he asked.

Solace gave a small shrug that Dare couldn't see. "You look troubled."

Dare opened his eyes. "I'm fine," he said. "Thank you for your concern." His voice held only a surprising sincerity.

Solace smiled, staying beside Dare until the lift passed through the cloud cover and reached the top of the mountain. Above them rose the mountain peak and the Aerie, the seat of the Cabinet of Aethir. The huge stairs leading up to it were carved directly into the mountain. The rest of the building emerged from the rock above, competing with the peak for height. Beside the Aerie, a long, windowless building snaked around the north side of the mountain, spiraling halfway up the peak.

"That's the library," Verity said with an upward nod. "But we should announce ourselves to the Cabinet, since we're here on official business. Lorekeeper Harrow's sent word to the head Archivist for the Aerie."

Dare groaned. "That could take hours."

"We need to do this right," Verity insisted. "Just because you're impatient doesn't mean we can sidestep protocols."

Drystan tapped her on the arm and gestured to the library. "Why don't they get started on the research?" Verity was about to repeat herself when he added, "*We're* here on official business, Vee. Dare and Solace aren't. They can get started, and we'll meet them when we're done."

Verity looked from Drystan's gentle eyes to Dare's eager grin to Solace's pleasant smile that showed how much he just wanted to help. With a sigh, she nodded. "Alright." She pointed a finger at Dare and Solace. "Stay together." She focused on Dare. "And keep out of trouble."

Dare turned the collar of his coat up against the wind as Verity and Drystan climbed the stairs to the Aerie. "I can't believe she agreed to leave the two of us alone," he said with a chuckle.

Solace let out a breathy laugh as he said, "I can't believe you're excited about doing research."

"I'm not." Dare gestured after the Wardens. "I'm excited about not having to wade through hours of bureaucratic bullshit."

The library foyer was surprisingly well-lit for not having any windows. A small set of steps led to a sunken circular lobby with chairs and tables of varying sizes scattered along its edges. Behind the central front desk, shelves shot outward to form hallways into the stacks like spokes from a wheel.

An older woman sat at the front desk, flipping through a massive volume.

"Good afternoon," Dare said.

The woman peered at them over the top of her glasses. Solace shrank from the stare, but Dare stepped forward and clasped his hands on the desk.

"Could you please point us in the direction of your religious texts?" He smiled as sweetly as he could. "We're missionaries," he added, trusting that to explain away their travel-stained clothing. "We're looking for more information about the Lord Ainam's glorious battle against Vire's evil forces in the last age."

"Oh, of course," the old librarian said, brightening as soon as the word *missionaries* passed Dare's lips. "Here, please, allow me to escort you."

"Thank you." Dare gave an appropriately humble bow. "You're too kind."

She pulled a small lantern from behind her desk and turned a nob on the side. A tiny orb of light appeared within the glass. Holding the lantern, she led them through the dim, winding corridors of the library. She eventually deposited Dare and Solace at a long table at the edge of an open reading area much like the foyer. The tables were each lit with small lanterns like the one the librarian carried, giving the whole space a warm glow without heat or flame.

As the older woman moved into the stacks with a promise to return with some primers to get them started, Solace leaned across the table to Dare. "How did you know that would work? Claiming to be missionaries of Ainam?"

Dare grinned. "Her pendant," he said. "It's the symbol of Ainam, but it's worn nearly smooth in the center. I took a chance that she was devout."

Solace dropped his pack beside the table. "That was lucky."

Dare draped his coat over a chair as the librarian returned and set a stack of tomes on the table.

"You young men just let me know if you need anything else," she said. She gestured down one of the long aisles. "Additional volumes on the subject can be found down that way. Ainam's blessings to you both."

"Ainam bless you," Dare said, giving her another small bow as she left them to their research. He picked up the first book on the stack, glanced at the title, and tossed it to Solace before grabbing the next one and cracking it open. "We'd better get started."

Dare and Solace were still poring over the tomes three hours later, breaking the silence only when one of them found something of interest, which wasn't nearly as often as Dare would have liked. Solace had braved the stacks once already, returning with half a dozen more books and some wide, flat cases used for storing loose parchments.

Dare leaned back, his legs stretched out on the table with a heavy tome open on his lap. The book outlined an alternate myth for the creation of the world. Most myths held that the four elemental gods—Taerna, Lanara, Aetherann, and Pyrannis—gave birth to the world and all the creatures in it, including Ainam and

Vire as the gods of good and evil respectively. This scholar, however, proposed a different theory: while the old gods created the world and its myriad creatures, Ainam and Vire were born of something else, something beyond the elemental gods' design.

The elemental gods of balance do not consent to the control sought by the outsider gods of order and chaos.

Dare read the passage again. *Order and chaos* . . . Not good and evil, not light and darkness as was often attributed, but order and chaos. That was new. He jotted a note before closing the book and dropping it on the table. It landed with an echoing *thud*. Solace's head jerked up from the loose parchments he was studying.

"This one's interesting," Dare said, shoving the book across the table toward Solace. He pushed himself to his feet, arching his back in a stretch.

Solace swapped the book for his pile of parchments, sliding them across to Dare. "Look at these," he said.

Dare leaned over the worn parchment and faded ink, pulling one of the lanterns a little closer. The tiniest jolt zapped his fingers when he touched it, more surprising than painful.

Of course the damn thing's magic.

The pages were from an illuminated text, with beautiful, ornate designs painted across each one. The text itself was in a runic script that Dare couldn't read. "What am I looking at? Can you read this?"

Solace shook his head. "Look at the designs."

Dare flipped back to the first page. The top was adorned with a wonderfully detailed tree, with leaves of gold filigree and roots that extended down the margins. The second page was covered in clouds and mountain peaks. The third, wreathed in amber and golden flame that curled around the crumbling edges. The fourth page was a stunning mosaic of blues and greens, aqua and turquoise, all swirling into a breaking wave.

"There's one for each of the old gods," Dare said. "Taerna, Aetherann, Pyrannis, and Lanara. Earth, air, fire, water." But there was nothing resembling a weapon or a war. "Solace, what are you seeing that I'm not?"

"I don't know," he conceded. "I keep coming back to it. Like there's something here if only I could read it. Look at the fifth page."

"Fifth page?" Dare flipped over Lanara's page and, sure enough, a fifth lay beneath it. Two eyes adorned the top. Two eyes, each with stars for the irises against a backdrop of twilight. The dark pupils at their centers were black as midnight and carried within them the weight of a world. Something itched at the back of Dare's mind, like a thought that hadn't quite taken shape.

"What do you think?"

Solace's question startled Dare out of his thoughts, yanking his attention away from those beautifully painted eyes. "I, uh . . ." He blinked hard, forcing himself to focus. "Is this for Ainam?"

Solace shrugged. "There's an analysis here that says so," he said, tossing another loose page toward Dare. "But I've never heard of Ainam being described with eyes like that."

"Forgive me, Solace, but . . . would you know if you had?"

The young man's shoulders slumped and a twinge of guilt tightened in Dare's chest. "Maybe not," Solace said quietly, "but if that's Ainam, where's Vire?"

Dare flipped the other four pages back on top of the last, burying those eyes beneath the elements. "True," he said. "Where there's one, there's always the other." He considered the possibilities. "Maybe there's a page missing."

No, that's not right.

"Maybe." Solace rubbed at his face.

No . . .

"Maybe we both need a break." Dare shook his head, trying to collect his wandering thoughts. There had to be a missing page if there was no Vire. They were equal and opposite, forever at war with one another. Two sides of the same coin. One simply didn't exist without the other.

Dare gestured to the book he'd slid toward Solace. "I'm going to see if there's more by this scholar," he said. "He's got a different premise than the others."

He picked up one of the flameless lanterns, ignoring the small zaps against his skin, and headed down one of the aisles, following the librarian's directions. The smell of old parchment and ink filled his nose as he wandered deeper into the endless stacks.

Occasionally, Dare slid a book a little off the shelf, glancing at the cover before pushing it back into place and continuing on, skimming the titles on the spines. After a few minutes he spotted *On the Machinations of the Divine.* Dare pulled it from the shelf. It was by Liam Mercer, the same scholar as the book he'd left with Solace. That sounded promising.

Dare cradled it in the crook of his arm, trailing his fingers along the leather-bound books on the shelf. The monotonous smoothness was interrupted toward the end of the row by one volume bound in a rough fabric that scratched against his fingers. He stopped and slid it from its spot. *The War for Balance: A History.* He checked the author's name. *Liam Mercer.*

Perfect.

Taking it with him, Dare rounded the corner. A shiver ran down his spine as he stepped into the next row. He stopped, searching the darkness beyond the small circle of lantern light.

He inhaled sharply, the air heavy and thick, almost stifling, like he couldn't quite get a full breath.

What in Vire's hells?

The edges of the books he carried were sharper where they pressed against his arm, the corners of the shelves a little too angled.

No, not Vire . . .

He needed to get back to Solace. Right now. Dare turned to run and almost collided with a broad-chested man who had stepped into the aisle behind him. Dare's lantern clattered to the floor as he stopped short.

"Whoa, easy. Didn't mean to scare you." The man stooped to pick up the light and held it out.

The man's short black hair and sharp, steel gray eyes were illuminated by the soft glow of the lantern, but so, too, was the thick scar encircling his throat.

CHAPTER 25

Fuck.

Dare kept his face neutral. "Sorry," he said, reaching for his lantern. "Didn't see you there."

Don't let him touch you, said a quiet voice somewhere in his mind. His hand twitched back for a moment before he carefully took the light.

Corvin Crosse carried his own small lantern and was wearing his Westholden dress uniform: deep crimson with gold stripes down the outside of the arms and legs.

So he was here on official business then. That didn't bode well.

"I haven't seen anyone else researching in this part of the library," the captain said.

Dare resisted the urge to pull the books against his chest. Movement like that would only attract Crosse's attention. Instead, he took a casual step back. "I'm a missionary," he said. The air was oppressive and thick, cloying at him as he spoke, as though it wanted to climb into his throat and suffocate him from the inside. "I've always enjoyed some of the ancient myths of the gods."

Corvin gave a warm smile, like they were old friends. "That's a passion of mine as well," he said gently, hushed tones for such a sacred topic. He regarded Dare, holding up the light to get a better look at him. "You seem familiar, friend. Have we met before?"

"I don't think so," Dare said. "I get that a lot though. Just one of those faces, I guess." He cleared his throat against the building pressure. "Are you here for anything in particular?"

"A little of this, a little of that," Corvin said. "Today, I'm looking for *The War for Balance* and *Beskajna dan Solara.*"

"You don't say?" Dare shifted so the spines of the books he held faced away from the captain.

Corvin turned toward the shelves to his left. "I find the works of Liam Mercer particularly intriguing. He wrote of a weapon created by the elemental gods hundreds of years ago, during the divine war. The old gods tried to overthrow the Lord Ainam." He glanced back at Dare, eyes alight in wonder. "Can you believe it? Ainam prevailed, of course. My theory is the old gods foolishly sank so much of their power into creating the weapon that they had no choice but to relinquish control of the world and abandon it to His glory." He held the lantern up to study the titles on the shelf. "But, according to Mercer, the weapon was lost after the war. I believe it still exists. And I believe the key to controlling it is somewhere in his works."

Dare forced a smile. "Control an ancient weapon of the gods?" he asked, trying to sound more curious than terrified. "Interesting, but it sounds a bit like the beginning of a morality tale on pride."

Corvin waved a dismissive hand. "Not at all," he said. "Can you imagine it? A weapon with the power of the elements? It could flatten cities. And if we use it in Ainam's name? Think of the good we could do!" He shook his head, looking almost sheepish as he calmed his excitement. "I'm sorry. As I said, it's something I'm quite passionate about."

Dare's gut was knotted over itself, and he had to fight to stay upright as the very air pressed in around him. It was getting harder to breathe. He had to get back to Solace. He had to get back to the Wardens and get the fuck out of here.

But Corvin blocked his route. He could try to circle around, but the stacks were full of turns that didn't make sense unless you already knew where you were going. Dare couldn't risk getting turned around in here, not when Corvin could stumble across Solace at any moment.

"That sounds fascinating. I'll have to look for those," Dare said.

Corvin stepped into the aisle he needed, browsing the shelves. "I'll let you know when I've finished with them."

Dare took the opportunity to follow, giving a noncommittal grunt of interest. Maybe if he could skirt behind Corvin, he could get to Solace.

"Nice talking with you," Dare managed as he cleared the captain's other side. Every angle around him felt too sharp, too perfect.

"Dare, are you back here?" Verity called. A light bobbed near the end of the aisle.

Corvin turned as Verity rounded the end of the row holding one of the flameless lanterns, the light glinting off her arms.

Go, now!

"I know you," Crosse breathed, his brow furrowing. The confusion was replaced by fury as soon as Drystan appeared behind her. "*You!*" The captain's face twisted with rage as his focus shifted toward Dare, who was still far too close for Dare's liking. "*That's* where I felt you before. In Port Merrick." Crosse lunged toward him, eyes flashing. "Where *is it?!*"

RUN!

Dare sprinted toward the Wardens, narrowly avoiding the grab. Verity set her feet, one hand moving to the hilt of her sword as the other shoved the lantern into Drystan's arms. "Grab Solace. Get out of here."

Drystan was running before she finished the order.

"Solace?" Crosse practically cackled as Dare ran toward Verity. "You brought it here. And you *named* it?"

Dare flew past Verity, still clutching the two books. A crash echoed behind him as he rounded the end of the shelves and sprinted down the next row. Dare slowed just enough to turn when the row ended at a perpendicular aisle. He bounced off the shelves and pushed himself forward.

The table where he and Solace had been researching came into view at the end of the corridor. It was empty save for some scattered books and papers. He had to trust that Solace was already with Drystan. Dare emerged into the open space, skidding to a stop against the table.

Verity. She was still back there somewhere with Crosse.

Back in Westhold, she'd taken down three soldiers before Dare had been able to get to his feet. *She can handle him,* he tried to convince himself as he wrapped his coat around the books he carried.

No, she can't, came the reply from the back of his mind.

Shit. Dare threw the parcel into his pack and stood, bracing himself to charge back toward Verity and Captain Crosse.

As he shouldered his pack, Verity backed out of the stacks, though she only took a step before something struck her in the chest and launched her over the table. She collided with Dare. They crashed to the floor in a tangled heap.

Verity groaned as she pushed herself up, drawing her broken sword before reaching down to grasp Dare by the forearm. She pulled him up, his skin tingling where she touched him.

"What *is* he?" Dare gasped, his vision swimming from the impact.

"I don't know."

"What am I?" Corvin stepped out from the shadows of the stacks, his eyes wild, mouth contorted in a maniacal grin. "I am the right hand of a god." He stalked toward them. "The Lord Ainam has chosen me as His agent in this world. I am doing His holy work. I am His will made manifest."

Oh, fuck . . . Somehow, it was true. Somehow, this man had been blessed by a god. And Dare and Verity and Drystan were all that stood between him and Solace, the weapon he hunted.

And Corvin was researching how to control it—control *Solace*. What would happen if Corvin got his hands on him again?

Verity stepped in front of Dare, placing her body between him and Corvin. "I'll hold him off," she said over her shoulder. "Go, find Drystan. Get Solace out of here."

Magic flared around her as she charged forward. Dare's knees nearly buckled with the sudden force of it. Pyrannis's flames, she was an instrument of death. Her every movement was swift and lethal, arcane power erupting and pouring out of her like lava.

And none of it mattered.

Corvin Crosse, in his pristine, crimson uniform, with empty hands and a madman's grin, weathered her fury. He dodged her sword blows like he was sidestepping a novice in the training ring. And the magic that billowed out of Verity—that Dare had to brace himself against so it wouldn't knock him over from twenty feet away—didn't even slow Corvin down.

Dare watched helplessly from the far side of the space, trying to find some opening in Corvin's defense. As Verity stepped back to gather herself for another attack, something shifted in Corvin's features. A slight change in his countenance as the Warden paused.

He's going to kill her.

Corvin drew his hand back as Verity pushed forward. There would only be one chance at this.

Now!

Dare bolted toward the table, sliding over the top of it and scattering the remaining books and parchments in his wake. His hand landed on the one small lantern left on the table, and when his feet touched the floor on the other side, he dropped to one knee and hurled the lantern forward as hard as he could.

It entered Verity's corona of magic, its flameless glow magnified by her power into a blinding radiance that should have burned out as quickly as it flared.

Should have, but didn't.

Even from this distance, the sharp and nauseating tightness of Corvin's power clawed at Dare's chest as *something* shot from his outstretched fingers and struck the lantern. It stopped in mid-flare—in mid-*flight*.

Dare ran to Verity. Flinging his arm around her waist, he pulled her into one of the aisles. Behind them, Corvin roared.

Verity's magic subsided as Dare grabbed her, but not before it crashed into him like a million burning needles. He stumbled and fell, his knees striking the floor hard. He pressed his knuckles against the smooth stone, trying to move.

Get up.

He tried again to push himself up, but all he could do was groan into the floor, every muscle in his body clenched tight.

Get. Up.

"Dare! Get up!" Verity's hands slid under his arms and hauled him to his feet. "Run!" She tugged him along, pulling him in close.

Light still poured out of the lantern, illuminating the surrounding rows, as bright as daylight.

"I'm alright," Dare mumbled, patting her hand that was hooked under his shoulder.

Verity didn't let him go. And he was grateful for it. Although his nerves were calming and the prickling sensation abating, his legs still trembled. He wasn't sure he'd be able to keep up with her.

"I've never seen anything like that," Verity said as they ran.

Dare stumbled, but she held him upright. "Maybe you should have tried kneeing him in the balls again."

She ignored him, though her grip on his arm tightened as they turned one corner, then another.

Dare inhaled sharply as a stifling pressure encompassed him. "Verity," he gasped, grabbing at her hand, his chest tightening painfully. "He's here."

"Tell me where the weapon is," Corvin said, "and I'll let you live so that you may see the glory of Ainam's divine plan."

Verity stopped at the end cap. A pulse of power erupted from her hand. Corvin's feet slid against the stone as the power rammed into him. As he regained his balance, Verity gripped the edge of the shelves tightly. Dare swung around to the other side, leaning into the shelves and shoving them with all his strength in the direction she was pulling.

Another surge of Verity's magic washed over him.

With the whine of twisting metal and the scrape of stone, the entire shelf, with its hundreds of books and tomes, crashed onto Corvin.

Dare grabbed Verity's arm where she braced it against the opposite shelf. "Come on!" He spared one look over his shoulder, to the toppled shelves and the bent metal supports at their base, the holes in the stone floor where they'd been bolted down.

They ran toward the front of the library, Dare leading the way now and Verity close behind. The grinding screech of metal against stone tore through the air. They had to get outside. There was no way a Westholden Captain would attack innocent bystanders in a foreign city. Especially in Aethir.

Right?

The walls closed in around Dare again as he burst out of the darkened stacks and into the well-lit foyer of the library. The angles of the steps and furniture were too sharp and the floor seemed to warp beneath his feet. Dare lost his balance on the stairs and pitched forward. He tucked himself into a roll just as he reached the front desk where the old librarian sat.

She stood at the commotion, and as Dare fell, that clawing, oppressive weight sailed over his head and struck her. Her skin turned ashy and gray, her face frozen in horror, one hand clutching at the pendant around her neck. Even her hair was perfectly suspended, unmoving, with strands flung wildly into the air.

Is that what had held the thrown lantern aloft, its flare undimmed? Would that have struck Verity if Dare hadn't acted on instinct?

Dare scrambled to his feet as the other patrons screamed and ran for the door. Verity spun, a wordless yell tearing from her as she launched another wave of power behind them. Dare's knees shook and buckled, but he caught himself against one of the plush reading chairs.

At the entrance to the stacks, Corvin Crosse ran into an invisible wall. He launched himself at it, but it held fast.

Verity grabbed Dare's hand. "Are you alright?"

He didn't answer. He could only watch as Corvin placed his hand against the wall blocking his path and pushed. His hand moved forward a few inches, then sprang back. He set his other hand against it and leaned forward, fingers digging into the forces that held him back.

He was going to *claw* his way through.

Dare squeezed her hand. "Verity . . ."

"I don't know how long that's going to stop him," she panted. Verity pulled him through the doors and into the crisp air of the Reach. "Stay close to me."

CHAPTER 26

DRYSTAN AND SOLACE SPRINTED across the upper tier of the Reach. Drystan's heart thundered in his chest as he scanned the tier for the contingent of Westholden soldiers he'd been expecting as soon as he'd seen Crosse. But nothing seemed out of place as they ran through the square at the front of the Aerie.

"I don't see them," Solace called, but he wasn't talking about the soldiers. "Drystan! We can't leave them."

Drystan kept moving, hefting his and Verity's packs higher onto his shoulders. He had to get Solace somewhere safe. Then he could—

"Drystan!" Solace shouted again. "We have to stop!"

Satisfied that there were no soldiers in sight, Drystan slowed. "We can't stay here," he said as Solace came up alongside him.

"We can't leave them," Solace said again. "We have to go back!"

Drystan checked over his shoulder, hoping for a sign of Verity and Dare. Nothing.

Dammit. Come on, Vee . . .

He gestured for Solace to follow him across the square. "We can't go back," Drystan said, positioning himself at the corner of a shop. It had a good vantage point to the library doors. They could linger there without calling attention to themselves. And the alleyway behind them would provide a quick escape. "We can't risk Westhold catching you, but we can wait for them here."

"How many?" Solace asked, moving into the alley behind Drystan.

He focused on the library's entrance. "Just one. While you were with them, did you ever meet a man named Corvin Crosse?"

Solace went still. "He's here?"

Drystan nodded, sparing a glance at the young man. He'd gone deathly pale. "Solace, what do you know about him?"

He was staring somewhere in the middle distance, not at Drystan, but another time and place. "He . . ." Solace drew his bottom lip between his teeth. "He's the one who . . ." He set a trembling hand against his chest.

And Drystan understood. "I'm not going to let him take you," he said. "Hey!" He grabbed the front of Solace's shirt, forcing the young man to focus on him instead of whatever memory had him near to panicking. "Listen to me. I'm *not* going to let him take you."

Solace nodded, leaning back against the alley wall and slowing his breathing. "Thank you," he whispered.

Drystan returned his attention to the library. *Come on*, he pleaded. *Please.* He offered a prayer to Pyrannis that Verity and Dare would make it out. But why was it taking so long?

At last the library doors flew open. Several people ran from the building before Verity emerged at a sprint, pulling Dare along by the arm. He stumbled, trying to keep up.

They didn't look hurt as far as he could tell. Drystan cupped his hands around his mouth and sent a bird trill echoing across the square.

The tightness in his chest eased when Verity spotted him, though it returned just as quickly as her steps faltered when she neared their position.

Drystan caught her as she fell into him, fear rising in his throat. He pulled her against his chest and swung around the corner into the alley. "What happened?"

Dare followed, bracing himself against the wall. He stared at Verity, a hand twitching toward her before he drew it back, rubbing at his face as he struggled to catch his breath.

Drystan gripped Verity's shoulders and pulled back so he could look her over. She swayed a little on her feet, and her normally sharp eyes seemed hazy and unfocused.

"I'm alright," she mumbled, pressing her palm against her forehead.

Drystan knew what she'd done. She'd pushed herself too hard, called upon too much of her magic. He encircled her with his arms again, holding her against him.

"What in the hells happened in there?" he asked Dare. If Verity had used this much of her power . . . "Is he dead?"

Dare shook his head. "No, but she slowed him down."

Slowed him down? That was it? A chill ran through him. Verity had expended that much energy and only managed to *slow him down?*

Verity tensed in his arms. "It won't hold for long," she said, trying to push weakly out of Drystan's grip. He didn't let her.

Dare peered around the corner, no doubt ensuring Crosse wasn't on their heels. "We have to get out of the city," he said. His eyes, always so calculating, softened with worry as they flicked once to Verity and then up to Drystan. "Is she going to be alright?"

Drystan nodded over the top of her head. "She needs to rest for a few hours, but she'll be fine."

"I'm right here, you know," Verity muttered into the fabric of his shirt. He couldn't help but smile.

Relief washed across the mercenary's face. "Then we need to find a place to hide, and fast. We can leave the city tonight."

Drystan slid a hand behind Verity's knees and scooped her into his arms. He expected her to argue, but her fingers only tightened around the front of his shirt.

His heart lurched. How close had she come to not making it out of that building? It must have been the force of her will alone that carried her out of there, pulling Dare along behind. Drystan knew just how strong her will could be. His arms tensed, holding her closer.

Dare moved past him, leading the way through the alley. Drystan turned to follow but caught Solace staring at Verity, at how she was cradled in his arms.

"She'll be alright, Solace," he said. "I promise you, she'll be fine, but we have to get out of here."

Solace nodded and stooped to pick up Verity's pack from where Drystan had dropped it, but the uncertainty didn't leave his face as he followed Dare into the city.

Thanks to Dare, they were able to drop down a tier and find an out-of-the-way inn without attracting much attention. Drystan lowered Verity to her feet before they stepped into the bustling common room, though he kept his arm slung around her.

"Dare . . ." Solace's voice was hushed as they crossed toward the front desk. "What kind of inn is this?"

It was the wariness in the question that made Drystan look—really look—around the common room. People were milling about, eating and drinking, as one would expect. But there, a woman wearing next to nothing perched on another woman's lap as she nuzzled her neck, and there, two people sat close, their hands roaming each other's bodies with an intimacy that was not common in most public places. As Drystan scanned the room, there were more private acts being conducted very, *very* publicly.

"It's the kind of inn a man like the dear captain wouldn't set foot in," Dare said. He smiled warmly at the bubbly young woman behind the counter. "We're in need of rooms for the night," he said, his voice dropping playfully.

The young woman twirled her dark hair around her fingers. "Of course," she said, taking in the four of them. "How many rooms? Just the one?"

"Two please," Dare said. He slid his arm around Solace's waist, pulling himself closer to the larger man. Solace tensed for a moment before he casually, almost *possessively*, set his arm around Dare's shoulders.

Drystan scratched at the corner of his mouth to hide his grin. *Well played.*

The girl at the desk smiled and set two brass keys on the counter. "Here you go. Enjoy your stay!"

Dare paid and palmed both keys. "Thank you, dear. Oh, and by the way . . ." He pushed one more gold coin across the desk. "If anyone asks, we were never here." He gestured to himself and Drystan. "Our wives would have our heads."

The young woman took the coin and winked, her eyes dancing with the conspiracy of it. "Not to worry, love" she said. "My lips are sealed."

Dare winked back. "You're a peach."

When they reached their rooms at the top of the stairs, Dare unlocked the door to the first and all four of them stepped inside. It was cramped, with little more than a bed against one wall, a dresser, and a small side table. Drystan helped Verity to the bed. She hadn't said anything since the alley, and her head drooped as he laid her back against the pillows.

"I think I know what happened in Port Merrick," Dare said from where he stood by the window. "Corvin Crosse has been blessed by Ainam. Chosen."

"Chosen?" The word echoed through Drystan. "Like what Lorekeeper Harrow was talking about? Granted the power of a god?"

Dare nodded. "That's what Corvin said himself, and given what I just saw back there, I'm inclined to believe him." He crossed his arms over his chest, his face grave. "Drystan, Verity was incredible, but she could hardly touch him. And he had this . . . power. It seemed like it froze things in place. Objects, people, whatever. Anything it hit just *stopped*. We barely got out of there."

Solace swallowed. "He calls it stasis," he said, his voice barely more than a whisper. Drystan hadn't seen him this closed off since they were still in the Westholden tunnels. "I've seen him use it. It's just like you said, it stops all movement." He wiped his palms on his pants. "It's . . . *very* lethal."

Drystan turned to Verity and found her sound asleep. "What was he even doing at the library?" he mumbled, half to himself.

"Same as us." Dare removed a cloth bundle from his knapsack and un-wrapped two books from within the confines of his coat, setting them on the small table. "He's researching the weapon." He tapped the cover of the top book. "He was looking for this one specifically, as well as another by the same scholar. He mentioned trying to find a way to . . ." Dare's eyes flicked to Solace almost apologetically. "To control it."

Solace drew a shuddering breath and wrapped his arms around his stomach, like the very idea was nauseating. Hells, Drystan found it unsettling and he wasn't the one being controlled.

"There's one other thing," Dare said, rubbing the back of his neck. "He believes the weapon was forged by the elemental gods."

"Harrow thought that could be the case," Drystan said. "Which one?"

Dare shook his head. "As in, all four of them. According to Crosse, it was made to challenge Ainam. He said they used so much of their power to create the weapon that it weakened them, which is why Ainam won the war."

Drystan sat on the edge of the bed and rubbed at his knee. "A weapon powerful enough to challenge Ainam himself? If that's true . . ." He looked at Solace, at the anguish on his young face, and he couldn't finish the thought aloud.

If that's true, that kind of power could decimate the continent.

"Then you were right," Drystan said instead. "We have to leave the city. We'll leave as soon as she wakes up."

"I'll stay with her," Dare said, handing Drystan the second key. "You go with Solace."

He didn't want to leave Verity, but he knew what Dare was getting at. If they were found, Solace's safety was critical. Dare wouldn't be able to protect him, and with Verity down, it would be up to Drystan.

He hated it, but he couldn't argue with the logic. Drystan looked down at his best friend, his family, the only person he had in this world. He leaned in and brushed his thumb lightly against Verity's cheek. "Alright," he said, and finally took the key from Dare. "Let me know when she wakes up."

Solace grabbed the two books and followed Drystan to the room next door. He set the books on the little table before sinking onto the bed.

"They could have died." His shoulders hunched as his elbows rested on his knees. "Because of me."

"No," Drystan said. "Not a single bit of this is your fault." He crouched down so he could meet Solace's gaze. "Things are shit, and I know you want to find someone to blame for everything that's happening to you. Trust me, I get that. Probably better than most. But you need to focus that blame where it belongs. It belongs with Westhold. It belongs with Corvin Crosse."

Solace's lips thinned, a muscle tensing in his jaw.

"And before you start thinking that you've dragged us into this, we're here helping you because we choose to. Because it's the right thing to do. None of this is your fault, Solace."

The young man studied him, a ghost of a smile on his lips. "Thank you, Drystan. It means a lot knowing I have the three of you as friends."

"You're welcome." He rose and moved to take up a vigil at the window. "Why don't you get some rest? I'll keep an eye out."

Solace pulled a small stack of books and parchments from his knapsack and placed them next to the two from Dare. "Actually, I think I'd rather read."

Drystan grinned and turned back, grabbing one of the volumes off the table. "You know what," he said. "Me too."

CHAPTER 27

DARE SAT IN THE single chair in the room and leaned his head back against the wall. He wished he'd asked Solace to leave him one of the books so he'd have something to focus on besides replaying the events in the library over and over in his mind. He could go ask him for one now; Solace and Drystan were right next door, but he didn't want to leave Verity alone.

She lay asleep on the bed. Nearly four hours had passed since Drystan had carried her here. Four hours since she had protected Solace—protected all of them—from Corvin Crosse, and had drained herself nearly to unconsciousness to do it.

Dare had been there with her. He'd been struggling to keep himself standing in the wake of the power flaring from her and Crosse, but he'd been there. She'd put herself between him and Crosse without hesitation, and Dare hadn't had the decency to notice what it had cost her to keep them moving.

To keep Crosse from killing them both.

He ran through the whole thing again, analyzing every step, every move. Had he missed some sign of her fatigue when she grabbed him? Or had she really been that good at hiding her exhaustion, only letting it surface when she knew for certain they were safe? Dare suspected it was the latter, but he wasn't so full of himself to think there wasn't a chance it could be the former. Even so, could he have done something differently? Could he have helped her somehow?

Fabric rustled on the bed, and Dare opened his eyes. The Warden stirred in her sleep, a crease appearing between her brows. He crossed to the bed, sitting on the edge near her feet. Her breath quickened as she shifted again. He didn't want to leave her to whatever nightmare she was having, but he also didn't want to startle her awake. He wasn't eager for a steel backhand to his face if she lashed out. Dare set his hand gently on her shin.

She jolted onto her elbows, taking in the empty room. "Wha—"

"Everyone's f—"

"Where's Drystan? Solace?"

"—fine." He raised his hands, hoping to convey calm. "They're together, right next door." He pointed to the wall adjoining their two rooms. "We're safe. At least for now. You got us out."

Verity sank against the bed and rubbed at her face. "Vire's hells," she muttered into her hands.

Dare couldn't help himself. "I do believe that may be the first time I've ever heard you curse, my lady Warden." The look she shot him between her fingers made his heart lighten.

Good, she's feeling better.

"Do you want me to get Drystan?" he asked.

Verity pushed herself up slowly and swung her legs over the side of the bed. She took a few deep breaths and flexed her fingers slowly, as if testing the motion.

"I couldn't stop him," she said, still staring at her hands.

"You stopped him from finding Solace," Dare said, scooting closer. "And you saved my ass. A fact for which I am eternally grateful."

She glanced at him sidelong.

"What?" He let a playful grin dance across his face. "I happen to like my ass. I've been told it's one of my nicer features."

Verity swung a backhanded slap into Dare's shoulder, but there was a glint of amusement as she rolled her eyes. It reminded him of his banter with Finn back in Valda. Not Caleb or Almestra—those two never appreciated his gibes, had always taken them far too seriously. But Finn got it, got *him*, as much as anyone on this half of the continent did.

"Do you want me to get Drystan?" he asked again. This time, she nodded.

"Dare?" She sounded so tired, so *small*, that it stopped him before he reached the door.

"Yes?"

"Thank you," she said quietly, wrapping her arms around her middle. Her dark auburn hair was a mess, half falling out of her braid, and she still looked so tired and worn. She was no longer the indomitable Warden of the Flame he'd met a few weeks ago in Valda. She was just a person. One who had given everything she had to defeat an enemy. And it hadn't been enough.

"You're welcome, Verity."

✹

When he returned with Drystan and Solace in tow, Verity was on her feet, pacing the small room like a caged animal, though she blew out a long breath when she saw them. Drystan immediately drew her into a hug, his broad shoulders losing their tension.

Dare returned to his seat at the edge of the bed, while Solace crossed to the window, giving Verity's shoulder a squeeze on his way by.

"How are you feeling?" he asked.

The Warden spared him a warm smile. "Much better, thank you." She surveyed the men in the room. "We need a plan. What do we know?"

Drystan spun the chair around and straddled it, leaning his arms against the back. He recounted everything they'd learned so far about the weapon and Corvin Crosse. Much to Dare's frustration, there wasn't anything he didn't already know. He'd hoped the Wardens' trip to the Aerie had turned up something useful, but the information obtained from the Master Archivist hadn't been worth the time it took to see him. Though he'd promised to fit them into his schedule for a more thorough discussion later in the week.

Dare muttered a curse under his breath. The whole mess was giving him a headache. "We can't stay in the city," he said when Drystan was finished. "It's too dangerous with Crosse here. And I don't even want to think about the political implications of there being a uniformed Westholden officer in the capital of Aethir, of all fucking places." He dismissed the thought with a shake of his head. "Regardless, we still need to figure out how this weapon might be bound to Solace and what in the hells we can do to separate them again. So the question is, where do we go?"

Drystan shrugged. "Back to Whitehollow?"

Dare winced, gently massaging the ache building along the base of his skull. "I could be wrong, but"—he gestured toward Verity, where most of her brand was visible—"I'm pretty sure Crosse made Verity as a Warden. He might expect us to head there. And besides, it's only a matter of time before Valda starts hunting us, if they're not already, and that'll be the first place they look. We need somewhere we can lay low."

While he spoke, Verity started digging through her knapsack. She pulled out a map and unrolled it on the bed beside Dare. "Here," Verity said, tapping the map.

Dare peered over her outstretched arm. The spot was about a day's ride beyond the eastern edge of the Crescent Mountains. "Fallwood? What's that?"

"Just a small town. It's nothing special." She traced a finger from the Reach. "But there are a few passes that cut through the mountains. This route here will drop us into Bremmaran just northwest of Fallwood."

"The mountains would be better than heading west into the Basin," Drystan agreed. "The sight lines westward from the Reach are incredible—we'd be spotted as soon as daylight crested over the peaks, no matter what time of night we leave. But heading east . . ." He crossed to the bed, studying the map over Verity's shoulder. "It's a good idea, Vee."

A small town whose only distinguishing characteristic was its placement on a major road connecting two kingdoms. Just enough people would pass through there that four travelers wouldn't be out of place. It would give them a chance to regroup, figure things out, plan their next move. It was a damn good plan, and the best one they were likely to get. So why was Dare's stomach starting to knot up?

He lifted his head from the map. "Solace?" he said. "What do you think?"

Solace hugged his arms tightly around himself. He was scared and alone, with two Wardens and a Crimson Brother as the only people looking out for him. Good plan or not, this was Solace's life they were deciding.

He studied Dare from his place by the window. "I trust you," he said.

The weight of those words landed in Dare's chest like a blow. *I trust you.* Those three words brought him back home, a kid again. A flash of Gregor smiling nervously with his ice-blue eyes, another of Jaelyn in the darkened woods beyond his family home.

I trust you.

"I trust all of you," Solace continued, pulling Dare out of his daydream. "I'll follow where you lead."

CHAPTER 28

IN THE GRAY LIGHT of dawn, as the mountain city was still shrouded in mist, Drystan and the others retrieved their horses from the bottom tier of the city and quietly left the Reach through the eastern gate. Not many people tended to take that path, as it led directly into the snow-covered slopes of the Crescent Mountains. As a result, it was little more than a narrow archway with a single iron gate. The guards on patrol waved them through without a second glance.

Drystan kept his bow slung across his lap as they traversed the first leg of the pass into Bremmaran. They were well-stocked for the journey, with warmer clothing and plenty of food thanks to a little excursion Dare undertook while everyone else was asleep. Verity had been furious with him, though Dare had calmly pointed out that there were extenuating circumstances and that, had there been a shop open early enough for him to secure provisions the legal way, he would have gladly done so . . . if for no other reason than to keep Verity off his back.

Drystan had been amused more than anything else, partially at Verity's outrage. He had to admit, he was intrigued by Dare and the line he walked between right and wrong, selfish and selfless. Whereas Drystan had always found himself squarely on one side of the line or the other, Dare straddled it with apparent ease. But Drystan had spent most of his youth around cruel, selfish men—had needed to become one to survive—and so he could see through the mask Dare wore. Even if Verity couldn't.

A gentle wind blew the snow across the trail beneath the overcast sky. Every shift of the snow had Drystan spinning around to ensure Corvin Crosse wasn't following, but so far, there'd been no sign of the captain.

The extra sleep before they left had Verity looking much better, though she was far from completely recovered. It would take several more days of rest before she was back to her full strength, so their planned week of rest and research in Fallwood was perfect. And after the last few weeks, laying low in a small town after traveling through the Crescent Mountains—and enjoying their stunning views—sounded almost like a vacation.

On the morning of their second day, they rode in something akin to a companionable silence. The only sound for a long while was the crunch of their horses' hooves against the snow-packed ground. Drystan had spent so much time getting Verity and Dare to work together and stop trying to kill each other that he wasn't sure what to do with himself now that they actually seemed to be getting along.

From his spot at the back of the group, Drystan observed the others as they rode. Dare had gone ahead, watching the steep, jagged outcroppings above them as they entered a sloping valley. Verity was next, her broken sword on her hip as it always was. Her braid bounced a little with each step, the morning sunlight bringing out the shades of red intertwined with brown. Solace rode only a few steps behind her. He'd been quiet since they left the Reach, even more so than usual. Occasionally he patted his horse's mane as it followed the path, and a soft, wordless song would float back to Drystan, just at the edge of his hearing.

Drystan took a hand from his bow and rubbed at his knee, at the deep-set ache in the joint that started whenever the weather turned wet or cold. Although the sun shone brightly in a clear sky, a chill wind blew through the mountain pass. He tried to stretch his leg out a little in the saddle, but there wasn't much he could do until they stopped next. Though honestly, it was likely to give him trouble until they were safely through the mountains.

He suspected Verity was feeling a similar ache in her arm, as was often the case when his knee acted up. No sooner had the thought crossed his mind, than she rotated her right shoulder and stretched her elbow, her fingers moving to where her pale skin met the gleaming silver steel of her forearm.

As the slope leveled into a long, narrow stretch between the mountains, pounding hooves pulled Drystan's attention. Dare spurred his horse back their way, galloping at a dangerous clip across the packed snow. Drystan's grip tightened on his bow.

"Go!" Dare shouted urgently. "It's an am—"

An arrow struck his horse in its left flank. It stopped short, launching Dare over its head. He rolled with the fall, tumbling for a distance before he could scramble to his feet.

Drystan nocked an arrow and drew, scanning the valley for where the arrow had come from. But the sun was rising between the mountains and reflecting off the snow and ice in the pass. It was nearly impossible to see anything on the slopes.

Two more arrows narrowly missed Dare, ricocheting off the rocks on either side of him as he ran. "Verity!" he shouted. "*Go!*"

Verity tugged hard on the reins, wheeling her horse around. But she stopped just as soon as she began, and the horse reared up. Drystan spared a quick glance over his shoulder and cursed.

Six figures dressed in white and gray, their faces hidden behind hoods and masks, stepped around some of the larger boulders they'd passed. Two of them lifted crossbows to take aim at Verity, swords glinting on their hips, while the other four wielded spears and stalked forward with calm malice.

Drystan loosed his arrow, striking one of the crossbow-wielding—what even were they? Bandits?—in the shoulder. Staggering back, the bandit dropped the crossbow and drew his sword with his good arm. No, they couldn't be bandits. Not with that discipline. They were too well-trained for common highwaymen.

Dare feinted left and then hooked right as an arrow whizzed over his shoulder. He was only twenty feet away from Verity when she leapt from her horse and planted her feet in the snow. She raised her arms in a familiar motion as an arrow flew straight toward her. It bounced harmlessly off the air mere inches from her face.

The barrier deflected another arrow, though this one had been aimed at Drystan. He gasped as he realized Verity had erected a wall of force that shielded not just herself, but all of them. It spanned the entire width of the pass and stretched at least fifteen feet high, given where another arrow ricocheted.

But Dare was on the wrong side of the barrier—he'd collide with it, the same as the arrows, before Drystan could shout a warning.

And yet he didn't. Dare stumbled, almost losing his balance as he bolted past Verity, but the invisible wall didn't stop him.

Somehow, Verity had made sure the barrier would only stop the arrows and not Dare. Drystan's mind reeled. She'd been dabbling with a theory for it back in Whitehollow—to adjust the spell to account for velocity—but Drystan had never seen her enact it.

A stream of curses poured out of Dare as he skidded to a stop, spotting the armed brigands blocking the path out of the valley.

Solace pulled back to Drystan's position, his horse stamping the ground. Drystan drew his sword from where it was strapped to his horse's flank and handed the hilt to Solace. "Take this. Find some cover. Keep your head down."

"Drystan!" Verity yelled, her voice a steady, booming command. "The archers!"

Drystan didn't see where Solace went, but he nocked another arrow from the quiver on his hip and leapt down from his horse. He ran for a large boulder along one side of the valley floor, just beyond Verity's barrier.

But where were they? He could barely see anything past the glare.

There! An arrow sailed toward Verity and bounced harmlessly off the barrier. Drystan followed its trajectory back to a cluster of rocks high on the opposite wall of the valley. Almost impossibly high. He squinted against the glare. At the briefest hint of movement, he fired. The arrow clattered against the stone.

The answering volley came in the form of two arrows, one from either side of the pass. Both bounced off the boulder he crouched behind. Drystan stood and loosed another arrow in the direction of the first. This time, there was no *clack* of the arrow striking the rock, no return fire from that side of the pass.

Got one.

Pressing his back against the boulder, Drystan spared a glance toward the others.

Verity had charged the other brigand with a crossbow, who had dropped it in favor of the sword strapped to his hip. She parried a thrust, spinning the attacker into the path of a large man with a spear. The spear hit the other's leg, and he dropped like a stone, clutching at the wound. But the one Drystan had struck in the shoulder and a second man with a spear circled her.

Nearby, Dare was dealing with the third spear-wielding bandit, who was doing his damnedest to keep Dare at a distance. Every dodge and sidestep ushered Dare farther away from Verity. He slashed inward between the strikes, a dagger in each hand, but wasn't able to close the distance. Given Dare's frenetic dodging and ducking, Drystan worried just how long he could keep it up. Especially with the last bandit, a woman by the look of her build, stalking toward him, spear at the ready.

Drystan nocked an arrow and took aim, but Solace stepped into view, taking the woman's attention away from Dare before she could get to him.

No!

With Drystan's sword in hand, Solace blocked each spear thrust. Every movement was crisp and clean. Efficient. It was as though the muscle memory from another time, another place, had taken over. Drystan waited for an opening, but they were clustered too close together. A shot at either of the brigands would risk hitting one of his friends.

Drystan turned his focus to the other archer hiding in the pass. Verity's force wall would fail soon. There was no way she could hold something of that size for very long, especially now, when she was still recovering from the fight with Crosse.

He was running out of time, but he couldn't see anything along the rocky slope of the pass. He leaned out from his cover behind the boulder, hoping to catch a glimpse of anything at all.

Pain erupted in his shoulder, and he spun from the impact, falling against the rocks. He cursed loudly and gripped the shaft of the arrow. He couldn't lift his bow with an arrow in his shoulder, and he didn't have time to work the arrowhead out properly. He gritted his teeth to stop from screaming, though a guttural growl escaped his throat as he tore the arrow free.

Drystan swallowed the nausea that followed. He knew where the archer was now. His own bow had fallen at his feet, but he bent to retrieve it, his shoulder screaming at him with every movement. Drystan nocked an arrow, stepped around the boulder again, and fired. But his arm buckled as he released the string, and the arrow crashed harmlessly into the rocks.

He stepped further out to get a better angle, nocked, drew, fired. Another ricochet. Drystan's shoulder raged, and the grip of the bow was slick with blood as he lowered it. He was still out in the open. A subtle movement of white and gray signaled where someone crouched behind the rocks.

The archer appeared on the slope above Drystan, his bow already nocked with an arrow. From his perch, he had a clear shot at Drystan. The bandit drew back the string and took aim. Drystan reached for an arrow, nocked it as he raised his bow, groaning with the effort, bile rising in his throat. His arrow loosed, piercing through the archer's throat. Only then did the bandit's arrow fly and sail wide, through the space where Verity's barrier had been.

Drystan's arm dropped, his bow slipping from his bloodied fingers to land in the snow. The fight was still happening behind him. He couldn't see Dare or Solace anymore. He didn't know where they had gone. But Verity . . .

One of her attackers lay slain nearby, but the remaining three encircled her. She parried and blocked their coordinated strikes with practiced skill and natural grace.

But he knew her like he knew himself—better, probably—and he could see the drag in her movements, how close their strikes were coming. She was still exhausted, and they were wearing her down even more.

Maybe if he could get a clean shot on one of them . . . Drystan reached down to collect his bow. A surge of pain tore through his arm as he picked it up, his fingers barely able to tighten around the grip. He tried to raise it, to take aim, but another wave of nausea crashed into him, and the bow hardly moved.

As Drystan tried to force his deadened arm to respond, Verity kicked one of the men in the knee, sending him sprawling. But he was on his feet again too soon. Verity didn't see him rise. She'd shifted her attention to the other two men and didn't see he was stepping around behind her.

Vee . . .

Drystan bolted across the valley floor. His shoulder burned and bled, leaving a trail of crimson in his wake, and his knee ached as he willed his legs to move faster. The man behind Verity raised his sword. Gods, she couldn't see him as she killed one of the others, her blade in his throat. Drystan shifted his bow to his other hand and threw himself forward.

He could do this. He could do something—*anything*. Anything that would deflect the sword, that would stop it from striking her. Anything would be enough. Pyrannis knew, she had saved his life. More than once. He could do this for her. He would pay whatever cost. He just needed it to be enough.

The sword slid through his upheld bow as though it were made of paper, but Drystan knew.

He knew it was enough.

✳

The ambush was waiting for them in the valley. As soon as he saw the six assassins blocking their escape, Dare drew two of his daggers. He wasn't about to lay down and die in this frozen, gods-forsaken mountain pass.

But fighting—the kind where your opponent is *armed*, and is facing you, trying to kill you just as much as you're trying to kill them—was never one of his strengths. And this particular miscreant, who stood at least a head taller than Dare, had a reach with his spear that was wholly unfair, especially when compared to his daggers.

Vire's fucking demons. Dare dodged several spear thrusts, the point dangerously close to his face. He shrugged out of his coat, letting it fall into the snow. The last thing he needed was for the heavy length to tangle him up or slow him down. The cold air of the mountain pass whipped through his shirt, biting into his skin.

Not far away, Verity was surrounded. How many was that—*four*? And Drystan would be dealing with the archers. Surely Dare could handle one frustratingly long-limbed assassin on his own.

He leapt back as another spear thrust threatened to skewer him. Something glinted to his right.

A second assassin stalked toward him, a wicked glimmer in her dark eyes, the only feature he could see beneath the hood and mask.

Fuck.

Every awkward block, every diving roll out of the way was taking Dare further away from the others. He was on his own. He would have no help from Verity or Drystan or—

—Solace?

He was there, harrying the second assassin and attracting her attention, pulling her away from Dare unless she wanted a sword through her back.

The wall of a man in front of Dare lunged forward. Dare twisted and tried to duck in close, slashing at the assassin while he was outstretched. But the spear swung around, the shaft clocking him on the side of the head as he tried to gain the advantage.

Dare staggered, doing his best to regain his footing, but his attacker didn't let him. The assassin slashed, the tip of the spear slicing across Dare's arm, tracing a thin line of red. He inhaled sharply between his teeth.

But . . . that should have been much worse. Given where he'd been standing, there was no way—

"Are you just *fucking* with me?" Dare shouted, taking the opportunity to step out of range. "Ainam's holy ass, if you're going to kill me, just get it over with."

The man laughed, the sound muffled in the gray and white cloth wrapped around his face, but it was low and rough. And familiar. The laugh brought Dare back to Valda, back to the Raven and Hart.

Dare straightened, his daggers falling to his sides. "Caleb?"

Caleb Tarneth pulled the cloth down away from his face, the anonymity it provided unnecessary now. "Morning, Dare."

"What the fuck—what is this?"

Caleb set the butt of the spear in the snow, shifting his weight to lean on it. "I would have thought that part was obvious," he said casually, like they weren't in the middle of fighting for their lives.

Well, Dare figured, *I suppose* he's *not . . .*

"The Council wants you dead," Caleb continued.

"The Council?" How'd the Council find them so soon? And *here*, of all places?

Tanithe. The Council's spymaster must have tracked him, but how?

"You took the weapon, idiot," Caleb said, mistaking the question for confusion as to their reasoning. He always took things too literally. "And instead of bringing it back to Valda, you're running off with it. Not a smart move, Dare. Even for you."

He pointed his dagger at Caleb. "Since when do you work for the Valdane Council?"

Caleb grinned broadly. Gods, Dare was really looking forward to sending his dagger through his throat later. "Since they have very deep pockets," Caleb said.

Dare scoffed. "And it seems I'm not the only one who's in them . . ."

The clang of blades echoed through the pass. Dare glanced quickly toward Verity, unwilling to take his eyes off Caleb for more than a moment. She was still surrounded by three of the assassins, but was fending them off beautifully. Dare's heart sank. They were Brothers. They were all Crimson Brothers.

To his right, Solace parried another spear thrust from the woman who had glared at him with hatred and malice. The one who'd wanted to help Caleb murder him.

"You dragged Almestra into this?" His grip tightened on his daggers. "Anyone else I know?"

"Are you kidding?" Caleb laughed. "She practically begged me to come along. They all did." His steel gray eyes wandered over Dare, appraising his value. "They're paying me a lot of money to be rid of the lot of you." A wicked smile spread across his lips, his teeth bared. "But killing *you*? Shit, I would've done that for free."

Caleb stepped back as his hands slid down the shaft of the spear. He spun it end over end in a fluid arc.

Dare took his shot. He flipped the dagger in his hand, gripping it by the blade. But his fingers were stiff from the cold, and he wasn't quick enough. Fast as a viper, Caleb shifted his grip and hurled the spear forward.

Pain crashed into Dare, stealing the breath from his lungs. But it dissipated as quickly as it struck, replaced by an icy chill that radiated from his chest and across his back as he slammed into the ground. His hand shaking, Dare grabbed the spear, a stark line, like a ship's mast, against the bright blue sky. He followed the wooden shaft until it passed through his shirt, into his chest. Blood welled in his mouth.

Not into. Through.

That thought was fleeting. But then all thoughts were fleeting.

Dare's vision darkened as his head tilted, and he watched Caleb fall to the ground, his dagger buried to the hilt in the bastard's throat.

<hr>

Boots crunched in the snow along with a flurry of movement behind her as Verity withdrew her sword from the bandit. She angled her head in time to see a blade descending toward her. She spun, but she couldn't raise her sword in time to parry it. She braced herself for the searing pain that was about to land.

It didn't come.

Drystan's bow snapped in two as an arc of crimson stained the snow. Verity drove the broken point of her sword through the assassin's heart.

The last attacker lunged, no doubt hoping to take advantage of her split attention. But . . .

But that was Drystan's blood at her feet.

Verity held up a hand and the assassin stopped as if running into a wall. She felt the tug of exhaustion drawing on her magic, but she didn't care. Not now. Not when that was Drystan's blood in the snow.

She whispered the familiar words and shoved her hand outward. The assassin careened into the rocks with a sickening *crack*. When she lowered her hand, he fell to the ground like a rag doll.

In a split second, Verity's eyes swept the valley. She saw no one. No one left standing.

Except Drystan.

He stood a few feet away, as though in the seconds it had taken her to dispatch the last two assassins, it had taken him that long to realize what had happened.

Verity moved to him, trying not to think about how much blood was staining the ground. An arrow wound in his shoulder was bleeding freely, the blood running in rivulets down his arm, dripping from his fingers that hung limp at his side. His other hand touched his chest . . .

When he saw her, he smiled. "Vee . . ."

Drystan's legs buckled. Verity dropped her sword and caught him, sliding her arms under his. "Drystan!" She held him up, his body pressed against her. "No. No, please."

Gently, Verity laid him down in the snow. She pressed her hands to his chest, but the blood welled up around her fingers. The wound was massive, extending from his left shoulder, above his collarbone, to the bottom of his ribs on his right side. And it was deep. The dark blood pulsed out with every breath, every beat of his heart.

Verity ripped off her cloak and pressed it to as much of the wound as she could cover, focusing her efforts on the deep gash near his neck. "Drystan, look at me."

He obeyed.

"Drystan, you have to listen to me. Hold on, alright? I just—I need—" Her voice was shrill as she ran through every spell she knew, every bit of magic she'd ever conjured or researched or read about.

No one had ever healed the body with magic. It was impossible.

But still Verity ran through every rote, every theory. There had to be something. Someone must have missed something. She could do it. She could figure it out. She just needed time.

"You have to stay with me," she commanded. "That's an order, Warden. Do you hear me?"

Drystan coughed, and his entire body rocked with the spasm of it. "I hear you," he said. Blood stained his lips, his tongue. He drew a ragged breath and placed his hand over hers. "I hear you, Vee."

Verity pressed the cloak against him with all her strength, but it was already soaked through with blood. There had to be something. She couldn't lose him. She couldn't.

His eyes began to flutter closed and Verity slid a hand behind his head. "Drystan!"

He opened his eyes, though the effort seemed monumental.

"I need you. I can't—" Her throat closed around the words. "I can't *do* this. I need you."

"You don't," he said, barely a whisper of breath. "All stories end."

"Your story's not over," she cried, still leaning against the wound, hoping, praying.

She had to help him, to save him. She couldn't fail this time, not again, but his life was slipping through her fingers and she couldn't grip it tightly enough. Her eyes burned. She couldn't breathe.

"Stay with me. Drystan, *please!*"

A ghost of a smile graced his lips. "I will," he said. "Always . . . and forever." He brushed a thumb against Verity's cheek, wiping away a tear that had slipped down. "I'm so . . . proud of you, Vee."

One hand still cradling his head, Verity leaned forward and pressed her forehead to his. "Wherever you're going," she whispered, "I will find you there, brother. I promise you."

When she pulled back, his eyes were closed.

And they did not open again.

CHAPTER 29

ALL AROUND HER, BODIES lay. Verity hardly noticed them as she cradled Drystan in her arms. It was the second time in her life, she had the wherewithal to consider, however briefly, that she held the body of a man who had given his life to save hers. But she knew this one's name. He had been her best friend and had, in fact, saved her more than once, though none had been so direct as the last. She wondered, again briefly, if he knew how many times he'd saved her over the years.

"Verity," Solace's gentle voice called. It echoed through the silent pass. "I need your help over here."

She needed to go. Solace was alive. She needed to help him. But she couldn't bring herself to lay Drystan onto the hard, frozen ground. Not yet. She held him close, pulling his body against her chest as her tears fell into his hair.

"Verity. I need you."

"A moment more," she choked out. "Please."

"Verity." His tone was urgent. "It can't wait a moment."

She drew a long, deep breath, letting the icy air fill her lungs until they burned. Then she slid herself out from under Drystan's body and set him carefully on the cold earth. The steel of her fingertips was like ice as she wiped the tears from her cheeks, and she welcomed that brief discomfort.

I'm still alive, she reminded herself as she picked up her sword and sheathed it. *And there may be something else I can do. Solace needs my help.* She willed her legs to carry her away from Drystan.

A rocky outcropping hid Solace—and three bodies in the snow—from view. There was a man with a dagger in his throat, a woman lying in a pool of blood, and another man with the haft of a spear plunged through his chest, pinning him to the ground. Solace crouched beside the last. She blinked away the remaining tears.

"Dare." Verity knelt beside Solace. "You're sure he's alive?" All color had drained from his face, and she couldn't see any wisps of breath. Surely at this angle the spear must have pierced his lungs, his heart.

"Barely," Solace said. "I . . ." He flexed his fingers, like there was an itch he needed to scratch but couldn't. "I think I can help him. But I can't . . . I . . ." His frown deepened. His brows knit as though he was trying to recall some memory on the tip of his tongue. "I need you to break the Binding spell."

She swallowed, her throat burning like it was filled with shards of glass.

"Verity, I think I can heal him, but I need—"

She gripped Solace's arm before he could finish speaking—before she could finish thinking—and spoke the memorized words for a Banishment. The emptiness in her heart served as a bottomless void that allowed the power in her core to flow unimpeded by thought or emotion. She hadn't fully recovered from her fight in the Reach, and the ambush had drained her further, but she channeled as much power as she could muster. And yet the emptiness was so complete that she didn't even feel the exhaustion closing in. She almost felt . . . stronger. *More* than she had been. And she let that power flow through her hand and into Solace.

The world fell silent. Her heart pounded in her ears. Neither of them moved.

"Solace?"

He was somewhere else, staring at something she couldn't see.

She tightened her grip on his arm. "Did it—?"

He blinked, and his eyes were rimmed with tears as they regained their focus. He picked up a sword from by his side—Drystan's sword—and sliced clean through the spear's haft a little bit above where it pierced Dare.

Before Verity could wrap her mind around how he'd sliced through solid wood like it was cheese, Solace spoke.

"Help me lift him up," he said, all timid uncertainty gone. He hooked an arm under Dare's shoulder and the other under his knee.

Verity circled to Dare's other side and did the same. Together they cradled his body and lifted him off the spear.

"Hold him upright," Solace instructed.

Verity shifted to kneel in front of Dare, her arms slung under his to hold him up as his head rested against her shoulder.

The shaft of the spear had stopped him from losing too much blood at first, but now that it was removed, her legs were soon warm and wet as the wounds on his chest and back bled freely.

"Solace, he's bleeding out." His skin was so pale it was almost blue in the cold, and she silently willed some of her warmth to flow into him. She didn't dare use magic to warm him. Whatever Solace thought he could do, he'd better do it soon.

Hold on.

"I know," Solace said. He placed one hand on Dare's back and the other on his chest, directly over the wounds. He closed his eyes, and an intense heat radiated from his hands. After a few moments, Solace withdrew. The bleeding had stopped. "Hold him," he said. "Tightly."

Dare's back arched violently, nearly sending him falling out of Verity's arms as he cried out, but she tightened her grip and held him. The spasm ended as abruptly as it started, his weight collapsing against her. His chest rose and fell gently as he breathed.

He groaned softly into her shoulder.

It shouldn't have been possible. It *wasn't* possible. And yet . . . "Dare?" Her voice almost failed.

Solace smiled, though it diminished slightly as he touched Dare's neck with the back of his hand. "We need to get him somewhere warmer," he said. "Soon."

"Dare," she said again, more firmly this time.

His voice was strained. "What?"

"Can you stand?"

A gruff sound came from somewhere near Verity's shoulder. Was he *laughing?* "Sure," he said after a moment. "Why not?"

Together, she and Solace got him to his feet, though he leaned against her heavily. She didn't ask if he was alright. It was clear he wasn't; his breathing sounded wrong, and he groaned in pain if they tried to move too quickly. But he was alive.

"Verity?"

She tried not to think about how weak he sounded as he spoke toward the ground, barely able to hold his head up as she helped him along. "Yes?"

"We need to get you some gloves. Your hands are like fucking icicles."

A laugh escaped her, brief and fleeting, as relief washed through her chest for an instant. Dare was alive. Solace was alive.

But Drystan lay ahead of them, cold and lifeless in the snow.

Verity stopped. "Can you bring him back?" she asked. She couldn't look at Solace. Or Dare.

Solace stepped forward and crouched, setting a hand on Drystan's chest. The slightest flicker of hope rushed into her. He'd brought Dare back from the edge of death. Maybe . . . *Maybe*—

But Solace bowed his head. "No," he said. "He's gone. I'm sorry."

Verity nodded, that momentary hope swallowed by the vast emptiness in her chest. She was grateful Dare chose that time to be silent.

Solace led them up a steep incline on the far end of the valley, promising that there was a cave ahead where they would be able to make camp. Verity didn't ask how he knew.

Whatever miracle Solace had worked on Dare had saved his life, but he was far from fully healed. It took them nearly half an hour to get him out of the valley.

"It's just ahead, I promise," Solace said when they needed to carry Dare the last ten yards.

Verity couldn't see the cave until they were practically on top of it, but there it was, right where Solace had said. Its narrow entrance opened into a wide, circular space with plenty of room for them to make camp.

Inside the cave, they propped Dare up against the wall farthest from the entrance, and Solace draped his cloak over him. Verity didn't know what had happened to Dare's midnight blue coat, and her own cloak . . .

Dare's eyes were shut tight as he tried to steady his breathing. Sweat glistened on his too-pale skin. He hadn't said anything to her since they left the pass. Another minor miracle.

Solace set his hand on Verity's shoulder. "We need to gather up our supplies and check the assassins for anything useful. Do you want to stay here with him while I—"

"No," she said quickly. "No, I'll come with you." She ignored Solace's pointed look. She needed to keep moving. No one was going to find this little cavern, and Dare would be fine for a couple of hours while they collected their gear and scrounged up some firewood. And maybe they'd be able to learn something about who had attacked them.

About who had killed Drystan.

✹

Verity gathered up their packs and the stray pieces of their gear that had been strewn about the valley when their horses had been killed. Solace ventured a short distance out of the pass, back the way they'd come. He returned with an arm full of twigs and pinecones from the evergreen trees that managed to take root in the cold, rocky terrain of the mountains.

"I'm going to start a fire at the cave," he said. "I'll be right back."

While he was gone, Verity collected what she could, though she carefully avoided the section of the pass where four assassins lay in the snow near one fallen Warden. She had to keep moving forward. If she stopped, she wasn't sure she would be able to keep going. And they needed to keep going.

"Verity," Solace said, startling her. She hadn't noticed he'd come back.

She turned to find him holding a sword in its scabbard. Drystan's sword.

"Drystan gave me this when the ambush started," he said quickly, like he needed to rush through the explanation of why he had the blade in his possession. He was staring at the ground. "It took me a bit to find the scabbard. But . . ." He held the sword out for her.

Verity swallowed around the lump in her throat. "Put it with the rest of the gear," she said sharply.

"I thought you might—"

"I'm going to check the archers. Can you finish down here?" Exhaustion was seeping into her bones. And there was something else there too, somewhere deep,

220

but she wouldn't let herself examine that too closely. Not yet. There was still work to do. "Please," she added.

Solace fidgeted, then lowered his arm. "Of course," he said, tucking the sword in close. "Consider it done."

Verity trudged up one side of the slope, focusing on the burning in her muscles. Ahead, an arrow lay against the rocks, its gray fletching almost blending in with the stone. She stooped to pick it up and found it snapped in half. She discarded it and continued on.

Behind an outcropping much higher up the slope than she'd expected, one of the archers lay on the ground, a bow beside her and one of Drystan's arrows lodged in her side, just above her hip.

She was still alive.

Verity stared down at the unconscious woman, a small pool of red coloring the snow around her. She could just leave her there, couldn't she? She'd be dead come nightfall. It would be easy to just walk away. Pretend she hadn't noticed the little clouds of breath. She had tried to kill them, after all. They had killed Drystan. On the valley floor, Solace was examining one of the bodies. She could walk away.

No one would know.

Verity pulled the cloth down away from the woman's face. Soft cheekbones met flushed cheeks and a small, rounded chin. Her nose was narrow and had the smallest upturn at the end. Wisps of golden hair stuck out from under the fitted hood that kept most of it tucked away. And she was young. Gods, she looked young. Had the girl even seen her twentieth year yet?

They had killed Drystan. It would be some measure of justice, wouldn't it? And yet . . .

Verity inhaled deeply. "Solace," she called. "This one is alive."

The woman was slender and a fair bit shorter than Verity. Between her and Solace, they were easily able to carry the assassin back to the cave, which had grown comfortably warm from the fire Solace had lit earlier. Dare was slumped against the far wall, asleep. They laid the woman down not too far from him, careful of the arrow that still protruded from her side.

The campfire burned in the center of the cave, the high ceiling taking the smoke up and away through some invisible cracks. Verity took a length of twine from her bag and bound the woman's wrists together. She paused, then bound her ankles together as well.

"Solace, can you help me with her wound?" Verity asked quietly.

He nodded, inching closer until he was kneeling beside the assassin.

With the precision of someone who had done this very thing more times than she cared to count, Verity extracted the arrowhead from the soft flesh of the woman's side. Blood oozed from the hole left behind, but Solace placed his palm over it without hesitation. When he removed it, the wound was covered over with white, splotchy scarring, like a small burn.

Verity wanted to study it, to figure out what magic Solace had done to heal her. And Dare. But her attention fixated on the arrow in her hand. The head was standard craftsmanship, but the fletching . . . Drystan had taken great care with the fletchings of all his arrows. He made them himself, whenever he had the time. This one was one of his. Verity traced her fingers along the edge of the gray feathers, which flitted softly against the metal of her fingertips.

"Thank you," she said, casting a quick glance toward Solace. "For both of them."

"I'm sorry I couldn't help him too. I wanted to. He—"

"I'll get the rest of the gear," she said, her throat tight. "Stay here in case she wakes up."

Verity made a few more trips back and forth between the cave and the valley floor, collecting the rest of the items they'd been able to salvage or scavenge from the assassins, and then set about making their camp for the night. Or the next several nights, most likely. To what extent Dare's injuries would linger after Solace's healing was still unknown. Maybe once she could talk to him, she could assess his status for herself.

But she wasn't in a hurry to talk to Dare. Something about the thought of speaking to him right now, of hearing his callous, sarcastic voice, made her jaw clench. Thankfully, he was still unconscious when she got back.

She appreciated having something to do with her hands and politely refused Solace's request to help with anything. He seemed to understand and simply nodded and said he would gather some more firewood before it got dark. He left before she could object, not that she planned to.

She nearly had the camp arranged to her satisfaction when the woman groaned. Verity moved to her, steel arms crossed over her chest. The young woman's amber eyes were wide as she took in her current situation, widening still further with each new observation: her bound hands and feet, Dare slumped against the rocks nearby, Verity, Verity's arms.

"Do you know me?" Verity asked. She brought the commanding tone to her voice with ease.

The girl shook her head.

"But you know who I am."

A nod this time. "Y-you're a Warden," the girl said. Her voice was soft, with a slight tremor to it. She gestured with her head toward where Dare still slept. "Is he dead?"

"That's what you're worried about right now? I would think you'd be a bit more concerned for yourself."

The girl swallowed, then wet her lips. "Is he dead?" she asked again.

"No," Verity said. "Though not for your lack of trying."

The girl drew a slow, steadying breath. "Are you going to kill me?"

"No. I think enough people have died today, don't you?"

The assassin nodded.

Verity hadn't expected that. She crouched, studying the young woman for a moment. Her fingers flexed, the soft sound of metal gliding against metal filling the silence.

Then she said, as softly as the whirring of her joints, "Tell me everything."

CHAPTER 30

VERITY ENSURED THE WOULD-BE assassin's bonds were secure before she and
Solace returned to the valley one final time.

They didn't have any tools, so they buried Drystan beneath rocks and stones.
Solace didn't speak as they worked, and Verity was grateful.

Night drifted in silently before they were finished, bringing with it a rising
wind and a deeper chill, but the cave served well to shelter them and their campfire
from the biting cold. The young woman had fallen asleep while they were gone,
her back to the fire. Dare was still unconscious and hadn't moved from where
they'd propped him against the back wall of the cave hours ago. Solace offered
to take the first watch, but Verity insisted on it herself. It was better to have
something to focus on.

Verity paced for a time, watching the area outside the cave from their perch
up the mountain slope. Eventually though, her curiosity finally outweighed her
desire to keep her distance.

Dare still slept, his breathing shallow but steady. The cloak Solace had draped
over him had fallen into his lap. He still wore the blood-soaked shirt, which had
turned brown as it dried, and through the tear in the front of it, a splotchy white
scar was visible on his chest.

How had Solace managed what he had? She'd seen a few devout followers
of Ainam perform healing miracles before, but it never left that sort of scarring.
Verity crouched silently in front of Dare to get a closer look. She moved the torn
fabric of his shirt to the side, peeling it gently from where the dried blood stuck
to his skin. Roughly the size of Solace's palm, the knot of white flesh was centered

where the spear had pierced clean through the middle of Dare's chest. It looked like it had been cauterized.

Dare set his hand on hers, so gentle she barely felt the pressure of it.

"Verity . . ." His normally bright, mischievous eyes were darkened and dulled with pain.

She looked away as her throat tightened. "I didn't mean to wake you. I wanted to check how it was healing." She pulled her hand back, but he held onto it.

He smiled weakly. "Liar."

She wasn't ready to talk to him. *Not now.*

"One of them survived," she said, hoping to keep him from saying much else. She nodded toward where the woman slept. "She's tied up. We know who sent them."

"I already know who sent them," he whispered. He didn't acknowledge the sleeping assassin.

"Well, now we both know."

"I'm sorry."

That was it. There was no joke, no jab, no snide comment. Just a quiet sincerity that twisted her stomach and made her eyes burn.

"Why?" She refused to look at him, though he still held her hand.

The question hung in the air between them, floating like a fog of breath in the cold.

"Because," he said at last. "Because I'm here instead of him."

Verity tore her hand from his grasp. "Don't talk about him," she bit out. Her chest ached, but she pushed it down, ignored it, tried to bury it beneath frozen stones as she had buried him only a few hours ago.

She thought she could hold herself together until they were safe and she had time to mourn him in peace, but it was welling up already—the emptiness, the loss. This was not a conversation she wanted to have, not right now. Maybe not ever. And certainly not with Dare.

"I know you two were very close."

"You don't know anything," she snapped.

It wasn't fair. She didn't want to think about any of it—of the years they'd traveled together, the bond they shared, forged by fire and heartbreak and pain.

She didn't want to remember the weight of his hand on her shoulder, how no matter what they'd been through, what they'd lost, that one gesture always comforted her, grounded her. But there was no hand on her shoulder now, and its absence sent her adrift. They had both lost so much, but losing *him* was never something she was meant to endure.

Verity gritted her teeth. She had no intention of breaking down now.

"I know you buried your best friend today," Dare continued, heedless of how much she didn't want him to speak. "And I know that you and Solace saved my life somehow."

Her chest was so tight she couldn't breathe.

Dare inhaled deeply, then winced, his eyes shutting tight as he hissed the air out between his teeth. He leaned his head back against the wall of the cavern, the firelight dancing across his face. "I know you're now stuck with me for some time longer, and I know I owe you a great debt, my lady Warden."

Dear sacred flames of Pyrannis, stop talking, you bastard. You living, breathing bastard.

"Verity, he—"

"Shut *up!*" She stood, seething with rage. Her whole body shook. If he wouldn't be silent, then she would leave. She could walk in the blessedly quiet dark for a while. "Vire take you," she cursed, an edge in her voice, low and hard.

"Someday," Dare said softly between labored breaths. "But not today."

"Well, it should have been today." The words were barbed and coated with venom. "It should have been you." She stormed out into the cold, leaving him behind with nothing but his own shadow flickering on the wall.

Verity didn't stray far from the cave, but Dare was asleep again when she returned. Or at least he was pretending to be. She didn't care which it was.

The exhaustion she'd been ignoring since the battle was finally taking hold. She woke Solace so he could keep watch over the camp before she curled up on her blanket to sleep.

✹

She had lain on that small cot for so long, she was sure it had become a part of her. A sad replacement, she remembered thinking then, for the parts of her she'd lost. It had been weeks since she had been found in the rubble of the College of Magi and brought to this place, and yet her arms still burned in her dreams and in her waking hours alike. She would flex her fingers and feel the skin crack and blister, but when she would look down, she would see only the empty space they once occupied. Some mornings, she'd awaken to an itch on her face or her shoulder, and she would move to scratch it. She would feel her elbow bend and her hand extend. But nothing would happen, and she'd remember with sudden horror that she had no hand to extend, no fingers to scratch.

It was in those moments of terror or anguish, or simply when she felt like there was nothing left for her in this world, that he always came, crutching his way slowly over to her bedside. He sat for hours and just talked. Often he read to her or told her stories of home and jokes he'd heard in some tavern a lifetime ago. Other times, he talked about his own horrible turn of fate that had brought him to the Wardens. He'd never expected anything and had never asked anything of her. He would sit and talk, and she would listen.

She didn't say a word to him in those first weeks. Never even gave her name, and he never asked for it, though he had given his freely the first day they met. And then one day, when he hobbled to her bedside and pulled up the small stool he always sat on, she spoke. She told him a story of a knight with no name, a broken sword, and an explosion of fire. It was the first time she had spoken it aloud to anyone, and she cried as she told the story. And he leaned in and brushed his thumb across her cheek, wiping away her tears.

She dreamt of those moments that night, after she and Solace buried him in the valley. She dreamt about how, when they were both well enough, they'd ridden together across the continent so she could learn what was needed to replace the arms she'd lost with ones of steel plates and gears. She dreamt about how the first sensation she felt after the Binding ritual was complete was him holding her hand. She had cried then too. And she dreamt about the day she took her Warden's oath and how he'd stood beside her, proud and beaming like an older brother.

Chapter 31

THERE HAD BEEN DARKNESS as Dare slept, but then it had become a Darkness—a suffocating void with the total absence of being. The Darkness was so encompassing that it swallowed him. Panic gripped him as those same Black Gates resolved in front of him. The Gates he'd seen after Caleb's spear ran him through.

And he was back there again, standing in that endless white expanse, reliving—if it could even be called that—the same moments again.

Just as before, the only thing marring the perfect landscape of white was an enormous, looming black iron gate. A coldness spiraled out from Dare's chest, but he could stand, and he could breathe.

"I know why I'm here . . ." a familiar voice said. Drystan stood beside him, staring at the massive wall of wrought iron before them. He glanced sidelong at Dare. "But what are *you* doing here?"

When Dare spoke, his own voice was rough and somewhat muffled, as though his mouth was full of ash. "I wasn't fast enough." He touched the spot on his chest where the spear had been. "What about you?"

"I was protecting Vee."

Incredibly, Dare laughed. "That ought to teach you." When Drystan didn't look amused, Dare put his hands up reflexively. "I just mean she's tough. She can protect herself."

Drystan's eyes lowered and slowly drifted back toward the Gates.

"Can't she?" The question came out much quieter than Dare intended.

The Warden shook his head, one hand absently rubbing at the curve where his shoulder met his neck. "Not from this."

"So . . . it's over?" Dare's hands fell limp at his sides. "We lost?"

"Verity is still alive," Drystan said. "And if Solace is too, then it's not over. Not yet."

Grinding metal cut through the perfectly still air as the Gates drifted open just far enough for a figure to step through. It was a man, or a near approximation of one, smallish in stature, wearing a tailored black suit. He carried a large, leather-bound tome open in one hand and a black, raven's-feather quill in the other. He strode forward with the purposefulness of someone who was very busy and had other much more important things to be doing.

"Darcy Wilhaven and Drystan Serah," the man said, indifference dripping from his voice. He didn't look up, letting out a long, deep sigh as he flipped a page in his book.

Drystan nudged Dare's elbow. *Darcy?* he mouthed.

Before Dare could react beyond his ears going hot, the small man spoke. "Alright, well, since I'm overloaded on souls as it is, let's hurry up and get you two processed." He thumbed another page or two in his ledger, then held the book out toward Dare, offering him the quill. "Sign here."

Instinctively, Dare took the quill, but he paused when he looked down at the book. There it was, in midnight black ink and the finest script he'd ever seen: his name. **Darcy Wilhaven**. He could feel the beating of his heart as he held the quill. One beat. Another. He wasn't ready for that to end.

"Sign," the man said again, exasperation leaking into his voice. "I've got another fifty souls already waiting."

Not yet.

No, not yet.

"Not yet," he said aloud.

The man finally looked up at Dare. "What?"

"What?" Drystan echoed.

Dare took a breath. "I said, not yet. I'm not ready."

"That choice is not yours, Mr. Wilhaven," the man said, pushing the ledger closer to Dare. "*Sign.*"

He set his most sincere smile on his face. "Then I want to make a deal." There were always stories of people making deals with Death in order to be sent back, with a task to complete. Surely, he could talk his way out of this.

Another beat of his heart. Another.

A presence joined them where they stood upon Death's doorstep. Dare saw nothing, but he felt it as surely as the breath in his lungs, and he knew with that same certainty precisely what it was.

A shudder ran through Drystan; the Warden had felt it too. The small man's eyes fluttered closed, and as quickly as the presence appeared, it was gone.

"No," the man with the book said. "There will be no deal."

The breath left Dare's lungs as though he'd been punched. His hope deflated. *No ... I'm not ready.*

Drystan's hand was on his shoulder. "It's alright," he said, his voice calm and steady. With his other hand, he slipped the quill from Dare's fingers. "All stories end." Drystan's grip on his shoulder tightened before he turned back to the man. To the ledger. "I'll sign."

The man flipped a few pages in the book and held it open.

"Wait . . ." Dare said. "Drystan, you can't."

"I've had a good run." Drystan touched quill to parchment. "I've already had my second chance." The ink scrawled across the page as he signed his name. "I only hope it mattered."

Dare could hardly think. "Mattered?"

"I hope I did enough to make my second chance matter."

"But . . ."

But Drystan's flesh turned ashy and gray. Cracks appeared on his hands, his face. Flecks of him drifted off, carried on some unseen, unfelt breeze toward the Black Gates.

"Was it worth it?" Dare blurted out. "Saving her? Was it worth the price, your life for hers?"

He saw the smile flash across Drystan's face, even as it began to dissolve. It was simple and true. Peaceful. His voice was barely an echo, and here, in his dream, Drystan never answered him. But Dare knew what Drystan had said at the Gates, everything he'd fought to say before his voice was nothing but a whisper on the wind. And he knew, now, that he would remember all of it for as long as he lived.

Then there was nothing left of Drystan but ash.

Dare swallowed around the lump in his throat as he regarded the man with the book, who held the quill out to him a second time.

"Sign. It is all that is left."

Dare reached for the quill, a tremor running through his fingers. He balled his hand into a fist.

"Sign, Mr. Wilhaven. *We are inevitable.*"

A burning in Dare's chest penetrated his awareness as it replaced every trace of the endless cold that had taken hold of him in this place. He stared, wide-eyed, at the man with the ledger who, curiously enough, was staring wide-eyed right back.

The man opened his mouth, but whatever he was about to say never made it to Dare's consciousness before he was torn away from Death's Gates and into darkness.

Although that had been the moment he'd suddenly found himself in Verity's arms, confused and wracked with pain unlike anything he'd ever felt before, here he fell into the empty nothingness of dream, falling and falling for forever in an instant.

The fear welled up again, clawing at him, encompassing him as he considered whether this emptiness was what waited for him—what had been waiting for Drystan—on the other side of those Gates.

Dare jerked awake and instantly regretted the involuntary movement. His hand flew to his chest. He was cold and clammy with sweat, and as his fingers brushed the ragged scar, he shivered, sending another wave of pain through him. He couldn't keep himself from crying out.

Whatever the power that had saved him from Death's Gates, it hadn't fixed everything. His skin was patched, sure, but inside, Dare was still a mess. Gods above and below, everything hurt.

But it was morning. And he was alive.

"Dare?"

He froze at the woman's voice that was far too hushed and timid to be Verity. He squinted, his eyes adjusting to the thin rays of sunlight filtering in through the mouth of the cave. There was no sign of Verity or Solace, though their bedrolls and other gear were still laid out from the night before. At least they weren't planning on leaving him behind. Yet.

A small form was curled up near the fire, which had died down to little more than smoldering embers.

"Are you alright?" the woman asked.

The assassin. The survivor that Verity and Solace had brought back to the cave, who they'd let live so they could learn who had attacked them and . . . and who had killed Drystan.

No, no, no . . .

Dare blinked away his grief and confusion at how the voice could be here, but the woman pressed her bound hands into the dirt and pushed herself up to sit on the side of her hip, giving him a view of her face.

"No," he said aloud.

Finn Garrison watched him, worry creasing her brow. "Dare," she said again. "Are you—"

"What the fuck are you doing here?" he snapped, clenching his jaw against the pain that followed. But he already knew the answer. Caleb had been there, and Almestra too. Of course Finn would be on the same job. He should have figured it out earlier—if he'd thought harder about it, he would have—but he hadn't wanted to, and now the realization shot through him like his dagger through Caleb's throat.

"It was an accident," she said quickly.

"You *accidentally* tried to kill me? Fucking hell, Finn, at least give me the courtesy of not treating me like a complete idiot."

"It was a mistake," she amended. "Caleb said—"

"Caleb is dead," he spat. "I killed him."

Finn swallowed, taking a steadying breath. "I didn't know you were going to be here."

Seeing her here made his chest ache. He managed to keep his voice steady as he asked, "What did Caleb tell you about the job?"

Finn held his gaze. "He said there was a bounty on a small group traveling near Aetherann's Reach. He said they'd be tough, but the payout was worth it. We were nearly there, but two nights ago Caleb received word that the group had left the Reach and was traveling through the pass into Bremmaran."

"Two nights ago?" Dare blinked. That was the same night they'd made the plan themselves. "Received word from who?"

Finn shook her head. "I don't know."

"What else did he say about it?"

"Nothing," she said.

"What other information did he have on the targets?"

"He didn't say. I swear."

Dare willed the mask of indifference to slide over his features. He'd already let her see too much. Dammit, he was better than that. But he'd gotten too trusting in Valda—too careless—and so her involvement cut far deeper than Caleb and Almestra's betrayal. Theirs he should have seen coming, but this was *Finn*.

"So he didn't say," Dare said, his voice cold. "And you didn't ask."

Finn didn't look away. "He promised me a promotion when we got back if I did this job with him," she said. "You know how he is . . . *was*. I thought I could finally get out from under him. Finally become a full member of the Brothers without having to get into his bed."

Dare's mouth twitched at the remark, at the casual way she said it. He did know how Caleb was. He'd seen how he treated his subordinates in the guild, especially the women. He'd seen what he asked of them, expected of them, *demanded* of them as if it was his right as their commander. It had sickened Dare every day. Could he really blame her for wanting to get away from that?

His face softened despite his efforts to maintain the false, cold neutrality. "You tried to kill me, Finn."

"I know," she said, and her voice trembled a little but still, she didn't look away. "I'm sorry, Dare." When he didn't say anything, she added, "I did get shot, if that makes you feel any better." She gestured with her head toward the bloody hole in her shirt, bunched near her hip.

"It doesn't." He eyed the blood stain on her shirt. "Alright, maybe a little, but not that much." A smile was beginning to tug on the corner of his mouth, but he fought it back.

"Are we still friends?"

The question caught him off guard. Had they been friends? Dare wasn't sure he ever really had any. At least, not in Valda.

"I always thought we were sort of friends," she added sheepishly. His confusion must have been more evident than he intended. "I saw how you always stepped in when Caleb was . . . well, when he was being *Caleb*. You always sat between us at the Raven and Hart. Or pretended that you were walking home the same way I was after a late night so I wouldn't be alone with him."

"I *was* walking home."

Finn arched an eyebrow at him. "You're not the only one who gathers information for a living, Dare. I know you don't live anywhere near the chapter house."

He sighed, the anger and heartache in his chest receding. She had him figured out. Perhaps he wasn't as subtle as he thought he was. Or perhaps she was more clever than he had given her credit for. But the thought of what Caleb could do had always set him on edge. Even if he hadn't actually done it to Finn, Dare had seen it in Caleb's eyes—he was capable of it. Dare couldn't allow something like that to happen if he had anything to say about it. Not ever.

"I know I never said it before," Finn went on. "And it seems pretty awkward to be saying it right now . . . but thank you. For all the times I caught you doing those things, and for all the ones that you probably managed without me noticing. Thank you. And even if you don't feel the same way about me, even if you never did, I'm your friend, Dare." She pushed her hair out of her eyes with her bound hands. "I hope you can believe me when I say that I never would have come if I knew it was you. And I never would have fired a single arrow if I'd recognized you out there. I swear to you."

Dare sighed again. The frustration and anger were still bubbling beneath the surface, but they were no longer directed at her. She truly hadn't known. "I believe you," he said at last.

Finn finally looked away, her shoulders dipping. "Do you know why Caleb had a contract to kill you?"

"I have some idea," Dare said, wincing. That would be a story for another time. Maybe. Although probably the less Finn knew about Solace and the Valdane Council, the better. "And I suspect this is not going to be the last run-in we have with his employers." He leaned his head against the stone wall. Even the conversation had exhausted him, and he'd only just woken up.

"I'm glad you're not dead," Finn said.

Dare's lips quirked up, though his heart still hurt. "Thanks. I'll ask Verity to untie you when she gets back."

"It's alright," she said. "I'd prefer to earn her trust, if I can. She has even more reason to doubt me than you do."

"Fair enough." He couldn't argue with that.

They were silent for a long time, Dare nodding in and out of sleep, before Finn spoke again. "The one who died," she said carefully. "What was his name?"

Dare's throat tightened. He didn't trust himself enough to look at Finn, so he stared at the dying embers of the fire. "Drystan," he said. The name was scarcely more than a whisper. "Drystan Serah. He was a Warden of the Flame." His eyes burned, and the fire blurred in his vision. "And he was my friend."

CHAPTER 32

VERITY SPENT MOST OF the day poring over everything Dare and Solace had smuggled out of the library in the Reach, searching them for more clues about the weapon and how to sever Solace's connection to it.

Solace busied himself tending to Dare, using whatever powers he possessed to heal his lingering injuries. He hummed while he worked, and more than once Verity caught him humming the song she'd taught him shortly after they'd left Whitehollow.

The assassin, Finn, kept to herself mostly, though she sometimes spoke with Dare when Solace wasn't with him, or when he wasn't asleep. Dare slept a lot, sometimes drifting in and out of consciousness while Solace worked on him.

Late that afternoon, Verity sifted through the loose pages of the illuminated manuscript Solace had taken. Four of the five pages each had a beautiful representation of the elements of the old gods, but the last page was adorned with violet, star-filled eyes. She studied the runic language they were written in. It looked like Ancient Pyrrinese. Maybe? It had been years since her ancient linguistics classes at the College.

The bottom of that fifth page did have some symbols she recognized, however. Four swirling glyphs, one for each of the Four, set within a circle, like the old preacher's pendant that day in Port Merrick. And just like the pendant, there were no symbols for Ainam or Vire. She flipped to the other pages, but each of them only had the glyph of the corresponding god.

"

No matter how many times she looked at those pages, she was getting nowhere. She set them aside and opened one of the books instead, rolling her neck to release the tension, though it didn't help.

"Any luck?" Solace asked, joining Verity at the mouth of the cave where the light was better.

She shook her head. "Not really. What about with you?" She gave an upward nod toward the back of the cave. "How is he?"

"Asleep." Solace wiped his hands on his thighs.

"Do you think he can travel tomorrow?" Verity asked. "We need to keep moving."

Solace tilted his head back and forth as though weighing the possibility. "Probably. Though I don't know how fast he'll be able to move, or for how long," he admitted. "I think he needs one more day to fully recover."

Verity muttered a few words with a quick gesture, even as the fingers of her other hand tightened around the spine of the book. The world around them went eerily silent as she cast a sphere around the two of them that blocked sound from passing through. Nothing in or out. The cave wasn't that big, and she didn't want Finn overhearing their conversation. "Could he make it to Fallwood?" she asked Solace. "We could resupply there like we planned. That could give you the extra time you need."

He considered it, glancing toward where Dare lay somewhere in the shadows. "That could work," he said. His voice softened. "I'm sorry I haven't been able to do more."

"You're doing what you can." It was more than she'd ever thought was possible. And if Solace had been near Drystan instead of on the other side of the pass with Dare . . . Verity tried to focus on the book in her lap.

"The girl's concerned about him," Solace said.

Verity had kept Finn's hands bound for everyone's safety, despite Dare's protests otherwise, though she untied the ropes around her ankles. The young woman hardly seemed like much of a threat without a weapon, but Verity wasn't going to take any chances.

"Dare said they knew each other back in Valda," Verity said.

"If she's concerned for his well-being, I don't think we have to worry about her. It seems like she just got caught up in this."

Verity sighed. "I can't think about that right now, Solace. That's not a risk I can take."

He nodded and picked up another one of the books, though he didn't open it. His fingers traced over the embossed title on the spine. *The War for Balance.*

"How are *you* feeling, Solace?" she asked, a gentle heat flushing her cheeks. With everything that had happened, Verity hadn't thought to check in with him. "After I removed the Binding spell, have there been any other . . . effects?"

Lorekeeper Harrow had warned that removing the spell on Solace could be dangerous, and yet Verity hadn't even thought twice about it when he said he could save Dare's life. She hadn't wanted to lose anyone else that day and so had acted on instinct, but she needed to regain her composure before she made any other lapses in judgment.

Solace nodded slowly, turning the book over in his hands. "I . . . remembered."

She closed the book and set her elbows on her knees, leaning toward him. "What do you remember?"

"Not everything," he said. "Just pieces. But . . . I remember entering a massive room . . . it was filled with skeletons, like some huge battle had happened there. And there was one body in the center of it all. Everything else seemed to spiral out from that spot. And it had . . . it had the head of a spear, about a foot long, inside it." Solace's throat bobbed and he stared at the book in his hands. "Not like he'd been stabbed. I mean it was *inside* him. Inside his ribcage, resting along his spine. I remember thinking that seemed so strange. The spear was plain, ordinary, but it looked new. I remember I reached in, under the corpse's ribs, and I picked it up."

He raised his eyes to look at Verity. The gray within them was more muted today, overpowered by the swirls of color and the glitter of silver. "I think that was it," he said, his voice hushed despite the wall of silence. "*That* was the weapon. I think I was just . . . a man, and then I picked up the weapon without realizing what it was."

Verity had been holding her breath as Solace spoke, and blew it out in one long exhale. "What happened after?"

Solace grimaced as he tried to pull up the memories from wherever they'd been hidden. "I . . . I remember there was pain, but not physical pain. It was as if . . . it felt like my soul was burning. I don't even know if that makes sense. But I felt incredible pain and then . . . then I didn't feel anything."

Verity swallowed, almost afraid to ask the question. "What happened to the spear?"

Solace touched his chest. "I can feel it . . ."

So it *was* inside him now, bound to him body and soul, just as Lorekeeper Harrow suggested. A chill ran down the back of her neck. "Were you there alone?"

"No," he said, but his tone tilted up at the end. "I don't think so." His brows drew together. "No," he repeated, more certain this time. "No, Crosse was there. He cast the Binding spell."

Verity hesitated. Had Solace been there *with* Crosse, or did Crosse arrive there on his own? And if Crosse had the kind of power needed for the Binding spell, was that before or after he was Chosen by Ainam? "Do . . . you remember your name?" she asked gently.

Solace shook his head.

"Do you remember anything else? Anything from before you found the spear?"

"No, but . . . I can feel its power now." He swallowed hard and looked away from her, searching for words. "It's like an immense part of me has been walled off, and all I have left is this tiny little room. With the Binding spell Crosse put on me before, I couldn't reach anything on the other side. But now there's a hole in the wall, and I can reach my hand through to pull some of that power in. But . . . each time I do, more of it spills through the hole, onto my side." His voice wavered as he said, "Verity, I don't know what will happen when there's no room left for *me*."

She reached forward and took both of Solace's hands in hers. "I won't let that happen," she said. She wasn't sure how—gods, she wasn't sure what to do with any of this. "I don't know the spell Crosse used, so I can't fix what I undid, but we'll get this thing out of you before . . ." She couldn't finish that thought. "We'll find the answer to this, I promise. It's in these books somewhere. I know it is. But I think you should try not to use any more of that power. Not unless it's absolutely necessary, understand?"

Solace squeezed her hands and nodded. "I need to use it at least one more time," he said, glancing over his shoulder toward where Dare slept on the other side of the cave, Finn beside him. "I think after that he'll be alright. Then I'll stop."

She pressed her lips together. She didn't like the risk, but what other choice did they have? "Alright," she said. "Now help me figure out what in Vire's hells we need to do."

Verity let the sound barrier dissipate, and they spent the next few hours going through the tomes, talking out passages while they still had enough light to read by.

"With magical objects," Verity muttered, almost to herself, "a mage has to add their own magical energy to it, until there's a balance between their power and the object's, before the mage can destroy it." *You have to add magic to destroy magic,* as Dare had said that day in Port Merrick. "What if divine magic is the same?"

"You're saying that if the weapon was created by the four elemental gods, then their same power could unmake it?" Solace asked.

Verity looked quickly toward where Dare and Finn lay on the other side of the cave. They were both asleep. "Yes, exactly."

"But how? No one has seen any sign of the Four in hundreds of years."

"Here." Verity turned the book so Solace could see the page. "This says there are places that are intrinsically tied to the elemental gods, cities that the legends say were founded by each of them. The Reach is said to be connected to Aetherann. It looks like Embercliff in Pyrrah was tied to Pyrannis, the city of Taernfane in Drahkonia to Taerna, and Neoma in the Southern Islands to Lanara. According to this, those cities are places where the connection between the gods and the mortal realm is strongest, serving as conduits for their power to reach into the world."

Solace scanned the page Verity held out to him. "You think they still are? Even now?"

"I don't know, but if they are, maybe there's something there we can use. Something that might help."

"Dare said that in the Reach, Crosse told him the old gods used their power to create the weapon, and they were weakened because of it." Solace bit the inside of his cheek. "What if they poured too much of their power into it? What if that's why they haven't been heard from since then?"

Verity's brows rose. "You mean, what if they're dead?"

"No," he said quickly. "No, I mean, what if they're asleep?"

An idea was beginning to form in her mind, along with the old, familiar excitement that came from working on a new theory. "If that's true . . . if placing their power into the weapon caused them to fall into a kind of torpor . . . then maybe returning that power to them could wake them up."

Solace nodded, his eyes alight with his own excitement at the idea. "Returning it to them through one of these conduits. Their places of power."

It wasn't much, but it was more than they had before. And this, at least, would give them a direction, if not an actual plan.

"We'd still have to figure out how to get their power—the weapon—out of you," Verity said. "But it's a start."

Solace frowned. "It's worth a try, but we just left the Reach. And I don't think it's safe to go back. Not with Crosse still looking for me."

"No, we can't go back there," Verity agreed. She weighed their options. "We should head to Taernfane."

His mouth quirked to the side as he considered. "Isn't Embercliff closer?"

"It is," Verity conceded, "but who knows where their allegiances lie, and that city is notoriously difficult to get into. If they refuse to let us in, we'd be out of luck and even farther away from the others. Neoma's too dangerous *and* too far away, so that doesn't seem wise." At the questioning look from Solace, she added, "It's a pirate haven now."

Solace tilted his head back, staring up at the cave ceiling. "That doesn't leave us much room for error." He breathed a heavy sigh. "What do you know about Taernfane? How do you like our odds?"

Despite the weight of the task before them, Solace's timidness had dissipated in the wake of the Binding spell. He'd taken charge with healing Dare and finding them a safe place while he recovered. He was eager to put the work in to solve the problem and was asking the right questions.

Was this confidence more of his own personality shining through now that the spell had been removed, or was it more of the weapon's power? She hoped it was the former.

"I've passed through Taernfane a couple of times but never stayed for very long," Verity said. "The king of Drahkonia has a reputation for being honorable. And reasonable. I don't think I've heard so much as an ugly rumor about him, and he's been in power for what, twenty years? If we're going to attempt a miracle without angering a monarch, I think we have a decent chance of reasoning with him."

She pulled out the map and laid it over the books that were splayed on the ground. "From Fallwood, we can follow the mountains south and east to Brookshire and cross the river there into Drahkonia."

Solace studied the map. "Without the horses, it'll take us the better part of a week to get to Brookshire. And it's at least that far again to Taernfane. Not to mention we still have Westhold and Valda looking for me."

Something deep inside Verity thrummed at the idea of having a goal. At having something to do besides wallow and wait for their enemies to find them again. "Then we'd better head out first thing tomorrow."

CHAPTER 33

THAT NIGHT, VERITY COULDN'T sleep. She sat at the mouth of the cavern, just at the edge of the firelight, listening to the sounds of the nocturnal animals going about their business while her companions slept. They had a direction now and it gave her something to focus on, but she was eager to be out of these damned mountains.

The snowy landscape was stunning, lit only by the full moon overhead, but movement pulled her focus back into the cave. Solace crept toward her, his footsteps light.

"There's a storm coming," he whispered, joining her at the cave entrance. "We should leave before dawn."

"What makes you say that? The sky's clear," Verity said, nodding up at the stars.

Solace glanced toward the sky and gave a small shrug, rubbing at one arm. "I don't know. It just feels like something's coming."

Verity wanted to push back, to say that they should wait for daylight, but Solace had done more than one impossible thing since she'd banished the Binding spell. Suddenly, predicting the weather didn't seem so far beyond the realm of possibility.

By midafternoon, the rolling foothills of Bremmaran greeted them. Darkening storm clouds and raging winds chased them out of the mountains as Verity led their prisoner by a rope looped around her bound hands and Solace kept Dare moving.

Dare's flagging steps and Solace's worried expression had Verity searching for shelter for the better part of the last two hours without success. And they still had at least another hour to Fallwood.

"We need shelter now," Solace said, casting a sharp glance back toward the encroaching storm.

"Over there." Finn gave an upward nod toward a darkened building offset from the road, the surrounding fields overgrown and untended. "It looks abandoned."

As they moved closer, Verity surveyed the old farmhouse. Even with the hole in the roof, it would protect them from the weather much more than anything they could cobble together in the open.

The inside was covered in a thick layer of dust and detritus, but it would serve their purposes well enough.

"I've slept in worse," Finn said, one of her shoulders rising. "We should collect some firewood before the storm hits." As Verity handed the end of the rope to Solace, Finn added, "Let me come with you. Four hands are better than two."

With the threatening clouds overhead, Verity acquiesced. Together they gathered enough dry fuel to keep the fire burning through the evening and night, making it back to the crumbling farmhouse as the first rain drops began to fall and the sky opened up. What was almost certainly a blizzard in the mountains was a heavy rain in the foothills. It poured in through the hole in the roof, leaving the air chill and damp.

That evening, Solace worked his strange healing magic one last time on Dare, who fell asleep just after Solace began. Verity knew sleep wouldn't come easily that night, so she set herself by the window to keep watch as the darkness settled outside.

✸

As Verity debated whether she should try to force herself to sleep in the hours left before dawn, a quiet groan near the cracked hearth pulled her attention. The main room of the farmhouse was large enough for each of them to have a small amount of space to themselves, and as Verity inched closer to the source of the noise, she found Dare stirring fitfully in his sleep. His hair was matted to his forehead with sweat, and his face twisted as he battled something frightening in his dreams.

She hesitated, watching him. Verity knew this particular discomfort all too well. She crouched beside him and gently touched his shoulder.

Dare startled awake, his muscles tensing as he was halfway to sitting up, propped on one elbow. When he saw Verity, her hand still on his shoulder, he collapsed back onto his blanket and rubbed at his chest.

"You were having a nightmare," she whispered.

Dare nodded, his hands drifting to his eyes. He pressed down with his palms, as though he could keep the visions at bay if he pushed hard enough. "Did I wake you?" he groaned.

"No, I couldn't sleep."

He slid his hands through his sweat-soaked hair and clasped them behind his head, staring at the ceiling. He drew a shuddering breath. "Thanks," he said.

Verity set her hands on her knees as if to stand, but something stopped her. The two of them had hardly spoken over the last three days, not since he'd apologized to her—apologized for surviving—and she'd snapped at him and said she wished he hadn't. Her stomach twisted at the thought.

Especially because she wasn't entirely sure she hadn't meant it.

And yet . . . How many times had she awoken in a cold sweat? How many times had Drystan talked her through her own nightmares?

So she stayed. "Do you want to talk about it?"

"No," Dare said quietly. "I really don't." His voice trembled a little.

How many times had Drystan stayed by her side when she hadn't felt like talking? "I sometimes have nightmares too," Verity said, flexing her fingers absently. "Drystan . . ." Her throat tightened around his name. "He always helps—helped—me through the worst of them." She took a breath to steady herself. She hadn't expected this to be so hard. Drystan was the only person she'd ever talked to about her nightmares. She looked down at her hands, which had clenched into fists.

She felt Dare's eyes on her and looked up. He was looking at her hands too. He rolled onto his side and propped his head up with his hand. "I'll tell you mine if you tell me yours."

Her lips tightened. She wanted to walk away. But where would she be if Drystan hadn't done this for her? "Usually, I'm back at the College. During the Westholden attack. I was getting ready to graduate." She crossed her legs and sat on the ground beside Dare's blanket. She couldn't look at him. "The soldiers snuck in while everyone was asleep. I found out later they'd sent assassins to take out the headmasters before the soldiers started in on the students. It was a massacre."

"I'd heard rumors," Dare said gently. "How did you survive it?"

Verity stared at her hands. "One of the guards who worked there tried to get me out. He . . . they killed him. They were going to kill me too." An image of laughing soldiers reached her mind. She blinked hard, pushing it away. "I tried to drive them back, but . . . I wanted to hurt them. I wanted to make them pay." She focused on the interlocking plates of her fingers, picturing the tiny gears inside that responded to her intentions to move them, to wiggle her fingers or ball her fists. "I thought I could do anything back then, even in that moment, even though I was so scared that I hadn't thought to do a single thing to stop the soldiers from killing that guard. I tried to create a wall of fire to drive them back. To burn them."

"I didn't think it was possible to create fire from nothing," he said carefully.

"It's exceptionally difficult to do," she said. "It's one thing to generate sufficient heat to ignite something flammable, but to create fire without a source of fuel . . . You have to literally ignite the air."

"What happened?"

Verity gave a helpless shrug. "I ignited the air. I created an explosion so massive it decimated the College." She held up her left hand. With her right, she tapped the steel of her shoulder. "The fire destroyed my entire arm. I was lucky I didn't incinerate myself." Her voice caught in her throat. It was still hard to talk about, even after all this time. She swallowed, turning at last to Dare. She would face this.

Dare didn't speak. She thought at first it was pity in his eyes, but it was something else. Admiration? No, that couldn't be it.

"I was buried under the building I collapsed. I didn't know how long it was, but later the Wardens told me it had been three days. Three days, buried with the corpses of everyone who'd just died there. The soldiers trying to kill me, the guard trying to save me, my friends who had been asleep in their beds—they were all dead. But I was still alive. Trapped in there with them." If she listened for it, she could still hear the crashing of stone and the screams of the soldiers as they burned.

"The Wardens found you?" Dare asked.

She nodded. "They pulled me out." She touched her fingers to her right arm, to the scarred seam just below her elbow where steel plates met flesh. "My forearm was crushed when the building collapsed. They removed it to save my life. I couldn't travel far, so they moved me to one of their camps, just across the border into Weryn."

Verity blinked back the tears that burned her eyes, threatening to fall. "I used to wish that they would have left me there. Just let me die there, buried in the tomb I made for myself. In my dreams I still see it. I see the bloody bodies and the soldiers turning to ash as I burned us all alive." One hand touched her chest. "Sometimes I can still feel him pressing me back into the wall, using his body to shield me, even as they shattered his sword and ran him through." Verity dropped her hands into her lap, staring down at her open palms. "I can still feel his blood on my hands."

"You carry his sword still?" Dare's whispered voice was small, reverent. "The guard's?"

"I picked it up after he fell," she said. "I was still clutching it when the Wardens pulled me out." She took a sharp inhale of breath and blinked again, tearing herself out of the dark memories before she could spiral into them any further. "But I dreamt of that day every night for months after. And then, after a while, it was a couple of times a week. They came less and less over time."

"When did they stop?"

"They haven't," she said honestly. "I still have them sometimes. It's been years, but . . . But it gets easier."

He took a slow, steadying breath. "My turn then, I suppose."

He wasn't ready. Verity recognized the look on his face. He wasn't ready to talk about it. She could guess at what had triggered the nightmares for him, but she wouldn't push him. She had done her part. She had let him know that she had her own experiences that she was still dealing with, and that she would be an ear when he needed one. Just as Drystan had done for her so many years ago.

"You don't have to talk about it if you don't want to." She shifted her weight to stand. "Just know that you can tell me. Whenever you're ready."

Dare's hand on her knee stopped her. "Thank you. And I will. But I owe you something at least." He levered himself carefully so he was sitting up cross-legged, as she was. "Ask me something, any one question you want. I'll answer truthfully."

Verity had to admit, there were a number of things she was curious about, but it was late and . . . and yet she knew she still wouldn't be able to sleep. Perhaps she could let this be a distraction. Just for tonight. After a moment she asked, "Why didn't you ever study magic?"

Dare blew out his breath as though she had punched him in the gut, but a faint smile graced his lips. "Right for the heart, my lady Warden?"

"Perceptives are always natural Channels," she added, undeterred. "It would have been so easy for you. Why didn't you try?"

He dragged his fingers through his hair, smoothing it back away from his face. "My parents were . . . conniving. My father always took an interest in my brother, but my mother—I was *hers*. She groomed me into exactly what she wanted."

"Wait," Verity interjected. "You have a brother?"

"Only one question answered tonight," he said with a wink. "But yes, I have an older brother. He was the perfect son, and I was . . . ." Dare held out his arms as though that should give some indication of the problem. "Anyway, my mother had a gift for magic, which she used to her distinct advantage at every opportunity. When she and my father realized I was a Perceptive . . ." He nearly stumbled over the word. "It was nothing but endless prodding, endless tests to gauge my abilities. They needed to know *exactly* what I was capable of so they could use it. Use me."

Verity swallowed, her stomach tightening into a knot. "How old were you?"

"I was six, I think, when it started. Maybe seven."

She drew her knees up to her chest. "That sounds horrible."

"It was." he said. "It is." He chewed on his lower lip as he found the words. "I've heard it's different for everyone—for each Perceptive, I mean—but for me, magic feels terrible. It always has."

"Captain Gil said that for her, different types of magical energy appear as different colors," Verity said. "Is it like that for you too? Do they feel different?"

Dare nodded, his shoulders slouching. "They do. But none of them are pleasant. Depending on the magic, it can make me feel sick, or shaky, or like I'm being stabbed by thousands of needles."

Verity was almost afraid to ask, but she had to know. "Your parents . . . ?"

His hands clenched where they rested in his lap. "They knew how it made me feel, and they did it to me all the same. I fought them on it every step of the way, though. They told me I was being selfish." He gave a soft, humorless chuckle. "My brother used to tell me that it wouldn't be so bad if I just did what they wanted, but . . . I couldn't. I think in some ways that would've been worse. It would've felt like giving up. So instead, I started to read. And I started to lie. I'd already learned *how* from my mother, but I started using it against her. Vire's fucking demons, I lied my ass off." He ran his fingers through his hair again. "Did you know that, in rare instances, a person who presents as a Perceptive in their youth can lose that ability and all natural ability to channel magic at puberty?"

Verity nodded. She remembered reading that in school. Remembered thinking how horrible that must be, to have a great gift like that and then to lose it. She had never considered that what she thought was a gift might feel more like a curse.

He smiled, but it didn't quite reach his eyes. "Imagine my parents' disappointment when they found that I fell into that small population."

"What did they do?"

"They tested me for another year until they were certain I had no Perceptive or channeling abilities left whatsoever. My mother would even try to surprise me by casting something near me, or even on me when I wasn't expecting it. I got a lot of practice hiding what I was feeling." He shrugged one shoulder, just a little gesture, as though the whole ordeal had been nothing at all.

How many feelings was he hiding now?

"But by the time I was fourteen or so, they finally gave up on their dreams of having an archmage in their pocket. My mother went back to manipulating me to do her bidding the old way, but by then the curtain had been pulled back. I had seen them for what they were. Some things, you can't ever *un*see."

"Did you have anyone else back home? Anyone you could talk to?"

Dare held up a hand, waggling a finger at her with a gentle *tsk*. "I said any *one* question. You've already asked me . . ." He made a show of counting on his fingers. "Seven. Let's save some of the mystery for another day, huh? If I tell you much more, I'll lose that undefinable quality you find so endearing."

Verity snorted a laugh.

He smiled. "Thank you, my lady Warden."

"Get some sleep," Verity said as she stood. "We have a long way to travel tomorrow."

Dare stretched out on his blanket, rolling onto his back. "Where to?"

"Taernfane."

Dare angled his head toward her. "In Drahkonia?"

"Last I checked."

He narrowed his eyes at her, but they glinted with amusement. "Verity, that's at least two hundred miles from here."

"I know, but it's the best option we have."

Dare leaned up onto his elbows again. "Best option for what?" He studied her for a moment, but it was easy to keep her face neutral in the dark. "What did I miss while I was busy not dying?"

"I'll tell you in the morning," she said. "Rest. You're still recovering."

His mouth twisted as though he were considering an argument, but in the end he only nodded. "Good night, Verity."

"Good night."

Verity found an open spot a bit away from the others and laid out her blanket, even though her mind was still too restless for sleep, too full of thoughts and questions. She would never have guessed at what Dare had endured growing up. And Solace . . . what had his life been like before it had been so irrevocably altered? And then there was Finn, who had now been swept up, at least tangentially, in this whole mess. What were they going to do with her?

And Drystan . . . would he be proud of her? Verity imagined him sitting beside her. What would he have said?

Nice work, Vee. You reached out your hand. That's all you can do. You've been there, and you know how hard it is, but you also know there's a path through it. And you can show him where it is, if he needs help finding it.

I don't know how to do this without you, she imagined telling him.

You don't need me, he would have said. *You're stronger than you think you are.* He'd told her that many times in those first months at the Wardens' camp. *You're stronger than you realize.*

She missed him so badly her heart ached whenever she thought about him, which was every moment. She was alive, and he was gone. He was *gone.* It had only been a few days . . . How was she meant to live with this pain for the rest of her life? He had filled the fissure in her soul that had cracked at the College, and she could already feel the edges of that wound peeling back to expose all the damaged pieces underneath. She had managed to mend or work with—or maybe work *despite*—those broken bits for years, but now they were splintering again, shredding the patches she'd managed to stitch over them.

But she had to hold those fractured pieces together until this was over. When this was done and they'd freed Solace and destroyed the weapon, then—only then—would she allow herself to break.

CHAPTER 34

Morning filtered into the old farmhouse through the hole in the roof, tendrils of sunlight catching the floating motes of dust. Verity woke to the sounds of movement and quiet shuffling nearby.

Dare had been the first to wake and was tentatively using the wall to push himself to his feet.

"Are you alright?" Verity asked, starting toward him. He'd barely been able to stand on his own the day before, and that had been before the hours of travel out of the mountains.

He held his hand up to stop her. "It's fine," he said as he slowly straightened to his full height. "I'm surprisingly alright, considering I was impaled a few days ago." He grinned at Verity. "Now, tell me more about why we're headed to Taernfane."

"We're going to Taernfane?" Finn asked from her spot on the floor nearby. Apparently she'd been awake as well.

Verity rolled her eyes at Dare. "Anything else you'd like to announce about our plan?"

Dare scoffed. "Please, she's obviously coming with us."

"No, she's not," Verity countered, crossing her arms.

"Really?" He mirrored her pose, setting her on edge. "What's your plan? Send her back to Valda so they can use her to find us?"

Solace was awake too, she noticed, and listened silently. He knew Verity didn't have a plan yet for what to do with the surviving assassin.

"She tried to kill us a few days ago," Verity reminded them.

"I know," Dare said. "But I trust her."

Heat rose in Verity's chest as she advanced another step toward Dare, satisfaction sparking in her when he flinched. "You *trust* her?" she said. "She was part of a group of assassins that tried to kill us. Tried to kill *you*. I would've thought you'd care about that part, if nothing else."

Dare didn't react, that obnoxious, blank expression falling like a curtain over his features. Knowing how he'd learned it didn't make it annoy her any less. To her right, Finn watched them carefully, biting her tongue so hard Verity wouldn't have been surprised if she spat blood. Solace, too, stayed silent.

Dare leaned against the wall, crossing one leg behind the other like he was bored. "*She* didn't kill anyone, Verity. She took a bad job. That doesn't make her a bad person."

"No, it gives her bad judgment, which is just as dangerous. How many *bad jobs* did you take for the Valdane Council?"

She regretted the words as soon as they met the air. He'd told her about his work for the Council in confidence, and she threw it back in his face. Finn's mouth fell open.

Solace tensed, a hand moving to his chest. "You were working for Valda?"

"I *was*," Dare said, and although he watched Verity with the same lazy, half-lidded gaze, a muscle clenched in his jaw. "Then what path would you suggest?" he asked, his tone icy.

"We'll take her as far as Brookshire." Verity squared her shoulders, calling on the commanding tone she used with the recruits in Whitehollow. This was not up for discussion.

"Brookshire?" Something flashed across Dare's face before he reined it in again, letting her see nothing of what was going on in his mind.

"Yes," she snapped. "It's far enough away that even if she runs back to the Valdane Council or gets a message to them, we'll be too far for them to do anything about it." She studied him, but he simply stared back at her, his expression still frustratingly blank. "Is that a problem?"

Dare huffed a laugh, looking away from Verity at last. "Only that I'm wanted there," he said, kicking at a piece of debris.

"You're wanted in Brookshire?" Solace asked.

"Yes. Well, technically I'm wanted in the whole duchy, but since Brookshire is the capital of the duchy, yes, I'm wanted in Brookshire."

"You're wanted in the entirety of Duchy Wilhaven?" Now it was Verity's turn to scoff. "Of course you are. What'd you do?"

"Does it matter?" Dare asked.

"It might." Wardens had sway with local governments. Depending on the nature of his crimes, she could defer his arrest until after their mission if he was caught. But they wouldn't be there long enough for him to find trouble. Or for trouble to find him.

The corner of Dare's mouth curved upward in one of his infuriating smirks. "You could say I did a bad job."

Verity seethed but didn't respond. Fine, if that was how he wanted to play it, he could deal with it himself. The rage in her gut was beginning to boil again.

Solace spoke up. "Can we go around?"

"No," Verity said without hesitation. She rattled off everything she'd already thought through, directing it all at Dare. "Brookshire controls the main passage from Bremmaran into Drahkonia. The only way *around* Duchy Wilhaven is to get through two mountain ranges into Southreach and through the Red Forest. Assuming we manage to not be massacred by the shifters, we'd then have to cross the Ragebrook, which is a serious endeavor. Even if we managed all of that without trouble, the detour would add at least a week. So, no. We will travel southeast along the edge of the mountains, through Brookshire, and across the Ravensfall River into Drahkonia. And we will be depositing our wayward assassin in Brookshire on our way through. Is. That. Understood?"

Dare smiled, all teeth and no warmth. "Of course, my lady Warden."

"We'll leave in an hour." Before any further arguments could be raised, Verity stuffed her blanket into her pack and headed outside. She sat on the stoop and pulled out one of the books, sifting through the pages again. She needed something to focus her mind, to calm the fire in her chest.

Nearly an hour later, she was rereading a passage for the seventh time and trying to wrap her mind around it when a voice floated over her shoulder from the doorway. "Do you want to tell me what that was about?"

She breathed out a sigh and didn't bother looking up at Dare. "I'm a little busy."

"Reading the same page over and over?"

"Don't you have anything better to do than pester me?"

"Not a thing," he said. His smirk was audible as he crouched on the step beside her and peered over her shoulder. "What're you stuck on?"

"It's in High Aethirian," she said sharply. "So I don't think you're going to be much help."

"Show me," he prompted. "Maybe talking it out will help it make sense."

Verity lifted her face toward the sky, closing her eyes. This was his way of trying to get back at her, wasn't it? "Dare, I'm really not in the mood. Could you *please—*"

"Humor me, Warden."

With another loud, resigned sigh, Verity turned her attention to the book on her lap. "Fine. This passage says that the elemental gods of balance pooled their power to create a weapon which they used to fight against order and chaos."

"Order and chaos being Ainam and Vire here, right?" Dare asked.

"Right. But I don't understand this part. It says *only ichor freely given to the channel of the gods would make it*, but that doesn't make sense. If they already made the weapon, why would someone need to give them ichor to make it again?"

Dare leaned in closer, staring at the sections Verity had pointed out to him. "Hm," he muttered.

She rolled her eyes as he made a point of studying the text. "Happy now?"

"Yes," he said, still staring at the page. "Thank you." He reached over her shoulder and pointed at the first passage she had indicated, his fingers sliding along one of the lines. "This is a poetic construction, so *althora* negates *linarthi* in this case. It says *ichor freely given to the channel of the gods would* un*make the weapon.*"

Poetic construction? They hadn't exactly covered High Aethirian poetry at the College. "Unmake the weapon," she repeated. "That's it! That's what we need. But, *ichor freely given*? What is that? Blood?" Blood could carry power, like when she channeled through others. It made sense.

Dare scanned the next few lines. "I don't know. That's all it says."

"Dammit. It's got to be in here somewhere." She stared down at the text, but her cheeks began to burn as the full weight of what he had just done sank in. "You can read High Aethirian. How in Vire's hells can *you* read High Aethirian?"

"I told you," he whispered in her ear. "You'd be surprised at what I'm good at." He continued reading the book over her shoulder. "My mother thought she was going to have an archmage in the family, remember?"

Verity rolled her shoulder hard to shoo him away. "You must be feeling better," she said, "if you're already back to making a game out of irritating me."

Dare scooted away, but instead of leaving her alone as she'd hoped, he sat beside her. "I am. But you must be feeling worse if you're back to this shit."

Verity slammed the book closed. "What *shit*?"

"All of this." He waved in her direction. "This *I'm in charge, follow my orders, I'm better than everyone* shit."

"Someone needs to be in charge," she snapped. "You think it should be *you*?"

"Fuck no!" He laughed the words out, but there was a bitter edge to it. "But we're a team, Verity."

"You don't do teams, remember? You work alone. You said so the first day we met."

"In case you haven't noticed, we don't have much of a choice," he shot back. "You think I like being caught up in this shit with you?"

The heat across her face spread to her ears and down her neck. Dare hung his head. "Fuck," he muttered. "Vee, I—"

"Do *not* call me that," she barked.

"Verity," he amended. "I didn't mean—"

"You did." She stuffed the book into her pack. "I told you to stay in White-hollow. You didn't listen, and now you nearly got yourself killed. Maybe it's time you head back."

Dare gave another forced laugh. "You're fucking joking. I'm not leaving. I'm in this, Warden, whether you like it or not. Whether *I* like it or not. You're stuck with me."

I know you're now stuck with me for some time longer. He'd said that to her the night she buried Drystan. She hadn't wanted to hear it then either.

Verity stood, staring daggers down at Dare. "To be clear," she said, her voice flat, "we're going to Brookshire. I understand that you're wanted there, and I don't care. Lying to people, tricking people into believing you're something you're not is what you're good at, isn't it? So make them think you're someone else. But if you get yourself caught, don't expect me to save you." She flung her pack over her shoulder and started toward the road. "You're on your own."

CHAPTER 35

THEY TOOK AN HOUR or two to resupply in Fallwood, though no one in town had any horses to spare, leaving them no choice but to travel on foot. Verity led the way along the northern edge of the Mistvale Mountains, keeping their pace as fast as the four of them could manage. Westhold had been in the Reach, with Valda in the pass out of the mountains. Although it would take time for the assassins' failure to reach Valda, and although it was unlikely that either the Council or Corvin Crosse would be able to guess their next destination, Solace was eager to keep moving. He didn't want to take any chances, and Verity agreed with him.

The journey took five days. Five days traveling in the tense, heavy silence of loss. Drystan's absence weighed on Verity, as did Dare's presence. She tried not to think too much about either. She focused instead on their immediate goal: getting to Brookshire.

Finn proved herself useful as they traveled, offering to help whenever they stopped to make camp. Not wanting the extra attention having a prisoner might attract, Verity had untied Finn's hands when they arrived in Fallwood on the first day, and she hadn't bothered tying her up again. Finn was also curious, asking Verity lots of questions about herself and about the Wardens. Verity answered tersely, if at all.

It was late morning when they finally entered Brookshire, which sat nestled in a valley between two mountain ranges, bordered on three sides by rivers. Just to the south of the city, the three rivers came together into a spectacular waterfall that formed the Ragebrook. The roaring of the falls provided a backdrop of sound everywhere in the city.

Brookshire reminded Verity a little of Whitehollow, with its wide streets made for carts transporting goods to market. Given its position on the nearby rivers and the gap between the mountain ranges, Brookshire had quickly become a prominent trade city, connecting the kingdom of Bremmaran with Drahkonia and Southreach. The buildings were a mixture of stone and wood, with a rounded architectural style that was reminiscent of a quaint town rather than a bustling city.

Verity and Solace agreed they would spend the day in the city, restock their gear, and obtain horses for the next leg of their journey to Taernfane. They could take a little time to rest and start out tomorrow morning, leaving Finn behind in the city with no easy way back to Valda.

Dare found them an inn and paid for two rooms for the night. When they went upstairs to stow their gear, Verity took stock of what they had remaining from the trek, composing a mental list of what they'd need. "Solace, why don't you stay here and guard Finn," she said. "Dare, I need your help getting provisions."

"Finn doesn't need guarding," Dare said quickly, tossing the new cloak he'd picked up in Fallwood onto one of the beds. "Take her with you instead."

Verity pinched the bridge of her nose, trying to ease the tension that started in her head every time he spoke. "I'm not in the mood to argue with you. I could use you. You know this city."

"Yes, and this city knows me."

"The faster we get this done," she said, setting her hands on her hips, "the faster you can lie low for the rest of the day."

"Verity, I'm not fucking around—"

"Neither am I," she snapped, her voice rising. "You think I'm suggesting this for the fun of it? Stop being ridiculous. We'll be gone before anyone even realizes you're here."

Dare bit the inside of his cheek as he snatched his discarded cloak.

✸

Brookshire's market square was crowded, but Dare navigated deftly through the shops and stalls, keeping his hood up and stopping only to marvel quietly about one thing or another that had changed since the last time he was here.

In the center of the square an enormous fountain stood. Carved in stone atop it was a man, larger than life, standing over a field of others, as though he was victorious in battle. The figure was stabbing down at the people at his feet with—

"Is that a lightning bolt?" Verity asked.

Dare followed her gaze to the fountain and laughed. "Sure is. That monstrosity depicts Ainam smiting evil-doers while worshipers gather at his feet."

Verity cringed as she skirted around the fountain and stopped at a fruit stall. Dare came up beside her, leaning against one of the poles that held up the stall's awning. "There used to be a bakery," he said with an upward nod down the street to their right, "just down that way. We should see if it's still there." He toed the ground with his boot as a wistful smile floated across his lips. "They had the best apple tarts, especially this time of year."

Verity had to admit, a fresh-baked apple tart sounded delightful, but they weren't here to enjoy themselves. She couldn't lose focus. Not now. "We don't have time for that," she said, paying the man working the stall for a small sack of apples. "We have a job to do."

Dare straightened and pushed away from the pole, his smile fading. "As you wish, my lady Warden." He took only a step before he stopped again. "Vire's demons," he muttered, "just my fucking luck."

Verity turned as two burly city guards approached.

Dare spun to retreat, but more guards appeared, flanking him. Dare side-stepped away from Verity, putting a few strangers between the two of them. He had time only to shoot her a look that seemed to say *I told you* before one of the guards spoke, his voice cutting through the thrum of the crowd.

"You're to come with us, sir. You're wanted."

Dammit! Verity did not have the patience for this. Whatever mess he found himself in now, Dare had better talk himself out of it. This was *his* problem. She wasn't about to get involved. Still, she found herself tracking the guards' movements as they approached him.

Shoppers and passers-by all stopped as a circle opened up, giving the guards and their quarry a wide berth. Verity moved with the crowd, taking a couple of steps back.

Dare set a perfect smile on his face. "Ah, good morning." He pitched his voice to carry across the square as well. "You're looking well. Where are we headed?"

Verity kept to the edge of the circle, waiting for Dare to make a move. However, the guard didn't smile or return the warm greeting. Instead, he grabbed Dare by the arm as one of the other guards approached with a pair of iron shackles connected by a solid bar about a foot long.

Dare didn't try to pull away as they snapped the shackles on his wrists. "Is this really necessary?"

Verity tensed as the guard laughed. "I think you know that it is," he said.

The guard gripped the metal bar in his meaty hand, and Verity's chest tightened. Dare wasn't fighting back. He wasn't trying to run or smooth talk his way out of this. But why? Several of the guards had their hands resting on the hilts of their swords, and all were grinning wickedly as the head guard gave the bar connecting Dare's shackles a sharp, sudden tug forward. Dare stumbled, his hood sliding off. She knew then what he must have already known—they were taking him, one way or another, and they were waiting for the slightest provocation to drag him away by force.

Gods dammit, Dare! Frustration pulsed through her as Verity pushed forward, into the circle where the guards were dragging him away.

"Stop!" she commanded, her head held high. As she moved, she pulled aside the collar of her shirt, revealing the Warden's brand on her chest. Even though this would be a simple fix, the fact that she couldn't manage to keep herself out of it was grating on her nerves.

The guards saluted, surprise coloring their faces, though the leader recovered quickly. "Warden," he said, trying and failing not to sound alarmed.

Dare's lips twisted into a smirk, and Verity had to resist the urge to glare at him. "This man is with me. He is a vital part of an urgent mission." There, that would take care of it. She could deal with the bureaucracy of getting him formally released later. That would be easy enough, considering—

"My apologies, Warden," the guard said. "But he's wanted here."

No public official could refuse a reasonable request made by a Warden, including commandeering assistance from the local populace. That included city guards. They had to release him if she asked. "Whatever his crimes," she insisted, "release him into my custody. I swear on my honor as a Warden of the Flame that I will return him to stand trial after our business is concluded."

"My orders come from Duke Wilhaven himself," the guard said, dragging Dare away down the central market street. "You'll have to petition him directly."

What? If they weren't city guards . . . If they were the duke's personal soldiers, then they weren't considered public officials. Wardens had no jurisdiction over private soldiers. She had no authority.

Oh, no . . .

Dare's smirk faded into a gentle smile, even as they pulled him away. "Keep going, Verity!" he called, the crowd filling in between them. "Finn can help you. You can trust her!" And then he was gone, around the corner and out of sight.

Slowly people resumed their daily activities, the circle closing around Verity. She stared after where Dare and the guards had disappeared. She had no power to get him out. She hadn't realized the kind of trouble he was courting. She had thought he could . . .

Heart pounding, Verity grabbed the sack of provisions they'd been collecting all afternoon and ran back to the inn where they'd left Solace with Finn.

Chapter 36

When the guards searched Dare before throwing him into the cell, he hadn't expected them to be so damn thorough. He'd been certain at least the backup lock picks in the sole of his boot would survive their scrutiny, but he'd been sorely mistaken.

A few torches lined the walls—hardly enough to illuminate the hallway—and an unpleasant, musty odor permeated the entire area. In each of the cells, a narrow slit in the wall near the ceiling revealed the clear afternoon sky and let in a tiny sliver of daylight. Hopefully it wouldn't rain later. A cool dampness hung in the air, and as he sat on the bare stone floor, Dare tried not to remember what it was like in the colder months. He hoped he wouldn't be around long enough to see it.

He closed his eyes. It was important that he maintain his smug, aloof image, even here. *Especially* here. They wouldn't catch him pacing the cell like a caged animal. He wouldn't give them the satisfaction. So he might as well get some rest while he was at it.

Or try to.

His thoughts kept wending back to Verity and Finn and Solace. Their trip out of the mountains had been long and tense. Verity had barely spoken to him except when she'd felt the need to order him to do something, like get firewood or keep watch.

And there'd been no evening stories or jokes by the campfire. Drystan had always started those.

You're on your own. That was how his last real conversation with Verity ended. *If you get yourself caught, don't expect me to come save you.*

And that was precisely what had happened.

He'd been surprised Verity had even spoken up before the duke's personal guard had dragged him away. She'd probably only done it so she could tell Solace she'd tried to help. Then she could convince him to leave Dare behind.

Would Solace even need that much convincing? What was Dare to him anyway? To any of them? He pulled his cloak tightly around himself. At least they'd left him that, though his coat had been lost in the pass back in the Crescent Mountains.

The least of what they'd lost there.

❋

Hours passed before footsteps echoed in the stone corridor outside his cell.

That would be Dorian.

That's how these things always played out. Dorian Wilhaven, the duke's eldest son and heir to the duchy, was always sent to talk to him first. When the sound stopped just beyond the iron bars, Dare waited for Dorian's chiding tone.

It didn't come.

"Darcy."

The voice was soft and kind. Not Dorian's at all, but painfully familiar all the same. Dare jolted to his feet almost as fast as he could open his eyes, his calm demeanor evaporating.

"Gregor." It was almost a whisper, a quiet utterance of disbelief.

The man standing on the other side of the bars gave a sad, tight-lipped smile. Vire help him, Gregor hadn't changed a bit. He was about the same height as Dare, though not as lean, with short, sandy hair, parted on the side in the more traditional fashion of the duchy. His ice-blue eyes glinted in the torchlight behind a pair of wire-framed glasses. On the breast pocket of his dark, well-tailored suit, among the silver embroidered accents, was the stag sigil of House Wilhaven, below which hung the image of a scroll crossed with a quill.

"House secretary?" Dare asked, nodding toward the sigil. He took the moment to still his racing thoughts. "When did they put you in charge? And why am I locked up?"

His childhood friend glanced down at the sigil on his chest. "Five years, this autumn," he said, touching it lightly with his thumb. "After my father passed. The duke said who better to advise him than his late-advisor's son." His smile grew somewhat wistful.

"I'm sorry," Dare said, meaning it. "I didn't know."

"It's alright. How could you have known? You've been gone eleven years."

Of course. How *could* he have known? "Eleven years?" Dare said quietly. "Has it been that long?"

"Yes," Gregor said. "It has. And you're locked up because you and I both know the window in your old room has a trick latch, and His Grace doesn't want you vanishing before he's had a chance to talk to you." After a quiet sigh, he extended an open hand through the bars. "It's good to see you, Darcy."

Dare crossed the distance quickly and clasped Gregor's hand. He wasn't expecting Gregor to pull him into an embrace, one arm snaking through the bars to wrap around Dare's shoulders. Even with the cold iron between them, he allowed himself to relax, just slightly. "It's been a long time," Dare said. "I'm sorry for that too."

"You always said you wouldn't ever come back, but I always thought . . ." Gregor pulled away, shaking his head as he huffed the barest breath of a laugh. "I don't know what I thought." He cleared his throat, tempering his features into something flat and professional, the picture of an employee doing their duty. "But that's not why I'm here."

Dare crossed his arms over his chest. "Why are you here then? I was expecting a lecture from Dorian."

"Darcy, he . . ." Gregor sighed and looked down at the floor, the control of his expression slipping for a moment. "He took ill after last Harvest and . . . Darcy, I'm sorry."

The hard stone wall smacked Dare in the shoulder as he fell into it, the whole world tilting with the weight of Gregor's words. His heart crashed into his stomach. "Dorian is dead?"

"Yes. This past winter."

It had been nearly a year then? Nearly a year and he hadn't known. Dare's knees buckled. He slid down the wall until he was seated on the floor again. "My brother is dead?"

"Yes."

Dare had always thought him invincible. He leaned his head against the stone and looked over to his friend, his dearest friend for as long as he could remember. "Why am I here, Gregor?"

"Your father has missed you all these years and wants the chance to reconcile."

Dare watched Gregor smooth the front of his suit jacket, his fingers fidgeting with the hem. "You were always a terrible liar."

Gregor sighed. He slipped his glasses off and cleaned the lenses with a small cloth from his pocket. "You are now the sole heir."

"Vire's unholy shit, you're joking, right? My father's fucking joking."

"Your father ordered you be brought home. The fact that you turned up in town today was . . . fortuitous. We've been searching for you for months."

Dare raised a brow. "*We*?"

Gregor replaced his glasses before meeting Dare's eyes again. "The duke has made it a priority."

"Was Dorian's body even cold before my father started planning his succession?"

"That's not fair." Gregor clasped his hands behind his back.

"You'll forgive me if I have little desire to be fair at this particular moment."

They both fell silent, neither looking at the other. When Gregor spoke next, his voice was still somber, but there was a note of heartache to it that clawed at Dare's chest.

"I wish it were under different circumstances, but I'm glad you're home, Darcy."

"I'm not home," Dare said, staring at the wall opposite him. It was as much to himself as it was to Gregor. He needed to find a way out so he could help Solace. If Verity hadn't already left without him.

Gregor turned to leave. "All the same."

"Am I a prisoner?" Dare called after him.

Gregor paused in the shadows of the hall and sighed again but didn't look back. "Your father told me, should you ask that question, I am to say, *that depends entirely on you.*"

Dare listened to Gregor's footsteps retreating up the corridor until the only sound left was his own heartbeat. "Eleven years . . ." he said to the empty space, "four months, and seventeen days."

Chapter 37

Verity burst into their rented room at the Ragebrook Inn, dropping the supplies carelessly by the small table, a few of the apples rolling out onto the floor.

Solace, standing by the window, turned with a start, one hand moving to rub at his chest, as Finn jumped to her feet from where she'd been reclining on the bed.

"What happened?" she asked.

Verity closed the door hard and leaned against it.

Solace looked at the closed door. "Where's Dare?"

Verity inhaled deeply. What could she even tell him? "Solace, can I speak with you privately for a moment?"

Solace glanced between the two women as Finn stepped closer.

"Verity, I want to help," she said. "If something happened to Dare, let me help. Please."

Finn can help you, Dare had said as the guard dragged him away.

Solace nodded toward Finn. "I think we can trust her."

You can trust her.

Verity didn't know what to do.

"She's been trying to help ever since . . ." His soft voice faded.

Verity's thoughts supplied the rest. *Ever since the mountains . . . Ever since Drystan died.* It was as though Verity's tether had been broken there and now she was drifting, scarcely sure which way was forward. The only things she knew for certain were that moving backward wasn't an option, and she couldn't do this alone. If Dare and Solace both trusted Finn, perhaps it was time for Verity to put her own reservations aside and trust *them*.

When she finished telling them what had happened in the market, Finn pulled her away from the door. "Come on," Finn said. "We're going to need a drink."

Downstairs, Solace led Verity to an open table while Finn scurried to the bar. "It isn't your fault," Solace said.

"I chose the route. He said he didn't want to travel through Brookshire, and I didn't listen."

"You didn't have a choice, Verity. It was the fastest route by at least a week."

Finn returned with three tankards of some kind of ale. She set one down in front of Verity before taking a seat beside her and sliding a second drink over to Solace.

Verity took a swig of ale, the flavor and slight fizz making her nose scrunch up. She never did care for it. "And now how long will we be delayed while we petition to get him released?"

Finn set a hand on the metal of Verity's forearm. "We'll figure it out," she said. "Do you have any idea why he was arrested?"

A cheerful, if direct, voice rose up from nearby. "Technically, he wasn't arrested."

A woman sat with a bearded man at the next table over. The man was staring at the mug between his hands, not paying any attention to the conversation, but the woman leaned back in her chair, watching Verity with large, dark eyes. Her skin was a deep brown, marked by several small scars, and her tightly curled hair was pulled back from her face with a strip of black fabric. She smiled at Verity, white teeth flashing.

"I'm sorry to eavesdrop," she said. "But we were in the market earlier and couldn't help but notice the two of you."

Verity hid her grimace. They had made quite a scene this morning.

"That wasn't the city guard that took him away," the woman continued. "Those were Duke Wilhaven's men."

Verity shifted in her chair, one finger tapping against the top of the table. "Yes, we know."

"Then you should also know Duke and Duchess Wilhaven are arguably the most powerful people in the entire kingdom of Bremmaran." The woman glanced to her companion, who still stared at his mug. He gave no indication he was even listening. "Except for the king," she added, mostly to herself. "Maybe."

Verity forced a smile and favored the stranger with a wave. "Thanks for the tip," she said sharply. She turned back to Solace and Finn. "We'll submit an appeal to the duke and see if we can have him released into the custody of the Wardens."

The woman slid into the empty chair between Verity and Solace. "The duke isn't going to just let him go," she said, lowering her voice. "You know that, right?"

Verity's jaw tightened. This stranger needed to mind her own business. "Whatever he's done to earn Duke Wilhaven's attention, I'm sure that—"

"Wait." The woman leaned in further. "You don't know?"

That didn't sound promising. Verity swallowed. Her irritation with the eavesdropping stranger waned. Or, at least, drifted to a more familiar target.

Gods above, what did he do?

But Solace was the one who spoke. "Hold on, how do you know Dare?"

The woman's dark brows drew together. "Dare?" After a moment, her eyes widened as something seemed to slide into place in her memory. She shook her head, her curls swaying. "Oh, that stupid son of a bitch."

Verity's patience was wearing thin. "What did he *do*?"

"The only thing he did was leave." The woman dropped her voice. "Your friend *Dare* is Lord Darcy Wilhaven, second son of the Duke and Duchess Wilhaven."

Verity fell back into her chair as though she'd been slapped in the face. A lord? Dare was a *lord*?

Finn gaped. "You're shitting me."

"Believe me"—the woman leaned back in her chair again—"I wish I was."

"How do you know that?" Verity asked, not bothering to hide her suspicion.

"I grew up here," the woman said.

Solace blew out a breath, shoulders drawing in. "He never said anything . . . Finn, did you . . . ?"

"It never came up," Finn said quietly.

Verity shook her head, dropping her hand against the table with a solid *thunk* and trying to ignore the tightening in her throat, the pang in her chest.

She hadn't known. He hadn't told her.

"It doesn't change anything," Verity said. "We still need to get him out."

"I'd like to help," the woman said, sliding her chair closer to Verity. "I know this city, and I still have friends here. I think we can help you, Warden." At Verity's hesitation, the woman stuck out her hand. "I'm Jae Aleissandra." She gave an upward nod to the man at the other table. "That's Lucien Longshadow. You have my word that we'll do what we can."

At the introduction, the man stood and took the seat between Finn and Solace. The corded muscles of his arms strained at the sleeves of his shirt as he leaned his elbows on the table, his dark hair falling to frame his face and trace the line of a scar that curved through his beard down the right side of his jaw. "I swear it as well," he said brusquely.

If these two knew their way around the city the way Jae claimed to and could truly help them free Dare, it would certainly put them in a better position to make it out of the city in one piece. But . . . "Why?" Verity asked, studying the two strangers. "Why help us?"

Jae surveyed the room, her gaze hesitating on Lucien before landing on Verity. "Darcy and I knew each other when we were young. I was his friend once."

Verity's lips quirked to the side. Could they really afford to turn down aid, especially with so much relying on them getting to Taernfane?

"You know I'm a Warden," she said to Jae, bringing forward all the commanding presence she could muster. Lucien shifted in his chair, sitting up a little straighter, gold eyes focusing on her face for the first time. "Then you also know that an oath sworn in the presence of a Warden is binding."

"I do," Jae said. "And I swear to help you."

Lucien nodded, his assent sounding like a grunt deep in his throat. "As do I."

"Me too," Finn added quickly. "I swear it too."

Verity turned to her. She'd almost forgotten the mercenary was sitting on her other side. "What?"

"I swear to help you get Dare out of here and . . ." She glanced at Solace. "Whatever comes after that."

Verity had been careful not to share too many details about their mission in front of her, but Finn had deduced it had something to do with Solace. Dare's voice echoed in her mind. *Finn can help you . . . You can trust her.*

Solace had a small smile on his lips, and he nodded when their eyes met. "We could use the help, Verity."

He wasn't wrong, but Finn was an assassin, and Verity had only just met these two. She knew nothing about them, and they conveniently turned up at just the right moment.

Could she trust them? Did she have a choice? It wasn't like they had any better options, and Solace was right—they could use the help.

And if they swore an oath . . .

"I need to think about this," Verity said, pushing back from the table. "If you're serious about helping us," she said to Jae and Lucien, "meet us here tomorrow morning. I'll have an answer by then." Her lips pressed together as Solace caught her eye.

"Verity, can we—"

"Tomorrow," she said, holding up her hand. "We'll figure it out tomorrow."

Jae and Lucien bid them good night and left for their own lodgings, promising to return in the morning.

Finn downed what was left in her mug in one long swallow. "I did not see that coming," she said, slamming the tankard onto the table. "I need another drink."

When Finn crossed to the bar, Solace leaned across the table. "Verity, I think we should trust them."

Her mind was already swimming with dozens of scenarios; she didn't think she could handle any more possibilities. But there was such an urgency to Solace's voice, the tension in his shoulders . . . "What makes you say that?"

He let out a long sigh. "I don't know how to explain it. I just . . . I feel like they're telling the truth. I think they really do want to help." One hand drifted slowly to his chest as he spoke. He'd been doing that more and more lately.

Since the mountain pass.

Verity drummed her fingers against the table. "I'll keep that in mind," she said quietly.

He looked like he wanted to say more, but Finn returned to the table with another drink, and Solace bit back whatever it was.

"I was just thinking," Finn said, settling back into the chair beside Verity. "I'm never letting Dare get away with not buying the drinks *ever* again."

That night, Verity and Finn settled into their shared room while Solace went to the room he should have been sharing with Dare.

Verity turned the same thoughts over and over in her mind. The idea of trusting them—any of them—was tying her stomach into a knot. But her options were limited. They needed help, and quickly. It was only a matter of time before Valda or Westhold caught up with them again.

She sat on the edge of one of the narrow beds, fingers slowly unbraiding her hair and letting the silken strands fall down her back.

"I understand why you don't want to trust me," Finn said from where she lay on the other bed. "And I don't know why you need to get Solace to Taernfane, but I can tell what you're doing means an awful lot to him. It's very selfless of you."

"It's the right thing to do," Verity said. "And if we can't figure out how to help him, a lot of people are going to die."

"Still," Finn said, propping herself up on her elbow. "I don't know many people who would willingly go through so much trouble for someone else. Regardless of what was at stake."

"You just offered to," Verity said, using her fingers to comb through a few snarls in her hair. "And you don't know anything about it."

"Yeah, but my motives are hardly selfless," she said, picking at a stray thread on her blanket. And yet there was a glint of determination on her youthful features. "I owe you for saving my life in the pass. And I owe Dare for . . . a lot of things. And I want you to trust me. I want to help."

Verity studied her from across the room. "Forgive me, but *wanting to help* without expecting payment still isn't something I'm used to hearing from mercenaries."

Finn's mouth twitched. "Yeah, but it's funny . . ." She rolled onto her back and stared at the ceiling. "Wanting to help is actually why I became a mercenary."

"Really? How so?"

"I grew up in Valda, at the Holy Order of Ainam's Home for Orphaned Children."

"Oh," Verity said. "I'm sorry."

Finn waved a dismissive hand, glancing over out of the corner of her eye. "It's alright—that's not the point. When I was about thirteen, Matron Nora started finding parcels on the back steps early in the mornings. Sometimes it was a few coins, sometimes just a loaf of bread. At first we got them once a month, but then they came as often as once a week. Always before dawn, and there was never a note."

Verity stretched out on the bed as she listened.

"The kids at the orphanage got so excited every time these little parcels arrived. But I wanted to know where they came from. I became obsessed with trying to figure it out." Finn turned to look at her across the room, her eyes sparkling with mischief in the lantern light. "I started trying to stay up all night so I could see where they were coming from. One night, I saw someone in a hooded cloak come to the back door and leave a package! Trying to catch them in the act became a game to me, and I started to make up stories about who they were."

Her lips drew up in an infectious grin, and Verity couldn't help but smile as well, caught up in the tale.

"I imagined that they were an adventurer who would go on grand quests. They'd come back to Valda with a bounty of gold and jewels and want to share their spoils. I imagined that maybe whoever it was had grown up at an orphanage too, and maybe this was their way of repaying Matron Nora's kindness."

A muscle ticked in Finn's jaw and she turned away, focusing on the ceiling again. "Before long, the gifts got larger. I remember one time the matron said there was enough gold to feed all the kids for a whole week. I dreamed of the adventures they must go on, and I wanted to be just like them." Her throat worked as she swallowed. "Lanara's tears, I've never told anyone this before. It sounds silly saying it out loud."

"No," Verity said quickly, pushing herself up. "No, it doesn't sound silly at all." She crossed the small room and sat on the edge of Finn's bed. "What did you do?"

"I did what any obsessed teenager would do," Finn said with an embarrassed chuckle. "I drove the matron crazy with my *training*, as I called it. Anything I could do to pretend that I was a great adventurer like our stranger." She smiled wistfully. "That's what we always called them. Our stranger. *Our stranger came again last night. What gifts did our stranger leave this time?*" Finn shook her head. "Gods, I'd almost forgotten about that," she muttered.

"Anyway, when I left the orphanage, I was determined to be just like our stranger. I wanted to make a difference. You know, be a part of something bigger than myself. So after a couple of false starts, I joined the Crimson Brothers. I thought maybe that was finally my chance." She grimaced, the expression contorting her young face. "I'm clearly still a really bad judge of that stuff."

Verity wasn't sure why she cared about Finn's story, but she wanted to know the ending. Drystan's smile flashed in her mind. "How long did your stranger keep bringing packages?" she asked.

"I left when I turned eighteen, and he'd been coming for five years by then, though last I heard, he was still doing it, another five years later. And meanwhile, I'm . . ." She trailed off, wiping her eyes with the back of her hand, blinking back tears before they could fall. "Sorry, I'm sure you didn't need to hear me going on and on tonight."

Verity's chest tightened. "No, it's fine" she said, and she found she had trouble getting the words out. She set her hand on top of Finn's slender fingers. "Thank you for sharing that with me, Finn."

Finn looked down at where their hands touched. Heat flashed across Verity's face as she pulled away, an apology stalling on her lips.

Finn gave a shy smile. "Fionna," she said.

"What?"

"My name. I hate it," she added quickly, "and no one calls me that, but I guess I just wanted you to know. My real name's Fionna."

"I . . ." Verity's stomach fluttered. "Thank you. That means a lot. Truly." She didn't know what else to say.

"I don't want to keep any secrets," Finn said. She smiled again, her eyes glinting. "Good night, Warden."

Verity stood quickly. "Good night, Finn." She crossed back to her own bed, snuffing the lantern on the tiny nightstand before climbing beneath the blankets. She lay awake for a long while, listening to the sound of Finn's breathing slow into the quiet rhythm of sleep.

Her thoughts drifted to Drystan. Gods, she missed his advice right now. Should she trust Finn and these two strangers she just met? Was it the right thing to do?

She heard Drystan's voice in her head. *Give them a chance.* It was what he always said whenever he thought she was judging someone too quickly. He'd said it about Dare too. *Give him a chance, Vee.*

Verity's last thought before she fell asleep was how Drystan had always been right. Every time.

CHAPTER 38

VERITY DESCENDED THE STAIRS the next morning to find Jae and Lucien, just as they'd promised. After some debate over how much to tell them, Solace finally convinced her that, if the three of them were swearing an oath, they'd better know exactly what they were getting into. And so Verity explained everything—about why they needed to get to Taernfane and who was hunting them.

To Verity's surprise, all three of them still swore to help in whatever way they could. With that out of the way, they all agreed Verity should speak with Duke Wilhaven about Dare. Jae left quickly, already having some ideas of where she could start gathering information in the city, and Finn went with her.

"Solace, I think you'd better stay here and lay low," Verity said after the two women left. "I don't think we can risk you getting found out."

"If what you said is true," Lucien said, "he shouldn't be alone. I'll stay with him."

Solace opened his mouth to argue but stopped. After what looked like a brief internal debate, he nodded, his jaw clenched.

"I know you want to help," Verity said. "But as far as we are from Valda and Westhold—"

"It's not nearly far enough." Solace gave her a tight-lipped smile. "I know. I'll stay put."

The sun had just dipped below the buildings when Verity trudged back to the Ragebrook Inn. She'd spent the morning at the duke's offices in the city center, trying to get a meeting. Unfortunately, His Grace was working from his manor today, but she could be added to His Grace's schedule next month. The afternoon was subsequently spent at the duke's manor on the northern edge of the city, where she was told to funnel all requests through the central offices. Bureaucratic nonsense. She hoped Finn and Jae had better luck.

As she pushed open the heavy door to the inn, the smell of roasting meat and root vegetables wafted around her. Her stomach rumbled. With all her fruitless efforts trying to speak with Duke Wilhaven, Verity had forgotten to eat. She ordered a meal and joined Lucien and Solace at one of the tables in the back where they were currently entrenched in a game of cards.

She took the seat beside Solace, who was humming softly to himself as he looked over his hand of cards. Verity recognized the tune almost immediately as the song Drystan had sung on their journey to the Reach.

"Are they back yet?" she asked.

Lucien laid a card down. "Not yet."

Solace drew a card from the pile in the center of the table and winced before turning his attention to Verity. "Any luck?"

"None." Sighing, she set her elbows on the table. "I just need to *talk* to him."

Solace played a card and nodded to Lucien. "We'll figure it out, Verity," he said. "I only wish I could *do* something."

A memory flashed in her mind, of her and Drystan stuck in an inn room in Port Merrick, and how frustrated she'd been. She'd hated feeling so useless.

"I know," she said, taking a bite of food. "But keeping yourself safe is what I need you to do."

"I know," he said quietly.

Lucien played another card. Solace groaned, tossing his cards onto the table. Verity glimpsed a ghost of a smile beneath Lucien's beard as he swept up the cards and shuffled.

"Thank you for staying," she said to Lucien around another bite.

Lucien shrugged one of his broad shoulders. "It's fine." His voice was a low rumble.

"Still," she continued, "I'm sure you must have been bored."

"He's not really the city type," Jae said, appearing behind Lucien. She nudged him along with the friendly taunt. He glared at her but didn't argue as he dealt another hand of cards between him and Solace. Jae set her own plate of food on the table beside him, smiling sweetly. "But," she added, turning to Verity, her face suddenly serious, "out on the road, or if shit gets nasty, there's no one I'd rather have at my back."

Lucien snorted, but he didn't argue that point either.

Jae waved to get someone's attention at the bar, and Verity craned her neck to see Finn on her way over with her own dinner.

Jae tore a piece of bread and dipped it in the sauce on her plate. "Let me guess. You couldn't get a meeting with the duke."

Verity shook her head. "Nothing."

Finn took the seat on Verity's other side. "I think we figured out why," she said, her lips pressing into a thin line.

"Apparently the duke's eldest son died last year," Jae said around the hunk of bread in her mouth. "He must be planning to make Darcy his heir."

Heir to Duchy Wilhaven? Verity considered it as she chewed and swallowed a bite of meat. Dare had made it clear that he didn't get along well with his parents, but for a second son to have a chance at an inheritance like that . . . at that kind of power . . .

How well did she really know him?

"Would he want that?" Solace asked, voicing Verity's thoughts, his card game with Lucien forgotten. He looked from Jae to Finn. "Would Dare *want* to be a duke?"

If it was something that he wanted, maybe they could find a way to complete the mission without him. Somehow.

Jae shook her head, dark curls swaying. "Hells no. Not a chance. If he's being named heir, I'd wager the duke's fortune it's against his will." She paused a moment before adding, "Unless he's *really* changed . . ."

Finn stabbed at a piece of meat on her plate, her shoulders tense. "There's no way," she said. She shoved a stray lock of golden hair behind her ear, but the wisps just fell right back into her face. "I can't imagine him ever wanting something like that." She pushed the food around her plate without actually taking a bite. "Besides, he wouldn't just walk away from this." She looked at Verity and then down at her dinner. "Not after everything."

Something chafed within Verity. It wasn't right. As irritated as she was with Dare, no one deserved to have their fate determined by someone else, to be forced into something against their will.

"I have a friend who used to work in the duke's manor," Jae said. "Probably still does. I'll reach out and see if we can get you that meeting."

A spark seemed to kindle in Solace's eyes. "We can't leave him here, Verity."

Determination was building in her chest, and as she met Solace's gaze, a fire flared to life within her. "We're not going to."

Verity tried to get a meeting again the next day and received the same response: a month out was all His Grace's schedule would allow, regardless of how urgent she insisted her business was. That evening she returned to the inn even later than she had the first night. She climbed the stairs toward the room she'd been sharing with Finn, though she paused at the door across the hall. Solace would be there.

Before she could knock to check on him, the door swung open. "Are you alright?" Solace asked. His ashy brown hair fell into his face, and he braced one arm against the door. Behind him, Finn looked up from where she'd been hunched over an open book.

"I'm fine," Verity said, mostly truthfully. Her stomach grumbled at having gone the day without food—again—and her legs wanted to carry her to her bed and no further. "What are you two working on?"

"More research."

Finn rose and joined Solace in the doorway, her small frame ducking easily under his arm. "Solace showed me the books he stole—"

"For the last time, I didn't *steal* them," he grumbled, a flush of red coloring his cheeks.

Finn waved him off. "The books from the library that he took without permission."

Solace huffed, resigned.

Verity's lips tugged into a grin; she could see why Dare and Finn were friends. "Find anything new?"

"Not yet," Finn conceded, crossing her arms over her chest. She eyed Verity. "You forgot to eat again today, didn't you?"

Verity's face heated. "I didn't *forget*."

But Solace and Finn exchanged a look. Some wordless decision was reached between them with only an arched brow from Solace and a nod from Finn. "Come on," Finn said, taking Verity's hand and spinning her back toward the stairs.

"Where are we going?" Verity asked, too tired to do anything other than let herself be pulled along. Behind them, Solace closed the door before he followed.

"To get you some dinner," Finn said, shooting Verity a smile over her shoulder. "If you're not going to take care of yourself, we will."

"I'm fine," she protested.

"Verity," Solace chided gently, "I can hear your stomach growling from here."

Downstairs, Finn settled her at a table while Solace crossed to the bar. "He doesn't have to do that," Verity said helplessly.

"He wants to," Finn said. "You're doing so much for him. He wants to be able to help you too."

Her chest tightened, and a prickling sensation teased at the corners of her eyes. "He said that?"

"He didn't have to."

Solace returned balancing two plates of food in one hand and three mugs in the other. He distributed the mugs before setting one plate of bread, meat, and cheese in front of Verity and the other, which contained assorted puff pastries, between him and Finn for them to share.

Solace and Finn talked and laughed while Verity ate. Something lightened in her chest as she watched them, like a crushing pressure was . . . not *lifted* exactly, but perhaps *eased*.

They were looking out for her. They had her back. And that feeling was like a comforting weight around her shoulders.

Chapter 39

Verity awoke the next morning to the sun slanting in through the window, falling across her face. She'd slept much later than she intended, but her body must have needed the rest. She rose and dressed, rebraiding her hair over her shoulder. Finn was gone, though how she left without Verity hearing her in the small room was a mystery. Verity took a few minutes to stretch and loosen her muscles before she headed downstairs.

Jae and Lucien were at a table, finishing up their breakfast. Lucien grunted a greeting as he tore into some bacon.

"Finn said you'd probably be down soon," Jae said around a mouthful of food. "She just left."

As Verity sat, Jae slid a mug of something dark over to her. Immediately, the scent of coffee hit her, clearing out the last cobwebs of sleep. It was delightful.

"Isn't that yours?" Verity asked, though she leaned toward the mug to inhale the scent more deeply. Steam curled from the contents.

"Nope, Finn left it for you."

Verity smiled as she wrapped her fingers around the mug and pulled it closer. "Any luck yesterday with your friend at the duke's manor?" she asked.

"I was able to make contact," Jae said. "We've officially got help on the inside. And they confirmed Duke Wilhaven plans to force Darcy into succeeding him. The duke's keeping him under lock and key."

Verity frowned into her coffee. "Dammit."

The innkeeper arrived at their table a moment later holding an envelope with a wax seal. He set it in front of Verity.

"What's this?" she asked.

"Message got left for *the Warden* this morning. That's you, ain't it?"

At Verity's nod, he returned to his post at the bar.

Verity looked to Jae and Lucien as Jae leaned over, peering at the seal.

"A stag," Jae said, wiping her mouth with the back of her hand. "That's Duke Wilhaven's seal."

Verity tore the envelope open and read the finely scripted letter inside. "It's an invitation," she said, blinking back her surprise. "Duke Wilhaven is inviting me to dinner. Tonight." She cast a quick glance at Jae. "Your friend works fast." Perhaps her friend was someone with the duchess's ear? Like a trusted maid servant or the like. How else would she be invited to dinner at the manor the very day after Jae had reached out?

Jae leaned back in her chair and let out a low whistle. "We've got to get you something to wear."

"I'll just wear this," she said, rereading the letter again, ensuring she grasped all the details. *Tonight. Sundown. Wilhaven Manor. The Duke and Duchess require your presence . . .* This was her chance to petition the duke directly for Dare's release.

A low rumbling sound made its way into her consciousness, and she realized that Lucien was trying—and failing—to contain a chuckle.

"What?"

Jae was covering her mouth to stifle her own laugh, but her eyes twinkled with amusement.

Verity looked down at herself, her functional but stained traveling clothes, her muddy, worn boots, her sword strapped to her hip.

"Duke and Duchess Wilhaven are . . ." Jae considered her next words carefully. "Conceited. And vain. And assholes. If you want to have any chance of appealing to their higher logic, you're first going to have to appeal to their base nature."

"I don't have anything nicer than this," Verity said, gesturing to what she was currently wearing.

"Don't worry." Jae's lips slid into a positively feline grin. "I know just the place."

Jae and Verity had gone back and forth on whether to cover up her arms or to show them off. Verity had never felt ashamed of them, but she recognized that in some situations it was better to be discreet, although, as Dare had once pointed out, subtlety was never a strength of hers. By the end of the afternoon, she and Jae had agreed that her goal should be to command respect, both as a woman and as a Warden.

Verity still wasn't sure about the dress, even as Jae helped her into it that evening and despite her assurances that it was perfect. Jae had called in three favors to get the dress and the jewelry Verity now wore, including the silver teardrop pendant that fell along her plunging neckline. The dress was sleeveless, with a fitted bodice and a skirt that flared from her hips. The flowing deep green fabric glittered and pooled around her as she sat in her room. Beneath the skirt, her leg bounced.

"Hold still," Jae said from behind her, sliding another pin into Verity's hair. After a moment she added, "You're going to blow them away tonight. How do you feel?"

"Strange," Verity admitted. Her fingers brushed against one of the silver earrings on the table beside her. The small emeralds sparkled in the flickering lantern light. "It's been a long time since I . . ." Her hands smoothed her skirt.

"Dressed like a *lady*?" Jae supplied, placing an almost mocking emphasis on the word.

Verity laughed, some of the tension releasing from her back and shoulder. "Did you ever dress like this?" she asked.

Jae pulled more of Verity's hair up, twisting it elegantly before pinning it on her head. "Oh yes. Well, never anything so sophisticated," Jae said. "I was always running around outside, getting scraped knees. My mother got so frustrated every time I ripped a hole in one of my skirts. What about you?"

The corner of Verity's mouth curved slightly. "I used to enjoy wearing fancy dresses when I was young." But that was a long time ago, a different version of herself.

Jae added one more pin to Verity's hair, securing the last strands in place. "There. Let me look at you."

Verity rose and ran her fingers over the shimmering skirts again, unsure what else to do with her hands.

Jae picked up the earrings from the table and slid them through the old holes in Verity's ears. "They're not going to know what hit them," she said, grinning. "Let's go."

Heading downstairs, Lucien nearly choked on his ale while Solace simply stared at her, his mouth hanging open. Only Finn stood with a smile and met her halfway across the room.

Verity eyed the two men over Finn's shoulder. "I'm not used to all this," she whispered, gesturing to herself. "I feel ridiculous." She must have looked it too, judging by Lucien and Solace's reactions. She wanted the comforting weight of her sword on her hip, not a bodice hugging her waist or yards of fabric flowing around her legs.

Finn reached up and adjusted one of the pins in Verity's hair to capture a stray wisp that had fallen out of place. "You look incredible," she said, a little breathless. Heat rushed to Verity's face. Before she could say anything, Finn stepped back, waving a hand toward the door. "You'd better go. You don't want to be late."

✽

Wilhaven Manor stood on the northernmost edge of the city, on a small bluff that gave a lovely view of the whole of Brookshire, as well as the tumultuous falls to the south. The sun cast long shadows across the manor grounds as Verity stood on the front steps. She smoothed out the front of her dress before lifting the bronze knocker on the door and letting it fall.

It was only a few seconds before the heavy door swung open. The man on the other side had sandy blond hair, smoothed and parted to the side, and wire-rimmed glasses. On the left breast of his dark blue suit coat was a large silver pin of a stag's head with a scroll and quill hanging beneath it. Silver embroidery wove along the lapels and down the outside seam of the trousers.

The man stepped back and bowed low, gesturing Verity inside with a sweep of his arm. "Good evening, Warden," he said, straightening. "It's a pleasure to meet you. I am Gregor Thalesen, house secretary to the Duke and Duchess Wilhaven. As you are an honored guest of His Grace, I am at your disposal. Should you require anything at all while you are visiting, please do not hesitate to ask."

Verity smiled and gave a quick dip of a curtsy. "Thank you," she said as he closed the door behind her.

The foyer of the manor extended before her, with a grand staircase sweeping upward on the left side of the hall. A set of large, ornately carved doors stood at the base of the stairs. To the right of the staircase, a long hall reached deep into the heart of the house, with other rooms and smaller hallways branching from it. A round table of dark wood sat in the center of the white and black checkered marble floor, with an elaborate bouquet of flowers arranged in a gradient of white to blue to violet. The scent of apples and cloves swirled through her nose, and she breathed in the wonderful scent of autumn.

The secretary smiled warmly. The gentle features of his face gave him a youthful countenance, but he carried himself with the practiced ease of someone who had been working in this place for a long time. "Please, Warden, if you would follow me, I'll escort you to the dining room."

Verity nodded and fell into step behind him as he led her through the manor. "Forgive my ignorance," she said as they walked, "but what does a house secretary do?"

"I handle all day-to-day affairs of the household," he said, as though he were quite used to answering that question, "including all official correspondence and scheduling for His Grace."

Verity considered what *day-to-day affairs* must look like in a manor this size. And one that ruled over this city and the surrounding duchy—arguably the most powerful in the kingdom of Bremmaran. "That seems like an awfully important position to be relegated to answering the door and escorting dinner guests," she mused.

"Personal guests of His Grace fall under my purview," he said. "And where important guests such as yourself are involved, I prefer to see to their needs personally."

As they reached another set of huge doors, their dark surfaces intricately carved and inlaid with gold, the secretary paused with his hand on the latch. He hesitated, shoulders sagging.

"What is it?" Verity asked. "Please, speak your mind."

He let his hand fall from the door. "You're a companion of Lord Darcy's, yes? A friend of his?"

"Yes," she said, before she had a moment to think. But it must be true, she realized. Why else would she be here? "Yes," she said again, more firmly this time. "I'm his friend."

The secretary smiled a little. Just a faint, delicate curve of his lips. "I'm glad," he said softly.

He reached for the door again, but Verity set her hand against it, stopping him. "Have you worked here long?" she asked. "I mean, did you know him well? Da—Lord Darcy?" The name felt strange in her mouth.

"Yes, I knew him well," he said. "My father was house secretary before me. I grew up in this house."

"Oh," Verity said, taking her hand from the door. "Thank you, Secretary."

"Please, call me Gregor."

He led her into the dining room, which was nearly as expansive as the foyer, with vaulted ceilings and two crystal chandeliers hanging above the massive table, their candles alight and bathing the entire room in a soft, sparkling glow. The room could easily seat twenty or more dinner guests, but Verity noted that only four place settings were clustered together; one at the head of the table, two to the right and one to the left. Four place settings. One for her, the duke, the duchess, and . . .

It was probably too much to hope that the fourth would be for Dare. Maybe an advisor of some kind? Or perhaps Gregor would take the fourth seat? Aside from her and Gregor, the room was empty.

"May I offer you something to drink, Warden?" he asked. "Wine?"

Verity forced a smile. "Yes, thank you," she said. Anything to calm her nerves. Who was she trying to fool here? She should never have let Jae talk her into this ridiculous dress. She was out of her depth. For about the hundredth time in the last week she found herself wishing Drystan were here. He would have charmed the duke into letting Dare go without breaking a sweat. Pyrannis's flames, it was hot in here.

Gregor bowed and crossed to a credenza of carved ivory on the far side of the room. It was laden with several bottles of wine, two decanters of liquor, and glasses of various styles. He brought her a generous glass of red wine and didn't flinch when her fingertips brushed against his hand. In fact, he hadn't reacted to her mechanical arms at all. Verity was impressed. Most people tended to gawk at least a little, especially when they were on full display, as they were tonight.

She took a long sip of wine. It was heavier than she was expecting, and a little sharp, but pleasant all the same. She knew nothing about wine, though, and was dreading the thought of possibly having to make small talk when one of the large doors swung open. A man entered.

Verity focused on how she was standing in her long dress, how she held the wine glass—gently but not as though she was afraid to break it. She needed to make the right first impression with the duke. She needed to convey confidence and authority, but her stomach turned over on itself, and she was certain she only looked uncomfortable and out of place.

The man wore a fine suit in a deep midnight blue, like Gregor's, though even from here she could see that it was lined with intricate gold embroidery where Gregor's suit had simple lines of silver. Beyond the clothing, she noted only that he was too young to be Duke Wilhaven, so she concentrated on presenting an outwardly collected and confident front.

Gregor bowed to the newcomer. "Good evening, Lord Darcy," he said. "I believe you already know Warden Verity Corallan."

Verity nearly dropped her glass as her attention whipped to Dare. Where there was nearly always some stubble on his chin, now his face was clean-shaven, and the sides of his hair were pulled back, leaving the rest of it to fall along his neck.

The last time she'd seen him, he'd been weeks on the road, dirty and unkempt, looking for all the world the part he chose to play—the part she'd believed he truly was—the scoundrel.

And the last time they'd *really* spoken, she'd said some things she regretted. But looking at him here, in this fancy dining room, dressed in finery, he certainly looked the part of a noble's son.

Which version of him is the real one?

She wondered whether she'd even seen the real version of him yet.

Dare had crossed to her by the time she regained her composure. He took her hand in his own, bowed low over it, perfect and graceful as any highborn lord, and brushed a kiss against the top of her knuckles. "Good evening, my lady Warden," he said. Something flashed through his hazel eyes, though his face was calm and poised. "I'm delighted to see you here."

CHAPTER 40

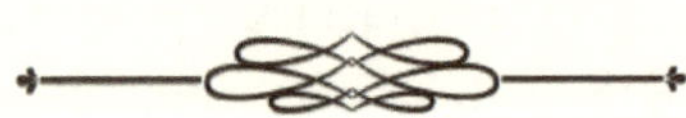

AND HE WAS. VIRE'S fucking hells, he was. Even as Dare fell into character—the tone, the manner, all of it falling into place around him, nestling into the grooves of his body like an old suit—even with this part he needed to play tonight, he wove in that little thread of truth.

Still, he couldn't help the flutter of amusement in his chest as Verity stared at him with the same dumbfounded surprise he'd wiped from his own face only a moment ago. When Dare had entered the dining room, he'd expected to see his glowering parents, not Verity in a floor-length gown drinking a glass of wine with Gregor. He'd only ever seen her in her rugged traveling clothes, but tonight she was stunning. The dress of forest green satin was overlaid with a sheer, glimmering material that reflected the candlelight like she was wading through diamonds. Her dark auburn locks were piled on top of her head, ringlets falling toward, but not touching, her bare shoulders. Never had he been so grateful to see her make a spectacle of herself. She looked incredible.

But that wasn't why his heart nearly stopped when he saw her.

She was *here*. She came.

"I see I'm not the only one who cleans up well," he quipped. The bewilderment on her face vanished, replaced by a flicker of irritation as she pulled her hand away. He flashed her a grin before he spotted the bar on the other side of the room. "I'm almost certainly going to be in need of a drink for this."

He let his attention fall on Gregor for the first time. Dare hated this role, but it was important. Especially tonight. There was too much at stake. "Whiskey, neat," he said. There was no mistaking it for anything other than a command.

Gregor bowed and crossed to the bar. When he stepped away, Verity angled her head. "Why didn't you tell me?" she said coolly. "About all this?"

"What would it have changed?" Dare said. "You were right. We couldn't avoid the city. I knew it could be trouble, but I—I miscalculated. I didn't think they would be *looking* for me. Not after all this time."

"You should have told me."

Maybe, he conceded. *Maybe I should have.*

Gregor returned with a snifter of whiskey three fingers high. Dare smiled, and as he took the glass, he touched Gregor's elbow with his other hand. He would allow himself this small moment. "Thank you," he said quietly.

Gregor returned the smile, restrained but genuine, that one spot beneath his right eye dimpling as it always did when he smiled and meant it.

Two servants entered, flanking either side of the entranceway as they held the doors open. A third servant followed, and his voice carried through the open dining room as he announced, "His Grace, Duke Horace Wilhaven and Her Grace, Duchess Lillian Wilhaven."

All the air rushed out of the room. The momentary lightness in Dare's chest dissipated, replaced by a lead weight as his parents appeared. His mother's gloved arm was draped delicately through his father's, and the candlelight glinted off the golden circlets of office that adorned each of their heads. Aside from the silver in their hair and the more pronounced lines around their stern eyes and mouths, they looked exactly as they had the last time Dare saw them.

All at once, his parents' collective stare fell on him. Dare's stomach tightened into a knot, but he kept his face carefully neutral. His mother, fair skinned and strikingly beautiful even still, left his father's side and floated across the room to him, head held high as any queen.

"Oh, my sweet boy," she sobbed. "Oh, Dars. How I've missed you!"

Dare moved his drink out of the way as she threw her arms around his neck, draping herself over him. He caught her with his hand around her waist, her lavender perfume cloying at his nose. It was exactly the same as it had always been, and in a blink he was a child again, clinging to her skirts, looking for her approval.

"You know, I've been here for three days, Mother," he said quietly, keeping his tone gentle and controlled. "You could have come to visit downstairs." He let the implication hang in the air.

"Sweetheart," his mother said, her voice dripping with sincerity. "You know that was for your own good."

Acid burned in his chest. How many times had he heard that after one of his mother's punishments?

"We needed to make sure you gave us a chance to talk to you without running off again, darling."

Bristling, Dare took a step back. She still clung to his arm as Dare's father approached them. The duke's sharp, angular features swept across the room, taking in Dare and Verity both. He was tall, like Dare's brother had been, with darker skin than Dare's. His deep mahogany hair was streaked through with silver, concentrated at the temples and speckled through his beard.

"Hello, sir," Dare said, his back going rigid. Even after so many years away, how had he not outgrown that instinctive reaction to seeing his father?

The duke only nodded to his son before holding his hand out to Verity. "Warden," he said. There was no warmth in his tone but then, there never was. "A pleasure to meet you."

Verity took his hand with a graceful curtsy. "The pleasure is mine, Your Grace."

Not bad, Warden, Dare thought, impressed.

Dare's father didn't release Verity's hand, instead turning it over to study her palm. "Interesting," he said, as though it were quite the opposite. "Mechanical or magical?"

Dare's hand tensed around his drink, but Verity simply bowed her head graciously. "A combination," she said.

The duke released her hand with a vague grunt of interest and gestured to the table. "Please, sit." He moved with cold efficiency and took the seat at the head of the table without waiting for anyone.

"Incredible!" the duchess gushed as Gregor slid out the chair immediately to the duke's right for her. "And it's so brave of you to have them out in the open as you do."

Dare groaned quietly. "Mother . . ."

She released Dare's arm and sat with a little flourish of her gloved hands. "What? It's a compliment, dear. If it were me, I'd be so self-conscious I'm certain I'd hardly be capable of being seen in public."

Verity curtsied to the duchess, a smile drawn tight across her lips. "Thank you, Your Grace."

Dare stepped to the chair across from his mother and pulled it back. "Warden," he said, smiling at Verity. "Would you care to sit?"

Verity stepped into place, letting Dare push the chair in for her. He then took the last empty seat beside his mother.

The duchess set her hand on Dare's, and something pricked at his skin, sending goosebumps up his arms. On his mother's gloved hand sat a sapphire stone the size of a gold piece. It was held in place by a gold bracelet and a delicate golden chain looped around her middle finger. The center of the gem swirled with its own gentle movement. His mother's periapt thrummed with magical energy against the back of his hand. Dare could scarcely remember a time in his life when she wasn't wearing it. He hated that godsdamned thing.

"I'm so grateful to have you back home, sweetheart," she said.

Dare forced a smile, even as the words sent a ripple of dread through him.

Gregor served a glass of wine to both the duke and the duchess before bowing low and positioning himself beside the smaller door in the back, toward the kitchen. Soon afterwards, additional servants entered with steaming bowls of soup.

"Now," his father said sharply, commanding everyone's attention with that single word. He turned his focus to Verity. "Warden, I understand you claim my son is working for you on some important business, is that right?"

The way he talked down to her made Dare's blood boil.

"He's working with me, yes, Your Grace," she said. "It's quite an urgent matter."

"I see."

He said nothing else, and Verity didn't press the matter. *Good,* Dare thought. *Let him lead.*

They made painful small talk over the next two courses, mostly led by his mother, who scarcely waited for an answer before moving to the next inane topic, until Dare was clawing at the walls to get out.

A Warden of the Flame, that must be so interesting!

Tell me about your family.

What lovely weather the valley has been having, wouldn't you say?

Though his face remained as passive as ever, Dare caught Verity eying him both times he stood to refill his whiskey. Her brows drew together the second time. He raised his glass to her in silent salute before pouring himself another three fingers full. He brought the bottle of red wine with him and refilled Verity's glass to a healthy level.

She didn't stop him, though her narrowed eyes were practically screaming, *That's not what I meant.*

I know, he answered with the curve of his lips.

As the staff brought out the fourth course, the duke leaned his elbows on the table. He clasped his hands together, golden rings sparkling in the candlelight. He stared intently at Verity. "Tell me about this *important business* for which you so urgently need my son."

Verity looked across the table at Dare, who had been in mid-sip of his whiskey. He shifted his head left just a fraction of an inch, the most he could do. He couldn't risk either of his parents catching his reaction. He hoped it was enough for Verity.

"I'm afraid I can't say," she said, shifting her gaze casually back to the duke. "But your son and I are under orders from the Wardens of the Flame, and I can assure you it is a matter of utmost urgency. A matter of life or death, Your Grace."

"Whose life or death?" His sharp gaze was pinned to Verity. Dare had been on the receiving end of that stare more times than he could count.

The Warden held up to it admirably. "Possibly everyone's, Your Grace."

His father barked a laugh, loud and harsh. "And that is all you will say on the matter?"

"My apologies, but I can only discuss the specifics when there is a dire need."

"Ah . . ." his father murmured.

Shit. Dare took another gulp of his whiskey.

The duke smiled, a slash of white against his deep bronze skin. "But you see, Warden, there is a dire need. My eldest son, Dorian, died tragically last winter."

"Ainam bless his soul," his mother said quietly, her hand squeezing Dare's knee under the table. He tried not to tense under her touch.

"And so now you mean to take my only son and heir away from his home and his duty on some secretive mission to Vire knows where . . ."

"Darling, language."

"Without so much as telling me what you need him *for*? We have a duchy to run, with murderous shifters from the Red Forest darkening our doorstep."

"Rampaging monsters, all of them," the duchess interjected.

His father ignored her. "I'm sorry, Warden, but we've indulged our son's proclivities—his fantasies—for far too long. I cannot even consider granting your petition without more information on the matter at hand."

Dare leaned forward, careful to maintain his perfectly crafted courtier's tone, though he wanted to do nothing but run. "Father, if you would understand what's at stake—"

His father slammed his fist down on the table, rattling the glasses and silverware with the impact. Dare flinched. Although he'd been quite accustomed to his father's temper, the suddenness with which it could erupt still caught him off guard.

"What's at *stake*," the duke bellowed, turning that blazing stare on his son, "is my city, my duchy. You are my heir, and I will not have you running off to play hero when your duty is here, to your family! Not without being able to judge for myself the nature of this *important business* you claim to be on."

Dare forced himself not to look away under the weight of his father's glare.

"How do I know this isn't one of your tricks?" his father went on. "Your lies? I think your Warden had better find herself another scoundrel. Certainly your lot are easy enough to come by."

Seething inside, Dare willed his face to remain calm, flat, emotionless. He refused to let his father see that he could still rattle him after all this time.

"Lord Darcy . . ." It was Verity. That name sounded so strange coming from her. He never wanted to hear her use it ever again, but at the same time he greatly appreciated her keeping his other name away from his parents. It was the first thing he'd ever had that was *his*. It was *his* name, and they couldn't take it from him. He held his father's gaze for another long moment until she said again, "Darcy."

When he finally looked at Verity, she let the unspoken question hang in the air between them.

His jaw tightened. What choice did they have? Maybe, just *maybe*, if his father understood what they were up against, he would let him go, even if it was with the expectation that Dare would come back when the job was done. That would buy him time, at least. Time to figure something else out. Or to run. Again. They had no other choice.

Dare nodded.

Starting with their crossing into Westhold, Verity told the whole story of how they found Solace and rescued him, how they barely escaped the Reach, and how they lost one of their companions in the mountain pass as they traversed into Bremmaran. She omitted Dare's own brush with death, for which he was also grateful. Pointing out the danger to his life wouldn't work in their favor. He didn't interject as she spoke, only giving the occasional encouraging nod when she looked his way.

As Verity neared the end of the tale, Dare caught Gregor watching him from his post by the servants' door. He couldn't read Gregor's face from this distance—and besides, Gregor was almost as skilled at masking his expressions as Dare was himself—but he locked eyes with Dare as Verity finished their story. Dare couldn't look away until his mother set her hand on the inside of his elbow. Even through his jacket, the energy of her jeweled periapt tickled his skin.

"How terribly horrific that must have been for you, Darcy," she said, squeezing the crook of his arm. He had long ago stopped interpreting the gesture as one of love and now recognized it for what it had always been: a manipulation born out of possessiveness, out of the idea that he was her son and so she *owned* him. He was *hers*.

And yet his chest still ached every time.

The duke remained silent for a long time after Verity finished speaking. "I see," he said at last. "This is valuable information, Warden. I appreciate you being so forthcoming. I will consider your petition and make my decision tomorrow."

Something flickered within Dare. Hope? Could he dare to hope his father would be reasonable and let him go?

"Thank you, Your Grace," Verity said. She flashed Dare an encouraging smile across the table.

The final course of the meal passed in a tense silence, until at last his father stood without any warning or pretense. "You have given me much to think about, Warden," he said. He extended his hand to his wife, who took it and rose from her chair as well.

Dare found himself rising with them out of some old habit. He bowed to his father before his mother threw her arms around Dare's neck again and kissed him on the cheek. "I love you, Darcy," she said. "I am so very happy to have you home again."

For lack of anything else to do with his hands, Dare gave his mother a gentle hug as she embraced him, along with a noncommittal "Hmm."

Verity stood and curtsied to them both as Duke and Duchess Wilhaven moved toward the main doors of the dining room.

"One more thing," the duke said, and Dare stiffened reflexively. "You may stay upstairs in the manor tonight, Darcy. Do not make me regret my generosity."

Generosity? Arrogant bastard. Dare gave another formal bow. "Of course, Father. Understood."

The servants worked to clear the table as soon as his parents departed. Dare caught Verity's shoulders relax, and as much as he wanted to do the same, he couldn't yet. The manor always had too many eyes and ears.

He drained the last of the liquor in his glass. He wanted to thank her for coming here, for petitioning his father. For trying to help him. But the servants were puttering around, and he couldn't say everything he wanted.

Gregor appeared beside them, politely gesturing Verity toward the door. "Warden, may I escort you out?"

Dare saw his chance and reached for it. "Secretary," he said, his voice sharp. "Attend to your duties here. I'll show the Warden out."

Maybe he'd be able to find a moment to talk . . .

"Of course, my lord," Gregor said with a quick bow. "Since you will be staying in the manor this evening, my lord, may I suggest taking a nightcap in the library after you've bid the Warden farewell? It is quite peaceful this time of night."

The corner of Dare's mouth threatened to curl into a bemused grin, but he tamped it down. The game. It was all part of the game they had to play. "Thank you, Secretary," he said. "I may do that." He offered Verity his arm. "Would you allow me the honor of escorting you out, my lady Warden?"

"Yes, thank you." Her hand slid into the circle of his arm as she favored Gregor with a smile. Gregor bowed to them both and returned to his work.

Dare led her through the halls of the manor until they neared the front door. Passing the grand staircase, he guided Verity toward the room at the bottom of the stairs. Gregor's message had been received: *The library will be empty if you need a private place to talk.* Without a word, Dare slipped inside, Verity still on his arm.

CHAPTER 41

VERITY'S HAND FELL FROM Dare's arm as they entered a massive chamber with ceilings that stretched at least to the second floor of the manor. Shelves filled with books covered every wall, with a narrow wooden staircase on either side that curved up to the second tier where a catwalk allowed access to even more volumes and tomes.

The library was warmly lit by lanterns on several small tables, as well as golden sconces along the walls. The smell of leather, old parchment, ink, and lantern oil assailed her. She inhaled deeply, welcoming the enchanting mix of scents. It was practically the opposite of the narrow, twisting aisles of the library in the Reach. It reminded her instead of the library at the College of Magi, where she had spent countless hours studying.

Tables, couches, overstuffed armchairs, and secluded benches were scattered throughout the room, providing lots of places to sit. Or hide. Verity could imagine a young Dare playing hide-and-seek with his brother or pretending to fight dragons on the stairs. The image brought a smile to her lips.

Dare closed the door, blowing out a long breath.

"We'll figure this out, one way or the other," Verity said, her voice hushed. "But what did your father mean? About staying in the manor tonight? Where have you—"

"You came," he breathed, shoving his hands into his pockets. It was a casual gesture, but the tension in his body was unmistakable.

Her shoulders sagged. "Of course. I'm not leaving this city without you, Dare." Her heart ached at the hope in his eyes.

"I'm sorry for what they said about you earlier. About your arms." He leaned back against the door. He looked tired.

"Thank you, but I've dealt with worse than that. I'm used to it by now."

"But you shouldn't have to be," he said softly.

She opened her mouth to say something else but shut it again, unable to find the words. What could she even say? She turned toward the open space of the library. "Do you think he'll agree?" she asked after a moment.

Dare pushed away from the door, striding toward one of the windows. "I honestly don't know. I'm amazed he even let you make your case. He's . . . he's the one person I can never get a read on," he admitted.

Dare was different here, and not just in the way he'd acted at dinner. Everything about him seemed worn and dimmed, as though being in this house drained the light from him. He was her friend, and he was hurting.

He had been hurting, she realized, all through their journey out of the mountains, from wounds she had caused.

When Dare looked at her again, he arched a brow. "What is it?"

Verity took a deep, steadying breath. "I wanted to say I'm sorry. For what I said before."

"It's alright. I'm grateful that you're here." He waved a dismissive hand. He smiled, too, but even that was a pale version of his usual bright grin.

Verity shook her head. "Not that, though I'm sorry for that too. I meant . . ." She paused. Why was this so difficult? "I'm sorry for what I said in the cave, the night that . . ." She stumbled before she could even say his name, and she couldn't bring herself to repeat what she'd said to Dare that night.

It should have been you.

"I was angry," she continued, looking anywhere but at him. "And I . . . reacted poorly. I'm sorry."

Dare had gone deathly still. When she worked up the nerve to face him again, his head was bowed, his face drained of color.

She took a hesitant step toward him. Then another. And another until she was standing right in front of him. "Dare?"

He startled as she said his name, though he didn't speak. He looked pale and tired. And scared.

"What's wrong?" she asked.

"You were right," he whispered, his voice hoarse.

Her heart cracked. "No, Dare, I—"

"It should have been me, Verity." His eyes glittered like the shimmer of her dress in the candlelight.

"No, no, it wasn't you. I couldn't save him." She blurted out the thoughts that had been plaguing her since the mountain pass. "I should have been able to do something, but I couldn't. I couldn't save him."

"It was his decision."

Verity stilled. "What do you mean?"

"He knew what he was doing," Dare said. "He *chose* to save you."

But he'd been on the other side of the valley. "You don't know that. You can't." There was no way he could've seen—

"I do."

"You *can't*."

Dare loosed a quiet sigh. "Verity, before you saved my life—before Solace pulled me back—I saw the Black Gates. *Death's* Gates. And I wasn't there alone."

Verity stared at him, unable to move as he paused to draw a breath, his eyes searching hers. Her stomach folded over itself.

"Drystan was there with me."

She shook her head again, the dangling ringlets of her hair bouncing. That was impossible. "Dare, why are you—?"

"I asked him what had happened, why he was there. He said he'd saved you. And then this . . . man . . . appeared with a ledger and told us to sign our names."

The room was stifling. Verity took a step away from him, but he followed as the words tumbled out of him in a torrent.

"He handed me a quill and—shit, Verity, I was so scared. I've never been so scared in all my life. I just kept thinking that I wasn't ready." He set a hand on his chest, as though feeling the rhythm of his heart. His hands were trembling. "I hesitated. I was standing there, holding the quill, and I couldn't do it. I couldn't."

Her chest tightened. She had never seen Dare so rattled, and she wasn't sure she wanted to hear what came next. "Stop," she whispered.

But he pressed on like he hadn't even heard her. Perhaps he hadn't. "I hesitated. And Drystan took the quill from me. He signed his name in that book. Then he . . . he was gone. And that's when Solace pulled me back, and I woke up in your arms and . . ."

"No," she said. Dare stepped toward her, but she retreated. "No, you're wrong." Her mind was racing. "It was a dream."

He crossed the distance she had tried to place between them and gripped her hands. "I see it in my dreams still, my nightmares, but . . ."

This was the subject of his nightmares? She had told him he could talk to her, that he could tell her about them whenever he was ready, but this? "It's impossible," she said sharply. "That wasn't him. Not really."

Dare's hands were still shaking as they held hers. "It was him, Verity. He told me . . . He said that all stories end."

The words landed like a blow. *Drystan's* words. One of the last things he ever said to her. "You're lying," she whispered, blinking back tears that she refused to let fall.

His grip tightened on her fingers. "I asked him if it was worth it. If saving you was worth the price he paid." She made half an effort to pull her hands away, but he held fast. "He smiled. We were standing there before Death's Gates, and he *smiled*. Do you know what he said? *Always*. He said it would always be worth it. He only wished he could tell you how strong you are. Drystan said you're the strongest person he knows—so much stronger than you think you are. And—" Dare's voice cracked, but he swallowed and pushed forward. "And he said he was grateful for the years he knew you—the years he had the honor of being your brother. And he was grateful he could do this for you. With his last breath, he wondered if you knew how many times you had saved him."

Her eyes burned as she tore her hands away. "You're *lying*!" she gritted out, even though she knew in her heart those were Drystan's words. How often had he told her that? *You're stronger than you think you are, Vee.*

"I have never lied to you, Verity. Not once. And I don't plan to start now." Dare stood before her, open and raw in a way she'd never seen. For the first time, she could read every emotion on his face. His weariness and sorrow, pain and heartache were all laid bare.

He held his hands out to his sides. "So you see now, you were right." He closed his eyes, his lashes brushing his cheeks as tears slid down. "It *should* have been me. I should have signed my damned name. Maybe if I had . . . maybe Solace could have saved *him* instead of me." Dare sank to his knees, eyes pleading. "I'm sorry, my lady Warden. Verity. I'm sorry. I'm sorry."

Too many thoughts flew through her mind, welling up inside her chest. She wanted to scream and strike him, to hug him, to cry and tell him it wasn't his fault, and to blame him for the rest of her life.

It was too much, and she couldn't wade through it all. So she ran. She opened the library door, and then the front door of the manor, and she ran.

Chapter 42

NOT A SINGLE THING was going how Dare had anticipated. He hadn't expected Verity to be here, and he hadn't expected his father to listen to anything she had to say. And he certainly hadn't expected Verity to apologize to him.

Dare didn't blame her for what she'd said in the cave. She'd just lost her best friend. Dare tried to think about how he'd feel if he lost Jaelyn or Gregor. They'd been his only friends growing up, and in a way he'd lost them when he left home, but he'd always been able to comfort himself with the hope that they were both still living in the safety of Brookshire. That they would almost certainly outlive him.

But if Dare knew without a doubt that they were gone? If he had to hold Gregor while . . . If he had to watch him . . .

He swallowed, pushing the thought away. Dare couldn't even fathom what that would do to him—who he would have to become just to get through that and come out the other side. And so he didn't blame Verity for what she'd said.

He did, however, blame himself for chasing her off. He'd wanted to tell her about the Black Gates. Ever since that night when she'd shared her story with him, he wanted to tell her. But he couldn't find the words that night, and between that night and this one, he'd found a hundred excuses not to tell her.

But when Verity apologized, the words had tumbled out before he could even think about what he was saying, let alone how it sounded. And she ran.

He didn't blame her for that either.

Dare pulled himself into one of the plush armchairs of the library and slumped against the cushions. Would she come back for him? There was still the possibility they'd swayed his father. He hadn't kicked Verity out directly, which was a minor miracle in its own right. Though Dare knew that if Verity swore an oath to bring him back, he'd have another problem on his hands.

That would be a problem for another day.

Today, Dare needed to figure out a way out of this. Assuming Verity wouldn't be packing for Taernfane tonight. He rubbed his face with his hands.

Fuck.

Dare wasn't sure how long he sat in that chair feeling sorry for himself, but eventually the voice in the back of his mind began goading him.

Your one night of freedom and you're going to spend it sulking like a child?

His father's final words at dinner floated into his memory: *You may stay upstairs in the manor tonight. Don't make me regret my generosity.*

Whether he'd make his father regret it remained to be seen, but Dare would at least take advantage of the time. He pulled a taper candle and a brass holder from one of the desk drawers, lit it from one of the lanterns, and left the library behind.

He wandered the halls of what had once been his home, the small candle lighting his way, though he still knew every hall and door by rote. Not much had changed from his memory, even if everything looked a little smaller, a little less imposing than it had in his youth. It was funny how time could soften some edges but not others.

Dare considered heading to his old room but instead found himself in front of a different door, equally familiar. There was a heavy *click* as he turned the handle. It was unlocked. He stood for a few moments, his hand pressing down on the latch, deciding whether or not he actually wanted to enter.

The door swung open on silent hinges. This room, it seemed, hadn't changed at all. The four-post bed with the wood and wrought iron chest at its foot stood where they always had, as did the bookshelf full of well-worn tomes, and the large, oak writing desk. Above the fireplace hung a sword crossed over a shield with the stag emblem of the Wilhavens.

It was all exactly as he remembered it. Dare breathed in the scent of the room, moss and cedar.

He lit the small lamp on his brother's writing desk. There was still oil in it, and the glow from the wick created a soft light throughout the room. Papers lay about the desk, some in neat stacks with others haphazardly splayed, as though their owner had been in the middle of poring over them and had been interrupted.

Dare traced his fingers along the smooth edge of the desk, finding the one rough patch that his brother always fiddled with when something was weighing on him. A nervous tic.

Then his fingers slid a little further to the right and found the hidden latch. A small compartment popped open. He sat in the cushioned chair to get a better view of the contents. An envelope, crisp and white, lay undisturbed inside, and on the front, written in Dorian's fine handwriting, was a single name. Dare's breath snagged in his throat.

Darcy.

His hand trembled as he plucked the envelope from its hidden spot. The wax seal on the back was unbroken. When had this been written? Had no one known to look here? He supposed not. As far as Dare knew, he'd been the only one besides his brother who knew about the secret compartment. Dare hadn't even been certain that Dorian knew that *he* knew, and yet . . .

Dare broke the wax seal. He wasn't sure he wanted to read it, but something urged him onward. He unfolded the note.

My dear brother, Darcy: In writing this letter, I realize I have no way to get it to you and, as such, have no way of knowing whether you will ever read it. I suppose I have to trust that if the fates deem it appropriate for you to know of its contents, they will find a way to get it to you. Darcy, if you are reading this, I want you to know that I am sorry.

Dare blinked. He wasn't sure he'd ever heard his brother speak those words.

I am sorry that I was not a better older brother to you. It should have been my duty—it <u>was</u> my duty—to protect you, to keep you safe. I told myself for years that I tried, that I did what I could. Yet those thoughts are foolish platitudes. I know in my heart that I did not protect you in the way that I should have. You were a child, *and they took advantage of you. They took advantage of us both, but I had resigned myself to it a long time ago. I should not have let it continue with you.*

Wherever your feet carried you these last years, I hope that you found what you needed. I hope that you found a family who took care of you. And I hope that you can one day forgive me for leaving you to the wolves when I should have been the one to keep you from them. Though in writing this, I don't know whether I am able to forgive myself.

Tears pricked Dare's eyes as he read the last line.

A weak man can swim far, so long as he swims with the current. It takes a strong man to swim against the current and still arrive at his destination. You were always the stronger of us, Darcy.

Your brother, Dorian

Dare sat in his brother's chair, his fingers crumpling the edges of the paper. Dorian *had* tried to help him, as best he knew how. Dare had known it then too. He never blamed his brother for any of it.

He wished he could tell him.

The latch on the door clicked, pulling him out of his thoughts. One hand pocketed the letter while the other closed the hidden drawer. The door swung open, and Gregor stood in the doorway, his formal attire as neat as ever, except that the top button of his shirt was undone. The only indication that he was off duty.

"I thought I might find you in here," he said.

Dare slid the chair away from the desk, angling it toward the door. "You did?"

Gregor closed the door behind him. "No," he said with a sheepish grin. "Truthfully this was the fifth place I checked for you." He chuckled, looking somewhat embarrassed, and pulled a bottle out from behind his back. "I thought maybe you could use a drink."

"Lanara's shining tits, yes!"

Smiling, Gregor handed the bottle to Dare, who studied the label.

"Gregor, this is fifty years old," Dare said.

"I know."

"My father will be furious if he finds out we drank half a bottle of his best liquor."

Gregor's cheek dimpled as he said, "Then we'd better finish it and make sure he never finds the bottle."

Dare laughed, long and deep. It had been a very long time since he had laughed like that. "Is that any way for the house secretary to speak about his lord's libations?"

Popping the cork, he took a swig directly from the bottle. The liquor warmed his throat all the way down, settling like a small hearthstone in his gut. He closed his eyes as the warmth radiated through him. "Now *that* is a good whiskey," he said, offering it back to Gregor.

Gregor took a sip, coughing and sputtering a little as the liquor hit the back of his throat.

Dare laughed again.

"It just went down the wrong way," Gregor wheezed, taking another longer swig before giving Dare a decidedly *there, see?* look to indicate that he was, in fact, capable of holding his liquor.

And just like that, the roles they'd both been playing since Dare's capture in the market three days ago melted away. They were no longer the dutiful house secretary and the duke's wayward son. It was just *Gregor* sitting with him, and he could finally just be himself.

Gregor slid some of the papers to one side and leaned against the edge of the desk, handing the bottle back to Dare. He slipped off his glasses and began cleaning the lenses with a small cloth from his jacket pocket. "I'm glad you're h—here," he said quietly.

Dare couldn't help but wonder whether *here* was truly the word Gregor had been about to say.

Regardless, he wished he could return the sentiment. "I'm glad to see *you*," he opted for instead, elbowing Gregor's thigh where he was propped against the desk. Another swallow of the aged liquor flowed down through his chest, warming him further.

Gregor swiped the bottle back from Dare before he offered it, and Dare shot him a look of quiet indignance. Gregor ignored it as he took another drink. "Do you remember the last time we snuck a bottle of your father's alcohol?"

Dare was already nodding, a smile creeping over his lips, having anticipated the question from the start. "I do. We hid in the crawl space under the back stairs and tried to see who could drink it the fastest." He shook his head at the recollection. "The cook found us because we couldn't stop hiccupping."

"And giggling," amended Gregor.

Dare chortled. "And giggling! Oh gods, what was her name?"

"Bethany," Gregor supplied without hesitation.

"Yes, of course," Dare said, sobering a little. "Bethany. She was always so nice."

Gregor stared at him like he'd grown a second head. "She used to chase us with a wooden spoon and leave welts on our asses that lasted days."

"I know, but she always let me have extra dessert after my midweek lessons."

Now it was Gregor's turn to chuckle. "Lucky! All she ever gave me was a stern look." Dare reached for the bottle, but Gregor took another long swig of it before handing it back.

Dare took another drink, unable to stop himself from smiling against the lip of the bottle. It was like no time at all had passed between them. Could it really be like this? Could they really pick up exactly where they'd left off before he'd run away? His chest tightened at the thought of the time they'd lost.

The warmth had floated from his belly to his chest to his head in the time they'd been talking, the bottle of liquor already showing a noticeable dent in its contents. Dare pushed himself to his feet, staggering one step forward at the sudden rush to his head as it combined with everything he'd already drunk at dinner. Gregor reached out a hand to steady him, setting it against his upper arm. The touch was so familiar, and yet it had been so long since he'd felt it.

Dare's smile turned wistful. "Let's get out of here," he said, taking one more look about the room, the note from Dorian heavy in his pocket. "This place is like a museum."

Gregor extinguished the brass lamp while Dare picked up the taper candle, leaving his brother's room to continue collecting dust.

CHAPTER 43

DARE WAS CERTAIN IT was after midnight, and it seemed no one else was awake at this hour. At least, not along the path Gregor took as he led the way through the darkened halls of Wilhaven Manor. Dare was acutely aware of which hallway Gregor skirted around, the one particular hall where light might still be glimpsed under one particular door, even at this time of night.

Gregor withdrew a small bronze key from his pocket and unlocked the suite of rooms reserved for the house secretary. Dare took another long sip of whiskey from the bottle he carried, swaying a little as he followed Gregor inside.

Inside, Gregor lit several lamps, bringing the space to life. It was different than he remembered it and yet undeniably familiar. The sitting room held a table with four wooden chairs, a sofa of a bright sapphire blue with walnut accents, and a matching armchair with a low table between them, all sitting atop a white rug of some sort of animal fur.

Gregor tossed another log in the fireplace against the far wall. The embers crackled, and more light flooded into the room as the dry wood caught and burned.

"You've made some changes," Dare said shedding his suit jacket. He draped it on a chair at a more intimate table for two with a chess board in mid-game. Black was winning from the look of it.

He plopped onto the sofa, stretching out to lay his head at one end while propping his feet up on the arm on the other side. He groaned as he settled into the plush cushions, reveling in the softness. It had been weeks since he'd slept in a bed. Although the couch was a long way off, it was still the most glorious thing he'd felt in a long time.

Gregor tugged off his own jacket. "If you're going to put your feet on my couch, at least take your shoes off, you heathen."

Dare kicked off the pristine leather shoes without bothering to sit up. "You haven't changed a bit," he muttered.

"Neither have you."

If only that were true.

Gregor nudged him up and slid onto the sofa, letting Dare settle his head on his lap. Dare's eyes were heavy as he held up the bottle for Gregor, who took it and drank another long swallow before draping his arm over the back of the couch. His other hand rested at Dare's head, fingers running lazily through his hair where it splayed across Gregor's leg.

Dare closed his eyes as the tension in his back and shoulders began to melt away. He willed himself to focus on nothing except the feeling of Gregor's leg beneath his head and the slow, idle movements of his fingers through his hair.

The next time Dare opened his eyes, the fire in the hearth was considerably lower. A fogginess clung to his mind, but it was a warm and pleasant combination of sleep and alcohol.

"You fell asleep," Gregor said gently, his hand now resting along the top of Dare's head.

"How long?"

Gregor shrugged one shoulder. "A while," he said. "I wasn't counting."

"You could have moved." Dare blinked blearily. "Or woken me up."

Gregor's hand began gliding through his hair again, lulling Dare's eyes closed despite his best efforts to stay conscious. "I know," he said. "But I didn't want to."

Dare woke to pale golden light streaming in through the windows. He still lay on the sofa, though a soft, wool blanket was draped over him. Gregor was gone, probably to his own bed. Dare had no sense of how early or late it was in the morning. The warm blanket slid away as he sat up, rubbing the sleep from his eyes. He felt reasonably good, like this was the first decent night's sleep he'd had since . . . he actually wasn't quite sure when. Certainly since all this mess started with the Valdane Council. It felt like ages ago.

Dare wandered down the hall that led away from the sitting room, taking a moment to admire the paintings hanging in simple frames along the wall. He passed a closed door on his right and another on his left before reaching the open door of Gregor's bedroom at the end. It was empty and pristine, the bed tidily made. Dare backtracked, his bare feet padding silently across the floor until he reached the first door and pushed it open.

The room beyond was like stepping into a different world. Light poured in through a wall of windows, falling across canvases, paper and paints, brushes and charcoal. A charcoal sketch, half finished, sat pinned over a canvas on the easel in the center of the room. Dare studied the curves and lines of the three faces shaded on the paper, their expressions suspended in laughter.

"Good morning."

Dare spun to find Gregor leaning against the frame of the door, arms crossed.

"I'd apologize for snooping," Dare said, turning back to the drawing, "but this is incredible."

"I guess seeing you again has me feeling a little nostalgic," Gregor mused. He nudged Dare's elbow. "Come on, I brought coffee."

He grudgingly left the drawing behind, following Gregor to the front sitting room. On the low table by the sofa sat a tray laden with a silver coffee pot, two mugs, small silver containers of cream and sugar, and a plate of pastries, including several of Dare's favorites.

Gregor flipped the mugs right-side up and poured the coffee. Dare sat, the rich, earthy scent hitting him as the dark liquid steamed and pooled into the cups. Gregor added some cream and sugar to both, stirred them with a gentle clink of the spoon against the porcelain cups, and sat beside Dare.

"What?" Gregor asked, and Dare realized he was grinning like a fool.

He dragged his fingers through his tousled hair. "Nothing. It's just . . ." What exactly could he say? "Thank you," he settled on after a time. "For the coffee. And letting me sleep."

"You seemed like you needed it."

Dare couldn't argue.

"I know things are complicated," Gregor said as Dare took a sip of the steaming coffee. "And it must feel like the whole world is resting on your shoulders. And based on what the Warden told your father last night, it sounds like it truly might be." He set a hand on Dare's knee. "I'm here if you want to talk about any of it. But if you'd rather spend some time pretending things are normal, I can do that too."

Dare searched those ice-blue eyes he hadn't seen for so many years. They'd known each other since they were children, for as long as either of them could remember. They had been close in age and so Gregor had been allowed to study alongside Dare for all those years. They had been . . . What *had* they been? He'd never felt the need to call it anything before, but whatever it was, it had been that way for forever.

Gregor had always looked out for him, always taken care of him. They had seen each other at their highest and their lowest, and when one of them was feeling lost or broken, the other had been there to find them, to help them put themselves back together.

What did I do in a past life to have deserved someone like you?

"I want to tell you," Dare said at last. "I want to tell you all of it. Every single thing I've done since I left, but I don't even know where to start." He set his mug down on the silver tray. "And I don't know that I can bear the thought of how you might look at me afterwards." He was always honest with Gregor. He didn't know how to not be. He never had to take off the mask he wore around others because it was never on when he was with him. "So can I just be here with you until reality comes knocking on your door to drag me back? Please?"

"Of course," Gregor said. "Whatever you want." He brushed a strand of hair out of Dare's face, letting his hand settle against his cheek. "But no matter what happened, I could never look at you any differently. I'm just glad to see you, for however long that might be. I've missed you, Darcy."

Dare leaned into the caress. "Gods, I've missed you too."

❊

They spent the next hour relaxing in each other's company, laughing at past stories, both old and more recent. Gregor sent a servant to retrieve a fresh set of clothes for Dare, who peeled off his rumpled shirt from the night before.

"Aetherann's breath," Gregor said. "What happened there?" His fingers gently touched the rough, uneven scar in the center of Dare's chest.

"A spear," Dare said. He turned so Gregor could see the matching scar on his back.

"Darcy . . ." Gregor whispered his name as though all the air had suddenly left the room. "How are you still breathing?"

"I don't know," he said honestly. "The man we were talking about last night—Solace—he saved my life."

Confusion creased Gregor's brow. "But the Warden said you only found him about a month ago."

"We did." Dare touched the scarred flesh on his chest. It still didn't quite feel real. His breath shuddered as he said, "This was a little over a week ago, when we were ambushed in the mountains."

"A week? That's . . . Darcy, that's impossible."

"Believe me, I know."

"If I ever meet this man," Gregor said, touching the scar again, "I'll have to thank him." His hand drifted to trace the lines of Dare's chest.

Dare closed his eyes against the memories of pain and the uncertainty of the road ahead. He tried to stand only in the present, here, with Gregor, feeling the touch of his uncalloused fingers against his bare chest. Here, he could pretend, even for just a little while, that nothing had changed.

And yet . . .

Everything had changed. Dare had left and become a different version of himself—one that had done a lot of things he wasn't proud of along the way. He wasn't sure even Gregor would understand. And then the Council and Tanithe had inserted themselves into his life, and everything had gone to shit.

Where did that leave him now?

Gregor's hand gripped his shoulder. "Hey," he said softly. "Where did you go just now?"

Dare inhaled a sharp breath to try to steady himself, but it all came rushing in, the thoughts spinning and spinning, coming faster than he could push them down again. He'd fucked everything up—first with Drystan and then last night with Verity. He squeezed his eyes shut as his heart pounded, his breath quickening.

And now he was *here*, in the one place he'd spent his life trying to escape, and every day Verity spent trying to help him was time lost in trying to save Solace. Assuming she even still wanted to help him after all he had done.

All he *hadn't* done.

"Darcy," Gregor's voice pierced his spiraling thoughts. "You're alright. Come on, you should get some proper sleep." A firm hand on Dare's elbow tugged him forward.

"It's morning," Dare managed, trying to push the thoughts, the dread, away again.

"You have somewhere to be?" Gregor asked, and Dare could hear the gentle smile as he spoke. He guided Dare to the room at the end of the hall and sat him on the edge of the bed. Gregor cupped his cheeks, tilting his face upward. A soft kiss, almost delicate, landed on Dare's brow. "Lie down," Gregor said, motioning toward the bed. "Sleep."

Dare did as he was instructed, lying his head on the pillow that smelled of vanilla and citrus. Gregor pulled the warm blanket over him and smoothed back a few strands of Dare's hair.

"I'll come back in a couple of hours, alright?"

He turned to leave, but Dare grabbed his hand. "Could you stay?" He felt foolish for even asking. Gregor almost certainly had work to do. "Please?"

And yet Gregor didn't hesitate as he removed his shoes and his coat and slid into the bed beside Dare, pulling him in close.

"I'm here," he whispered.

Dare was asleep a moment later.

A sharp knock on the door to Gregor's chambers penetrated Dare's awareness. Gregor was asleep, his chest pressed against Dare's back, his arm draped lazily over Dare's bare stomach.

Dare pretended he didn't hear it. He wanted to stay like this for a long while yet. He didn't even want Gregor to get up to answer the door, let alone have to deal with whatever might be waiting for him on the other side. He slid his hand over Gregor's and pulled it in closer, willing the world outside to disappear.

The knock sounded again, more insistent this time, and Gregor stirred. He moved to get out of bed, but Dare didn't let him go.

Not yet.

"I have to get that," Gregor whispered into Dare's ear.

"No, you don't," he countered.

"I do." He nuzzled a kiss against Dare's neck and slid his hand free. "I still work here."

There was a rustle of fabric as Gregor stood and grabbed his discarded coat. Then came the soft opening and closing of his bedroom door as he stepped into the front room.

Dare pulled the blanket over his head. Maybe the knock had nothing to do with him. Gregor was an important part of the household, after all. It could be any number of things. It wasn't necessarily about him. He could still have time.

"Darcy?" Gregor's voice called softly from the hall.

No, no, no, no.

"I'm sorry, Dars." He was standing beside the bed now. He rubbed Dare's shoulder through the blanket.

Not yet.

"Your father wants to see you."

Fuck.

CHAPTER 44

DARE PULLED THE BLANKET down with a groan. Despite everything, Gregor smiled down at him, although a cloud seemed to settle over his features. He held the fresh shirt they'd left by the sofa.

"What?" Dare asked, pushing himself up. He swung his legs over the edge of the bed.

Gregor sat beside him. "I'm here," he said. "No matter what happens, I'm here." He studied Dare for a moment before his brows drew close. "You know that, right? I'll do anything I can for you."

Dare took the clean shirt and slipped it over his head. "I know," he said. "You're the one person who always has."

He rolled his shoulders as he moved to the door, sliding on his shoes along the way. The duke's head guardsman, who'd caught him in the market his first day in town, was standing at attention just outside Gregor's chambers.

"Sigurd," Dare drawled, the mask of smug indifference sliding easily back into place. "So nice to see you again."

"His Grace is waiting for you in his study," the guardsman said. "The both of you."

Dare gave an overly formal bow and said, "Of course. Lead the way." But his blood was ice in his veins. Gregor fell into step behind them as Dare was led to the one hall, the one door, he dreaded more than anywhere else—even more than the cells beneath the manor.

Sigurd knocked.

"Enter."

The guardsman stepped inside and moved against the wall to let Dare and Gregor pass. "Lord Darcy Wilhaven and House Secretary Gregor Thalesen, Your Grace," Sigurd announced.

Crossing the threshold, Dare's heartbeat quickened. How many times had he been brought to this room against his will? How many times had he fled here scared or crying, and had run back to—

Gregor brushed the back of Dare's hand with his own. Scarcely a breath's length of contact, but it was enough. Enough to say, *I'm here.* Enough to steady Dare's resolve.

Towering bookshelves lined every wall save for the two enormous windows and the wide, low fireplace. A massive, dark-stained wooden desk sat in the middle of the expansive room, books and parchments stacked neatly in various piles across the top, with a quill and inkwell set beside a glass lamp. Behind the desk was a high-backed leather chair. That chair had always been so imposing in Dare's youth, like it would swallow him up if he got too close. Everything in this room had always made him feel so small.

In the chair, scribbling at a parchment with a simple black stylus, sat Dare's father. He didn't look up. Dare's mother stood beside the chair, one arm draped over the back while the other lightly caressed her husband's shoulder.

Two chairs sat on the near side of the desk, positioned for personal—though not *too* personal—conversation. Dare held his head high.

"Have a seat," his father said, still not looking at him. His mother hadn't looked up yet either, her attention fixed on her husband's work.

Gregor sat in the chair to the right, but Dare slid his hands into his pockets. "I'll stand."

The duke set down the quill and lifted the parchment, blowing on the ink to speed its drying. Then he handed it to his wife, who blew on it as well before rolling it up carefully, holding it between her delicate, gloved fingers. A pulse of energy swirled past Dare, the hair on his arms standing on end as the gemstone on the back of her hand flickered. The scroll disappeared in a puff of silver smoke.

At last, his parents turned their focus to him, and Dare's skin went cold and clammy under the weight of their stare. He schooled his face into passive boredom, ensuring neither of them glimpsed his discomfort.

"We have considered your situation," his father began, clasping his large, tanned hands on the desk, gold rings glittering. "We have decided it is no concern of ours and should be no concern of yours. You will remain here and take up your duties as my heir."

The weight of his father's words settled like a knot somewhere in Dare's chest. Just like that, they'd decided his fate. Callously, in an instant. His fists clenched in his pockets.

They can't, a voice breathed in the back of his mind.

"You can't do that," he managed.

"We can, and we have," his father said. That was it. No room for discussion or argument. His father's word was law. Always.

Fuck this.

"Then it seems we have no further business," Dare said, grateful that his voice remained steady. He gave half a bow, hands still in his pockets lest his parents see them shaking, and turned toward the door.

As Sigurd stepped in to block Dare's exit, his father said, "We're not finished here."

"We are," Dare snapped. "I'm leaving."

Sigurd didn't move.

"Please stay," his mother said, her voice like a caress. "I've missed you so much, Dars. We can make this work, I promise."

His shoulders sagged. *They're just words*, Dare reminded himself. *Empty fucking words.* There had been many beautiful promises, but none of them had ever meant anything. Not really.

Dammit, he knew this was one of her tricks, and yet his heart lurched. Vire's demons. He *knew* it, but he still longed for her approval. Her acceptance.

Her love.

And he thought of Gregor, of their quiet night together—the first in so long. The first of many, perhaps . . . if he stayed.

"Your Grace?" Gregor's voice cut into his thoughts.

Gods above and below, I've missed him . . .

"If I may, Your Grace."

"Secretary." The duke's tone was razor sharp. "You have thoughts on this matter?"

"I do."

"We have already made up our minds."

"Your Grace," Gregor pressed, "if you would but consider . . ."

Dare turned, eyes widening at the quiet, gentle defiance. It was unheard of. In all the years Dare had known him, Gregor had never spoken back to the duke. Not once.

"Lord Darcy is bound to assist the Warden in her mission. You could have her swear to return him after the job is done. She would be bound to comply, by the rules of her order."

"Out of the question," his father barked, his eyes flashing with warning.

Dare stared at Gregor, his heart pounding in his ears. *If I stay . . .*

Gregor met Dare's gaze. His eyes were pleading. Dare had seen that look before, the night he left Brookshire all those years ago. *Go*, it said. *Run.*

Dare swallowed hard, reining in his thoughts. He couldn't stay. Solace needed his help. Verity needed his help.

"You can't stop me from leaving," Dare said. He faced his father, squaring his shoulders. "What are you going to do? Lock me up until you die and I inherit the duchy?"

His father steepled his fingers, leaning on his desk. "If I have to."

"You can't force me to rule, you *fucking—*"

Dare's mother stepped forward and grabbed his jaw, silencing him. He'd been so focused on his father, he hadn't seen her reach for him. He'd forgotten which parent he had to thank for his speed.

Her nails dug into the soft flesh of his cheeks even through her gloves. "Darling, *language.*" She pulled his face down until he had no choice but to look her in the eye. "I will not tolerate this disrespect," she said. Her voice had lost all sugar and warmth, leaving behind only the cold cruelty that pierced him to his core. "Your father and I have many years yet before you will inherit your birthright. If you will not do your duty willingly, I have plenty of time to convince you otherwise."

She released him and returned to her husband's side. Dare tried to regain his wits and stop his knees from trembling.

The duke took the duchess's hand, a slow, predatory smile pulling across his lips. "Besides," he said, sliding into the deep, quiet tone that set every one of Dare's senses on alert. "It is no longer your concern."

A chill ran down the back of Dare's neck, and his palms began to sweat. *Verity.* His muscles tensed. "What did you do?"

His father's stare was cold and unfeeling.

Gods, Solace. They'd told him about Solace. "What the *fuck* did you do!"

"I've taken care of it." The duke nodded to Sigurd. "You needn't worry about your little mission anymore."

The guardsman grabbed Dare's elbow, but he tore his arm away, lunging at his father as the duchess's hand flew upward. Dare had been fast in his dash, but she'd been a hair's breadth faster.

The solid wall of her magic clipped Dare's chin, snapping his head back with the impact as it rose between her son and her husband. A roar tore from his throat, thousands of pinpricks of magic colliding with his body. He staggered straight into Sigurd's waiting arms, his vision reeling.

Gregor jumped to his feet but was met with a sharp glare from the duchess.

"Sit down or join him below."

Gregor lowered himself back down, his knuckles white where he gripped the arms of the chair.

"Take him away," his father ordered. "I suspect more time downstairs will see our son come to his senses."

No!

No, this cannot be the end.

Dare fought to wrench himself free, but Sigurd held him fast, his vise-like grip threatening to snap the bones in Dare's arms if he tested him.

"You can't do this!" Dare screamed.

"Oh, child," his mother said, a viper in the grass, the sickly sweet tone returning. "But we already have."

He clawed and shouted and kicked as Sigurd dragged him from the study, through the halls of the manor, down and down the winding stairs into the darkness below.

Chapter 45

VERITY SLOWED TO A brisk walk after she left the Wilhaven Manor grounds. With the bustle of the city quieted so late, the roar of the rivers clashing to the south ensured Brookshire was never completely silent. Walking through the darkened streets, Dare's words clung to her mind like the mist at the bottom of the falls.

Maybe Solace could have saved him *instead of me . . . I'm sorry . . .*

Drystan's absence was sharp, the wound still fresh, like another piece of herself had been cut away. Her thoughts wandered over the path that led her here, fixating on the choices she'd made along the way, analyzing everything that had happened in the last month. She turned it all over and over in her mind, like river stones, wearing them smooth.

When she returned to the Ragebrook Inn, Solace met her in the hallway outside their rented rooms. He opened his door just as she crested the top of the stairs. "Are you alright?" he asked, his voice thick with sleep and worry.

"I'm fine." How had he even heard her come in?

He studied her from his doorway as she moved to the room she shared with Finn, his brows knitting together. "What happened at the manor?"

"Nothing happened," she said, biting out the harsh whisper.

He leaned against the door frame, all signs of sleep disappearing. "I meant with dinner. Is the duke considering your request?"

Verity sighed, turning to him. Of course that was what he meant. "I don't know," she said truthfully. "He seems to be."

Solace gave her half a smile. "That's good." He was still watching her carefully. "Did you see Dare?"

The image of Dare on his knees, his head bowed with tears staining his cheeks flashed in her mind. She blinked hard against it as she said, "I saw him."

Solace stared at the space somewhere between them, his swirled eyes distant for a moment before he inhaled sharply and shook his head, focusing on her face. "We'll get him out of there, Verity. We have to."

She nodded, turning the latch to her room. "Good night, Solace."

No message came from Duke Wilhaven the next day. The following morning, Verity left early, heading north toward the sprawling manor at the edge of the city. She passed Jae and Lucien on their way to the inn, and Jae turned to keep pace with her, waving Lucien on.

"Tell me you're not heading where I think you're heading," Jae said, jogging to keep up with Verity's determined strides.

She didn't slow. "He said he'd have a decision yesterday."

"Marching on his house is *not* going to help your case," Jae argued. She stepped in front of Verity, blocking her path. "Duke Wilhaven is as big an asshole as I've ever met."

A man walking past grumbled something under his breath and glared at them.

Jae ignored him. "Pushing him is only going to make him delay even longer, just out of spite."

Verity's hands clenched at her sides, though she tried to calm the temper that was already flaring. "I can't just sit and do nothing."

"Give me a day to get a message through," Jae said. "If by midday tomorrow we still haven't heard, then by all means, storm the manor." As Verity forced herself to relax her fists, Jae slung an arm around her shoulders, spinning her back toward the inn. "And gods help the poor fool who gets in your way."

Jae and Lucien were waiting for Verity the next morning when she, Finn, and Solace went downstairs for breakfast.

"I haven't been able to get anything into or out of Wilhaven Manor," Jae said as the group collected around the table. "The place has been locked down since you left the other night."

And each day that passed reduced the hope that she had managed to sway Duke Wilhaven.

How many more days could they wait before she and Solace were forced to continue to Taernfane without him?

From his seat beside her, Solace set his hand on Verity's shoulder. "We're not going to leave him here."

And yet they could only delay so long before things were bound to get much, much worse.

"I could no sooner abandon him here as I could you," Solace continued. "I'm forever indebted to the both of you for what you've done for me—for what you're *still* doing for me. I won't turn my back when one of you is in need." He looked to each of the others. "I say if we don't hear back from Duke Wilhaven by the week's end, or if he says no, then we'll get Dare out ourselves."

By the week's end . . . *Three more days.*

On Verity's other side, Finn leaned forward, setting her elbows on the table. "How are we going to do that? We can't exactly launch a full-scale attack on the manor."

Verity shook her head. "No, it can't be anything like that," she agreed. "There are far too many innocent people that would get caught in the middle of any sort of assault." She rested her chin in her hand, the metal cold against her skin. "Besides, Wardens have to remain neutral. We can't get involved in any political affairs." She blew out a long breath, giving voice to one of the thoughts that had been plaguing her for the last few days. "I'm dangerously close to breaking my oath as it is. If we're going to do something, we'll need to be clever. Subtle. We need . . ."

We need Dare.

"Could we sneak him out?" Finn asked. "If we're fast, we could be well on our way before they even notice he's gone."

"It's the same problem," Verity said. "I would be interfering and therefore breaking my oath as a Warden. I can't."

"What if we do it?" Lucien asked, crossing his broad arms as he leaned back in his chair. "What if you and Solace started out for Taernfane, and the rest of us broke him out? Then you'd have nothing to do with it."

Jae arched one brow. "Lucien, that is downright devious." She gave him a playful backhanded slap against his muscled chest. "I'm proud of you!"

He grumbled something under his breath, but otherwise ignored her. Jae chuckled in delight.

"I'm not sure the technicality would matter in Duke Wilhaven's eyes," Verity said slowly. "Or the Wardens'. I've petitioned the duke for Dare's release. If Dare suddenly turns up missing, Duke Wilhaven's going to know I was involved, whether I was there or not." She hung her head, staring down at the table. There had to be something.

Finn slid her fingers into Verity's hand and squeezed. "We'll figure it out, Vee."

Verity lifted her head at the touch. At the familiar nickname on unfamiliar lips. A flash of crimson colored Finn's cheeks, and she pulled her hand away to tuck a stray lock of hair behind her ear.

"I'll use my power," Solace said, dropping his voice to a determined whisper. "Something to make a distraction so Dare can slip out. They can't blame you for—"

"You can't!" Verity snapped. She wasn't sure how much Solace might have shared with the others about how he felt when he used the gods-given—or gods-*stolen*—magic he possessed, but judging by the concern in Finn's eyes, he must have at least mentioned it to her. "We'll find another way."

"Verity, there may not be another way."

"Then we'll make one."

CHAPTER 46

FOUR DAYS PASSED IN the cold dark below Wilhaven Manor. Dare counted the passing days by the sun traveling across the window slit at the top of the cell and by the four plates of dry bread and water he'd been brought since being locked away again. He knew it was all part of their plan. Their game. They wouldn't starve him or hurt him; they would leave him there, alone, just long enough for him to crave comfort, interaction, real food. A drink.

Gods, I could use a drink.

He paced miles circling the inside of his cell. Whatever his parents had done, whatever message they'd sent, there was no chance it was anything other than vile. If Verity and Solace were still in Brookshire, he needed to warn them. But they couldn't still be in the city, could they? Not after all this time. Surely they must have cut their losses by now.

Yet every time Dare tried to calm his racing heart and still his body, every time he tried to convince himself that it was over, that it was time to give up, something pushed at the back of his mind, urging him on. So he paced, and he pried at the cell bars until his fingers bled.

By early afternoon on the fourth day, Dare had another idea. An incredibly stupid idea, if he was being honest with himself, but he was out of options. Not that he'd had many to begin with.

Anyone was capable of magic, under the proper circumstances. Certain attributes, like being a natural Channel, or being a Perceptive, made it significantly easier. He remembered reading in his youth about some Channels who had managed complex magical effects simply by *willing* them hard enough, without ever knowing the rotes or theories. Well, Dare had known some of the rotes, a few theories. Once.

Though he'd tried hard to forget.

Sitting on the floor, hands gripping the bars of his cell, Dare thought back to the library in the Reach, to their frantic run from Corvin Crosse. He thought about how Verity had used her magic to tear the metal shelves right out of the floor where they'd been bolted down. He focused on the memory of twisted metal, of how he'd felt when that power had pulsed out of Verity. Dare tightened his fingers around the iron bars and tried to focus the energy within him to pry the bars apart, twisting the metal, as she had done.

Nothing happened.

Dare tried again. And again. And again. He was a Perceptive, gods dammit all to Vire's fucking hells. He should be able to do this. He *needed* to do this. He tried over and over again, until his blood was pulsing in his ears and his hands were numb from straining against the bars. By the time the sun had set and darkness settled into the cell, all he had to show for his efforts was a migraine.

His head was still pounding as the moon rose through the window slit and footsteps echoed down the darkened corridor. Ignoring the throbbing in his temples and the base of his neck, Dare jumped to his feet, though he kept his distance from the bars until he could see who was approaching.

Gregor's soft voice came from the darkness. "Darcy?" When he reached the cell, the silver moonlight fell across his face.

Dare's shoulders slumped with relief. "Thank the gods," he breathed.

"I came as soon as I could get away," he said, keeping his voice hushed. "But I'm afraid I can't stay long. They've been keeping a very close eye. Are you alright?" Through the bars, Gregor held out a small, folded-over piece of dough about the size of his palm. Dare knew from childhood experience it would contain some sort of meat and vegetables.

Dare's mouth watered as he snatched the offered food from Gregor's outstretched hand. The little meat pie was browned and crispy on the edges but cold, though he didn't care in the least. He took a greedy bite, a quiet groan escaping his throat. "Thank you," he managed before devouring the rest of the pie in two more bites.

"Are you alright?" Gregor asked again.

Dare ignored the question, taking Gregor's hand between his own. "Have you heard anything?"

Gregor shook his head. "No, I still don't know what your father did, but there's been no word of anything. Darcy, your hands are shaking."

Shit. Dare gripped Gregor's hand tighter in the hopes of steadying his own. "Gregor, I need to get a message out."

"What's happened?" Gregor asked, focusing on Dare's hands, which still hadn't stopped trembling. "Talk to me. Did one of your parents come to see you?"

"Of course not," Dare said gruffly, pulling away to pace the cell. "That's not how they work, you know that." Every turn of his head sent a stabbing pain through his temples.

"I hate this," Gregor said, so softly that Dare barely heard him over the frantic pounding of his own heart. "Whenever they locked you down here, I always felt so powerless. I couldn't do anything to help you. And now . . ." He gave a humorless laugh. "I'm the duke's right hand and I *still* can't do anything. Not a damned thing."

Dare paused in his pacing, pressing a hand into the side of his head. "You make it sound like it was all the time," he muttered. "They only did it when I . . ."

He let the thought fall away, unsure of why, exactly, he was defending them. It was an old habit, like standing when his father entered a room, that he somehow hadn't outgrown.

"It was often enough," Gregor said through clenched teeth.

Dare crossed the small space. He pressed his forehead against the cold iron bars and grabbed Gregor's hand again. "And you *are* helping. More than you know. I just . . . I *need* to get a message to Verity. I need to warn her. Can you do that for me?"

"I can't," Gregor said. "Your father's having every letter I handle checked. He'll find any message I try to send on your behalf. Especially if it's to the Warden."

"I have an idea," Dare said, "and they'll be none the wiser." He was tired and hungry and everything ached, but even still, the edge of his mouth curled into a smirk. He couldn't help it. The thought of slipping something past his ever-watchful parents had always brought him a small thrill of pleasure, and apparently he hadn't outgrown that either. "Trust me, Gregor."

Gregor's cheek dimpled as he smiled just a little at those words. "I trust you, Darcy." He squeezed Dare's hand. "I'll always trust you."

CHAPTER 47

Jae strode beside Lucien through the market, the crowd parting around them like a river around a boulder. It was getting late. The shops and stalls were closing, and people were hurrying to make their purchases and get home before full dark. She hadn't been able to get any messages into or out of the manor in five days. Nobody was talking. The whole thing was a mess, with Darcy at the center of it.

As usual.

She'd recognized him the moment Duke Wilhaven's soldiers hauled him through the market square. As soon as his hood had fallen and she'd seen his face. Those eyes. That mouth.

That damned mouth.

This whole thing was insane. If someone had told her a month ago that she would be back in Brookshire, and that Darcy fucking Wilhaven would be there too, she would have kindly told them to fuck off. And yet here she was. Here they both were. Together. Well, not *together*, but . . .

"Are you alright?" Lucien asked as they moved east across the square.

"Of course," she said, maybe a little too quickly. "Why?"

He glanced at her sidelong. "Because I had to ask you three times before you answered."

Dammit.

"How long has it been since you've been back?" he asked.

"Too long," she grumbled. "Or not long enough . . . I'm not sure which."

"I'm sorry to be the one to drag you back."

Because he *was* the one who'd dragged her back. "Have you had any more visions?" she asked, lowering her voice.

Six weeks earlier, Lucien's nightmares had started. The two of them had just swung into Valda to see if they could pick up an odd job or two from any of their usual contacts when the first dream hit. He'd awoken with a start, drenched in sweat. When they started to head north to the Wilds, things only got worse. He'd nearly torn his bedroll in half during the last one before she convinced him to give up their current job and turn south. He'd finally told her about them then. Really told her, with details and everything. And when he described the gaudy fountain he saw in each of the dreams, Jae knew. They weren't just dreams. They were visions, and she knew where they had to go.

And standing in front of that gods-awful fountain in the center of Brook-shire was where she'd watched the duke's soldiers drag Darcy away.

Lucien shook his head, dark hair swaying against his shoulders. "Not since they arrested your lov—"

"Finish that sentence and I'll stab you."

The deep rumble of Lucien's laughter floated past her.

"But really?" she pressed, following Lucien as he turned down the next street, heading to the Ragebrook Inn so they could report their day's progress—or lack thereof—to Verity. "Nothing?"

"Nope."

"They just . . . stopped?"

"Yup."

"Why?"

A ripple of tension flitted through his shoulders. "How the hells should I know?"

"No, I know, but aren't you curious?"

"No." Lucien had picked up his pace now, and Jae had to jog to keep up.

Stubborn prick. "*Really?* So six weeks of visions that stop as suddenly as they start, and you're not in the least bit curious where they came from? Or why? *Visions*, Lucien. That's not something that just happens."

"Leave it alone, Jae," he growled.

She sped up and swung in front of him, forcing him to stop. She was grateful, in moments like this, to have been graced with height so she didn't have to look up at him. Though he was easily twice as broad as she was and could pick her up and move her out of the way if he had half a mind to. If she let him.

She met his eyes, which narrowed on her, bright yellow set against his olive skin. "When you grimace like that it makes you look old," she said. It was a lie. He didn't look old, not really. Even with the sneer he was giving her. Though admittedly he would look even younger without the beard. Or the scar. Or the pissy attitude.

"You're incredibly—"

"Endearing?" Jae offered helpfully. She smiled, angling her head as though she were a child trying to convince her parents to buy her a puppy.

"Annoying," Lucien finished, but the edge of a grin was starting to curl beneath the beard.

"Bitter old man," Jae shot back.

But Lucien wasn't listening to her anymore. He stepped around her, something pulling his attention like a hound to a fox.

"What is it?" Jae followed after him.

Lucien broke into a run and Jae sprinted to catch up. "The Warden," was all he said.

Sure enough, Jae spotted Verity ahead of them on the road, running through the thinning crowd as though something were chasing her. But she wasn't the type to run from danger.

So what danger was she running *toward*?

Lucien caught up to her easily. A word or two passed between them before he peeled away at the next side street.

Shit. Whatever was happening, it couldn't be good. Jae picked up the pace, trying to close the distance between her and the Warden.

Jae had nearly caught up to her when the Ragebrook Inn came into view. A mass of people was gathered around the front.

Oh shit.

Verity slowed, but only a little. She looked ready to throw herself through the crowd and charge into the building when Lucien stepped into her path. Verity slammed into him, but he simply absorbed the impact and caught her by the arms as Jae skidded to a stop beside them.

"He's gone," Lucien said, tightening his grip as she tried to push past him.

"Who?" Jae demanded, taking a moment to catch her breath. "Solace?"

"Let go of me," Verity ordered.

He did, and she stalked into the inn with Jae and Lucien on her heels.

"Warden, he's not here," Lucien repeated as they entered.

"You can't know that," Verity snapped.

He could. But Lucien didn't say so. And neither did Jae.

The place was a battlefield. Tables were overturned, chairs broken and . . . were those scorch marks on the wall?

"Fuck . . ." Jae murmured, drawing out the word as she took in the scene. "Gods, what about—"

Verity was already moving to the stairs, taking them two at a time with Lucien close behind, following like a shadow.

The damage upstairs was as bad as the lower level, with several holes through the wooden walls. One of the doors was at an angle, barely on its hinges, and Verity burst in, panting. Lucien stayed right with her, though Jae hung back by the door. The room was in tatters, with more scorch marks on the walls and on the floor. The bed was overturned, the window smashed.

"No, no, *no!*" Verity muttered to herself as she left the room as quickly as she entered, blowing past Jae. Verity bolted to the door across the hall, a loud *crack* sounding as she turned the latch and broke the flimsy lock. Jae stayed in the doorway of the ransacked room and peered after Verity.

The other room was empty. Not smashed or overturned, just empty.

Lucien stalked through the first room, sniffing the air. Jae wanted to help, but she knew better than to distract him when he got that look. Instead, she moved closer to Verity, keeping her across the hall to give Lucien a minute to do what he could.

"Verity, what happened?"

The Warden thrust a small piece of paper at Jae's chest, crumpled in her metal hand. The writing was in a familiar, scrawling script, but in a language she couldn't read. "What's this?"

"It's from Dare," Verity said, beginning to pace the room. "He wrote it in High Aethirian so the house secretary could get the note out without it being confiscated. It says that his parents did something to put the whole mission at risk, but he doesn't know what." Verity pushed past Jae and returned to Solace's room. "He said to get Solace out of the city, but I was too late. He's gone. They're gone."

She pivoted and punched the wall, putting another small hole through the wood. A shard of glass from the broken window fell to the floor and shattered.

Lucien crouched near the bed, looking at something on the floor. When he stood, he froze for a moment before sniffing the air again. He spun on his heels and ran to the window. Jae followed, shoving in beside him.

Night had snuck up on them all, but below the broken window, Finn lay struggling in an overgrown tangle of vines. She looked up at them, pausing in her attempts to free herself.

"Can I get a little help?"

Jae turned from the window, but Verity was already out the door, bolting down the hall.

What in the hells had the Wilhavens done now?

VERITY SPRINTED DOWN THE stairs and through the dwindling crowd, rounding first one corner and then the next into the alley behind the building. Finn lay in a thick bed of verdant green leaves and vines, which were wrapped around her arms and legs, refusing to loosen their grip no matter how hard she struggled.

Verity drew her sword and knelt beside Finn, sawing at the plants with the jagged edge of her broken blade. "Are you alright? What happened?"

"Solace!" Finn tugged harder at the vines. "Where's Solace?" Her face was scratched and her eyes red, but otherwise she seemed unharmed.

The tightness in Verity's chest began to ease but didn't release its grip. "What happened?" she demanded again. Jae and Lucien appeared around them, and Lucien easily hefted Finn to her feet as Verity sliced away the last of the vines.

"I don't know," Finn said, breathing hard. "I was with Solace—we were doing some research. A group of men kicked in the door and set on us. One of them—I don't know what he was, but he and Solace started to fight, and it was like nothing I've ever seen." She ran her hands through her disheveled hair, pulling out the tie that held it back. It fell in a mess around her shoulders, shards of glass clinking to the ground. "They started to overpower him. I tried to help, but Solace shoved me back. There was a burst of . . . wind? And the next thing I knew, I was stuck in this damn plant."

The pile of vines was beginning to wither and brown while Finn spoke, drying out far more quickly than ought to be natural. They definitely didn't belong here, the only spot of green in the otherwise wooden and stone alley.

"How many?" Lucien asked.

"Five, I think. Maybe six?"

"The man," Verity pressed. "The one that fought with Solace. What did he look like?"

Finn lifted her eyes as though searching for the memory of the man's face through the broken window above. "He was about the same size as Solace, with black hair." Her hand drifted to her throat. "He had a scar around his neck, like from a rope."

Corvin Crosse. The psychotic zealot of Ainam who had locked Solace up and planned to use him to wage war across the continent.

"You said . . ." Verity's voice was strained. "You . . . were doing research?"

"Yeah," Finn said. "Why?"

Verity swallowed hard, remembering the destroyed—and empty—room. "You had the books with you in Solace's room? All of them?"

"Everything but those weird pages with the runes on them," Finn said. "I left those with your gear since we can't read—" Her eyes widened. "Shit, are they—"

"Gone." Verity's shoulders shook as she tried to focus on her breathing. All Westhold needed was the weapon, and they would be unstoppable, decimating everything and everyone in their path. And now they had it. They had Solace.

A lot of people were going to die.

They couldn't have gotten far—not yet. Someone must have seen where they went. Verity ran to the front of the building, but the crowd had mostly dispersed. She asked as many people as she could, including the bartender who'd been working when the fight broke out upstairs, but no one had seen anything more than what Finn had described. She had no leads. Nothing.

A hand clasped her shoulder. It was Jae, with Lucien and Finn behind her. "We'll find him," she said. She glanced to Lucien, though he was already moving.

"I'm on it," he mumbled to Jae, as though answering a question she hadn't asked. "The usual signs."

Jae nodded and, before Verity could ask, he took off down the street, past the last of the stragglers still muttering about the night's excitement.

Verity stood in the darkness outside the inn. Despite Jae and Finn beside her, she felt utterly alone. She should have been here. Dare had known something was wrong; he'd gotten the message to her, but she hadn't been where she'd needed to be. If she'd been here, maybe she could have stopped them.

The hole inside her that had reopened when Drystan died stretched and yawned, sinking teeth and claws into the very center of her. She'd managed to hold it at bay for a time. She'd forced herself to focus on the mission—on Solace, and even Dare and Finn. They'd given her a purpose that kept her from peering too closely into that black, gaping pit inside herself. But now everything had crashed down in flames around her again. The fire and the darkness clawed at her, pulling her back down into that dark place.

He'd been the only one able to wrench her from it before, to stop her from falling.

Drystan.

He was the only reason she hadn't thrown herself into the river in the weeks and months after the College fell.

Drystan, I can't do this without you.

But he was gone. Sacrificed for her life.

And now Dare was gone.

And Solace was gone.

The weight of all the losses she'd suffered—that she'd *caused*—was strangling, suffocating.

Before she even realized what she was doing, Verity was running. She ran from Finn and Jae, ran from Dare and his family, ran from her failed promise to Solace that she would keep him safe. She tried to outrun the darkness, but still it was all around her, and she was drowning in it. She ran until the burning in her lungs outpaced the burning in her eyes.

She made it through the city gates by then, no one having dared stop her, and collapsed onto her knees just beyond the edge of the forest outside Brookshire's northwestern walls.

The damp seeped through her pants as she knelt in the moss and, for the first time since she'd laid Drystan's body in the snow of the mountain pass, Verity cried. She cried and raged, the hole in her center turning into a blaze that threatened to consume her.

A twig snapped close behind her. She knew she should stand, should face whoever was there. What if Corvin's men had found her? But she couldn't bring herself to stand. She couldn't bring herself to care.

"Verity?"

The worry in Finn's voice was audible and only served to draw another round of sobs from Verity. Arms swooped down around her, pulling her in. They were thin but strong—the arms of an archer. Verity let those arms hold her, leaning her head into Finn's shoulder as they knelt together at the edge of the woods.

Finn didn't say anything else. She held Verity, letting her cry all the pain and emptiness out of her, simply being a tether. Something Verity could hold on to. Something she could use to pull herself back.

When Verity had no tears left in her, and her sobs were reduced to shuddering breaths, she managed to say quietly, "You came after me?"

Lithe fingers brushed Verity's hair behind her ear as Finn still held her close. "We both did."

Verity lifted her head from Finn's shoulder enough to see Jae crouched a few feet away.

"We thought you might want to talk," Jae said. Her voice was tender and kind in a way Verity hadn't heard from the brusque woman before.

"There's nothing to say," Verity choked out. "I failed. It's that simple. I let everyone down."

"You haven't failed," Finn said, rubbing a hand along Verity's back.

"I have." She pulled away to look at Finn. "I couldn't save any of them! I couldn't save Solace, and I couldn't save Dare, and I couldn't save Drystan. And I couldn't save . . ." She choked on the lack of a name for the first person she'd ever failed and collapsed against Finn's shoulder. "I didn't know his name," she blurted out. "I never asked and he never said, because he didn't think I cared enough to know. And he was right. I didn't until it was too late. Until he was gone, and it was too late. It's over. I thought I could make a difference. I thought I could save people, but I *can't*." She gripped Finn's shirt as she cried into her. "It's over," she said again.

"You saved *me*," Finn whispered into Verity's hair. She stroked her back in slow, soothing circles. "It's only over if you give up."

Was there another choice? What was left?

"What assets do we have?" Finn went on, her voice as calm and placid as the circles she traced on Verity's back. "There's Jae with her inside information on Duke Wilhaven. There's Lucien with his general . . . grrr." She sneered, mimicking a growl.

Jae chuckled at the impression. "And he's already off tracking down the ones who did this. There's Finn. Didn't you say you can shoot?"

Finn nodded, though she said nothing further of her own abilities. "And there's you," she said to Verity. "A godsdamned Warden of the Flame and a mage on top of it. Verity, you're incredible." Finn's hands slid from around Verity and gripped her steel fingers, squeezing tightly. "What do you say we go rescue our wayward boys?"

"But Dare's parents are holding him hostage in that house," she said. "They won't let him go. And if we break him out and take him by force, or even without them seeing, they'll know it was me. I'll be kicked out of the Wardens for interfering."

How far was she prepared to go?

Finn tugged Verity to her feet. "So if we can't break him out," she said, her bright amber eyes glinting with mischief, "we'll get his parents to throw him out."

Jae rose, joining them. "He's their only heir," she said. "Why would they disown him?"

"I have an idea." Finn grimaced as she watched Verity. "But I don't think you're going to like it."

The dark pit within her was still there. Verity could feel it reaching into every part of her, but she pulled the edges tighter, stopping the spread for now. They might still have a chance.

"Whatever it is," Jae said, grinning, "count me in."

Verity gripped Finn's hand and nodded. "Alright, what's the plan?"

CHAPTER 49

VERITY WAITED IN A small copse of trees at the back edge of the Wilhaven estate as the sky lightened in the east. She'd been waiting since before dawn, when she and Jae had parted ways, Jae heading to make contact with her friend in the household without alerting the guards.

Verity crouched in the shadows, focusing on the manor and the side door beyond the little vegetable garden, which Jae had indicated would be her point of ingress if everything went as expected. It was a bigger *if* than Verity would have liked, but it was the best they had. She steadied her breathing. It wouldn't do any good to worry about Jae.

Or Dare.

She took another deep breath, holding it for a few seconds before releasing it slowly.

The door opened a crack, and Verity moved as quietly as she could across the grass and through the garden.

Gregor, the house secretary, stood at the door.

"You're Jae's contact?" Verity asked.

Gregor ushered her into a small work area off the kitchen. "We were all old friends," he said, his voice barely a whisper. "Before Darcy left." He guided her to a narrow, darkened hallway. "She told me the plan. You really think you can get him out?" Something like hope gleamed behind his wire-framed glasses. "For good?"

"I do," she said, managing to keep her voice steady. She had to focus if there was any hope of their plan working. And it *had* to work.

Gregor gestured down the hall. "That way, make your first left, then the next right, and through the door at the end." He handed her an iron key. "Follow the spiral staircase. He's the only one down there at present."

Verity tensed. "Down there *where*, exactly?" she asked.

"I'm supposed to say that it's used for storage and occasionally to hold someone to be transported into town for a trial." He hesitated a heartbeat. "It's a dungeon."

They have a dungeon below their family home. Her stomach knotted. *And they locked their own son in it.* She pushed the thought from her mind. "Thank you," she said.

His lips curved into a breath of a smile. "I'll make sure no one accidentally wanders into your path."

Verity followed his directions, unlocking the heavy door at the end of the hall. The air was chill and damp, the stairs slick as she descended into the dark. As Gregor had said, the dungeon cells lining the outer walls were empty. Narrow horizontal window slits near the ceiling let in a bit of the early morning light, and Verity could only imagine what else they let in.

She found him in the cell at the far end. Dare lay on the cold stone floor, not even a mat beneath him, with a tattered blanket pulled over his shoulders. His hair, stringy and knotted, hung over his face. Verity crouched when she reached his cell, her steel fingers clinking lightly against the iron as she grasped the bars.

"Dare," she whispered.

He lifted his head, peering at her through the tangles of his hair. "Verity," he breathed. It was almost a question, like he didn't quite believe that she was truly there. He scrambled across the stone floor on his knees, the filthy blanket falling away. His clothes had been fine once, but now they were wrinkled and stained, and nearly a week's worth of stubble was on his chin. "You shouldn't be here." His voice was hoarse, his lips pale and cracked. "But by all the gods, I'm glad you are."

"Dare—" She should say something about that night. He'd opened himself up to her, and she'd run from him. Later. They would talk after she got him out of there. She would find the words later. "I don't have much time."

"Did you get my message, did—"

"I got it, but . . . I couldn't stop them." Her voice cracked. "They took Solace. Corvin . . . he took Solace."

Dare set his head against the bars, his hair obscuring his face again. "Fuck."

"I'm sorry, I . . ."

"It's not your fault," Dare said before she could finish.

She shook her head. "But I—"

"Verity, listen to me." He looked up at her and squeezed her hand through the bars, a quiet resolve falling over his features. "This is not your fault. You didn't do this. My father did this. He sold us out and started a fucking war so he could keep me here. But Verity, you have to go. You have to get him back."

"We have a plan," she said, her voice firm and steady. "We have a plan to get you out of this and get Solace back." After a moment, she added the words Finn had spoken to her a few hours ago. "But I don't think you're going to like it."

Dare's eyes glittered in the dim light. "Tell me."

Back at the Ragebrook Inn, Verity descended the stairs to find Finn and Jae already waiting for her. It was an hour after dawn, and Finn had been planning to hit a few shops just as they opened so the group would have everything they'd need for their journey. She must have just come back.

"Morning," Finn called.

Verity's heart thrummed as she crossed the room to the two women. A bow was slung over Finn's shoulder, and a quiver of arrows hung on one slender hip. Jae was beside her with not one but two swords. One was strapped to her hip, and the other was across her back. Verity remembered Jae's words from a few days ago and smiled. *Gods help the poor fool who gets in your way.*

Vire help anyone who tried to stop them today. Verity wasn't sure any of the other gods would dare.

"When it's done, Jae and I will meet you just outside the southern gates," Finn said. "She found a sign from Lucien that they're heading south and west."

"Corvin must be taking him back to Westhold," Verity said. It was the opposite way they wanted to be heading.

Jae nodded, and as if knowing Verity's concern, said, "Once we get Solace back, we'll swing east again, toward Taernfane."

Verity searched their faces. There was no fear or doubt. They were ready to risk it all for this. For her and Dare and Solace. "You . . . don't have to do this," she said, looking between the two of them. "Neither of you have to do this. This isn't your fight."

Jae took one of Verity's hands in hers. "First of all," she said, "Lucien and I swore an oath to help you. Seems to me you still need some help, so I wouldn't count that as fulfilled just yet." A wicked grin flashed across her face. "And besides, I need to see the look on Darcy's face when he realizes I helped save his ass."

Finn clasped Verity's other hand. "Ignoring the fact that I owe the three of you my life, I told you before that I joined the Crimson Brothers because I wanted to be a part of something bigger than myself. When I stand at the Black Gates, I want to be able to look back on my life and say that I did something. That I made a difference in the world and left it a little bit better than I found it." She smiled, her eyes crinkling at the corners. "I can't think of a better way to make a difference in the world than by trying to help save it."

Verity stared at the two of them, bereft of anything at all to say. To have them at her back . . . she hadn't known how much it would mean. "Let's get out of here," she said when she found her voice again. "It's a long way to Taernfane, and we have quite the detour to make."

Verity passed through the manor's gates on foot, holding her head high. She'd decided to leave her sword and her traveling pack with Jae and Finn; she needed to stay light in case they had to flee, and coming in armed would send the wrong message. She could do this without anyone getting hurt.

She pounded on the front door, not bothering to use the knocker. A brief moment passed before it swung open. Gregor stood in the entryway, dressed in his formal suit with the silver embroidery. He was on duty.

"Good morning, Warden," he said, puzzled. He gave her a belated bow.

Verity returned it with only a curt nod. "Good morning, Secretary. I'm here to request an immediate audience with Duke Wilhaven."

"I'm sorry, but he's indisposed this morning. Perhaps you would like to schedule an appointment for another time?"

"Tell His Grace," she continued sharply, pitching her voice to carry the command through the manor halls, "that I have learned Duke Wilhaven has acted unlawfully toward a Warden of the Flame. I will not be leaving here until the situation is rectified."

Gregor stiffened. "I beg your pardon?"

Out of the corner of her eye, Verity caught one of the manor's staff poke their head around the corner and then quickly disappear.

"Do I need to repeat myself, Secretary?"

Gregor gave another more formal bow. "No, of course not, Warden. My apologies. Please, follow me. You may await His Grace in the library."

Verity followed him into the house, to the ornate oak door just before the grand staircase. He pushed the door open and gestured for Verity to enter.

"Wait here, please." He closed the door silently behind her.

Verity stilled her mind, stopping herself from dwelling on her past mistakes or on future concerns. She needed to focus on the present, on this moment. Forward was the direction open, she reminded herself. Verity positioned herself by one of the windows. There was nothing to do now but wait.

She didn't need to wait long. When next the library door swung open, it slammed into the wall. Duke Wilhaven stormed in, his long robes of office replaced with riding leathers and boots, as though he'd been about to go on a hunt. The thought of disrupting Duke Wilhaven's day sent a small thrill through her. Trailing behind the duke were two guardsmen followed by Gregor, who closed the door and stood off to the side, doing his best impression of a statue.

The guards flanked the duke across the room. "What is the meaning of this, Warden?" he barked.

Verity let a mask of indifference slide over her face, mimicking the one she'd seen on Dare in the moments when he'd been particularly infuriating. Judging by the rage that flashed in the duke's eyes, she guessed he was familiar with the look as well.

"Did your secretary not pass along my message?" she inquired coolly, not deigning to look toward Gregor. "I'm here to address your unlawful actions toward a Warden of the Flame."

"I have done nothing unlawful to you," he ground out. "*You* are the one overstepping your bounds here."

"My sincerest apologies if I wasn't clear," Verity said, keeping her voice flat and neutral. "You haven't done anything to *me*. But you are holding Darcy Wilhaven here against his will and without just cause, yes? I'm here to collect him."

"*Lord* Darcy Wilhaven," Gregor dutifully corrected from the door.

She knew he would take the bait. It was his job, after all. Verity kept her eyes on the duke. "*Warden* Darcy Wilhaven."

Duke Wilhaven scoffed, tossing his head back with palpable arrogance. It was almost enough to make Verity laugh aloud. She had seen that posturing before on Dare, when he was playing the part of the arrogant asshole. It seemed she had just found his source material for the role.

He snapped his fingers sharply at Gregor. "Bring him. Now."

Gregor bowed and ducked out of the room.

"What ridiculous scheme are you attempting now?" The duke sneered. "First you try begging for my help, then you think you can trick me with this charade?" He forced a laugh. "You're showing your desperation, Warden. It is most unbecoming."

Verity stood with her feet planted solidly beneath her shoulders, her hands clasped behind her. She smiled with her lips still pressed closed. "Your Grace, I would kindly ask you not to waste my time. Please release Warden Darcy Wilhaven to me so that we may continue on our mission."

"I will do no such thing," he snapped.

They glared at each other, neither willing to bend. The fury that had been simmering in the duke's hazel eyes was building to a roaring inferno, and although Verity's temper roiled within her, eager to face him head on, she remained calm and passive. She would be patient. She could wait him out.

When Gregor returned, he was followed by two more guards who marched Dare between them, his hands bound behind his back. Verity recognized the larger of the two from the market square their first day in Brookshire. The duchess floated along behind. Her gloved hands hovered around her mouth and throat in distress, the large blue jewel on the back of her hand glimmering.

The guards shoved Dare at Duke Wilhaven's feet. Unable to catch himself, Dare landed hard, his face striking the marble floor.

Verity suppressed the urge to go to his side. She stayed where she was, hands clasped, feet apart, face neutral. Gregor returned to his post by the door, but his eyes tracked Dare's every movement.

One of the guards flanking the duke grabbed the back of Dare's collar, hoisting him onto his knees in front of his father. Dare had looked terrible in the dim light of the dungeon a few hours ago, but seeing him now in the morning light streaming in through the windows, he looked even worse. He hadn't been tortured—Verity had seen *that* look before—but just . . . neglected. Tossed into the dungeon and left there.

Dare, to his credit, smiled, though blood trickled from a split on his lower lip. "Thank you for coming, my lady Warden."

She fought back the grin that threatened to push forward as Duke Wilhaven turned to face his son.

"What other pathetic story have you made up this time?" Disdain and disappointment oozed from his voice as he stared down the bridge of his nose at Dare. "Haven't you gotten this out of your system yet? Did you succeed at all your foolish dreams? You ran away and . . . did what, exactly? Rescued the maiden? Became the hero?" He cast a derisive glance at Verity. "Well, it seems the maiden is here to rescue you." He walked a tight circle around Dare where he knelt, hands shackled. "The only things you succeeded at were disappointing me and making a fool out of yourself. You can't be the hero when you run away like a coward."

Dare's mouth tightened into a thin line. He stared at the floor, and although he managed to keep up the calm exterior, Verity could see the mask starting to crumble, just a little. His father's words had hit their mark, even if Dare wouldn't show it.

Her stomach twisted. *He's wrong*, she wanted to tell him. She willed him to see it in her presence here. To feel it in the strength of her resolve. *Don't listen to him. He's wrong.*

"That's enough," Verity said, sliding back into the familiar, commanding tone. "Your Grace, it is a crime in every kingdom on this continent to imprison a Warden without just cause."

Duke Wilhaven wheeled on Verity, his rage erupting. "He is no Warden!" he roared.

She didn't flinch. She'd faced worse tantrums by worse men than this.

Dare laughed from the floor behind him, a low, tired chuckle.

Verity gestured toward him with the slightest upward nod of her head. "See for yourself."

Duke Wilhaven stormed the few steps to where Dare knelt and fisted the collar of his son's shirt. He yanked it downward with such force that the fabric tore, revealing the angry, red burn of two blades crossed over a brazier.

Dare smiled fiendishly as his father bellowed, "No. *No!*"

The duchess moved to where she could see the brand for herself. One gloved hand flew to her mouth. "Dars, what have you done?" she choked out.

The duke towered over Dare, raising his hand to strike. "That's impossible! It's a lie!"

Dare lifted his face to meet his father's wrath.

"I can assure you," Verity said, commanding his attention and stopping his hand, "it's real. And official, I'm afraid. I sent the missive by a Sending spell earlier this morning. They'll have the record of it on file in Whitehollow before long."

The duke's hand lowered, balling into a white-knuckled fist at his side.

"You have only two options now, Your Grace," she said with unhurried calm. "You can do as I've said and release your son to me, or you can face the consequences of imprisoning a Warden and refusing to comply with a lawful request to release him." She smiled that tight-lipped smile again. "The choice is yours, Your Grace. But like it or not, he *is* a Warden and is bound by that oath and all related laws." She paused, letting the understanding of what she was saying—of exactly what they'd done—float through them both. "He can hold no office," she recited. "He can inherit no lands or titles, and can swear allegiance to no person or group beyond the Wardens."

Indignance rippled from Duke Wilhaven like a storm. For a long moment no one moved. Finally, he gestured to his head guard, who grabbed Dare by the manacles and hauled him roughly to his feet. Dare tried to hide a wince as the motion wrenched his shoulders awkwardly. The guard took a ring of keys from his pocket and unlocked the shackles.

Rubbing at his wrists, Dare glanced at the guardsman over his shoulder. "Sigurd, a pleasure as always." He crossed to Verity and, taking her hand in his, placed an elaborate kiss on the metal plates of the top of her hand. "Thank you for the rescue, fair maiden."

She stifled a laugh at the vibrating rage emanating from both of his parents. He sure knew how to goad them into a state, she had to admit.

"After you, Warden," she said, gesturing to the door.

"Yes, of course. But before we go, would you be so kind as to banish the force wall my mother placed in front of the door? I do believe she intended to stun us with a rather unpleasant jolt."

Verity's brows rose in alarm as the duchess shed all pretense of worry or concern. She stared at Dare in pure, wild-eyed hatred, cruelty twisting her beautiful features. Verity took a step back at the sudden, terrifying shift, though Dare moved closer.

"Y-*you* . . ." she managed to say between shuddering breaths. "You never lost it, did you?"

Dare gave her a low bow. When he rose, he took up her gloved hand between both of his, his face tightening into heart-wrenching sincerity. "Mother, I can safely say that everything I ever learned about deception, I learned from you."

The duchess ripped her hand from his grip as though his touch was poison. "You selfish child. You were always a foolish, ungrateful boy! Always." She thrust her chin up, glaring at him with nothing but venom. "I don't *ever* want to see you again. Do you understand me, boy? You are dead to me." Even through her regal bearing, she was shaking with anger. "And don't you dare set one foot in this duchy again."

Dare ignored her barbs, though a muscle ticked in his jaw as he slid his hands into his pockets. He turned and gave a shorter bow to the seething duke. "Father," he said as he straightened. "Thank you for the hospitality."

Verity cast a Banishment spell, and Dare didn't look back at either of his parents as Gregor opened the door for them and followed them out, closing it behind.

But instead of turning toward the front door, Gregor pulled them down a long hallway and into a narrow servants' corridor.

"Aetherann's breath," he whispered to Verity as he adjusted his glasses. "You can be quite intimidating when you want to be."

Dare collapsed against the wall. "Pyrannis's flaming ass," he muttered, running his fingers through his hair.

Gregor checked back the way they'd come. "We weren't followed," he said, before giving Dare a playful elbow in the ribs. "You know, I don't think you're allowed to curse like that anymore, *Warden*."

"Ha ha," Dare said, exaggerating the syllables. "That wasn't part of the oath." He shot a look to Verity. "That's not part of the oath, right?"

She chuckled, relief washing over her. "We're purely secular now," she said, giving Dare a reassuring pat on the shoulder. "Of course, we do expect our members to act with a certain amount of decorum."

Dare returned the laugh, rubbing his hands over his face as though he was trying to make sure he wasn't dreaming. "I guess you're really stuck with me now."

"Not really," Verity replied, her lip curling. "There are plenty of other chapters on the continent that I can ship you off to when this is all over."

Dare blinked at her. "Was that a *joke*, my lady Warden?"

Gregor snickered. "You must be a bad influence on her."

"You know, I said exactly that!" Dare pushed off the wall, digging into his pocket. "Oh, by the way, Verity, could you please take this from me before it makes my whole side go numb?" He withdrew a sizable sapphire attached to delicate gold chains. Recognition sparked on Gregor's face.

"Her Grace's periapt?" he said, his voice tight. He shot Dare a piercing look. "You stole your mother's periapt?"

Dare gave a halfhearted shrug but flashed Gregor a wry smile as he held the stone out to Verity. "You'll have to charge it yourself so you can use it," he said to her, "but I figured you can put it to better use than she would."

She stared at the jewel. A periapt. A way to store magical energy. The implications for use—

"Verity, please just take it," he said sharply.

She snapped herself out of her wandering thoughts and reached for the gem. Dare dropped it into her palm and shook out his hand. But then his face softened. "Thank you both for what you did for me," he said.

Gregor smiled, though it was short-lived. "You know I would do anything for you. But you have to go." He gestured for them to follow him. Gregor took Dare by the hand, lacing their fingers together, and led them down a series of winding corridors until they came to the back entrance Verity had passed through in the earliest hours of the morning.

"This way," he said. "You can get to the woods from the northwest gate and then make your way back into the city, or around it. In case your father gets any crazy ideas, I don't want him knowing which way you left." Gregor withdrew a parcel wrapped in a piece of linen from beneath a low table. He handed it to Dare as he said, "I put a few things together for you. It's all I could manage without attracting attention. It's not much, I'm afraid."

Dare pulled Gregor in closer. "Gregor, I . . . uh . . ." He drew a shaking breath, his eyes darting to where their fingers were still entwined.

"Secretary, thank you for your help," Verity said quickly. "I'm forever in your debt." She slipped through the door and into the garden to give Dare a moment of peace. She leaned against the outside wall and tilted her face toward the morning sky. It worked. Now all they needed to do was get Solace back. *We're coming, Solace*, she said to the sky. *We'll find you.*

A minute later, the door opened a crack, and Dare slipped through, parcel in hand. "Let's go," he said, his voice hoarse. He didn't look at Verity as he left his family's estate behind.

He remained silent until Verity led him south, into the city proper, and they pushed through the morning crowd of shoppers in the market. Only then did Dare's voice float over her shoulder. "How did you manage this?" he asked. "How did you get in touch with Gregor?"

Verity smiled, though he couldn't see it. "I made some new friends while you were away."

"You? Made friends?" His tone just a little too incredulous for her liking.

Verity slowed until he came up alongside her and punched him in the arm, not too hard, but definitely not as gently as she could have. He laughed, rubbing his bicep as they cut down a side street.

"You should be grateful, considering."

"I am," he said softly. "I really am."

CHAPTER 50

OUTSIDE THE SOUTHERN GATES of Brookshire, Jae paced while Finn whittled a stick with her dagger, leaning against a nearby tree where they'd secured the four horses they'd acquired for the trip. The roar of the rivers was doing nothing to drown out the worry inside her head.

Lucien was off chasing down a Chosen of Ainam, and while Jae had no doubts about her friend's ability to take care of himself, Verity's description of Corvin Crosse and what he could do sent a chill down her spine.

And then there was the other tiny, little detail. She was about to see Darcy again. Or, more accurately, *he* was about to see *her* again. Why did that feel worse somehow? Her stomach was full of somersaulting butterflies as she walked back and forth along the road.

"It's taking too long," she muttered for probably the seventh time since they'd been waiting.

"It's fine," Finn said, also for the seventh time. "It hasn't even been two hours yet, and the manor's on the other side of the city. It's going to take them some time to get here."

She knew Finn was right—Jae had grown up in Brookshire and traversed the city many times—but it didn't settle the unease that had her so wound up. What if something had happened?

Jae cracked her knuckles and checked that her swords and daggers were securely attached and in their proper positions. She drew each blade an inch out of its sheath to test for any catch.

"It's *fine*," Finn repeated.

"I didn't say anything."

"No, but that's at least the fifth time you've checked your weapons." Finn finally looked up from the stick she was absently carving. "They're fine."

Jae returned to her pacing until she spotted two people passing through the southern gates. Sunlight glinted off the steel plates of Verity's arms, eliciting a quiet sigh from Jae. But beside the Warden . . .

When Jae spotted him in the market square more than a week ago, it had been like seeing a ghost, and now it was the same feeling all over again. She hadn't expected it to be so hard the second time.

She'd mourned his loss for months when he left, until she'd finally realized that she didn't actually need him. She didn't need anyone. She could make her own way in the world, and who she was had nothing to do with who she loved or whose bed she shared. It had been a difficult realization, but once she'd made it, she'd found that, while she'd still missed Darcy terribly, she'd been able to go on without him. More than that—she had thrived.

But now here he was again, and the two disparate parts of her life were about to collide.

Verity hailed them with a wave and sped her approach. Darcy—*Dare*, as he called himself now—followed. He hadn't seen her, or at least, hadn't recognized her yet.

Jae had told herself she would relish the look on his face when he saw her, when he realized who she was. But now that the moment was here, she was struck with another thought: What if he didn't recognize her? Or worse, what if he did and simply didn't care?

By the time they were in speaking distance, Dare had skidded to a stop, dumbfounded, mouth agape like a damned fool, like he was the one who had just seen a ghost. Jae could feel him watching her as she busied herself with untethering the leads and handing them off to Verity and Finn, who immediately turned tail and wandered away. Finn seemed to be finding something on her horse's tack quite fascinating.

They're no help.

Dare closed the rest of the distance to Jae as the other two left her to flounder. He looked truly terrible, and his clothes were filthy, his shirt torn at the collar. But it was definitely *his* face beneath the greasy, tangled hair and the grime, even if the lines had hardened over the years. Even if he wasn't as pretty as he'd been as a boy, even with a split lip and dark circles under his eyes, Jae's knees weakened, and she shifted her weight from foot to foot.

Theirs had always been a relationship of complications though, and so she jerked her chin toward the remaining horses. "We need to move," she said, but it came out much more quietly than she intended.

"Jaelyn."

Dammit all, she'd tried hard to steel herself for this moment, but her name on his tongue made her draw a shuddering breath. She tried to rein in her composure before it ran away entirely.

"You look like shit," she said.

He huffed a laugh so soft she barely heard it over the crashing water nearby. "Jaelyn . . . I, uh . . ."

She couldn't remember a time he'd ever been lost for words. She hadn't thought it was possible. She untied the last two horses, and he took the reins from her, his fingers brushing hers gently in the transition. She pulled her hand back a little too quickly, and there was a flicker in his eyes as he marked it.

"You're coming with us . . . ?" he asked.

"I am," she said, swinging herself onto her horse with practiced ease. She adjusted the placement of her blades. He marked those too. "We promised Verity we'd help."

Dare's throat worked as he swallowed. "We?"

"My . . . friend," she said, cringing at the unnecessary pause she left in the phrase. She'd tried to decide in the moment whether to say *friend* or *brother* and made a jumble of it instead. "Lucien. He's tracking Solace and the soldiers who took him. They're headed west."

Was that a flash of relief or jealousy in his eyes? Dammit, why was this so complicated?

Dare glanced briefly eastward, where Taernfane lay somewhere beyond the horizon. "So we double back once we find Solace?"

"That's the plan."

"Only four horses?" he asked.

Jae's back stiffened, a few of the flutters in her stomach turning into flickers of irritation. "Finn can double up with Solace when we find him," she said, leaving out the fact that Lucien preferred to travel on foot anyway. He didn't get on well with horses, though if they needed speed, Jae could always ride double with him long enough to get to safety. "It's more important that we're quick now, so we can catch up."

"We should put some distance between us and the city," Verity called from where she'd been keeping a respectable distance.

Dare nodded, though whether it was to Verity or Jae, she wasn't sure. He pulled himself into the saddle and urged his horse into a canter to ride beside Verity.

Jae galloped ahead, toward the southwest bridge leading over the Mistvale River into Southreach, keeping an eye out for signs from Lucien.

Jae had to agree with Verity's assessment. Distance was a very good idea.

CHAPTER 51

DARE LET HIS HORSE follow the road, his eyes fixed on Jaelyn's back as she led the way west. First Gregor, and now Jaelyn . . . Not to mention everything with his parents . . .

His heart threatened to stop beating every time he so much as attempted to wrap his mind around any of it, so he pushed it out of his thoughts for now. Instead, he focused on a different pain: the searing burn on his chest that marked him as a Warden of the Flame.

This is going to hurt, Verity had said early that morning, just before burning the brand into his skin. That had been agonizing enough, but under the circumstances, she'd had to use magic to do it. He'd managed not to scream from the pain, though he'd passed out as soon as she'd disappeared into the shadows, leaving him alone again.

Now, every jostle from his horse's gait rubbed his shirt against the burn, irritating it further. Dare didn't mind, though. Being out from under his parents was worth the pain.

And yet despite it all, his mother's words still wrapped around his heart like a vise.

You are dead to me. And don't you dare set one foot in this duchy again.

He had some idea of what she would do to him if he defied her banishment, and while he had no plans of ever going back, there was a vast difference between *won't* and *can't*.

Then there was the matter of Valda. Brookshire hadn't been Dare's home for a long time, but Valda had been, and now he couldn't go back there either. For the last decade, Dare had built a life for himself there, a life he was happy with. Then the Council, with Tanithe steering them, had threatened to destroy everything he'd worked for if he didn't do what they said. Tanithe had learned who he was and held that over him. If his name and his relation to Duke Wilhaven had gotten out in Valda, his work with the Crimson Brothers, his network of connections, everything he had worked so hard to build would have gone up in flames. So he had done what they asked of him. Every time. Every shitty job they sent him on. He'd done it all just to save his own ass.

But then he'd found Solace under the mountain in Westhold, and he'd known in that moment he was done following their orders, no matter what it cost him.

And it *had* cost him. It had cost all of them.

Dare's hand drifted to his chest, to the scar in the center that would always serve as a reminder of what they'd lost. And to the right of it, the Warden's brand blazed angrily, raw and blistered.

While one scar would remind him of what they'd lost, the other would remind him of what he'd gained.

"Dare!"

He startled and turned to find Verity studying him, her brow knit in concern. He got the impression that may not have been the first time she'd said his name. "Yeah?"

"Are you alright?"

He snorted a laugh. "That depends greatly on your definition, my lady Warden. But I'm alive, and I'm finally free of my family for good. So . . . yes. I'm alright."

She watched him sidelong, like she didn't quite believe him. "We've been riding for a bit," she said. "Let's take a break."

"I'm fine, Verity," he said. "We have some time we need to make up, as I understand it."

"We do," she said. "But you've been through hell. We can spare an hour to get you some food and a change of clothes. And we should put a bandage on the brand so it doesn't get infected." He opened his mouth to argue, but she cut him off. "Don't make me order you, Warden."

Dare's mouth twisted into a wry grin. "You're really going to enjoy this, aren't you?"

Verity whistled ahead to Jae, signaling for her to stop before she slowed her horse and moved to the edge of the road. "Oh, I *really* am."

Now that he had a moment to check, Dare discovered that the parcel Gregor gave him included some clothes, a warm wool cloak in a storm cloud gray, a loaf of bread, three apples, and a small roll of bandages with a tiny container of salve. Dare muttered a prayer to any gods who would listen to bless Gregor to the heavens and back.

Dare stripped out of his torn shirt and washed up before he applied the salve to the Warden's brand on his chest. The cooling ointment soothed the burn immediately, causing him to offer up another silent prayer.

"Let me help with that," Verity said as Dare started unrolling the bandages. "You need to cushion it first, otherwise it'll hurt like hell." She found a clean piece of cloth and folded it a few times to provide some padding.

"I'll yield to your Warden's expertise," he said, grateful for her aid.

Verity set the square of cloth over the brand. "Can we talk? About what happened in your parents' library the other night?" She took the bandages from Dare and moved his hand to hold the cloth in place.

The memory flooded back to him and, along with it, a vision of standing at the Black Gates with Drystan. "There's nothing to talk about," he said quietly.

She wrapped the bandages around his chest carefully, though not gently. Her metal fingers were not made for a healer's ministrations. He hid a wince as she worked.

"But I owe you an apology. I . . ." Her voice caught.

Dare set a hand over hers, pausing her work. "Verity, you have done more for me than almost anyone else I've ever known. I can't express what this"—he gestured to the open air around them—"means to me. You owe me *nothing*, my lady Warden. Certainly not an apology." His chest tightened, the scar from Solace's magic twinging. "But I . . ." He swallowed hard. "I owe you everything."

"You don't," she said, barely a whisper.

"Yes, I—"

"You *don't,*" she repeated, more forcefully this time. She resumed her work with the bandages, her honey brown eyes flicking down. "Drystan did what he thought was right. They were his choices to make. With me . . ." Her eyes met his for just a moment, and he stilled, barely breathing. "And with you. Drystan made those choices. Not you. What happened wasn't your fault, Dare." Her jaw clenched, and she finished tying off the bandage. "And it wasn't mine either."

✦

The group pressed on, Jaelyn leading the way until it grew too dark to follow whatever trail her friend Lucien left for her. When they stopped to make camp, Dare shared the food Gregor had packed for him.

Once the others were asleep, Dare circled the camp just outside the ring of firelight. The campfire flickered, logs snapping and sending tiny embers dancing into the clear night sky.

Verity had urged him to rest, to let the other three split the watches for the night, but he insisted. He needed something to do, something to focus on so he didn't focus so much on everything else.

Not that it helped.

Dare's movements were silent, precise, nothing more than whispers as he picked each step with care. It used to be what he was known for back in Valda. It was why certain people with certain types of jobs would seek him out.

But now . . .

"Darcy?"

He spun on his heels at the name he'd abandoned to find Jaelyn—the girl he'd abandoned—standing in the darkness. He hadn't heard her approach. Her dark skin seemed to soak up the night, and the firelight danced in her eyes and across her lips as she smiled at him. It wasn't a broad smile, but it was genuine. Gods, he hadn't realized how much he'd missed her smile.

"So, what should I call you now?" She arched one eyebrow. There was a small scar notched into it that hadn't been there when he'd seen her last.

"I'll answer to anything you want to call me," Dare said. He returned the smile, though hers faded.

"What about *lying son of a bitch*?"

Instinctively, the cool indifference began to creep over his face, but Dare let it fall away before it took hold. He wouldn't hide himself from her. Not anymore. "I didn't lie to you, Jaelyn."

"Jae," she corrected, then seemed to consider his words. "Fair," she conceded. "Then how about *coward*?"

The air flew out of Dare's lungs. *You can't be the hero when you run away like a coward.*

His father was right. Jae was right. He had been afraid. It had taken him years to build up the courage to leave, and the thought of having to face Jaelyn and tell her he was going had threatened to make him lose his nerve entirely. He hadn't thought he'd be able to look at her, into her beautiful deep brown eyes, and still walk away. And so he had simply run.

He had told Gregor he was leaving—he never could keep anything from Gregor—and that had been the hardest thing he'd ever done. He'd almost changed his mind as Gregor had hugged him and said goodbye. Dare had held on a little too long and was having trouble letting him go. His knapsack had lain at his feet, filled with some clothes, food, and what coin he'd been able to keep from his parents' watchful eyes. He'd been about to give up when Gregor had whispered in his ear to go. To run. He'd pulled himself out of Dare's embrace and placed a gentle kiss on his forehead, his eyes pleading for him to run.

And so Dare had left. He'd asked Gregor to get a message to Jaelyn, to say goodbye for him, but then he'd left. Like a coward.

"You're right," he said when he could find his breath again. "Can we talk?"

She set her hands on her hips. "You're supposed to be keeping watch."

"I am," he said. He held out a hand to her, a gesture he'd done hundreds of times. "Walk with me?"

She studied him, the open hand extended toward her, palm up, fingers gently curled, an invitation, a lifeline—for him at least, if not for her. She nodded, then strode past him, her arm brushing his outstretched hand.

Dare ran his fingers through his hair, letting out a long breath before he followed. Jae walked alongside him, her footfalls as silent as his own. She'd changed. Vire's demons, she'd changed. The swords with their grips worn from use, the hardness of her stare . . . Even her hair was different, all short, tight curls instead of long, neat braids. But the fire in her, the spirit . . . that had always been there.

It was why he'd loved her.

Dare let the silence sit between them. He knew what he wanted to say, but he couldn't find the words, so he soaked in that feeling of closeness, of being physically near her, for as long as he could.

"I thought you wanted to *talk*," she said after a while.

"I do," he said, sliding his hands into his pockets to keep himself from reaching for her hand again. The scent of jasmine and sage floated to him as he inhaled.

Some things had remained the same after all. His mind drifted back to secret meetings in darkened city streets, when he would wrap his arms around her and whisk her off to some hidden spot where they could be together. Where he would be surrounded by the scent of jasmine and sage.

"Do you still live in Brookshire?" It was an admittedly pathetic attempt to start a conversation, but he needed to buy himself more time to gather his wandering thoughts.

Jae snorted a laugh. "No, no, I left about a year after you did." She looked up at the night sky through the trees. "Right after you left, I decided I would go too. At first I thought I was leaving to find you. But as I started to save up some coin, and as the months went by, I realized that I just wanted to get out. But it took you leaving for me to see it. I was so happy for you when you left. And proud of you."

His heart twinged at her words.

"I was so proud of you that you finally got out of there. But Vire's fucking hells, Darcy, I was mad at you too. I cursed at you every day for months."

The corner of his mouth curved into a smile. "What made you stop?"

"Gregor. It took a while because I was so pissed off, but he reminded me that it was what we wanted, what he and I had been pushing you toward for so long." She cast a sidelong glance at him as she stepped over a fallen branch. "He can be very persistent."

"Yeah," Dare said with a quiet chuckle. "Yeah, he certainly can be."

To his surprise, Jae laughed with him, and the sound was like hearing music for the first time, not realizing what he'd been missing in the silence.

"Do you remember what I used to tell you?" she asked. "Before you left?"

The question threw him off. He hadn't expected her to remember. It had always seemed like such a small thing for her, but for him . . . for him it had meant everything. It had meant *hope*.

"I do." A flush of warmth flooded his cheeks. "You used to tell me that I could be anything I dared to be."

"I didn't mean for you to take me so literally, *Dare*," she teased, elbowing him in the ribs.

This, he thought. *Lanara's tears, I've missed this.* He drew a breath and dragged his fingers through his hair again. *I've missed* her.

"I would've gone with you, you know. If you'd asked."

"I know," he admitted.

"Why didn't you?"

That was a question he'd spent many nights asking himself. "Because I thought you deserved better."

Jae stopped walking and studied him, her face going tight. "Whether I do or not, I think I should be the one who gets to make that decision, don't you?"

"I know," he said again.

"Darcy, you didn't say goodbye."

Dare held her gaze. He wouldn't run away again. "There are very few choices I've made in my life that I regret." When her brows rose in silent skepticism, he clarified, "I've made plenty of mistakes, and there have been plenty of things that I wish had gone differently, but there isn't much I truly regret. But leaving without telling you, without saying goodbye . . . without asking you to come with me . . . I think that's my biggest regret. Jaelyn . . ." He took a step closer. "*Jae*—I'm sorry."

"Now that," she said, her mouth twisting, "is something I never thought I'd hear."

He gave up on his restraint, hesitating for only a moment before he took her hand, wrapping his fingers around hers. The pads of her fingers were rough with calluses where there hadn't been any before.

Dare expected her to pull away, and when she didn't, he drew her hand to his lips. He brushed a soft kiss against the back of her hand, as he had done a hundred times. A thousand.

But that had been a lifetime ago.

"I'm sorry, Jae" he said again.

Dare held his breath as she leaned forward and set a gentle kiss on his cheek.

"You'd better not do it again," she said. It was equal parts promise and threat.

He nodded once. "I won't. And thank you. For helping get me out . . ." He couldn't stop the shadow of a smirk from flickering across his lips. "Again."

"Don't think for a moment the irony is lost on me."

He was sure he saw an answering smile tug at the corner of her mouth. Withdrawing her hand from his, Jae strode back toward the camp. "It's still your watch for another hour," she said over her shoulder.

Dare's hand was poised as though he still held hers, the scent of jasmine and sage surrounding him even as she walked away.

You're an idiot, he told himself.

He couldn't find a good reason to argue.

CHAPTER 52

GREGOR BUSIED HIMSELF WITH his duties, though the ache in his heart proved quite distracting. It had been a day—only a single day—since Darcy left with the Warden, and yet it felt as though an age had passed.

When Darcy had left the first time and the years ticked by, Gregor had doubted he would ever see him again. But then he had returned, briefly and brilliantly, only to disappear once more, this time for good, if the duchess's words were to be believed.

Gregor didn't doubt her resolve for a moment.

"Excuse me, Secretary," one of the house staff called. Gregor was thankful for the interruption. "Your presence is requested by His Grace in his study, to attend upon him and his guest."

Gregor frowned. "Guest? His Grace doesn't have any appointments today."

The servant wrung his hands, shrugging helplessly. "She said she had an appointment this morning, and when I confirmed with His Grace, he quite swiftly had me escort her to his study. And he requested your presence immediately."

The servant gave a quick bow and darted off as Gregor headed toward Duke Wilhaven's study. It wasn't so unusual to be summoned while he held a private meeting. As house secretary, Gregor was sometimes brought in to take notes or, rarely, to answer a question about something under his purview. It was more troubling that he'd somehow missed the appointment on the duke's agenda. But then he had been quite distracted these last few days.

When Gregor entered the study, Duke Wilhaven was pacing behind his desk. The duchess perched on the arm of her husband's chair, motionless save for her savage eyes, which tracked Gregor's movements. She had never liked him and often gifted him with withering glares when no one else was looking. As she watched him, one gloved hand absently rubbed at the other. Where her periapt used to sit.

The visitor reclined in the chair as though she owned it, slender legs crossed. Her flame-red hair fell loose about her narrow, black leather-clad shoulders. She, too, watched Gregor enter, though she studied him as one might a mouse or an insect.

Gregor gave the woman a polite nod and stood with his hands clasped loosely behind his back. "You asked to see me, Your Grace?"

Duke Wilhaven motioned for Gregor to sit in the chair beside the woman. Gregor obliged. No one spoke, though they all stared at Gregor—the stranger with curiosity, the duke with disinterest, and the duchess with malice.

The silence grew increasingly awkward. Just as Gregor was about to break protocol and ask what was going on, the woman scoffed. "This is him?"

His Grace nodded.

"Really?" She gave Gregor an appraising look halfway between amusement and disgust. "*This* is the object of your son's affection?"

Gregor shifted uncomfortably and pushed his glasses up the bridge of his nose with his thumb as the duke nodded again.

"Unfortunately yes. Ever since they were children." The disdain was plain on his face.

"Um, excuse me, Your Grace," Gregor said, smoothing the front of his suit coat. It was all he could do to maintain some semblance of propriety. "What is this about?"

His question was met with a startling cackle of laughter as the woman stood with languid grace and moved the short distance to Gregor. Her arm moved almost faster than he could register. A sharp blossom of pain radiated from his cheek before he could even flinch, and a *crack* echoed through his head, though he wasn't sure if it was from his cheekbone or just his glasses breaking. The blow nearly toppled him from the chair, his vision replaced with a hazy field of gray. As he reeled from the strike, vision still clouded, he was vaguely aware of the woman hauling him to his feet.

"Did you think we wouldn't figure it out?" the duke demanded. "Did you think I wouldn't realize you were helping the Warden?"

"Your Grace—" Gregor started. His vision cleared in time to see the duke glowering at him and a delicate smile curving the duchess's lips.

"You should know well enough by now," the duchess said coolly. "Loyalty is rewarded in our household. And disloyalty is punished most severely."

"Pleasure doing business with you," the woman cooed toward Duke Wilhaven, her fingers digging into Gregor's arm hard enough to bruise.

"Your Grace, *please!*"

A swirl of black enveloped him, and it was as though the world existed only as shadows that rippled past at breathtaking speed. He caught strange, haunting glimpses of the city flashing by, then the river crossings.

When the rushing stopped and the world returned to normal, Gregor's stomach lurched with the suddenness of it. They were outside, well beyond the walls of Brookshire by the look of it, standing in the shadow of a large tree. Still holding his arm in a tight grip, the woman pulled a dagger with her other hand and pressed the blade against the soft flesh under his chin.

Gregor didn't dare move and found himself staring into her piercing blue eyes. He couldn't breathe, couldn't think. His face throbbed from where she'd struck him.

"Who are you?" he managed. When he spoke, the point of the blade pressed a little harder against him. He tried not to think about how little pressure it would take for her to pierce his skin with that dagger.

"Forgive me, I've been so rude. You may call me Tanithe."

Gregor's mind raced, trying to find some pieces of the puzzle in the hopes of putting *something* together. She mentioned Darcy in the study. Could she be trying to use Gregor to find Darcy? If so, it had to have something to do with what he and the Warden had discussed with the duke, the divine weapon that could destroy the continent. It was the only explanation.

"What do you want with him?" he asked, trying and failing to keep the fear out of his voice.

"Oh, you are the clever one, aren't you," she purred. "I'm going to use you to barter. Or for bait. Whichever works in the moment."

Gregor swallowed. "Whatever you want, he won't trade it to you," he said, unwilling to let on exactly how much he knew.

Tanithe tilted her head back and laughed. "You severely underestimate your influence here."

She released his arm long enough to slide her long fingers up to the back of his head. She fisted his hair and gave it a sharp yank, exposing his throat to her. The dagger traced gentle lines along the sides of his neck.

"You think he won't do *anything* for you, Gregor Thalesen? For his childhood best friend, his lover, who he just reconnected with after so many long years apart?" She tightened her grip on his hair and pulled his head toward her. A drip of warm blood trailed down his neck, the dagger grazing him as her lips brushed his ear. The sickly-sweet scent of honeysuckle surrounded him, but there was something else beneath it. Something harsh and acrid, almost metallic. "Oh, buttercup, for you, he would burn down the world."

Chapter 53

Dare wasn't about to give up on helping Solace. Solace hadn't given up on him. They had to make up the lead Corvin had on them. For two days, they traveled as far as they could each day, stopping only once it got too dark to move safely and starting out again in the early light before dawn.

Dare's mind was a jumble of distracted thoughts as they followed Lucien's signs due west, despite the northward curve of the mountains. Solace had fallen into Westhold's hands because Dare had been too arrogant. Too proud. Regardless of Verity's insistence that they travel through Brookshire, Dare had thought he could slip through undetected. He hadn't thought he'd get caught, so he hadn't fully warned Verity of the risks, and Solace had paid the price.

They crested a small hill to find a forest of thick-trunked trees obscuring the horizon, the setting sun making the leaves glisten red as though they were wet with blood.

"We should stop for the night at the tree line," Jae said. "That's not somewhere we want to be caught after dark."

Dare eyed the trees again, their crimson leaves stretching for miles to the north and south. It wasn't just a trick of the light. "This is the Red Forest, isn't it?" he asked.

"Yes," Jae said. Her horse whinnied and stamped its front hooves as she checked that her swords were secured.

Even in Valda, people knew of the Red Forest and the threats that reportedly lay within. Most people in the city considered it little more than a folktale, but it was supposedly one of the places where the savage, monstrous shifters staked their claim, answering to no king or government and killing anyone who dared enter their domain.

Dare trotted his horse to stop alongside her. It was still strange to see Jae so heavily armed, and yet he couldn't help the swell of pride and the curiosity at what she would look like—how she would move—when she wielded those twin swords. He hoped, somewhat grimly, that he might get to see it one day. From a safe distance. So long as he wasn't her target.

Finn rode up on Jae's other side. "Are the stories true? That it's a forest of nightmares?"

"No," Jae said. "It's much worse."

"Have you been there before?" Finn asked.

"No, but I . . . know someone who has."

Finn stared at the forest looming in the distance. "Did they survive?"

Jae's voice was quiet, somber. "In a manner." She checked her swords again.

Dare suppressed a shudder.

"And you're certain Lucien's trail heads through it?" Verity asked. "There's no chance they could have gone around?"

"I'll know for sure when we get to the trees," Jae said, looking off into the distance, as though she might spot her friend on one of the sloping hills. "He'll leave a sign there to say which way he went. But the forest runs for miles. If Crosse is in a rush, going through is the fastest route."

"I'd heard the shifters were mobilizing," Verity said. "Up north in the Wilds. The Wardens were sending teams to help the villages along the border. Have you heard if it's happening here too?"

"Mobilizing?" Dare rubbed his hand along the back of his neck. "Now *that's* a thought. They're scarcely more than animals."

Jae glared at him. "We'd heard the same thing about the Wilds," she said to Verity. "Lucien and I were on our way to investigate the situation there when we were"—a muscle ticked in her jaw—"redirected to Brookshire."

As much as she'd changed, Dare still knew all her tells. There was something she wasn't saying.

"Alright." Verity looked to the three of them. "Jae, we'll follow your lead."

As Jae suggested, they made their camp for the night at the very edge of the Red Forest. She assured them the shifters were incredibly territorial and wouldn't have a problem with them sleeping within ten feet of their forest, but as soon as they set foot inside, all bets were off.

Dare lay near the dying embers of their small campfire. It was getting too cold at night to go without, but they kept the fire low to avoid giving away their position now that they were gaining ground. The four of them took to sleeping near each other for the extra warmth.

After Dare had woken Jae for her watch, a dull throbbing in his temples and at the base of his skull kept him awake. So he lay still, pretending to sleep so Jae wouldn't feel obligated to talk to him, and watched the night sky slowly lighten in the east.

Get up.

A rush of air blew through the camp, accompanied by branches snapping in the trees. Dare pushed himself up almost as fast as Jae was on her feet, though the ground felt unsteady beneath him, like his sense of balance was off kilter. He watched the trees to the west as he nudged Finn awake. At the same time, Jae stretched out her hand to rouse Verity.

"Something's here," Jae whispered. She drew one of her swords.

Dare crouched low and slid a dagger out of the sheath tucked under his blanket—one of several well-balanced blades that Finn had picked up for him before his rescue. He stalked toward the tree line, every muscle in his body tensed and ready.

Reality warped around him, though no one else seemed to notice.

"No need for blades," a female voice called out, low and sultry as it danced through the leaves. "I've come to strike a deal."

Dare's blood froze in his veins as a shadow moved and shifted at the edge of the trees, coalescing into human form. Tanithe Ash stepped forward into the ring of flickering firelight, scarcely more than a few feet from Dare and Jae. The shadows of the trees reached after her as though they wanted to keep her with them, holding her close. She was clad all in black leathers clinging to her curves, and Dare marked the hilts of at least six blades on her. Wisps of red hair poked out from beneath a black hood and her eyes, blazing with exhilaration, were locked on his.

Dare straightened, masking his dizziness. "What is it that you want, Tanithe?" He let boredom drip from his voice, though he remained balanced on the balls of his feet, ready to move. He lowered his blade, even as his fingers tightened their grip on the hilt.

Tanithe's lips parted in a sinful smile. "Oh, my dear," she purred. "I've come to collect what's mine."

"And what exactly do you think we have of yours?" Verity demanded. She had stepped forward, flanking Dare on his left, opposite Jae.

"The weapon, of course."

Jae growled, "Fuck you."

Tanithe smiled, as if noticing Jae for the first time. "Why hello, little lamb," she cooed.

Dare had to stop himself from stepping in front of Jae. Aside from the fact that Tanithe would find it far too amusing, Jae was just as likely to stab him for a move like that.

"You're a long way from where you're supposed to be." Tanithe looked over the campsite. "Where's your guard dog?"

"What makes you think I need one?" Jae snapped.

Tanithe ignored her, returning her attention to Dare. The hunger in her eyes made something inside him writhe. "Come now, love. A deal's a deal."

He huffed a disinterested laugh. "Please! That was your *demand*. The terms of your little game. I never agreed to shit."

Tanithe's smile grew unnaturally wide. "Then I guess it's lucky for me that I came with some new terms." She reached into the shadows behind her. A wave of dizziness rushed through Dare as they stretched toward her hand, caressing her arm, beckoning her back into their inky darkness. But she wrapped her hand around one of the shadows and, with another wobble of reality, pulled it forward until it took the shape of a person. "How about a trade?"

As the last tendrils of shadow floated away, the figure stood with his hands bound behind his back and a cloth hood over his head, covering his face. The man's white shirt was stained and half untucked from his dark trousers.

Tanithe gripped her captive by the elbow and tugged him roughly forward, displaying him to the group. When she yanked the hood from his head, Gregor's glasses fell into the grass. His blond hair, always so neat, was mussed and disheveled, and a black cloth was tied tightly around his mouth, clenched between his teeth. Even in the dim light, a bloom of purple colored his cheek.

Dare's heart clenched. It was hard to breathe.

Jae's whole body tensed, preparing to strike. "Don't you fucking touch him."

Dare shifted his hand, signaling for her to wait, just as Tanithe slithered a little behind Gregor, blocking her body with his.

"Oh, you too?" Tanithe said to Jae. The glint of a blade appeared at Gregor's throat, and he stiffened with the pressure of the point against his skin. "What do they see in you?" she murmured into his ear.

"We don't have the weapon," Dare said, his voice measured and even. He couldn't give away how important her captive was to them. To him. Even as Gregor's eyes were locked on his, wide and pleading—terrified. Even as blood welled under the point of Tanithe's dagger, beginning a slow trickle down Gregor's neck.

He needed to make her think he didn't care.

This is a dangerous game.

Dare took the gamble. "I'm afraid Corvin Crosse has it in his possession."

Verity stiffened.

"Corvin Crosse!" Tanithe erupted into cackling laughter. "That fucking sack of Ainam's distilled shit managed to get the weapon?"

"You know about Crosse?" Verity asked.

Tanithe rolled her eyes. "Of course. He's been a pain in my ass ever since he stuck his tongue up Ainam's."

Another stomach-churning pulse of vertigo pulled Dare down and in, but he forced himself to remain steady. The air was heavy, like no matter how much he tried, his lungs couldn't expand enough to get a full breath, like when he'd nearly run into Crosse in the Reach.

Wait . . . Crosse!

But where the stifling *wrongness* of Corvin Crosse had been sharp and angled, Tanithe's was spiraling and warping. And yet . . .

Yes.

"You're like him," Dare blurted out. "But you're not blessed by Ainam, are you?"

Tanithe laughed again, long and low, as though amused by a small child. "Oh, sweetheart," she drawled. "Are you just piecing that together now? How precious." The shadows behind her beckoned, lapping at her shoulders and at Gregor's arms.

Dare ignored her comment, just as he tried to ignore the tendrils grasping at Gregor. "Look, Crosse has the weapon and is taking it back to Westhold." He waved vaguely toward the expanse of forest behind Tanithe. "If you hurry, you can probably catch him."

She wrenched Gregor's arm behind his back, forcing out a muffled groan. Dare flinched, his heart splintering in his chest. Gregor's pain was his pain. Whatever she did to him, Dare would pay it back a hundredfold.

"Why don't you leave him here," he continued, forcing himself to focus. "He's a liability. Wouldn't you rather he slow us down instead of you?"

Tanithe clicked her tongue before drawing it across her parted lips. "Look at you, trying to be clever." She leaned in close to Gregor, her chin resting on his shoulder. "You won't slow me down, will you?" Her dagger traced a line down Gregor's cheek like a gentle caress, and his eyes pinched shut. She gave Dare another wicked smile. "And since you couldn't deliver, consider the offer expired."

No! Instinct overtook him. Dare lunged forward. Tanithe took one step into the trees, letting the shadows swallow her in a swirl of darkness as the whole world seemed to tilt and warp. Dare stumbled. An arrow flew over his shoulder, into the shadows as Tanithe disappeared. The hand on Gregor's arm yanked him back, a shout tearing past the cloth in his mouth. Dare stretched out his hand as he moved, but the shadows grasped at Gregor, pouring over him, spiraling over his shoulders.

Dare landed where Gregor had been standing, Jae and Verity still on either side. He had moved and they had moved with him, but it hadn't been enough. Dare stared into the shadows of the trees, now nothing more than darkened shades of gray in the pre-dawn light. Beneath his feet, the ground was steady.

They were gone.

He was gone.

Jae's voice trembled as she said, "We'll get him back."

Dare held onto the calm facade, the illusion of not caring what happened to Gregor, whether he lived or died by Tanithe's hand. Maybe if he gripped that mask tightly enough, he could will it to be true just long enough to get him back.

But all he could think about was the look of terror on Gregor's face as Tanithe held a blade to his throat. This wasn't his fight, and yet she had dragged him into it to get to Dare, to hurt him so she could get what she wanted.

It's my fault Gregor's in danger.

He dropped to his knees as the realization struck him, his resolve shattering into a hundred thousand shards. It was his fault. Gregor had been safe in Brookshire until Dare had shown up. He knelt in the grass, shaking. It was his fault. If she hurt Gregor—if she killed him—Dare would have no one to blame but himself.

Strong arms gripped his shoulders and pulled him into an embrace, warm and safe.

"Darcy," Jae whispered over the top of his head, her cheek resting against his hair as she held him close. "Dare . . ."

It was the first time she had called him that in earnest, and it settled something in him. His shoulders steadied despite his ragged, shuddering breaths.

"We will get him back," Jae said. She gently pushed him away, holding him at arms' length.

His hands lay in his lap, open and useless. He wasn't sure when he'd dropped the dagger. Why hadn't he used it? Could he have thrown it and struck her faster than she could have slit Gregor's throat?

Calloused hands cupped his cheeks, lifting his gaze until it fell on Jae. She held him there, and he was unable to look anywhere other than her face.

Growing up in and around Wilhaven Manor, he and Gregor and Jae had been inseparable, but she and Gregor had always been the best of friends. Looking at her now, Dare knew that her pain at losing him rivaled his own.

"I know you're worried about him, and it's clawing at you that he's in trouble. And I know that you think it's your fault," Jae said. "But you can't let the guilt drown you. I need you to take that pain and fear and *use* it."

Determination rose in him like the tide.

"We *will* get him back," she said again. "And we will make her pay for hurting him."

Before another thought could enter his mind, he threw his arms around Jae, pulling her into his chest, and her arms tightened around him. Something raw and molten solidified within him, like a newly forged blade tempered by being doused in water. If he fell apart now, if he broke, he wouldn't be able to help Gregor. Or Solace.

Jae rocked back on her heels and rose, bringing Dare with her.

Finn approached slowly, her bow slung over her shoulder. "Who the hells was that?"

"Her name is Tanithe Ash," Dare said, only a slight tremor in his voice. "She's the spymaster for the Valdane Council and, apparently, the Chosen of Vire."

Verity joined them, arms crossed over her chest, practically vibrating with tension. Dare could read the unspoken questions in that tension, in the doubt in her eyes as she studied them. Tanithe knew Dare and Jae both. A little too well. And Verity needed to know why.

Dare had his own questions for Jae about that point, but . . .

"This just got more complicated, didn't it?" Finn remarked, glancing toward Verity.

"The plan hasn't changed," Dare said. "We still have to catch up to Crosse and get Solace back."

"Except now we have a second Chosen to deal with," Finn said. "Or what if she gets there first? She just *disappeared* . . . what if she just reappears next to Crosse and disappears again with Solace?"

The Warden sighed. "Regardless, Dare's right. The plan hasn't changed." She stooped in the underbrush at the edge of the tree line and came back up with something cupped in her hand. She held it out to Dare.

His stomach lurched. Bile rose into his throat.

Gregor's glasses.

"We can't worry about all of the things that could be," Verity said.

With a steady hand, Dare took the glasses. The wire frames were bent on one side, and one of the lenses was cracked. He closed his fingers around them.

"We have a path to Crosse," Verity continued, "and as far as we know right now, he still has Solace. We have to continue with the expectation that hasn't changed."

"And if Tanithe's going after them," Jae added, "then we know where Gregor will be."

Dare slipped the glasses into an inner pocket of his shirt before crouching to pick up Jae's sword. "We need to move," he said. He held the sword out to her, hilt first. "Thank you," he added quietly.

"We'll get him back," she said again, softer this time, but no less fierce.

Dare met her intensity with his own. "Yes. We will."

CHAPTER 54

FOR YOU, HE WOULD burn down the world.

The words echoed in Gregor's mind as Tanithe dragged him from shadow to shadow. He held onto the image of Darcy's face, the calm, almost bored demeanor as he'd bantered with Tanithe. That was his skill. Gregor had seen it many times when they were children. Don't let on what you're thinking. Don't give away what really matters. But watching him in action now, after years—when both of their lives depended on it—it was like watching a master painter at work. Only the details he wanted shone through.

Gregor wished he could have told Darcy he loved him.

The cloth was tight between his teeth, and the ropes cut into his wrists. The rising sun illuminated the forest, and between the jarring starts and stops of Tanithe's magic, the blood-red leaves overhead told Gregor everything he needed to know about where they were. The Red Forest.

A chill ran through him. Anyone who entered the forest was promised death by the shifters—or at least, by the ones who still retained the power of human speech. Some had reverted too far into their bestial natures to maintain that level of thought, but then again, those shifters would kill anyone they came across regardless.

Gregor tried to track their location, but the world around them seemed to move at a different speed than their bodies, and the dissonance between the two made his head swim and twisted his stomach over itself. It almost made him wish for the darkness of the hood.

Every time they stopped, they were moving again before he could focus on his surroundings, speeding through the lifeless, colorless world. A few stops later, a wicked smile danced across Tanithe's lips as she whispered, "There you are."

Gregor turned to look, but his stomach lurched as they were moving again. After a few more stops, a wild howl tore through the silence. Then another. Shadows, howling, shadows, roars, shadows, Tanithe's throaty laugh.

The next time they stopped, they stayed put. Tanithe dropped into a low crouch, throwing Gregor to the ground at the base of a broad-trunked tree. She inhaled deeply. Then again.

She's catching her breath. Her strange power had limits.

"And now we wait to see what comes out to play," she muttered, her lilting voice dancing with the words like they were a children's rhyme.

Long minutes passed before a feral howl sounded through the trees. It was close. Even closer, men shouted in alarm.

Tanithe's eyes swirled with darkness. "Be a good little boy and wait here," she said, walking her fingers up Gregor's chest. "Or else the monsters are going to come and eat you all up." Her shadows swirled around her again, and she was gone.

Gregor leaned his shoulder against the tree. Growls and roars followed by cries tore through the forest. He whirled around, but without his glasses, he couldn't make out anything that was more than a few feet away. Dark, monstrous shapes stalked through the trees, and the smaller shapes of men fell beneath them.

His heartbeat pounded in his ears. The rough fibers of the rope binding his wrists cut deeper into his skin the more he tried to twist out of them. He could try to run, but how far would he get before Tanithe caught him again? Or one of the shifters did?

Gregor wasn't sure which thought scared him more.

A woman's shout pierced his awareness. Tanithe. "Fuck off, you mangy—"

Another roar of primal rage followed. If one of the creatures had Tanithe, now was his chance to escape. Gregor pushed off the tree with his shoulder, though his knees were shaking, and turned to run.

And stopped dead.

Dark fur and a snarling maw filled his field of vision as Gregor came face to face with the bestial form of a shifter.

Gregor staggered back and fell against the tree. He could barely shout with the cloth tight between his teeth. Not that it would matter. Who would hear him?

The shifter stalked forward on all fours, its hot breath washing over Gregor's face. It stood nearly as tall as Gregor at the shoulder—the perfect height to rip his throat out without even needing to stretch for it. Fangs as long as his fingers glistened in the beast's mouth. It inched closer to Gregor, who pressed harder against the tree. But he had nowhere to go.

In his mind, Gregor conjured an image of Darcy. If these were to be his last moments, he would not waste them on fear. He would think of Darcy and find the strength to face his end.

The creature sniffed him, snarling as its ears flattened against the deep gray fur of its head. The fur parted beneath its ear, revealing a scar curving down the side of the creature's face. Drawing a shaky breath, Gregor stared into its yellow eyes.

The monster took a single step back on massive paws, lowering its head. The fur began to slough off as its body shrank. Muscle seemed to melt away, revealing clothes. Dark hair fell to human shoulders, broad and muscular. The man before him straightened with a series of truly horrifying snaps and pops.

Were it not for the same yellow eyes and the scar running from temple to jaw along the man's face, Gregor wouldn't have believed he was the monster that had been standing before him a moment ago.

The shifter held up his hands, palms open. "I'm not going to hurt you," he said. He moved slowly, reaching toward Gregor, and pulled the gag out from between his teeth. "I'm here to help, alright?"

"Thank you," Gregor choked out, his lips cracking as he spoke. "You . . . you're . . ." His brain was having trouble forming words. He licked his lips, tasting copper.

"A shifter," the man said. He drew a serrated blade from his boot and pulled Gregor away from the tree, turning him around. The shifter began sawing through the rope binding his wrists.

"Do you have a name?" Gregor managed.

The shifter snorted. "Lucien," he said as the ropes fell away.

The snarls continued through the trees, but they'd grown more distant. The screaming had stopped, though Gregor could make out two human voices shouting in the distance, punctuated with what sounded like an explosion or a tree crashing to the ground.

"What's happening?" he asked with a groan, flexing his fingers slowly. His wrists were raw and bleeding.

The shifter gestured for him to follow. "Distraction," he said. "One she didn't think through." He sniffed the air and hooked left. "I have friends who should be somewhere nearby. I'll take you to them. But I need to find someone first." Lucien sniffed again and turned right.

Gregor followed—what choice did he have?—until the shifter held up a hand.

"Wait."

Something moved in the trees ahead. Lucien charged forward.

There was a blur of motion and startled shouts. Gregor took an instinctive step back as the sounds of a fight broke out. A pained grunt preceded a strangled scream. It broke off in the middle as something heavy hit the ground. Another short scuffle later, and a second body followed the first.

The shifter reemerged, growling something under his breath. Blood ran freely down his arm as he dragged an unconscious form out of the underbrush.

"A-Are you alright?" Gregor asked, watching as the blood dripped from Lucien's fingers.

The shifter's focus was on the man he'd found as he said, "It's fine." He crouched, checking the man over for injuries.

"But, your arm . . ." He trailed off as the gash across the shifter's forearm slowly knit together. "How . . . ?"

Lucien spared the briefest glance at the healing wound. "Shifters are hard to kill," he muttered before returning his attention to the man on the ground. "Believe me." He tapped the man's face a few times to try to rouse him, but he didn't stir.

Another roar sounded, a little closer than the last few. Lucien's head swiveled. "Shit." His yellow eyes settled on Gregor as he stood. "I'm going to need your help."

Gregor hesitated. He had no idea what was happening, but certainly this shifter could have killed him a dozen times already if he wanted to.

When he didn't answer right away, Lucien said, "What's your name?"

"Gregor."

The shifter cocked his head, one brow arching. "Gregor?" he repeated. "Jae's Gregor?"

His mind jerked like a wagon wheel catching on a stone. "You know Jaelyn?"

Lucien huffed something that might have been a laugh. "Yeah," he said gruffly. "I'm a friend of hers."

Nearby, a howl keened. Lucien jerked his head up, listening to the long, low tone. "Gregor, I need your help, and I'm going to need you to trust me, alright?"

He was a friend of Jaelyn's. He was a friend. "W-What do you need me to do?"

"I'm going to change," Lucien said. "Then I need you to help get him on my back and keep him there." A crash sounded in the trees behind them. "Can you do that?"

"*Change*?" Gregor asked. "You mean—"

It was too late.

It all happened in the space of a few seconds. Lucien's feet rooted to the ground, and it sounded as though all of his joints popped as muscle and sinew stretched and expanded. A guttural growl came through clenched teeth that sharpened as his mouth elongated into a lupine snout. He doubled over, setting his hands on the ground as claws, front and back, raked into the earth. Charcoal gray fur overtook his clothing, which melded into his new, monstrous form. Yellow eyes fixed on Gregor.

Gregor's knees shook, nearly dropping him into the underbrush, and he forgot how to breathe as some primal fear flooded through him. He tried to focus on what the shifter had said. He was a friend of Jaelyn's. If she trusted him, then Gregor could as well.

His resolve steadied his legs, his fear receding into the background of his thoughts as a new thought emerged at the fore. *If he's a friend of Jaelyn's,* Gregor considered, *that means she and Darcy and the Warden are somewhere nearby.*

He forced himself to draw a breath as Lucien angled toward where the man lay and flattened himself against the ground. He snorted impatiently at Gregor, who hadn't moved.

Gregor blinked and shook his head. He could do this. He stepped toward Lucien, hesitating as he walked around his muzzle. Lucien laid his chin on the ground as though saying, *See, I'm not going to eat you.*

Even with Lucien lying flat, Gregor struggled to heft the unconscious man onto Lucien's back. The man was larger than Gregor and solidly built, but Lucien shifted his weight to help where he could until finally the man was draped across the shifter's shoulders like a sack of flour.

"Now what?" Gregor asked.

Lucien angled his head toward his back.

"You're going to carry us both?"

The beast nodded.

Gregor lightly touched the gray fur, sending a shudder across the muscles of Lucien's back, like the beast was looking to shake off a fly. Gregor flinched, pulling his hand back, but Lucien snorted and gave another heavy nod.

He had to do this. He needed to get out of this forest. He needed to see Darcy again. Gregor gripped Lucien's fur tightly and pulled himself up. He leaned forward over the other man's body to hold him steady.

There was another series of howls behind them and another crash of trees. Lucien stamped one massive paw against the ground in a gesture Gregor imagined meant *hold on.*

He grabbed two fistfuls of Lucien's fur at the nape of his neck. "I'm ready," he said, his voice shaking. Then the shifter took off running.

The trees blurred past, but not in the disjointed way they had with Tanithe's shadows. There was a grace to the way the beast moved. It was remarkable that as fast as Lucien darted between the trees, Gregor barely felt the movement of his powerful legs carrying them toward safety.

Toward Jaelyn and Darcy. Toward his best friend and the man he loved.

Gregor tried not to think about it too much. Instead, he focused on keeping the stranger steady on Lucien's shoulders. He was afraid to hope that the danger had passed, that he might yet see Darcy again.

After a short time, Lucien let out a yip, like he was trying to get Gregor's attention.

"What is it?" he asked. As he lifted his head, his stomach dropped. Gregor could just make out a handful of dark shapes picking slowly through the trees ahead. But Lucien continued running toward the shapes, making no more effort to avoid them than perhaps giving them a wide berth.

Gregor squinted, trying to force his vision to focus at such a distance. Four horses. That was all he could make out. And if Lucien wasn't diverting around, he could guess who it would be.

He could *hope*.

A shout rose up from ahead. "Keep the horses back!" Jaelyn called. "Turn around!"

Lucien swung wide as he closed the distance and blew past the four travelers, much faster and more nimble through the dense woods than the horses. As they passed, Gregor heard the elegant blaspheming that only Darcy could accomplish. "What in Taerna's stone tits—"

"Follow him, you idiot," Jaelyn snapped.

Gregor's heart squeezed.

Once they broke through the tree line and into the open plains beyond, Lucien turned southeast, putting more distance between them and the Red Forest. Gregor wondered how long he would run before letting the others catch up.

The sun was overhead when another forest came into view, though this one had verdant green leaves rather than the foreboding crimson of the Red Forest. Lucien was at the edge of the trees before he finally trotted to a stop. Looking back, Gregor couldn't see anyone following. He hoped it was only that they hadn't caught up yet . . .

Gregor's legs and back ached from the ride as Lucien crouched and let him slide down. Once they had the man, still unconscious, on the ground as well, Lucien stood and shifted to his human form. Gregor turned his back, doing his best to ignore the sound of cracking bones and popping joints that accompanied the change.

The deep, distinctly human voice grumbled from behind him, "Here." He turned to find Lucien holding a water skin in his outstretched hand. Gregor took it gratefully and drank a long swallow.

Now that he had a moment to stop and breathe and *think*, his mind reeled, and the ache in his muscles settled into a bone-deep weariness. It was just past midday now. Tanithe had taken him in the early morning, but that was yesterday. He'd gone more than a day without sleep or food or water, save what Lucien had just given him. But it was over. The danger had passed . . .

The world seemed to sway beneath his feet.

"Ah," Lucien said as Gregor handed him back the water skin. He was looking the way they'd come, toward the crest of the low hill in the distance. Gregor spun, but couldn't see anything but a swath of pale green below bright blue.

"What?" Gregor asked, unable to keep the hope from his voice. "What is it?"

Lucien's broad hand clapped onto his shoulder. "Our friends."

Friends.

Jae. Darcy. He was safe.

The horses thundered toward them, slowing as they neared the tree line. Darcy reached him first, leaping from his horse before it had even fully stopped.

Safe.

Gregor's legs buckled. He landed on his knees in the grass, and Darcy was there, on his knees too, gripping Gregor firmly by the shoulders. He slid his hands down Gregor's arms.

"I'm alright," Gregor breathed, speaking as much to himself as he was to Darcy, though he inhaled sharply through his teeth as Darcy's hands found the wounds on his wrists.

"We'll patch you up," Darcy said, his voice tight. "We'll patch you up and get you back home, alright?" He took Gregor's face in his hands and drew him closer, setting his forehead against his. The motions were quick, almost frantic. "I'm sorry, Gregor. Gods above, I'm so sorry I got you into this. I'm sorry. Gods, I'm sorry."

Gregor shook his head. "No," he said. "I can't go back. They gave me to her." The words were coming harder than he anticipated. He set his hands on Darcy's shoulders as he pulled away just enough to look at him. "Your father. H-He made some sort of deal with her. Your parents, they . . . I can't go back."

Darcy's shoulders tensed, and his mouth became a thin line. "We'll get you somewhere safe. I can—"

"Darcy. You don't understand." He couldn't do it. Not again. "I'm not leaving."

Gregor was aware that the others had stopped their horses a short distance away, and Verity had moved toward the unconscious man Lucien had rescued along with Gregor.

"See to him," Gregor said, nodding toward the man. "I'll be right here."

Nearby, Lucien spoke to the Warden, his voice low. "We should be safe a little ways into the wood. Can you wake him?"

Verity's voice reached his ears, though Gregor was having trouble looking away from Darcy, who also hadn't moved yet. "What's wrong with him?"

"Don't know," Lucien said. "Found him like that. But he doesn't look hurt."

Darcy was still staring at Gregor, drinking him in like he was memorizing his face. "I thought I'd lost you," he said. "*Really* lost you."

"So did I," Gregor admitted.

A shadow blocked the sun, and Gregor tensed before realizing it was Jae, a roll of bandages in her hand. She nudged Darcy in the leg with her foot. "Verity needs you. I'll patch him up." When he didn't move right away, she said, "Go. I've got him."

Darcy let his hands fall and pushed himself to his feet. He smiled down at Gregor. "I'll be right back. Oh!" He reached into a pocket and withdrew Gregor's glasses. He handed them over with an apologetic smile. "I tried to straighten them out as best I could."

Gregor's heart warmed as he took the glasses, noting with some dismay the lens that had cracked when Tanithe struck him yesterday. He resisted the urge to touch his cheek. "Thank you," he said, carefully cleaning the lenses with the edge of his shirt before sliding them on.

As Darcy started toward the Warden, Jaelyn caught him by the elbow, her face stern. "Don't be an ass."

Darcy threw his hands up, affronted. "What'd I do?"

Gregor tried to suppress a smile, their bickering bringing with it a wave of nostalgia.

"Nothing yet." She gestured with her head toward the rest of the group. "Play nice."

"Why wouldn't I play nice?" Darcy inquired a little too innocently. "Because there's a shifter standing six feet away and no one mentioned this little detail earlier?"

From the other group, Lucien lifted his head from his conversation with the Warden and another woman, his eyes narrowing with predatory focus. The Warden, too, gave Darcy a withering look.

"Not that I'm complaining, mind you," Darcy added quickly.

Jaelyn gave Darcy a backhanded slap to his chest. "I said don't be an ass."

"I'm only saying," Darcy continued, "that judging by the look on Verity's face back there, I get the sense she didn't know about him either. Are we really not going to talk about that?"

Lucien crossed his arms over his broad chest as he watched Darcy.

Gregor started to say how Lucien had saved him, but Jaelyn gave an exasperated sigh. "What did you want him to say? *Hi, and oh by the way, I'm a shifter, but don't worry, I won't eat you—Promise!*"

"Um, yes, actually," Darcy countered. "That would have done the trick."

Jaelyn opened her mouth to snap something back at Darcy, but Lucien spoke first. "It's fine, Jae," he said, his voice a rumble in his throat. He turned to Verity. "I should have told you sooner."

Verity waved a dismissive hand at him. "I'm certain you have your reasons for keeping it a secret, and I don't blame you for that." She eyed Darcy. "Lucien's been nothing but helpful since the day you were arrested in Brookshire," she said. "And considering he just saved Solace and Gregor both, you could show him some respect."

Darcy blinked, the humorous, snarky expression disappearing. It was replaced with a humble sincerity as he crossed the short distance to Lucien. "They're right," he said. "That was unfair of me." He extended his hand to the shifter. "Thank you for your help, and for finding them. I owe you."

The women looked on in shock, though Gregor just smiled. Few ever got to see this side of Darcy. It was nice to see him finally letting others in.

Lucien seemed to consider Darcy for only a moment before he clasped his hand in a firm grip, grunting a wordless acceptance.

Jaelyn sighed and shook her head, the dark curls of her hair bouncing as the others turned their attention back to the unconscious man.

"Hi again," she said to Gregor, giving him a weary smile.

"Hi, Jae," he said. "It's been a long time."

She snorted a quiet laugh. "I just saw you two days ago."

"I know," Gregor said. "I meant before that." They hadn't really gotten a chance to catch up while they traded messages back and forth trying to help the Warden rescue Darcy. And it had been a while since her last letter home. "I've missed you."

Her smile softened, and she gave him a gentle hug. "I missed you too, Gregor. Can I see your wrists?"

He held out his arms as she unhooked a skin of water from her belt, wincing when she poured the cool liquid over his wrists. She took a small container out of a pouch on her belt and smeared some of the contents on two fingers. She worked swiftly, her fingers rubbing the poultice into the wounds with a surprising gentleness.

"Thank you," he said as she wrapped the bandages around his wrists.

"You're welcome." She studied his face a moment, then asked, "What could you possibly have to be smiling about right now?"

Gregor felt a heat rise to his cheeks. He hadn't realized he was smiling. But as he looked beyond Jae to where Darcy stood, he knew the reason. "We're together again," he said. "The three of us."

"Really?" Jae admonished. "That's why you're smiling? Because we're together—in the middle of this serious, catastrophic bullshit?"

Gregor's smile widened. "Yes," he said. "It is."

Verity appeared over Jae's shoulder and offered Gregor some dried meat, which he took with a gracious bow of his head. "Take a moment," she said. "But then we're going to move deeper into the forest." She turned to Jae. "From what Lucien says, they're not too close, and if they haven't managed to kill each other, it'll be helpful to have a little extra cover. They're not going to be happy about what happened."

"What about Solace?" Jae asked.

The Warden glanced to where the man still lay unconscious a few feet away. "I don't know," she said. "I'm wondering if this is something like the Binding spell he was under before. If it is, I might be able to banish it again."

Gregor looked to the man on the ground. *That* was Solace? The man who had a gods-made weapon inside him. The man who at least two nations were after.

The man who had saved Darcy's life.

Verity spared a quick smile at Gregor before returning to where Darcy traded quiet words with the woman Gregor didn't know. The Warden placed an artificed hand on Darcy's elbow, pulling his attention away from the unknown woman, who wandered to where Gregor sat with Jae.

He felt like an attraction on a sightseeing tour, what with everyone stopping by to talk to him, but he smiled politely at the young woman when she unslung her bow and crouched, introducing herself as *Finn*.

When Gregor introduced himself in turn, Finn's smile broadened. "I know. From Brookshire. And the plan." She bounced on her heels as she spoke, and Gregor found her youthful exuberance rather endearing. "Your name came up when we were figuring out what to do about Dare."

Gregor angled his head. "Dare?"

Jae rolled her eyes, though she was grinning. "Darcy. That's what he goes by now."

"Oh," he said as this new information worked its way into his exhausted mind. His gaze fell on Darcy, where he and Verity knelt around Solace. "I didn't know."

Darcy—*Dare*—looked up, as though sensing the topic of the conversation. "The three of you talking together is making me nervous," he called. "I fear no secrets are safe."

"What secrets?" Jae and Gregor said at the same time, feigning innocence.

Finn added quickly, "Oh, I know a few."

"Shit," Dare groaned.

The Warden smacked him in the shoulder with the back of her hand, drawing his attention back to more pressing issues.

Gregor laughed, a lightness filling his chest from how quickly they fell back into their old habits. Jae joined him only a moment before Dare did.

How long has it been since the three of us laughed together? he wondered.

He pushed the thought away. It didn't matter how long it had been. It only mattered that they were together now and that they'd found a moment of light amidst the encroaching darkness.

CHAPTER 55

VERITY KNELT BESIDE SOLACE. The immense relief she'd felt at realizing the literal monster galloping through the trees was *Lucien,* and that he was carrying both Gregor and Solace, was short-lived. She'd known something was wrong the moment they caught up and found Solace lying in the grass, unmoving. A panic had risen in her chest that he was dead. But Lucien had explained quickly that although Solace was alive, he hadn't been able to wake him.

She wasn't sure what had happened to Solace, but she suspected it had something to do with Crosse. He'd been the one to put the original Binding spell on Solace, but they didn't have time for her to do a Sight ritual to see if this was something similar. So she needed to rely on the next best thing.

Dare crouched on Solace's other side, looking up at Lucien. "Tell me everything you saw."

Lucien recounted how he'd been tracking Solace by scent and how Tanithe had appeared with Gregor, trailing a whole mess of angry, feral shifters. But she'd gotten caught up in her own distraction, it seemed, and she and Corvin had had to fight each other *and* the shifters. Lucien had used the chaos as an opportunity to get Solace and Gregor to safety.

Dare's throat worked, but he kept his mouth shut.

"Thank you," Verity said. "We wouldn't have found them—either of them—without you."

Lucien nodded. "Jae tells me Tanithe's the Chosen of Vire?"

Verity blew her breath out in a long sigh. "It certainly appears that way."

"I didn't realize," he said, his massive arms crossing over his chest. "We did odd jobs for her sometimes when we passed near Valda. Verity, I want you to know that if I'd known who—*what*—she was, I would never have worked for her."

Verity appreciated his candor. And she inwardly smiled at what was probably the most words she'd heard Lucien speak at one time. "Thank you," she said gently.

Lucien nodded again and took a few steps back, giving her space to work.

"That answers one question," Verity said to Dare, turning the early morning's encounter with Tanithe over in her mind. "What about you?"

"You want to talk about this now?" He gestured at Solace's unconscious body. "*Now?*"

Pressing her lips together, Verity looked down at Solace. Dare had a point. "So what do you think? Is it a Binding spell like before?"

Dare set one hand on Solace's shoulder, the other on his forehead. He closed his eyes. "It feels . . . similar . . . But there's something . . ." He trailed off as he shifted his hands to Solace's chest.

Verity tapped her fingertips against her elbow. If she could just figure out what Dare knew about Tanithe, she could put it to rest. "Tanithe knew you and Jae both," she said.

A crease appeared between Dare's brows.

"She's the one who's been blackmailing you, isn't she?"

"I'm trying to concentrate, Verity . . ."

"Why didn't you tell me she had this kind of power?"

Dare's eyes snapped open. "I didn't know. The only thing she—" He stopped in mid-thought, his face falling, eyes going round.

"What?" Verity urged.

"When we were in Whitehollow, she—" Dare yanked his hands from Solace's chest with a hiss of pain, shaking them out as though he'd been holding them against a flame.

"That bad?" Verity asked.

Dare flexed his fingers. "Yeah, it's that bad. It's stronger than it was before. A lot stronger. Do you think you can banish it again?"

"I will," she said. She would have to. But . . . "But about Tanithe."

"Fuck's sake, Verity."

"What did she do when we were in Whitehollow?"

Dare dragged his fingers through his hair. Verity didn't think he was going to answer, but finally he said, "After we first found Solace, the night before we met with the lorekeeper . . . Tanithe pulled me into a memory of hers while I was asleep. Like a dream."

Verity's hands tightened into fists. "She pulled you into a mindscape?"

Dare nodded, focusing again on Solace. "Yes. Can you banish the Binding spell or not?"

She set her hand on Solace, opening herself up as a channel. She spoke the words that helped focus the energy into the Banishment, as she'd done before, though she poured more of herself into it this time. If this Binding was stronger than the last, she would need a stronger Banishment to dispel it. But Solace didn't stir. She looked to Dare.

"I felt it," he said, answering her unspoken question. The spell had worked.

Verity studied Solace while Dare hovered a hand over him, checking to see if anything had changed.

It was interesting how boyhood seemed to linger in the gentle lines of his face, despite having a build that could easily belong to a soldier.

A soldier . . .

Was that why Crosse was with Solace when he stumbled on the weapon? Could Solace have been one of Crosse's soldiers? And if he got his hands on Solace again . . . or if Tanithe did. Tanithe Ash, spymaster for the Valdane Council, and Chosen of Vire. Who apparently had the ability to create mindscapes . . .

"She has mind magic and you didn't tell me?"

"You didn't exactly trust me at the time," Dare muttered, still focusing on Solace. "Besides, I thought I had it under control."

"Under control?" Verity scoffed. "Only a handful of mages have the ability to affect the mind through magic. Do you have any idea what someone like that can do?"

"Yes, Verity, I have an inkling." He pulled his hand away. "Nothing's changed. I don't think the Banishment was strong enough."

Verity stared at the canopy of trees overhead. What would it have changed if she'd known about Tanithe's magic earlier? Probably nothing, but she couldn't be sure. And that was the problem. But she didn't have time for this. Not right now. Verity pulled in her temper. She could almost feel Drystan's hand on her shoulder, steadying her.

"I'll try again," she said, drawing a deep breath. "And I'm sorry for pushing, it's just . . . no more secrets, please. Alright?"

Dare didn't respond. He was looking toward the others where they rested and ate, a small, secret smile on his lips.

"Dare, are you listening?"

He startled out of his reverie. "Hmm?"

"It must be really nice to see the both of them again," she said, even more of her frustration evaporating. Her chest tightened as a vision of Drystan sitting among them flashed in her mind.

Dare inhaled deeply. "That is a grand understatement, my lady Warden," he said, almost under his breath. "I never thought I'd see them again, and now . . ." He turned to Verity, catching himself as though he only just remembered she was there. "I'm sorry."

"It's alright." She gave him a wistful smile. "I'm happy for you." And she was, though her heart ached, a pang of jealousy. No turn of fate would let her see Drystan again.

"There'll be time to be happy later," he said, turning his full attention back to Verity and Solace. ". . . I hope."

"I'm going to do a stronger Banishment," Verity said. She shifted on her knees, preparing to try a second time.

"Use me as the Channel."

"What? No." Verity surprised herself with her own vehemence. Logically, it wasn't a terrible idea, but something in her chest raged at the thought. At the unknown risks of channeling from a Perceptive. At the risk of hurting him.

"Verity, we're running out of time. We can't travel with him like this. If we stay here too long, one or both of those really big problems following us are going to catch up."

She stared down at Solace. There had to be another option. "No, I'll just—"

"You're *just* going to be wasting your power if you keep trying on your own. Channeling from someone else is going to give you the best chance of breaking it now. You haven't finished charging my mother's periapt, so that's out. That leaves us."

Dare gestured vaguely to where the others were grouped in the grass nearby. "Shall I run down the list, my lady Warden? You saw that thing Lucien can turn into. I have a feeling we're going to need him for a fight before too long. And you'll need Finn's bow and Jae's swords before the end, just as much as you'll need Lucien's . . . whatever that is. Your magic *and* your fighting are the best I've ever seen—you can't tap yourself out." He dragged his fingers through his hair. "And Gregor's not a part of this," he added firmly. "So that leaves me."

When she opened her mouth to convince him otherwise, he continued, "Listen to me. I can't cast magic, and I'm not much good to you in a fight. And with the magic roiling off them, I'll be next to useless against either Corvin or Tanithe if they catch up to us." He flashed a wry smirk. "Unless you want me to try talking them to death."

"As truly obnoxious as your skills are in that area," she teased. But she shook her head. "Dare, we need you."

"You don't." He pointed toward where the Red Forest stood somewhere a few hours' hard ride away. "Not for that." Then he gestured down at Solace. "But for this? Verity, I'm a natural Channel, just like you. That's got to work better than using anyone else, right?"

Dammit, he was right.

Dare fidgeted where he crouched, picking at a stray blade of grass. "Just leave me with enough strength to hold myself on a horse so I'm not a liability."

"But I've never channeled from a Perceptive before," she went on. Could she make him understand the risk? "Under normal circumstances, it feels uncomfortable, and for the amount of power I'm going to need . . . it would be enough to leave someone feeling exhausted and weak, like a bad illness. But I honestly don't know how it'll make you feel. I'm going to be pulling raw, unfocused magic from you. It'll flow from your wellspring, *through* you as I draw it into me. At best it may feel like when I cast that Banishment through you in the tunnels."

Dare's hand flexed.

"But it's going to be more magic than that. I don't . . ." She reached across Solace and took his hand. "Dare, I don't know what that's going to do to you. You're—"

"I know," he said sharply, the slightest tremor in his voice. His hazel eyes flashed. "I know I'm not *normal circumstances*, Verity. I know I'm a Perceptive. I've known my whole life. I'm not going to run from this." He squeezed her hand. "I'm not going to let it stop me from helping Solace."

Verity had never seen him so determined. Except perhaps when she'd sworn him in as a Warden . . . "Alright."

Dare blew out a breath. "What do you need me to do?"

"Gather up the others," she said. "We'll explain the plan. Then sit here." She gestured to the grass beside her.

"This is crazy," she whispered when Dare left to gather the group. She was very skilled at channeling and could draw from Drystan to a precise degree, knowing exactly how much to take so he'd feel no worse than a little run down.

But with Dare? She could have a target in mind, but who knew how he would react. If she undershot, the Binding spell would still be in place, anything she took from him would be wasted, and she'd be unable to try again without taking too much of what he had left and likely knocking him unconscious. If she aimed too high to start with, same problem. And trading Solace's unconscious body for Dare's was only a mild improvement in that he'd be about fifty pounds less of dead weight.

When she looked up, the group had gathered around her and Solace, their faces grave. She explained the plan. "Anyone have a problem with this?" she asked. To her surprise, no one argued.

"I don't like it, but it's the best plan we've got," Finn said. She set her hand on Verity's shoulder and squeezed.

Dare sat beside Verity, watching her, waiting for his next instruction.

"Give me your hand," she said. "Blood works best, so I'm going to cut your arm, and then I'll begin to channel from you. If this Binding spell on Solace is as strong as we think it is, I'm going to need a lot of power." She paused for a moment, searching his eyes. "However you feel, don't fight against it, alright?"

Dare rolled up the sleeve of his shirt and extended his arm. He then drew a dagger from his belt and handed it to Verity. "You can do this," he said. "I trust you."

Over his head, Jae and Gregor exchanged a look. Verity couldn't read it beyond the obvious concern on their faces, but whatever passed between them, they both understood it without the need for words. As Verity took the blade from Dare, Jae knelt on his other side, and Gregor crouched behind him. Finn knelt beside Verity, laying her bow in the grass, and Lucien looked on from a short distance away.

When Verity had met Dare in that tavern in Valda, she had regarded him as nothing more than a brigand. Drystan had urged her to give him a chance, but she'd decided she'd known enough mercenaries that she didn't need to get to know this one. She'd decided he was beneath her and had treated him as such from the start. It was just how she'd been at the College all those years ago. She'd acted that way with everyone there. Including the guard who had saved her life.

If this was still her instinct, had she changed at all? All these years of trying to be good and help people—protect people—and in the end she was no different than when she was a pretentious teenager.

She trusted Drystan, had *always* trusted Drystan, but everyone else she kept at a distance, ordering them around as though she knew better.

But she didn't. Every plan she'd enacted had ended in disaster, and yet here they all were. They were all willing to help Solace and maybe, just *maybe*, reawaken the gods. Together.

Deep within Dare's eyes, a light shone. He was more than the masks he wore. He'd learned all of those to protect himself. That was how he kept others at a distance, but he'd let his guard down around her. Well before she'd earned his trust, he'd taken a chance on her. Even after she'd stomped on that offering, he'd done it again and again. She hadn't deserved it then. She wasn't sure she deserved it now.

In Brookshire, in the dining room of Wilhaven Manor, Verity had wondered if she'd met the real Dare yet. She knew now that she had. She'd met him in the little forest of birch trees in Westhold.

And now, he was a Warden of the Flame. Her brother.

"I'm sorry," she whispered as she drew the dagger across his forearm.

Dare inhaled sharply between his teeth, clenching his hand into a fist. Verity held onto his wrist as the blood welled to the surface where the skin parted. She dropped the dagger and clamped her hand over the wound. Verity steadied her breathing, opening herself up as a Channel to her own wellspring of magical energy. Then she began the incantation to siphon magic through the conduit now open before her, through Dare's blood in her hand.

There was a certain feeling that accompanied channeling large amounts of magic. Verity had always likened it to the sensation of having reality stretch out before her like a gentle slope, or drifting like a feather into a hole and watching the surface floating farther away.

Channeling from another created a similar effect in the caster, as the siphoned magic still needed to pass through the mage, even if it wasn't their own power to begin with.

If she was expecting a softly floating feather, channeling from Dare was like being fired from a slingshot off a cliff.

CHAPTER 56

THE BURNING KISS OF the blade slicing across Dare's arm evaporated as a hundred thousand needles jabbed into his heart, ricocheted inside his chest, and tore down his arm. His vision went white as he cried out. Every muscle in his body tensed. The magic flowing through him was like jagged shards of iron, and every instinct was telling him to pull away from Verity, to curl into a ball and close himself off from everything.

Verity's voice echoed in his mind. *Don't fight against it.*

He clenched his jaw, swallowing his screams. He reached out with his senses for something else to hold on to.

There. Somewhere through the blinding, needling pain, a pressure on his shoulder. Gentle and calming, like the first still breath after a storm. *I'm here*, it said. *I'm here.*

And there, another, gripping his knee. It was more forceful than the first, but steady, like the pressure deep underwater. *I'm here.*

Dare focused on those two disparate points, letting them anchor his consciousness.

Don't fight against it.

And so Dare stopped fighting.

The pain was still there if he looked for it, but it faded into the background. A vast, endless expanse stretched before him, and set against the midnight blackness that enveloped him were two eyes, the irises like a galaxy against violet sclera. His mind reeled at the sheer enormity of them. Dare had no sense of where his body was in the endless dark, but it could hardly be more than a speck of dust. The silent regard of those eyes peered into every aspect of him, every fragment of his being that made him who he was, and exposed it all, laying it bare.

And yet there was something familiar about them. Miraculously, Dare had enough sense about him to silently ask, *Should I know you?*

And, even more miraculously, the voice in his head replied.

Yes.

❁

Voices echoed around Dare. Distant. It was dark.

"What happened?" one of them said.

"I'm not sure," another replied.

"You said it would make him tired, not knock him out," the first voice said. "Is he going to be alright?"

"I don't know." The second again.

"You *don't know*?" the first shouted.

The second voice faltered. "I-I hope so. I've never felt anything like that."

The first voice said, "Dare, can you hear me?"

Yes . . . He wasn't sure if he managed to say it out loud.

A third voice floated to him on a soft breeze. "Darcy." A hand stroked his hair. "Look at me."

Dare's eyelids were weighted down with lead, but he forced them open. The world blurred and spun, and he couldn't orient where his body was, but Gregor's face stared down at him.

Gregor smiled, relief shining in his eyes.

Eyes. A vision—*memory?*—flashed in Dare's mind. Unearthly eyes weighing the measure of him.

Verity appeared above him. "Dare, can you move?"

Move? The idea was exhausting, but he tried. He lifted his head, and his vision swam. He figured out that he was lying on his back in the grass, though. That was a start. Dare managed to push himself onto his elbows, his arms shaking with the effort. He blinked away the blurriness and found Verity still staring at him.

"Did it work?" he asked. The effort of speaking was enough to lay him out flat again. His arms buckled. Dare fell, his head landing in Gregor's lap.

"It worked," Gregor said, smoothing Dare's sweat-slicked hair.

Dare tilted his head and spotted Solace, awake and exchanging words with Finn. Gods above and below, every movement was like wading through mud. He wanted to close his eyes and sleep for a week.

"Verity," Lucien's deep voice carried across the clearing. "We should move into the cover of the trees. Try to make some more headway before dark."

"We can give him a minute," Finn interjected. "He looks like he just went through the hells and back."

"Gee, thanks . . ." Dare groaned.

"I don't think a minute is going to make much of a difference for him," Jae said. She stepped into view over him. "Dare, we need you to try to get up now. I'll help you. Here. Take my hand."

He groaned again, unable to articulate exactly how much he wanted to do no such thing. He tried to roll onto his side, but his muscles didn't want to respond. "I can't . . ." he breathed.

"We need you," Gregor said firmly. He slid his hands under Dare's shoulders. "I'll help you too."

"I need sleep," Dare managed to say. It had worked. Solace was awake. He'd done his part. Now it was up to them. He closed his eyes. It would be alright. He could just rest for a while. And if Corvin or Tanithe found him . . . honestly, that sounded better than moving.

"Let's go, Warden," Verity said. Dare looked up. She had moved to stand next to Jae, holding out her hand as well, a sly smile on her lips. "That's an order."

Dare sighed. His thoughts were sluggish and his mouth, even more so. "I hate . . . all of you," he said, but he forced himself to grab both of the offered hands. Jae's grip was so solid it was almost a rival for Verity's as the two women hoisted him to his feet, along with Gregor's gentle hands under his shoulders. The world did a flip in Dare's vision as he stood, but his three friends kept him standing.

Gregor slipped himself under Dare's arm, supporting his weight across his shoulders. "I've got you," he whispered, his other arm sliding around Dare's waist.

"Didn't *you* just . . ." He took a breath. ". . . Get rescued?"

"I guess it's your turn," Gregor said. "*Again.*" The verbal jab was accompanied by a playful squeeze of his hand.

Dare snorted a laugh and let himself be guided toward the horses. The more weight he tried to put on them, the more the muscles in his legs trembled, and the effort of keeping his head upright was almost more than he could manage while also trying to walk. Or stand. Or breathe. But it helped, if he was being honest. Moving his mired limbs was starting to loosen them, and Gregor's arms around him reminded him why he needed to keep moving.

"I'll ride with him," Jae said as they reached Dare's horse.

"I'll do it," Finn piped up, jogging over. "I'm the lightest."

"It's been a while," Dare said to Gregor, "since two women . . . fought over me."

Gregor choked on a laugh while Jae favored him with a vulgar gesture. Finn cocked her arm back to slug him in the shoulder as she so often did, but apparently thought better of striking him in his current state. He doubted her care with him would last long, but he gave her a wink. Her eyes narrowed, and Dare was quite certain she was already plotting how she was going to get him back for that.

Jae dismissed him with a wave. "You can have him," she muttered to Finn. "I'll ride with Verity."

They managed to get him onto the horse, and Finn swung up behind him. Her arms encircled him as she grabbed the reins. "Lean against me if you need to," she said.

He was a good deal larger than Finn—almost everyone was—so he was surprised by how strong her arms were and how steady she felt behind him, though he knew he shouldn't be. She'd always been tougher than she looked.

Solace lingered behind the others, staring up at him. "Thank you for what you did," he said. "I owe you more than I can say."

Dare waved him off. "Let's just call it even," he said, tapping the center of his chest, his fingertips easily finding the knotted scar.

"Thank you all the same," Solace said.

Even through the crippling exhaustion, Dare felt the tug against his heart. He wasn't sure there was any way he could truly repay Solace, but he smiled down at his friend. His friend who had saved his life. His friend who had risked everything to try to help him. "You are most welcome, Solace."

It was slow going, but they traveled east for the rest of that day, until the sun had set behind the trees. Lucien guided them into a small clearing that would serve well enough for their camp. Finn hopped down from the horse, landing with a light bounce on the balls of her feet before she turned to help Dare down as well. He was pleasantly surprised to find that, despite the hours spent riding, his legs were sturdier now. She left her hands on his arms for a moment, until she seemed sure he was steady on his feet.

He tried to make himself useful, but as soon as he approached Verity and Jae where they were setting up camp, they both ordered him to sit his ass down—well, Verity pulled rank again, while Jae threatened to kick his ass if he didn't sit. Dare gave a mocking salute to one and blew a kiss to the other before he grabbed his blanket from one of the saddle bags and trudged off to find somewhere out of the way to rest.

He wasn't sitting long when Gregor approached, a slight hitch in his step and a small, wrapped parcel of food in one hand.

"How are you feeling?" Dare asked as Gregor lowered himself slowly to the ground, groaning the whole way.

"It's been a long while since I've spent that much time on horseback," Gregor said. "But I think I should be asking you that question."

Dare gave half a shrug. "Better, I guess, though I still feel like I'm doing everything underwater."

"Here," he said, handing Dare some dried meat from the little parcel. "Verity keeps feeding me. Eat something. Then sleep."

Dare chuckled as he took the offered food and eased himself down onto his blanket, one hand tucking behind his head. Out of the corner of his eye, he caught

Gregor watching his movements, worry lining his face. "Don't look at me like that," he said.

"Like what?"

"Like I'm broken."

"I know you're not broken." Gregor slid his glasses off and cleaned the cracked lenses. "I just hate seeing you hurting, Dare. I always have."

He startled. He hadn't told him that name, or anything about the life that was tied to it. But to hear Gregor say it—Aetherann's breath, it warmed something deep in his heart, something that had been dormant a long time.

"You don't have to call me that." It was almost a whisper.

"I know," Gregor said. "But I like it. It suits you."

Dare studied him, letting his gaze wander over Gregor, though it stalled on the bandages around his wrists, the bruise on his cheek. Gregor had been hurt because of him, had been gifted to Tanithe because Dare had pissed off her and his parents both. And if Corvin were to find out about him? What then?

It would be pure luck if they made it to Taernfane without running into the Chosen of either Ainam or Vire again. And Dare didn't doubt for a second that Tanithe would torture and kill Gregor for no reason other than to hurt Dare.

Gregor had always been the one to look after him. It was time he returned the favor. "You can't come with us, Gregor."

"What? Why not?"

He hated seeing the hurt in Gregor's eyes, the bewilderment on his face. Dare rolled onto his side and propped himself up on his elbow. He brushed his fingers lightly across Gregor's cheek. Gregor hissed in pain at the touch.

"I can't let you get hurt anymore," Dare said, trying to keep the sorrow from his voice. "Those two god-touched assholes are still after us. And I don't know what we're going to find when we reach Taernfane. I just . . . Gregor, I need to know that you're safe."

Gregor surveyed the camp. "That's not something you can guarantee," he said. "You thought I was safe back home, but . . ."

"I can't risk losing you."

"But you expect me to risk losing *you*?" Gregor snapped.

Dare's eyes widened. He'd never heard Gregor raise his voice.

"I've already lost you," he continued. "Twice now. I said goodbye and let you walk away, certain that I would never see you again. I did that twice, Dare." The intensity in Gregor's eyes was startling. "I will *not* do it a third time. I'm not leaving."

Dare couldn't help but laugh.

Gregor's mouth tightened into a thin line. "What is so funny?"

"You're too stubborn to know when to save your own ass," Dare said, shaking with laughter.

"And you're not?"

"Of course I am." Tears were gathering at the corner of his eyes. "Look at us! Two stubborn idiots, determined to do the right thing and die trying."

The corner of Gregor's mouth twitched, threatening a grin. "Don't you mean *or* die trying?"

Dare wiped at a tear, still laughing. "Vire's hells, I hope so, but I'm not optimistic." The frustration on Gregor's face was about to crack, so Dare prodded him in the ribs. "Will you at least try to keep yourself out of trouble?"

Gregor huffed. "Will you?"

"You know what I mean," he said. "If there's a fight—"

"I'll stay out of it," Gregor finished. "I know my own strengths. And weaknesses."

"Good." Dare settled back against the blanket. A fire was burning nearby, and the first stars were twinkling through the canopy of leaves rustling overhead. He watched the stars and listened to the whisper of Gregor's breathing beside him, allowing himself to finally relax now that he knew Gregor was safe.

Chapter 57

Sitting beside Dare, Gregor was quiet for a long time. He pushed his glasses up the bridge of his nose with his thumb while he watched the others. Jae was sitting by Lucien, who was speaking with Verity; Finn sat near Solace, the two of them eating in companionable silence, though Finn stole periodic glances at Verity.

Perhaps Gregor would speak with the Warden in the morning. If they were heading to Taernfane soon, his knowledge and training as a courtier could be helpful. He needed to make sure he was useful. He would not let himself become a burden to Dare or Jae—not to any of them. He would find some way to help.

His resolve set, he took a deep breath, steadying himself. He hated feeling like he was arguing with Dare, but he needed to make certain he was understood. "Look," he said at last. "I appreciate that you're worried about me. But I've worried about you too. Every day that you were gone, I wondered if you were still alive. I don't want to do that again. I want to stay and help. I want to stay with you." He looked down at Dare.

He was sound asleep.

Gregor chuckled to himself and draped his arms over his knees, rubbing absently at one of the bandages on his wrists. The ropes had cut deep. Even when the wounds healed, he would likely carry the scars for the rest of his life.

Sometime later, Jae plopped herself into the grass beside Gregor. She glanced over at Dare's sleeping form as she said, "How is he?"

"Incorrigible."

Jae laughed. "So, same as always?"

"Same as always."

Gregor took another bite of the food Verity had given him. Jae stretched out her long legs in the grass, leaning back on her hands. She had kept in touch with him after she left, but her letters were always vague, talking about the places she'd been, but not really what she was doing there. When she'd found him in Brookshire, he'd taken one look at her and started to get an idea of what she'd been up to.

Eventually, he said, "How did you get into all this?"

Jae eyed him sidelong. "To be honest with you, I'm not entirely sure. Lucien and I . . . It's complicated."

"Have you known him long?" he tried instead.

"I met him a little after I left home. We've traveled together ever since."

"You never mentioned him in your letters."

Jae half shrugged. "I didn't want you to worry about me," she said.

"You thought I'd be worried about you?"

She nudged his arm. "You've always been my best friend, so yeah. I thought you might worry."

Gregor's heart warmed in his chest. "Jae, since the moment I met you, there has been no doubt in my mind that you are capable of taking care of yourself."

She laughed aloud, then quickly covered her mouth, glancing over at Dare to make sure she didn't wake him. "Gregor, we met when we were six."

"I know. Go back to the complicated part about how you and Lucien ended up in Brookshire with the Warden."

"Lately, Lucien's been getting these dreams . . . visions, I guess. He felt like they were pulling him toward something, and when he told me about them, I realized they were leading us home. To Brookshire, I mean. We were . . ." She hesitated long enough that he turned to her. "We were working a job up north. For Tanithe. We didn't know what she was," Jae hurried to add.

"Visions?" Gregor asked, not allowing himself to focus on the part about Tanithe. "Is that something he's had before?"

"Never. As soon as we realized Lucien's dreams meant something, we dropped the job and traveled to Brookshire. We were in the square when Sigurd arrested Dare. When I saw him, I swear to all the gods alive and dead Gregor, I've never wanted to kiss someone and also punch them in the face as much as I did in that moment."

He snorted a laugh. "I understand."

"I don't think you do. You at least knew he was leaving," she said flatly. "You got to say goodbye."

"You know he had to leave," Gregor said after a long moment. "We'd both been begging him to go for months—years, even."

"That's not the point and you know it."

Gregor blew out a sigh. "Even that night, even as he was packed and ready, I had to beg him to leave. I could feel the hesitation in him. He was a hair's breadth away from changing his mind, Jae. And I was just as close to letting him." He closed his eyes, thinking back to that night. "But then I hugged him, and I could feel his ribs, the knobs of his spine. Staying was killing him. So I held him for as long as I could without losing my nerve, and then I told him to run. And when he asked me to get a message to you . . . I knew it wasn't fair to you, but I agreed."

"You didn't think I could let him go?"

"I didn't think *he* could let *you* go."

Jae glanced briefly to Dare again before leaning her head back to watch the stars through the trees. "Don't tell him yet, but I think I've forgiven him."

Gregor couldn't help the small smile from settling on his lips. "I won't. Do you still love him?" There never had been any secrets between him and Jae. He'd been happy for her when she'd fallen in love with Darcy, since Darcy had certainly been head-over-heels for her since he was twelve.

"A part of me always will," she said. "But I'm not the same girl anymore."

Gregor nodded. "I suppose we've all changed. Some more than others, perhaps."

"What about you?"

"What about me?"

"Do you still love him?"

He looked down to where Darcy—*Dare*—was lying on his back, one hand under his head, the other resting on his stomach, rising and falling slowly with his breath. His hair was longer than it had been when he'd left home, and there were faint lines on his face, around his eyes and mouth, that hadn't been there before.

But there, on his chin, was the scar from when the two of them were children and Dare had thought it wise to sprint down a dirt hill in the rain. He'd slipped and sliced his chin open on a rock. But there was another scar, too, on Dare's upper lip. That one Gregor wasn't familiar with. Beneath the open collar of his shirt was part of the raised, white scar from the spear that had almost killed him. So many scars. He would memorize them all, each one of them, if only he would be afforded the time.

"Gregor?"

He startled out of his daydream.

Jae was smiling at him. "You do, don't you."

Gregor gave a helpless shrug. "I don't know how not to."

She elbowed him playfully in the side, and he returned it in kind.

"So are you and Lucien . . . ?"

She laughed again, low and warm. "No, no," she said. "He's a dear friend, like you. Or even like an older brother, I suppose."

"How did you meet him?"

"I hadn't been gone long when I joined up with a caravan traveling through the mountains. He'd been brought on as a guide. The caravan got attacked by highwaymen. I think he took pity on me after that." She smiled a little, caught in the memory.

"Pity?" Gregor asked. "Why?"

"He saw me fight." Jae's eyes twinkled in the firelight. "He came over to me after we were safe and—I'll never forget this as long as I live—he said, *Um, miss, that's not how you fight.*" She dropped her voice to a lower register, mimicking Lucien's slow, deliberate pattern of speech. It sounded honed over many years of practice. "I looked him square in the eye and said, *This is how I fight.* He shook his head and said, *No, that may be how you fight, but that's not how anyone should fight.*

"He worked with me the rest of the time we were with the caravan, teaching me how to hold a sword whenever he had a chance. After we arrived in Weryn, I asked if I could hire him as a guide for the next leg of my journey. He agreed. That was almost ten years ago."

Gregor could only imagine the adventures they must have and couldn't deny the deep curiosity of wanting very much to see Jae wield the twin swords she carried. He could imagine her crashing against her opponents like a tidal wave, while Lucien . . . A shiver ran down Gregor's spine.

"And he's a . . . shifter?" Gregor asked, cringing at his own awkwardness.

To her credit, Jae simply eyed him. "Yes."

"How long has . . . has he . . ."

"Gregor, just ask the damn question."

He sighed. "Has he been like that for as long as you've known him?"

"Does it matter?" she asked.

"Not in the least," he said truthfully. "I'm curious. I've never met one before."

The side of her mouth quirked into a smile. "Of course you are. Yes, he was already a shifter when I met him."

Gregor considered this as he looked across the campsite to where Verity was chatting now with Solace and Finn. There was no sign of Lucien. "Do you know how he—"

Jae clicked her tongue before he could finish the question. "Gregor Thalesen," she chided. "That's not my story to tell."

A wave of heat colored his cheeks as she called him out, knowing exactly what he'd wanted to ask. "So is it all just folklore then?" he asked instead. "Just stories? That shifters are all feral barbarians at best and bloodthirsty beasts at worst?"

"No." The word escaped her so quick and sharp that it caught him off guard. "No, it's not folklore. They are monsters, in one sense of the word or the other. But Lucien's different. I trust him with my life."

Gregor considered the blurred ride through the trees that morning. Lucien hadn't needed to save him. He'd been there for Solace, but he'd stopped to help Gregor, even before he'd known they had mutual friends.

"I can see why," Gregor said. "I trust him with mine, too, for what that's worth. But do you know why he can be . . . as he is, or how, when seemingly no other shifters are?"

Jae gave half a shrug. "As far as I can tell, sheer force of will."

That answer didn't soothe Gregor's concern as much as he'd hoped.

Chapter 58

Verity awoke the next morning while most of the camp still slept. Lucien was nowhere in sight, but it was his turn to keep watch. He was likely patrolling somewhere nearby. He had quietly offered not to take a watch that night, in case anyone felt uncomfortable with it, but they'd all agreed little would make them feel safer than having Lucien guard them while they slept. Verity thought there might have been a soft smile on his face before he grumbled something to Jae and set about gathering more firewood.

Careful not to wake anyone, Verity opened her pack and withdrew the notes and parchments stored there. Corvin Crosse had stolen the books along with Solace, so now the strange runic writing was all they had left. She pored over her notes again. If the elemental gods were asleep and that was why no one had seen them in so long, could separating the weapon from Solace and destroying it truly return their power to them? Could that wake them up? She hoped their guess was right—that the conduit to Taerna's power in Taernfane could help destroy the weapon. Otherwise . . .

She didn't want to think about what *otherwise* might be.

She leafed through the loose pages written in the old language of the island of Pyrrah and decorated with the imagery of the elemental gods. A massive tree with spreading roots for Taerna, goddess of earth; clouds and an ice-blue sky for Aetherann, the god of air; golden flames for Pyrannis, the god of fire; and crashing waves for Lanara, goddess of water. She flipped to the fifth page, adorned with strange, star-laden eyes.

"What is that?"

Verity jumped at Gregor's voice over her shoulder.

"Sorry," he said, crouching beside her. He was looking much better for having slept. "I didn't mean to startle you."

"It's alright; I didn't realize anyone else was awake yet." She angled the pages toward him. "I don't suppose you can read Ancient Pyrrinese?"

Gregor adjusted his glasses. "I remember the alphabet," he said, eyes darting over the pages. "So I could sound it out phonetically, but translating would be beyond my skill, I'm afraid."

Even that was more than she had expected. There were very few people in the world who could read the dead language. Verity handed the parchments to him. "That's better than I've been able to do," she said. "How does a house secretary know the Ancient Pyrrinese alphabet?"

Gregor was already scanning the pages. "I've always been rather good with languages, but Duke Wilhaven insisted Darcy study all the old ones, including Pyrrinese. Though finding a tutor who knew enough to teach it was its own challenge, so we didn't make it very far. I can't promise I'll find anything useful."

"Anything you could tell us about it might help."

After several minutes reviewing the pages, Gregor flipped back and forth between a few of them. "Hmm . . ."

Verity leaned closer. "What is it?"

He drew his lower lip between his teeth as he studied the last parchment. "*Tykaras*," he said. He pointed to a word written in the runic language. "It's repeated multiple times throughout this page. But *only* on this one." He turned to the earlier pages, skimming them again. "It appears nowhere else, and there are no words on the others that behave in the same manner." He peered at Verity over the top of his glasses. "But I have no idea what it means."

Another piece of a puzzle where she wasn't even sure how many pieces there should be. She rubbed at her temples.

Gregor glanced at the pages of notes beside Verity, a slight smile on his lips. "What else do you have?"

✸

When the others woke, it was time to move out. As Verity placed the parchments and notes back into her knapsack, her metal fingers brushed against a small book. She pulled it out, fingers tightening on the green leather cover of the well-read tome. She held the book, wishing she could feel the texture of the binding, soft from repeated handling. She wished she could feel what Drystan felt when he'd held this book so many times.

She took slow, steadying breaths as she placed the book back in her pack. There were two things she needed to do before they started out.

Nearby, Dare was standing of his own free will, which was a vast improvement, although he still looked exhausted. "Does the word *tykaras* mean anything to you?" she asked, crossing to him.

Dare rubbed a hand across the back of his neck. "I don't think so. What is it?"

"Not sure," Verity said. "Gregor pulled it from one of the parchments from the library." She shrugged. "It was a long shot, but I thought I'd ask."

He flashed her a grin. "Happy to continue to disappoint," he said cheerfully.

Verity scoffed, though she returned the smile. "How are you feeling?"

"Oh, you know, like I got knocked on my ass by a magic ritual yesterday."

Verity sized him up, including the snarky tone. "You seem like you're doing just fine."

"Yes, well . . ." He looked across the camp. "I guess you could say I'm feeling very lucky today."

She extended her hand to him. "I'm glad you're still with us," she said.

His mouth twitched with what was certain to be some witty remark, but the playfulness winked out and, for a moment, Dare smiled. Not his usual smirk, but a true, sincere smile that danced in his eyes and scrunched them up at the corners. It might have been the first time she saw him truly happy.

He met her offered hand, clasping her steel forearm in a firm grip that surprised her. "Thank you, my lady Warden."

Verity rolled her eyes, turning toward where Finn and Solace were tending to the horses at the outer edge of the camp. "You just had to say that, didn't you?"

The playfulness returned as he called after her, "I really did."

"Solace," she said, ignoring Dare. "How are you today? Any lingering effects from the Binding spell?"

Solace was helping secure the gear to the horses, but he paused to give Verity a warm smile. Unlike Dare, his expressions were always genuine. Verity doubted he even knew how to keep what he was thinking or feeling from showing on his face. "Fine, thank you," he said quietly. "And no. Everything seems to be . . . as it was. Thank you again. I hate to think what Crosse would have done if . . ."

She set her hand on his broad shoulder. "I'm just glad we have you back." Her throat tightened as she said, "I was really worried about you."

He bowed his head. "Thank you, Verity."

She took a deep breath as she moved to one of the horses where much of their gear was already packed.

"Sorry," Solace said, following her. "Did I pack something you still needed?"

"No," she said absently, finding what she was looking for. She turned to Solace, offering him a longsword in its scabbard. "You should have this."

Solace's eyes widened as he stared at the sword. He didn't move to take it. "Verity . . ."

"Solace, I want you to have it. Drystan would want you to have it."

He swallowed hard. "Are you sure?"

She hadn't realized it until she stumbled across the worn book, but she was certain. The things that were his, like the book—like the sword—were meant to be used, not left in a pile to collect dust. Drystan would want his things to be put to use by the people he cared about.

"I'm sure. I can think of no one better to carry it."

A flush of pink colored Solace's cheeks as he wrapped his fingers around the scabbard, pulling it close to his chest. "I don't know what to say."

"You don't have to say anything," Verity said, a soft smile on her lips. "Would you mind gathering everyone up? We need to go over the plan."

Solace nodded. "Of course."

Finn wandered over once he'd stepped away and nudged her arm. "And what about you?"

"What about me?"

"I've been watching you check in with everyone," she said, hands coming to rest on her hips. "But what about you? How are *you*?"

Verity pushed a loose strand of hair behind her ear. "I don't know," she said truthfully. She'd been too scared to stop and think about it. Worried that if she stopped moving forward, she'd fall *down*, with no way to climb back up again.

"What are you excited about?" Finn asked.

"What?"

"After all this is done and you've finished saving the world, I mean. What are you looking forward to?"

Verity hesitated.

"Don't think too hard," Finn prompted. "What's the first thing that comes to mind?"

"I . . . Honestly, I think I'd go back to Embercliff," Verity said, surprising herself with her answer.

"Is it true you can see all the way to Kyleria from the cliffs?"

"On a clear day." Verity chuckled at Finn's excitement. "You've never been?"

She shook her head. "I've scarcely ever been out of Valda," she said. "Have you been to Embercliff much?"

"Just once a few years ago, for a mission with the Wardens. When you first land in their port, you have to take a lift up the cliffs to the city. The view of the Moontide Sea is remarkable. You're so high up that the sea looks like a pool of the brightest blue you can imagine. And all the boats look like diamonds scattered across the water." Verity inhaled deeply, almost able to smell the salt off the sea. "I'd like to go back there one day."

Finn watched her with interest. "That's incredible."

Verity wondered how Finn would react to seeing the Moontide Sea from such a height. She could almost picture the smile on her face, the wonder in her eyes at the ships glittering below. She held the image of it in her mind, her heart squeezing at the thought, though she wondered, too, why she could so clearly picture the look of delight. And why she wanted so badly to see it.

Since they'd arrived in Brookshire, Verity had been focused on protecting Solace and rescuing Dare. But Finn had been the one looking after *her*—making sure she ate, making sure she slept, giving her something to hold onto when she felt the darkness seeping in. Somehow through these recent disasters, Finn had supported her in a way no one else had.

"You should come with me."

"Really?" Finn asked, her face growing serious.

"Yes, when this is over, we'll go to Embercliff."

Finn's smile lit up her whole face, and Verity couldn't help but return it in kind.

❋

With everyone gathered around, they all looked to Verity. They were looking to her for a plan, and for reassurance that they were going to make it through this. She could feel the pressure of that responsibility bearing down on her. She straightened, refusing to bend under the weight. She wouldn't let them down. Not again.

"As you all know, we're heading to Taernfane," she said. "There's a tree in the center of the city that is supposedly a place of power for Taerna. The plan is to bring Solace to that tree so he can perform a sacrifice."

"What kind of sacrifice?" Finn asked, her brows drawing together.

"Blood, we think," Verity said. At Finn's concerned expression, she added quickly, "We're hoping a small amount will be enough."

"You're *hoping*?"

"Yes," she said. Her eyes met Solace's. "Like when I channel magic through someone else and the blood acts as a conduit. It's what we have to go on right now."

Finn crossed her arms over her chest but didn't say anything else. Verity wanted to reassure her that everything would be alright, but she had no idea if that were true. All she had right now was hope.

"Taerna's tree is in a park open to the public," Gregor said, "but it's technically within the palace grounds. If you want to avoid any unpleasant consequences after the fact, you should get permission from the Court."

Verity nodded. "Good idea."

"What about Tanithe and Crosse?" Jae asked.

"We have to hope we can get to Taernfane before they catch up to us," Verity said. "Maybe they haven't realized where we're headed."

"We should assume our dear Captain Corvin knows," Dare said. He leaned casually against a tree to Verity's left. "My father made some sort of a deal with him in exchange for Solace." The muscles along his jaw tightened. "We don't know how much he told him."

"And Tanithe," Gregor added, fiddling with the bandages around his wrists. "Your father made a deal with her too."

"Fucking asshole," Finn blurted out. As everyone looked her way, her fair skin turned an endearing shade of crimson. "Shit, sorry." She grimaced, giving Dare an apologetic half bow.

He laughed. "I've called him far worse, believe me." He focused on Verity. "We should probably assume they both know everything."

Verity set her hands on her hips as she continued thinking aloud. "And we need to consider the teleportation magic Tanithe has. I'll admit, I have no idea how it works."

"It's not teleportation," Gregor said, stepping forward. "Well, not strictly speaking. It wasn't instant transport from one place to the other. It was more like traveling very quickly in an ethereal state via contact with shadows. And it seemed to tire her. After a while, at least."

Although Dare's face showed nothing but thinly veiled pride, Verity only managed to stare at him, working through the implications of what Gregor had just said.

"Sorry," he added, shrinking back to Dare's side. "I was only able to see a little bit."

"No, Gregor," Verity said, shaking her head to clear the shock from her face. "No, that was perfect. We'll likely have to contend with her again before this is over. But with a little luck, maybe we can reach Taernfane before she tracks us down. Or at least before Corvin catches up to us too."

"With a little luck," Dare muttered, "maybe they killed each other in the Red Forest."

Verity forced a smile, though she felt less than optimistic about that possibility. More than likely, they were both still alive and very, very irritated. "A couple people should ride ahead," she said, looking across the faces of her six companions. "Two people can travel faster than seven, especially with only four horses. It'll give us a chance to explain what we need and warn the city of what might be following us."

"Then I should go," Gregor said without hesitation. Dare's eyes tracked him. "I can help arrange the audience with the court. His Gr—" He cleared his throat. "Duke Wilhaven had *aspirations*. He had me learn court etiquette for all the kingdoms on the continent."

Verity nodded. "Alright. And one more."

"You should go, Verity." Dare chewed the inside of his cheek. "Your presence as a Warden would give weight to Gregor's request."

He was right that having a Warden there would only help their cause, but she had sworn to keep Solace safe. He'd been taken once already because she hadn't been there to protect him.

"You're a Warden now too," she said. "You could go with him." That would make him happy, wouldn't it? To be able to stay with the person he cared about so deeply? "Besides, you're more persuasive than I am."

"Much more," Dare said. The corner of his mouth twisted upward, though it didn't quite reach his eyes. "But if we ran into trouble on the road, we'd be fucked. I'm not a fighter, Verity, and neither is Gregor. But you are. You can protect him and make sure he gets there safely." He paused and drew a deep breath. "Not to mention that I won't be able to keep up that kind of pace. Not right now."

Dare still leaned against the tree, but now that she was watching him, how had she missed the tension in his shoulders and his jaw as he spoke? Verity didn't doubt he intended to give the impression of nonchalance, but he was using the tree to keep himself standing. He hadn't recovered yet, regardless of how much he wanted to look like he had.

Finn adjusted the bow slung over her shoulder, her features hardening. She gave a quick look toward Jae and Lucien before looking up at Solace. "We'll make sure you get to Taernfane," she said. "I promise."

Jae nodded her agreement, and Lucien grunted his.

"See?" Dare said. "We'll be in good hands."

Solace looked down at the sword he clutched in his hands. Drystan's sword. "You have to go," he told Verity. "We'll be fine."

She nodded, an ember beginning to glow within her. It was something she hadn't felt in a long time, something that had been extinguished, now rekindled to life. "Alright. Gregor, you're with me. Everyone else, make for Taernfane as quickly but as *safely* as you can." Her eyes landed on Dare. "We'll meet you there."

CHAPTER 59

Dare was unsure what he should say or do. The group was splitting up to give their plan the best chance of success, but as he looked at Gregor, Dare wanted nothing more than to get him somewhere safe and leave him there, and also to never let him out of his sight again. These two conflicting desires, along with the acute awareness that he was currently doing neither of those things, knotted his stomach.

"Are you sure you want to do this?" he asked. "This isn't your fight."

"It is," Gregor said, a stillness settling over him. "It's all of ours."

He was right, and Dare hated it. That Verity would be the one with Gregor was, Dare was certain, the only reason he wasn't going completely out of his mind. He would trust no one else. He swallowed against the tightening in his throat as he held up a small dagger in a plain leather sheath. "I want you to take this with you."

Gregor's nose scrunched up. "I hardly know what to do with that."

"You studied blade work with Hammon back home, same as me." He'd known this would be a point of contention and had come prepared to argue.

"Yes, but I failed those lessons, remember? Hammon said I was a lost cause."

"Fine." Dare unsheathed the blade and held it, point up, between them. "Here's your new lesson." He touched the point gingerly with his finger. "This part is sharp. If someone is bothering you, shove the sharp part into them."

"Dare?"

"Yes?"

"*You're* bothering me." A slight dimple appeared under Gregor's eye as he held back a grin.

Dare gave him a wink, though his insides were still twisted up. He slid the dagger back into the sheath. "Just take it with you. Please."

"Alright, fine." Gregor's shoulders sagged as he held out his hand for it.

"It's a hidden blade," Dare said. "I'll show you." He pulled a narrow leather belt out from his pack. "Lift your shirt."

Sliding the sheath onto the belt, Dare tied it securely around Gregor's waist so the dagger was nestled, hilt down, against the small of his back.

"Now see if you can draw it."

Gregor let his shirt fall back into place and did as he was told. With an awkward tug, he drew the blade and presented it to Dare. "And without cutting myself."

"See, you're learning already!" Dare took the blade and secured it back into place for him. "Stay safe, Gregor," he said. "Stick close to Verity. She'll look out for you."

Gregor turned to face him. Dare opened his mouth but the words stalled in his throat. What could he even say? Not another goodbye.

Not again.

Before Dare could find his voice, Gregor pulled him close, tightening his arms around him. "I *will* see you there." Then he stepped away and turned toward the horse that had been picked out for him, one of the fastest they had. Gregor didn't look back as he mounted, nor as he and Verity disappeared into the trees, his movements charged with determination.

It was at least a three-day journey to Taernfane, assuming luck was on their side. If all went to plan, in three days, they'd all be together again, and Solace would be free.

Just three more days.

A hand on his shoulder pulled him back. "She'll keep him safe," Jae said.

"I know," he said, still watching where Gregor and Verity had long faded from view.

"He'll be alright, Dare."

"I know," he said again, though he didn't.

Jae tugged on his arm. "Come on. You're riding with me."

They only had two horses now, and even with Lucien keeping up on foot—or paw, as the case might be—they still needed to ride double, which was only going to wear the horses down faster. Which meant the journey to Taernfane would take longer. They might be able to get fresh horses, enough for each of them, in Finnigan's Forde. The Forde was the best place to cross the Ragebrook, and the only safe one. Then maybe they could make up the time—

"*Dare.*"

He turned to Jae.

"We need you to focus. The sooner we can finish packing up, the sooner we can start after them."

"Right," he said, casting one last look in the direction Gregor had gone. "Sorry." He still felt like shit from the day before, but dammit, he would see this through if it killed him. He clasped Jae's hand in his and drew it to his lips, placing a kiss on her knuckles. "I'm glad you're here, Jae," he said.

She smiled at him, gentle but bright, and something stilled in his chest, calming, settling. "Of course you are. I'm fucking delightful. Now let's go."

✸

Dare had hoped they'd be able to travel through some of the night. Although the moon would be little more than a sliver in the clear sky, the stars might provide enough light to ride by, at least for a little while.

Yet by sundown, he was drooping in the saddle, his energy waning to the point that he was fairly certain Jae was the only thing keeping him on the horse. It was nice, he had to admit. Being so close to her again, being surrounded by the scent of jasmine and sage, the warmth of her body against his back. Maybe if he just closed his eyes for a minute . . .

"We should stop," she said.

His head snapped up as he righted himself. "It's too early," he said. "We need to keep moving."

"You need to rest, Dare," Jae insisted. "You're clearly still recovering from yesterday."

Dare grumbled, glancing to where Solace rode with Finn. Lucien followed along behind but had no problems keeping up. The man, it seemed, could run for hours. "We can't afford the delay."

Jae grabbed the reins from him and signaled for the others to stop. "And how much of a delay are we going to have if you fall off the damn horse and break your neck? Or if you don't let yourself recover and the whole trip has to take even longer?"

Dare turned in the saddle to glower at her over his shoulder. "I really hate it when you're right."

Jae smiled sweetly. "I know. I would think you'd be used to it by now."

His eyes narrowed, though he had to tense his jaw to keep from grinning at her like a damn fool. "Fine," he said. "We'll stop here."

Jae hopped down first and dug one of the blankets out from the saddle bags. She spread it out, tamping down some of the tall grass. "Here," she said. "Lie here for a minute while we get things organized, then you can help with the rest of the setup."

Dare raised a skeptical brow. He wanted to make sure he did his fair share of the work around the camp.

"Rest for a minute," she said. "Trust me, you'll feel better and will be in a better position to help."

He sighed and dismounted. "Alright," he conceded. "Just for a minute, Jae."

"Just for a minute," she repeated.

Dare lay down on the blanket and was asleep by the time his head hit the ground.

CHAPTER 60

By the time Jae had finished unloading the gear from her saddle bag, Dare was already asleep, just as she'd hoped. Lucien's familiar presence joined her as she cleared some of the grass to make room for a campfire.

He watched her work. "Are you alright?" he asked, keeping his deep voice hushed, like a rumble of stones. "You've seemed . . ." His yellow eyes, focused and wary, darted to where Dare slept not far away. "Bothered."

Jae glanced to where Finn and Solace were tending the horses. She really didn't feel like being overheard, so she lowered her voice as well. "I didn't think it would bother me so much. Seeing him again, I mean. It's been so long, I thought it wouldn't matter. But it does, it's just . . . it's different than it was."

Lucien offered her one of his rare smiles. "I don't think it matters how many years have passed. Love has a way of lingering." He drew the hunting knife from his boot and began to help clear away some of the grass.

For as long as she had traveled with Lucien, there were still so many details she didn't know about his past. He didn't like to talk about it, as a rule, and although she understood why, it didn't stop her from asking the question now.

"How long has it been for you?"

The corner of his mouth twitched. "Would you believe I've lost count?"

"No," she said. "I wouldn't."

Crouching in the tall grass, Lucien held still, though his thumb rubbed along the inside of his third finger, where a ring might sit. "It was twenty years this past spring," he said.

Her brows drew up. She knew Lucien's shifter blood kept him healthy and young much longer than should be natural, but it was easy to forget that he was older than he looked.

Jae couldn't fathom still feeling that love for someone after so much time had passed. Not to mention knowing there was still so much time to be had. "Do you ever think about going back?"

His hand tightened around the knife, the leather straining with the strength of his grip, and Jae knew she was starting to tread into dangerous territory. "I used to," he said.

"But not anymore?"

"No."

"Why?"

"Partly because it's been so long," Lucien said, his voice even rougher than usual. "I don't know what I would find there anymore. We were about your age when I . . ." He scratched at his beard. Even after all this time, the words were still hard for him. "When everything happened."

She hesitated a moment. "And the other part?"

"I don't want them to see what I've become."

"I know I don't know them at all." Jae finished clearing the last of the grass away and stood, facing him. "But if it were me—"

"It's not," he said, the warning clear in the force with which he tucked his knife back into his boot.

"But *if* it were," she continued. She met his hard stare with her own. "I would be proud of you."

Lucien's lip twitched again, but his eyes narrowed on her. She straightened to her full height and didn't look away. He stood, the tension across his shoulders visible as he stalked away.

"I'm going to find something we can burn for a fire," he growled.

Jae didn't stop him. She didn't pretend to understand what it must be like for him, to have a literal monster living inside his skin, clawing and howling to get out. And to have sacrificed everything to keep the people he loved safe.

❋

Night crept in slowly with no trees or mountains to block the setting sun. They kept the fire as low as they could, given the lack of cover on the rolling hills. Jae tried to rouse Dare for dinner, but when he didn't wake after a rough nudge to his leg, they all agreed to let him sleep.

They divided up the night amongst the four of them, keeping an eye out for any dangers. When Finn woke Jae for her watch in the hours closest to dawn, Finn made no move toward her own blanket.

"I've got it," Jae said, tying her tight curls back away from her face. "You can go back to sleep."

Finn shrugged. "I'm up now. I thought maybe I'd just sit with you, if that's alright? Keep you company?"

As far as Jae was concerned, the young Crimson Brother had proved her worth several times over in Brookshire. She was unapologetically bold, and Jae liked that about her. Not to mention the idea of company was much better than sitting alone for the next few hours.

"I'd like that," she said.

Jae grabbed her swords, and they moved to where a few larger rocks stuck out of the ground a short distance from the fire. It was close enough that Jae could keep an eye on things, but not so close that they would wake anyone up. Jae brought her blanket with her, wrapping it around her shoulders in the crisp air of the early morning hours. Finn did the same.

Perched on the rocks, Jae surveyed the campsite, noting where each of the men were sleeping.

"You grew up in Brookshire?" Finn asked, pitching her voice low and quiet so it didn't carry too far through the still night. "With Dare and Gregor, right?"

Jae nodded. "Yeah, we all grew up together. I didn't live in the manor, but we were there so often, I might as well have." At the quizzical look from Finn, she continued, "My father was a baker and was contracted with Wilhaven Manor. We were there almost every morning and for any large events the Duke and Duchess held."

"What was it like?" Finn asked, leaning forward to rest her elbows on her knees. She pulled the blanket tighter around herself. "I'm trying to picture the two of them as children, and I just *can't*."

Jae drifted into those memories. Memories she hadn't let herself think on for years and years. To her surprise, her lips curled into a wistful smile. "The three of us were the best of friends," she said. "We were inseparable. Darcy and I were always coming up with some adventure or scheme and dragging poor Gregor along. Though I think he secretly loved it. As we grew up, Gregor was my closest friend. And Darcy . . ." She trailed off, her eyes drifting back to the camp, to where he lay asleep.

Finn followed her gaze. "You two were in love, right? Before he left?"

"Yeah. We were."

"I thought so," Finn said. "It's in the way he looks at you." There was a short pause before she asked, "Were Dare and Gregor in love back then too?"

"Oh, yes," she said. "For as long as I've known them."

"Can I ask . . . Did it ever bother you that he loved you and somcone else at the same time?"

Jae shrugged one shoulder. Truthfully, she had never thought to be bothered by it. Her relationship with Darcy was very different than what he had with Gregor. With her and Darcy there had been a longing between them that had clawed at her whenever they were apart. And when they were together, it was all passion and wild, untamed brilliance.

But it had always been different between Darcy and Gregor. They had known each other their whole lives. When they were together they just *were*. They never had any expectations or demands. Only the quiet serenity of two people who had been through their lowest moments together and loved each other anyway.

In Darcy's life, Jae was the hurricane and Gregor was the eye of the storm. Jae, tumultuous and exhilarating as the sea; Gregor, the safety and comfort of the harbor. They had each meant something different to Darcy, both equally crucial and beautiful. And in return, he had loved them both with his whole heart. Jae had never felt the need to limit that. Why should she tell someone how they should or should not love?

It had never felt like a competition between her and Gregor, although she was sometimes jealous of how simple and easy things always seemed to work between them.

"No," she said at last. "No, it never bothered me at all."

Near the fire, Dare startled awake and jumped to his feet. Jae leapt down from the rock, shedding the blanket as she drew her swords.

"Dare, what is it?" she called, no longer worrying about waking the others.

He spun toward her, staggering a step, one arm outstretched as though losing his balance.

Jae hadn't taken more than a step toward him when an arm clad in black snaked around his shoulders. Dare stiffened and a glint of metal at his throat caught the firelight.

"Take it easy," Tanithe crooned, her face appearing out of the shadows at Dare's shoulder. "There's no reason this needs to turn bloody." She leaned into Dare, whispering something in his ear. Whatever she said, he shut his eyes tight against it, his hands clenching into fists at his sides.

On the other side of the fire, Lucien was awake, crouching low to the ground, and Solace was slowly standing up, watching Tanithe's every move.

She spotted them and flashed Solace a grin full of teeth, the wisps of red hair sticking out of her hood like tendrils of flame. "Oh, there you are." She pressed herself against Dare's back as she said into his ear, "As fun as playtime with you is, my dear, I'm just here to get what's mine."

Shadows curled around her, enveloping her. Finn loosed an arrow. It sailed over Dare's shoulder, no more than an inch from his head. And struck nothing.

She was gone.

In the space of a breath, Jae knew three things with absolute certainty: Tanithe was going to reappear in the shadows around Solace; she was going to disappear again, taking him with her; and Jae was too far away to stop her.

Jae sprinted toward the camp as Finn reached for another arrow. Dare dropped to his knees, a hand grasping for something near his blanket. Lucien dug his heels into the earth and launched himself toward Solace, and in the space between one step and the next, his body snapped and shifted into a beast of muscle and fur and fangs.

The shadows coalesced behind Solace. He flicked his wrist at his side and stumbled forward a step as if struck from behind, and Tanithe, as she appeared behind him, was forced one step back. It wasn't much. Just a puff of wind pushing them apart a single step.

It wasn't much, but it was enough. Tanithe's arms wrapped around empty air.

Lucien leapt, claws ready to rend Tanithe into fleshy ribbons. His fangs glistened as he aimed for her throat. Her eyes widened, her shadows sliding over her to pull her away. But Lucien was there, practically on top of her. Jae willed her legs to move faster. A blade flashed and a yelp of pain echoed as the shadows engulfed them both.

"*Lucien!*" Jae screamed.

Hands caught her by the shoulders as she ran to the space where Lucien had landed. The empty space.

"We have to get out of here," Dare said.

She shoved him aside. A splatter of something dark colored the grass. Jae stooped to touch it, and her fingers came away wet. Blood. And that howl before they disappeared . . .

Fuck!

"Jae . . ." Solace stepped into her field of vision. "I—I didn't know he . . ."

Jae forced herself to be still despite her muscles practically vibrating with the need to tear Tanithe apart. "He knew what he was doing," she ground out. "Lucien never does anything without knowing the risks. He knew what he was doing."

"He bought us time," Dare said, appearing at her side. "Let's use it."

CHAPTER 61

BASED ON CERTAIN ASSUMPTIONS—THE weather was right for travel, the ferries at Finnigan's Forde were crossing the Ragebrook on schedule, and any other assorted delays, typical or unusual, didn't befall those on the road—it was a three-day ride from the forest in Southreach to the city of Taernfane in Drahkonia.

Verity and Gregor made it in two.

Luck was with them at the Forde, where Verity's sway as a Warden proved useful. They also rode through much of the night. The moon and stars provided some light to ride by, which Verity augmented with a small magical light. Not enough to draw attention or drain her ahead of their arrival in Taernfane but enough to light their way.

On the morning of the third day, the rising sun illuminated the city. Taernfane towered before them, set upon a lone hill in the middle of wide, fertile plains. Over the years, the prosperous city, with its gray brick buildings and broad green spaces, had splayed across the hill like a quilt draped over a table. It sprawled down the sides of the hill and extended to meet the farms and ranches that stretched around it for miles in all directions.

Verity charged across the pastures toward the city, Gregor just behind her. They slowed only when the road became more populated. Within the walls, traversing the long, sloping streets was slow going, and it was another couple of hours before Verity and Gregor stood in front of the palace gates at the top of the hill.

The gates, huge and white as though carved from antler, stood open wide, inviting anyone to wander into the beautiful gardens and winding paths of the outer courtyard. Among the plentiful shrubs and flowers in dozens of colors, a single tree stood apart in the center of the park. The path curved to either side of it, providing a wide berth, and the tree was partitioned off only with a cursory, knee-high fence of wrought iron.

Taerna's sacred tree was the focal point of the palace gardens and, in fact, the center around which the entire city was built. It stood at least fifty feet high, its canopy of branches casting out a net of shadows dozens of feet beyond the base. Its thick trunk was covered in rich, mossy brown bark, and the leaves above seemed to iridesce in shades of deep emerald, bright chartreuse, and warm sage, speckled throughout with bits of amber, honey yellow, and sepia.

Gregor blew out a breath. "Wow," he whispered.

"That is . . . amazing," Verity agreed. This was it. The conduit to Taerna, goddess of the earth. This could be the key to freeing Solace.

He just needed to make it here in one piece.

Many others stood in the broad shadows of the sacred tree. Some stood in awe, as Verity did, admiring the quiet majesty, while others simply enjoyed the offered shade.

Verity pushed forward and made her way to the palace proper. It took some time to be seen by anyone of importance—Gregor realized too late, he lamented, that his torn and travel-stained clothes were not helping him get the right people's attention—but before too long he was speaking with one of the king's advisors to request an audience. Between his knowledge of court etiquette and Verity's clout as a Warden of the Flame, they were promised an audience with the king in three hours. It would be enough time to get themselves cleaned up, the advisor politely suggested. Gregor bowed his thanks and led Verity back into the gardens.

"Three hours?" Verity kicked at a pebble on the path and it skittered into the grass.

"No, this is good," Gregor insisted, his pace quickening as he headed toward the city. "The fact that we'll even be seen today is an excellent sign. I wasn't sure we'd be able to get anything better than tomorrow."

Verity sighed. "Alright, so now what do we do?"

"We get ourselves cleaned up and we get something to eat," Gregor said. "And we get ready to speak with a king."

⬤

A bath, some new clothes, and a hearty meal later, and Verity and Gregor returned to the palace.

"What do you know about him?" Verity asked while they waited in the large entrance hall.

Gregor cleaned his glasses with the hem of his shirt, frowning at the broken lens. "By reputation, King Dominic is exceptionally fair and pragmatic," Gregor explained. He glanced around the empty hall before adding, "If a little rough around the edges. The kingdom just celebrated the twentieth anniversary of his coronation. He was only fifteen years old when he ascended the throne, but he's done well by his people."

Before Verity could ask what *rough around the edges* meant, they were summoned before the king. An attendant led them up a wide marble staircase and down a long corridor of white stone, with stunningly beautiful stained glass windows depicting scenes from the legends of Taernfane's founding. Through the doors at the end of the hall, crimson carpets lined the gray marble floor of the throne room.

Two armored guards in chain shirts and greaves stood at the foot of a raised dais, their armor a notable, yet exceptionally functional, departure from the more customary plate armor of a traditional king's guard.

The advisor Gregor had spoken with earlier in the day sat in a chair toward the left side of the platform. Two thrones stood in the center. The one closest to the advisor was empty, shrouded by a black funereal cloth, while the other was of simple construction, the aged wood taking on an almost gray tone. And on that throne sat the king.

King Dominic Drahkon had a broad stature, even seated, that reminded Verity of Solace. He sat upon his throne in much the same manner that a lion might lounge in a tree. The sleeves of his plain gray shirt were rolled up, displaying the corded muscles of his forearms. Black pants were tucked into black leather boots, scuffed and worn gray in patches.

The king studied them for a time, his intensely focused eyes watching their every move as they approached.

Verity had been concerned that she hadn't been asked to surrender her sword before entering the throne room, but now she saw why. A plain metal rack stood beside the throne, a sword resting on it. The black sheath was oiled and pristine but plain, and matched the leather of the grip. The only embellishment was the pommel—a single circular agate stone, light brown and mottled with splotches of darker brown and veins of mossy green.

Gregor bowed, low and formal.

"Rise," the king said before Gregor had gotten very far. Before Verity had even started. He tapped his unadorned fingers against the edge of the throne before rubbing at his neatly trimmed beard. "What news brings a Bremmari courtier and a Warden of the Flame to my House with such urgency?" The king's voice was a pleasant baritone, but there was no mistaking the presence in it. Nothing could disguise the simple truth that this man could command legions with a single word.

Gregor cleared his throat. "Your Majesty, thank you for seeing us. We come with dark tidings and an urgent request."

"Continue."

And so Gregor explained, as he had heard it explained in Brookshire, the entire story of Solace, who had unwittingly become a weapon of the gods.

As he told the tale, Verity kept silent. Gregor knew what he was doing. She would follow his lead. King Dominic shifted on his throne, setting both feet flat on the floor and leaning forward, his eyes fixed on Gregor.

Gregor told the king about their friends, who were riding toward Taernfane now, trying to outrun the agents of Ainam and Vire.

Dominic caught his advisor's eye and waved a hand toward the back of the throne room. The man stood and exited quickly.

"Our hope," Gregor continued, his voice grave, "is that the power of Taerna's sacred tree will help us separate the weapon from Solace and, if the lore is to be believed, awaken the gods."

King Dominic leaned back. "That's quite the story," he said, his tone neutral, unreadable. "And you say this divine weapon is on its way here now?"

"Yes, Your Majesty, escorted by another Warden of the Flame and three of our allies," Gregor said. "We humbly ask your permission to clear the palace gardens so that we may perform a sacrifice at your sacred tree."

"To awaken the gods."

Verity tensed. She still couldn't get a read on the king's reaction.

Gregor's throat bobbed. "We believe so, yes."

Dominic's hand was curled into a loose fist on the arm of the throne, his thumb scratching absently at the cuticles of his other fingers. "Did you look at Taerna's tree when you arrived?" he asked.

"Yes, Your Majesty."

"Did you notice anything about it?"

Gregor hesitated for a breath before saying, "Only its beauty, Your Majesty."

"It's dying."

Gregor startled, his propriety failing. "Dying? How?"

"The short answer," the king said, exhaling deeply, "is that no one knows. But the suspicion is that Taerna's power is fading."

Verity took a small step forward. "Is that even possible? For a god's power to fade?" Did that mean the tree was no longer connected to the gods?

Dominic shrugged almost casually. "That's the question, isn't it," he said. "There's been no sign of the elemental gods in, what, five hundred years? More? Priests of Ainam can work minor miracles at will, and yet no one who worships the old gods can do the same. People are beginning to believe that the old gods are just stories. That they never existed at all." He leaned forward again, setting his elbows on his knees. "If I hadn't grown up in the shade of that tree, I might feel the same. But I know the old gods are real, just as I know you're standing before me now. If what you say is true—that the gods have been slumbering these past hundreds of years—do you really think your friend will be able to wake them up?"

Gregor bowed his head. "We fervently hope so, Your Majesty."

The large doors at the end of the throne room opened and several sets of footfalls scuffed down the length of carpet.

"That's not much of a reassurance"—the king acknowledged whoever had just entered with a beckoning of his hand—"but sometimes hope is all we have. Interestingly, you are not the first ones to weave me this tale. Though the other had a decidedly different angle." He nodded toward Verity. "Specifically regarding the Warden and her friends."

The man approached, stopping a few feet from Gregor. Verity's mouth went dry as she took in the crimson and gold uniform, the man's black hair, piercing gray eyes, and the scar curving around his throat.

"Tell me, Warden," the king continued, "are you familiar with Captain Crosse?"

Verity grabbed Gregor by the elbow, jerking him closer to her. She positioned herself between him and Corvin Crosse as Corvin bowed deeply to Dominic. Dare was right; Duke Wilhaven must have told Crosse exactly where they were heading, and he'd come straight here after losing Solace in the Red Forest. And if he'd already managed to convince the king . . .

We're bringing Solace right to him.

"Your Majesty," Corvin said before Verity could answer the king's question. "You see now that I spoke the truth."

"What I *see*," King Dominic said, his words sharp, "is the Warden with metal arms you spoke of, but no other signs of the supposed holy war you were so adamant about."

Verity had never seen Corvin armed before this moment. Just as she hadn't been stripped of her weapon, neither had he. A massive two-handed sword was strapped to his back, its hilt gleaming silver over his shoulder.

The guards were armed too, of course, and would certainly draw their weapons at the slightest threat of violence from anyone. There was also the sword resting beside the king—the single most well-maintained object in the king's possession. No, if she drew her sword first, she would lose all hope of obtaining King Dominic's aid.

"He's lying," Verity interjected before Corvin could speak again. "He's the one who means to start a war. He's the agent of Ainam."

Corvin gave a short bow, his hand over his heart. "Aren't we all in service of the Lord Ainam?"

Gregor tapped Verity's hand where she still gripped his arm. She let him go, biting her tongue to keep herself from any further outbursts.

"Your Majesty," Gregor said, his tone calm and measured. "Captain Crosse has been hunting my companions across the continent. He kidnapped our friend, Solace, out of Brookshire and tried to take him back to Westhold under a Binding spell that kept him incapacitated."

"Purely out of necessity," Corvin said. "It was for the safety of my men, as well as the citizens of Brookshire. Their friend is a dangerous weapon that cannot be controlled save by highly trained scholars of the divine." He straightened the cuffs of his crimson jacket. "Westhold has known of the weapon's existence and has prepared for when the world would need to be protected from it. And from the agents of chaos who seek to wield it."

Verity seethed. "Agents of chaos?"

"Indeed," Corvin said, keeping his eyes fixed on the king. "I am here as a representative of order and justice, and seek only to keep the world safe."

Dominic considered his words, studying the man carefully. "And how do I know that keeping the world safe is what Westhold seeks as well? Your nation has not been known for their desire to keep the peace. What happens if you take this weapon back to your king, as you plan to do?"

"Your Majesty, Westhold wants only to bring order and safety to the citizens of the continent."

"Mmm . . ." The king scratched at his bearded chin. "Whether or not those citizens want it, eh?"

Corvin didn't respond.

The doors behind them slammed open. Corvin and Verity both spun, hands on their weapons, as King Dominic jumped to his feet.

A guard sprinted into the throne room. "Sire, something is attacking the city!"

"*Something* doesn't help me," the king shouted. "What is it?"

The guard shook his head, breathing hard. "I . . . shadows, sire. Creatures of shadow and bone."

Verity shot a look at Corvin, but the captain seemed just as surprised as she was.

Gregor grabbed Verity's arm. "It's her," he gasped. "Tanithe. She found us." His eyes widened in fear as his grip tightened.

The king grabbed his sword and slid it through a loop on his belt. "These better not be your friends," he muttered to Verity as he passed between her and Corvin. His two guardsmen fell into step behind him.

"It's not," Gregor said as the king strode past. "But I know who it is. I can help."

Without hesitation, Dominic motioned for Gregor to follow. "You're with me," he said.

Gregor nearly had to jog to keep up with the king's long strides, the guards on either side of him.

Verity's heart pounded in her chest. If Tanithe was here, had she found their friends on the road? No, she couldn't have. If she had, why would she be in Taernfane? Either she'd beaten them here or, at best, Dare and the others had managed to arrive just ahead of her. Either way, her friends were in danger.

The king, his guards, and Gregor were nearly to the open doors—with Corvin following not far behind. A hand on the grip of her sword, Verity bolted down the carpeted floor, catching up as they reached the hall beyond the throne room.

Just as a dark, hulking creature crashed through the stained glass window, skidding to a stop at the king's feet.

CHAPTER 62

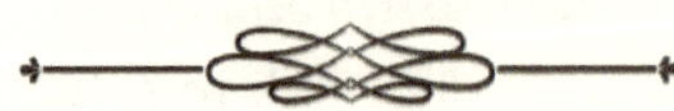

ONLY TWO THOUGHTS OCCUPIED Dare's mind throughout the hard ride to Taernfane, though he wavered between the two for most of it.

He's with Verity . . . He'll be fine.

She's with Gregor . . . She'll be fine.

They'd had luck at the Forde and secured four fresh horses after the crossing. Dare's strength had returned, enough at least that he was steadier on his horse, though he still saw those star-filled eyes every time he slept.

The sun was behind them when the city on the hill came into view. Approaching the gates, Solace urged them onward.

"She's close!" he shouted over the din of the horses' hooves. "I can feel her."

A knot formed in Dare's gut; he didn't have to ask who Solace meant.

They rushed through the city, slowing only enough to avoid getting arrested. The walls that surrounded the palace and its sprawling gardens soon came into view, Taerna's sacred tree standing proud in the center of it. Dare dismounted at the gates, aware of every person that passed them on the street. Jae hopped down from her horse and checked the draw of her swords.

Finn jogged up to him. "Do you see Verity?"

"No," he said, still watching the surrounding area. "But I don't think we can wait for her."

"What about getting permission from the king?" Finn asked.

"This is one of those situations where we're just going to have to ask for forgiveness instead."

At Dare's first step through the gates, the hair on his arms and the back of his neck stood on end. He reached for Jae.

As though sensing the same thing that tickled the edge of Dare's perception, Solace was already moving on Jae's other side. He shoved her hard, sending her toward Dare's outstretched hand.

Jae stumbled, crying out as she fell against him, a crossbow bolt in her chest.

Dare caught her and spun with the momentum of her fall, pulling her out of the garden and slamming his back hard into the stone wall. The bolt protruded from the left side of Jae's chest. It couldn't be more than an inch from her heart. Dare's stomach lurched. She should be dead. He hadn't been fast enough to reach her.

And if Solace hadn't . . .

It would be Jae's body in his arms.

Dare held Jae tight, panic flaring in him. Her breathing was coming in short, labored gasps. Her hand clutched his shirt, the cloth balled in her fist.

Chaos unfolded, screams rising up as people fled. Solace and Finn sprinted from the gardens. Finn hooked to the other side of the gate while Solace swung toward Dare and Jae.

"Help her," Dare pleaded, his voice breaking. "Please."

Solace grabbed Dare's dagger from the sheath on his belt and cut the fletchings off the end of the bolt. Jae bit back a scream as it jostled in her chest. Her knees buckled. Dare tightened his grip, holding her up. He wouldn't let her fall. Not ever.

"I've got you," he whispered, leaning his cheek against her hair. "I've got you."

Solace handed him the dagger, grabbed the bolt by the tip that pierced through her back, and pulled. Jae couldn't hold in the scream this time, but the bolt was out. Heat and magic radiated from Solace's hands as he set them over the wounds, front and back.

When Solace had used his magic to heal Dare, it had been such an oddly calming sensation that Dare hadn't been sure what to make of it, and it was the same now. The magic had a pleasant warmth to it, like sitting in front of a hearth on a cold day. It was like no other magic Dare had ever felt.

His eyes stung. *I should go*, he thought, still holding tightly onto Jae. *I should hand her to Solace and go. I need to find where that bolt came from. Solace is healing her. Go. I have to go.* But his arms wouldn't release their hold on her waist, and his feet wouldn't move. He needed to know she would be alright. He couldn't leave her until he knew.

At the gate, a guard rounded the corner toward the gardens and immediately fell, a crossbow bolt in his throat.

Solace's brow furrowed.

Dare could barely think. "What is it?"

The taller man kept his hands on Jae, the pleasant warmth still emanating from them, but the concern in his eyes made Dare's heart sink. "It's poisoned."

Dare swallowed down his fear. He only just got her back. He couldn't lose her. Not now. "Can you . . . ?"

"I can, but it will take me a little longer." He moved his hand from the wound on her back and wrapped it around her to support her weight. "Go with Finn. Find Tanithe."

I have to go.

He didn't move. He couldn't. There was so much he wanted to say. He had left without telling her all those years ago, and he'd never regretted anything more. If this was to be another goodbye . . .

"Dare!" Solace barked. "I will help her. I promise you. But you have to go."

This isn't goodbye. But . . . But the words tangled and stalled in his throat as he held onto Jae. *I have to go*, he told himself again.

And the voice in the back of his mind answered back, *Yes, you do.*

Dare kissed her forehead, beaded with sweat, and pried his shirt from her clenched fingers as he handed her to Solace.

Finn stood on the opposite side of the open gates. Her bow was drawn with an arrow nocked as she leaned around the corner, trying to catch a glimpse of where the attacks were coming from. She pulled back just as another bolt sailed past. Dare sprinted across the wide entranceway and slid to a stop beside her.

"Is she alright?" Finn demanded, her back pressed against the wall.

Dare sucked in a breath to steady himself. "She will be," he said. He tried to make himself believe it. "But those bolts are poisoned."

Finn cursed. "I saw Tanithe. She's somewhere along the battlements on the palace side, but I can't get a clear shot."

Dare pushed off the wall, rounding the corner into the gardens. "I'll draw her out."

Finn tried to grab him. "Dare, no!"

The gardens had quieted after the initial chaos. Bodies littered the ground, but most of the citizens who'd been in the courtyard had fled. Shouts still echoed from the city outside the walls, but here, his footsteps on the gravel path crunched loud in his ears.

Dare held his hands out at his sides, palms open. If Tanithe wanted him dead, that first shot would have been aimed at him. So either she didn't want to kill him, or she wanted to make him suffer first. Either way, she wouldn't shoot him now. Probably.

He walked along the central path toward the tree, watching the walls and the battlements on the far side of the gardens, searching for any movement. The whine of a bolt flying past his ear made him stop. A warning shot.

"Tanithe," Dare called across the courtyard. "Why don't you come out so we can talk?"

"Ugh, why do you always assume I want to *talk*?"

Dare set a lazy grin on his face. "Well, you haven't shot me yet." In the shadows on the far side, the bodies of several palace guards were slumped along the wall. No wonder the alarm hadn't been raised inside the palace yet. She'd killed everyone who came to check on the commotion. And if she was here . . .

Lucien . . .

"Can't a girl just appreciate a little wanton death and destruction?" she mused.

Dare began walking forward again. "Sure, but you and I both know you're not in it for the havoc. Speaking of havoc, that was quite a stunt you pulled out on the plains. What'd you do with Lucien?"

"The mongrel?" Tanithe's laugh echoed through the courtyard. "He'd been off his leash for far too long, so I put him down."

Dare's steps faltered.

"Are the dog euphemisms too subtle for you? This should help: I slit his throat."

He thought of Jae on the other side of the wall. The loss she would feel, the broken heart.

He would kill Tanithe for that. For that pain, and the pain she'd caused Gregor. "What do you want?"

"You know what I want, Dare." Her voice, like poisoned daggers hidden behind a layer of satin, sent a chill down his spine as it seemed to come from everywhere at once.

"I know," he said, ignoring the discomfort settling into his chest. Ignoring his fear and the worry over his friends. Would they survive this? If he could distract Tanithe long enough to give Finn a clear shot, then maybe . . . "You want the weapon," he continued. "For Valda. For the Council, right?"

Tanithe's laughter rang out, soft at first like chimes, then sharp and jagged, like shards of glass scattering across the cobblestones. "The *Council*? Valda is a pawn, you sweet, stupid child. Once I kill you, I'll take the weapon to Him."

Dare's blood turned to ice. Vire. She planned to give the weapon directly to Vire. But still, the mask of lazy, disinterested boredom remained as he walked closer. "And what do you get out of it?" he asked.

On top of the wall, the darkness shifted and took form. A hooded figure appeared at the edge of the shadows, and there was a glint of metal as Tanithe raised her crossbow.

"What do *I* get?" She was still so far away, and the leaves and branches of the sacred tree obscured the view, but she'd already proven that was hardly a problem for her aim. "Only the world."

Dare launched himself into a roll as the *twang* of a bow string sounded—behind him. An arrow flew over his head, between the branches, and into the shadows. Tanithe reeled back, a scream of rage and fury tearing from her as her own bolt loosed and sailed wide. Dare pushed himself to his feet as Tanithe wiped at a small streak of blood on her cheek.

The crossbow clattered onto the stones at her feet. "I will make sure you live just long enough to regret that, little girl," she sneered. She raised her arms and scattered something over the crenelations.

Small black stones rained down, erupting as they hit the grass at the base of the wall. Shadows twisted over sprouting amalgamations of bone and dust, pulling themselves onto four legs. They were all talons and feral bodies, with faces spawned from nightmares. Dozens of creatures charged through the gardens and into the city, though some stayed behind, circling within the courtyard walls.

Dare sprinted to the tree, leaping over the low fence. He didn't dare slow until he'd reached cover. He slammed into its trunk, his palms scraping against the rough bark. Power thrummed through his hands, sturdy and solid, with roots that stretched into the deepest parts of the world. He spun and leaned his back against it.

Finn appeared at the gates and let another arrow fly. It ricocheted harmlessly off the stone battlements, and she swore loudly. "Dare, get out of there!" she shouted as she ducked out of sight.

But he could still distract Tanithe. He could give Finn more time to get another shot. He could give Solace more time to heal Jae and get to the tree. It was the one thing he could do. He could give them all time.

Dare leaned around the side of the trunk, hoping to spot Tanithe. But as he cleared the tree, his only view was into the gaping maw of a shadow beast.

Tendrils of inky blackness dripped from its jaws like spittle as its eyes, specks of glowing red set into deep, empty sockets of bone and shadow, stared at him hungrily. Power pulsed from the creature in a dizzying spiral.

He grabbed his dagger, but it wouldn't be enough. He could never draw it in time. Someone shouted behind him. The shadow creature snarled and raised its head, only to be met with an arcing sword blow that crashed down into it like a tidal wave. The beast slammed into the tree roots.

"Try not to get yourself killed," Jae said, both swords drawn as she stood over the shadow creature that was slowly pushing itself up. She pivoted and thrust one sword straight through the creature's skull. It collapsed into a heap of bone and disintegrated into dust.

Relief flooded Dare's chest, both at her standing beside him and at the simple fact that these monsters could be killed. "Jae," he breathed. He searched for the words he still needed to say. "I . . ."

"Thank me later." She gave him a quick wink before she ran forward, charging one of the other shadow beasts along the walls.

Dare swung around the tree with her. If he could get onto the battlements, then maybe . . .

He made for the wall as Jae ran at the creature. It growled and leapt, crossing the shrinking distance far too quickly. A thunderous roar echoed through the courtyard and another huge beast, this one of fur and muscle, barreled into the monster at full speed, sending it slamming into the wall just ahead of Dare. There was a sickening crunch of bone, and the shadow creature dissolved. The monstrous beast snorted, fangs gleaming, as it stalked toward Jae, its gray fur matted with blood.

Dare stumbled back, but Jae lunged at it, her arms wide, burying her face in the thick fur of its shoulder. "Thank every single one of the fucking gods," Jae said, her swords nearly falling out of her hands. "Lucien!"

Dare puffed out a sigh. "Aetherann's bollocks," he said. "It's good to see you. We thought—"

A scream of rage erupted from the battlements. "You fucking mutt!" Tanithe shrieked. "I *killed* you!"

Lucien lifted his head, Jae's arms still wrapped around his neck, and growled so loud and deep that the ground rumbled.

Tanithe threw another stone at the ground, and a creature billowed from it. This one was twice the size of the others and spread massive wings of shadow and mist as it took to the sky. Jae released Lucien and stepped forward, swinging her twin blades at the ready.

The winged shadow beast swooped down and collided with Lucien in a flurry of bone and fur. Lucien roared as the creature dug its tenebrous talons into his shoulders and lifted him off the ground.

Dare hit the corner at a dead run. He leapt, setting a foot against one of the adjoining walls, and bounded to the other a little higher up. Back and forth until his hands gripped the top of the wall and he swung himself up and over the crenelations.

He landed in a crouch as the flying creature hurled Lucien through the massive stained glass window above him.

CHAPTER 63

VERITY GRIPPED HER SWORD before the creature was on its feet, but she didn't draw it. It stood, its shoulders nearly as tall as Verity was herself, and shook shards of glass from its dark fur. The guards and the king wheeled on it. King Dominic readied his sword.

"Wait!" Gregor stepped between Dominic and the beast, hands upraised, as Verity's mind raced to catch up. "Your Majesty, he's our friend."

Lucien's yellow eyes swept over the group before landing on Corvin. A rumble of a growl started deep in his chest as he lowered his head, teeth bared and ears pressed back. Shouting and screaming poured in through the broad expanse of the broken window.

Corvin held up his hands, a model of innocence that lasted for a breath before he thrust his open palm toward Lucien. Something struck the beast under the chin, snapping his head back and launching him through the window he'd shattered only moments before. His rage rattled the remaining windows of the hall.

Now that Corvin had started the fight, Verity was damn sure going to finish it. She slid into Corvin, gripping his outstretched wrist in one hand as she elbowed him hard in the ribs. The air flew out of him with a groan. She spun him around with her, putting their backs to the shattered window.

With Corvin behind her, Verity cast a wave of force at the floor, sending them both crashing into the gardens below. They landed hard in the grass, though Corvin broke her fall. She rolled off him, her chest aching for breath, but she forced herself to her feet and drew her sword before he had a chance to stand.

The gardens were carnage and chaos. Bodies were scattered across the ground and monsters made of shadow stalked through the courtyard, including an enormous creature with wings that circled above.

Crosse stood and drew his sword. Hot breath grazed the back of Verity's neck as Lucien's monstrous form stepped around her. Corvin's steel eyes darted between Warden and beast.

"I won't let you take him," Verity ground out between clenched teeth.

"The weapon's dangerous, Warden," Corvin said, circling her and Lucien slowly. "You'll come to understand this before the end. You'll beg me to take him." Between one blink and the next, his eyes began to glow with a pale light. Then he was moving on them, swinging that massive sword as though it weighed no more than a cavalry saber.

Verity dove out of the way. She rolled as she landed, putting some distance between her and Corvin as his sword cleaved inches deep into the ground. She snatched a shield from one of the fallen palace guards. She slipped her arm into the strap, raising the shield just as Corvin brought the blade down.

The shield deflected the blow, her arm vibrating with the impact. He swung again, just as fast, just as hard, and Verity leapt out of the way. Lucien lunged at Corvin, mighty jaws open, ready to rip his throat out. But the shifter bounced harmlessly off his target, some sort of force stopping him mere inches from Corvin's body. Lucien lunged again. The invisible armor around Corvin held, but the strength of the attack pushed him back a step.

Corvin swung, aiming across Verity's torso. She ducked beneath the blade and charged into the opening. Her sword was a blur of motion as she unleashed strike after strike after strike at him, hoping to keep him off balance.

The Westholden captain parried each one, his blade—longer than Verity was tall—moving with an unnatural speed for something of that size. Lucien moved to circle behind him, but Corvin spun away from them both. He slashed toward Lucien to drive him back. Lucien yowled as flecks of hot blood splattered against Verity's face. Fear lodged in her throat, but he was still standing, blood running freely down his snout to drip into the grass.

Corvin leapt, his sword swinging for Verity's head. He was so *fast*. Verity barely raised her shield in time, and the force of the impact drove her to one knee.

Verity tightened her grip on the shield and muttered a quiet incantation. Corvin wasted no time. His next strike crashed down on her, but Verity stood into the blow. Her shield absorbed the force and reflected it back at Corvin, sending him stumbling.

In that moment, Drystan's voice was as clear as if he were standing beside her. *You've got this, Vee.*

And as Corvin regained his balance and his glowing gray eyes met hers, she charged.

Dare ran along the wall, scanning the battlements for Tanithe. She wasn't where he'd last seen her. Overhead, a roar sounded, and Lucien flew back out through the same window, followed closely by Verity holding onto—

Is that Crosse?

They slammed into the ground, sending dirt and grass scattering. Dare stepped into the shadows of the palace walls as the flying creature took another pass over the gardens.

It let out a shriek that made the ground tremble, several amber leaves shaking loose from Tacrna's tree. Throughout the courtyard were piles of dark gray dust, one or more arrows sticking out of the ground beside each one. Disintegrated shadow beasts.

Nice shooting, Finn.

On the far side of the garden, Solace and Jae headed toward the tree, while Verity and Lucien battled Corvin a short distance away. Dare focused on the battlements. The best way he could help them was to find Tanithe before she did more damage.

With his next step, the stones warped beneath his feet. His vision wobbled as pain pulsed in his temples. Dare set his hand on the palace wall to steady himself.

Little Darcy Wilhaven, Tanithe cooed, caressing his mind like a lover. *Too scared to join the fight?*

He scanned the battlements again, but there was no sign of her. *Stop trying to read my mind.* He kept his thoughts calm.

Tanithe's voice drawled along the base of his skull where a dull ache was building. *Make me . . .*

Dare rubbed at his eyes with his thumb and forefinger, hoping to get the world to stop spinning.

Talons sunk into his mind, cultivating a pounding headache in their wake. *Let's see what lovely goodies you have for me in here.*

Dare gritted his teeth. *Get. Out.*

Tanithe dug in harder, rooting around inside his head. As his knees buckled, he leaned against the wall for balance.

Oh! Oh, my dear, sweet little lordling . . . Tanithe's grin scraped against the inside of his skull. *Are you really so . . . Perceptive . . . ?* Her laughter echoed in roiling waves. *I'm impressed that you've kept this little gem hidden from me, my pet. But what fun we'll have now that I know.*

Dare shut his eyes against the pain, but her laughter crashed through his mind, sending fragmented shards of magic bouncing into every corner of his brain. His knees slammed into the stones as he fell, and he pressed his hands into his temples, trying to ease the pressure. He couldn't see. He couldn't stand. He spiraled inward, searching for something to hold onto, to steady himself.

I am here, the voice in the back of his mind said. *Let me help you.*

Tanithe's echoing laughter trailed off. *What is that?* Her voice was almost . . . hesitant.

Dare struggled to focus. *I . . . I don't . . .*

I am here, that small voice said again. The voice that, up until this moment, he'd thought was his own. *Will you let me in?*

He's mine, Tanithe bellowed, her mental talons digging in deeper.

Dare doubled over, falling through the overwhelming agony, spiraling in and down, and so he stretched his consciousness toward that voice with every piece of himself he could gather and said, *Yes.*

Against the back of his eyelids, a pair of eyes flashed, immense and star-filled.

As though a trap had been sprung, a wall of night slammed down around his mind. It sat tight against him like a suit of armor and yet seemed to stretch on and on for miles. For eons. The pain abated as the world slowly stopped spinning. His mind was still.

Quiet.

A calmness settled into Dare's chest, pumping through his body with every beat of his heart, even as the battle raged below and screaming still drifted up from the city on the wind.

As his vision cleared, he was still kneeling on the battlements along the top of the garden wall. "What in the name of—"

Over the courtyard, the shadow drake shrieked as it circled on wings of pure darkness.

Later.

All thoughts of Tanithe had been pushed out of his mind along with her presence. Dare stood and sprinted along the wall toward Solace and Jae.

And Taerna's tree.

Gregor stared at the broken window where Lucien, Verity and Captain Crosse had just disappeared.

"You have exactly ten seconds to explain," King Dominic demanded.

Hoping to out-pace the growing suspicion on the king's face, Gregor explained about Lucien and what he knew about Tanithe's shadows.

Dominic signaled his guards and strode down the hall, shouting orders to rally his soldiers. "I want these shadow creatures out of my city." None of the guards seemed concerned that their king meant to lead the defense of the city himself.

Gregor followed. "I should come with you."

The king didn't slow as he called over his shoulder, "Can you fight?"

Gregor's hesitation was answer enough.

"You've done your job," Dominic said. "You've advised me. Now go back to the throne room. There's a door behind the throne that leads to a secure chamber. Lock yourself in until I return." And then he was gone, down the stairs and through the archway below. Out into the city—his city—to protect his people.

Gregor stood alone at the top of the stairs, listening to the shouts and screams that filtered in from outside. Had he really done his job? Had he done everything he could to help? He tried to imagine what Duke Wilhaven would have done in this situation.

"Probably cower while his people were slaughtered in the street."

Gregor startled, the too-familiar voice driving a spike of fear through him. He spun around, and she was there—right *there*—her outstretched hand waiting to receive his throat as he turned. He tried to flinch back, but Tanithe Ash caught hold of him, her nails like talons gripping along the sides of his neck, pinching between the tendons.

A strangled cry escaped him. He grasped at her fingers, trying to pry them away from his throat.

"If I can't have *him*," she said quietly, almost to herself. "I'll have to make do with you." She took a single step toward the stairs. The edge of the top step brushed Gregor's heel as she leaned him backward. She had only to let him go to send him toppling down the marble staircase.

"Too easy," she purred, pulling him closer.

He clawed at her hand, trying to get a breath. Instead of dropping him as he feared, she turned and hurled him through the hallway. Gregor landed hard on his side and rolled a short distance, his shoulder screaming from the impact. He lay there, gasping and choking as the air flowed into his lungs again. Tanithe's footfalls sounded gently on the long carpet.

Gregor sucked in another lungful of air, coughing hard. His shoulder throbbed as he tried to push himself up, but Tanithe grabbed him by the front of his shirt and hauled him to his feet like he was nothing. Like he was a doll.

Fear closed like a vise around his heart. He couldn't stop her. She could do whatever she wanted to him.

With a hand gripping his collar, she drove him across the hallway, slamming his back into the wall. Gregor's vision went white as his head connected with the smooth stone. Tanithe leaned in, her body pressing against his, pinning him. One arm rested casually beside his head while she slid her other arm under his chin, pressing his head back. Her scent filled his nose—warm honeysuckle in springtime, but with a sharpness buried beneath the surface. Tanithe grinned into his upturned face, eyes manic.

"Aw, did your friends leave you all alone?" she whispered, her breath tickling his ear. "While they're off dancing with Ainam's lackey, or trying to stop my demons from ransacking the city, do they know where you are?" She pressed herself tighter against him, her knee between his legs. "Poor little Gregor," she cooed. "I wonder . . . Do they even remember that you're here?"

Gregor couldn't move. Panic gripped his heart as surely as she gripped him. Tanithe traced the outer shell of his ear with her fingernail. He tried to lean his head away from her touch, but she was everywhere, encompassing him in darkness and—

Shadows. It wasn't just a trick of her presence and the terror clawing at him, but *her* shadows—the ones she used for traveling. She was going to take him away again. He struggled to get out of her grip, but she only leaned her forearm harder against his throat, cutting off his breath again. He grabbed at her arm, at her shoulders, at the wall, but found no give.

Darcy . . . Help me . . .

There was no help. No one could help him. She was right. They were all occupied with the fight outside, and he was here. Alone. With her.

"Shall we see how things are going out there?" she purred, leaning in so that her lips brushed against his neck. "We can always have some fun while we wait for them to kill each other."

Gregor went still, something hard pressing against the small of his back. He slid his hand along the wall, his shoulder protesting as he reached back.

The shadows coalesced around them both, their chill seeping into his bones. Gregor drew Dare's hidden dagger and thrust it blindly forward. His stomach twisted over itself at the squish of flesh and scrape of the blade against bone. He couldn't keep his grip on the hilt as Tanithe staggered back with a howl of rage. He almost fell to the floor as she pulled away.

Through the flickering darkness surrounding her, the dagger stuck out from between her ribs, buried to the hilt.

As her body dissolved into shadow, her wild eyes locked on his. "You . . ." Tanithe sneered through clenched teeth. "I will kill you, Gregor Thalesen. I swear it."

She vanished as Gregor fell back, steadying himself against the wall. The long hallway was empty in both directions. He could go left, toward the throne room and the safety King Dominic had offered, or right, down the stairs and toward the battle. Toward his friends and Darcy.

Gregor turned and ran, taking the stairs as fast as he could.

Verity and Lucien traded blow after blow with Corvin, though his attacks were relentless. He was faster than should have ever been possible. The force redirection spell on her shield was helping, but it wouldn't last forever.

As Lucien harried him, Corvin's attention darted behind Verity. A wicked smile danced across his lips. "You've brought me my prize, Warden."

Solace.

Verity spared a glance over her shoulder. Solace was moving toward the tree with Jae, their swords drawn and ready.

They'd made it. Verity just needed to keep Corvin busy. She sidestepped, shoving a thrust of magical force toward him. If she could draw his attention, maybe Lucien could flank him.

"It's too late!" she shouted. "I won't let you touch him."

Corvin shook his head, his face sorrowful. "The Lord Ainam helps those in need, even when the hour grows late and all hope seems lost."

He spun his sword and stabbed it into the earth. The air hardened around him in a sphere that expanded outward, driving Verity and Lucien back several feet. Lucien snarled.

Corvin clasped his hands around the hilt of his sword and began to chant.

Verity launched a Banishment at the sphere before charging forward, but it still pushed her away.

"*Verity!*"

She whirled at Solace's anguished scream. He'd stopped in the middle of the path, clutching his chest.

Lucien barked a warning as Solace's eyes flashed with an inner light. Jae stepped back, her swords rising slightly to level at him.

Solace's face went slack, all emotion slipping away as he turned to regard Jae with silent indifference. He raised his hand, and vines sprang out of the ground, grasping for Jae. She dove to the side, rolling to land on her feet a short distance away, only to have to flatten herself to the ground as shards of ice flew through the space where she'd been standing.

"What did you do?" Verity screamed at Corvin. He'd stopped chanting and was watching the scene from within his shielded sphere.

"I've set it free," the Chosen of Ainam said gravely. "The weapon has been unleashed." His steel gray eyes, still shining, locked onto Verity. "I told you, Warden. You will beg me to take him away before the end. Only I can control it now."

CHAPTER 64

ABOVE THE COURTYARD, THE winged shadow beast circled, shrieking at Corvin. Verity ducked behind her shield as Solace tore through the gardens, shooting fire and ice at anything that moved.

The creature in the sky swooped at Corvin, talons extended, but not even that demonic creature of chaos could penetrate the shell that still surrounded him.

But Corvin winced when the beast collided with the shield. He was channeling whatever divine power he had to hold it up. That meant it was breakable.

That meant Verity could break it.

Verity sheathed her sword and reached into her pocket, closing her hand around the periapt she'd been carrying since they'd fled Brookshire. She emptied her mind, focusing inward to the wellspring of power at her center.

The hole of sorrow and misery that had torn open when Drystan died greeted her. It sat within her like a bottomless pit. She'd done everything she could to ignore it, to push it down, to keep herself from falling in. But now, as Verity stared into that blackness, she let herself fall. Nothing would distract her. No fears or worries or grief would block the flow of power when the time came.

There was a blur of motion as Dare dove off the high walls. He rolled to his feet as a sharp gust of wind pelted him with debris. The shadow creature banked and dove toward Jae.

She tried to twist away from the monster, but it caught her arm in its dark, bony talons and pulled her into the sky. Jae swung at it with the sword in her free hand, but the beast held her so precariously that she couldn't get a good strike.

A dagger was in Dare's hand, poised to throw, but the beast was already too high for him to reach.

Verity knew she should feel something, but the bleak nothingness had swallowed her with such immediacy that she could only watch as the monster lifted Jae high into the air.

Lucien growled as he circled Corvin, a beast stalking its prey.

Corvin looked to the sky and tilted his head, considering. "What's that expression," he mused to no one in particular, "about two birds?" He raised his hand toward the creature. Toward Jae.

Much like the librarian in the Reach ages ago, the creature's swirls of mist and shadow began to harden. It spasmed as the stasis magic spread through it, dropping Jae from its talons only a moment before its wings stopped beating and it, too, began to plummet.

Dare shouted something, but Verity couldn't hear him over Lucien's roar. Solace moved his hand, and the grass and earth beneath Dare bucked, sending him sprawling. Lucien charged past Verity, aiming for where Jae was about to collide with the ground.

Verity let the emptiness take root, opening herself up to it fully. It was an absence—Drystan's absence. She couldn't save him, but she could use her grief to do this for her friends now. She could save them.

A little more. She just needed to let go a little more.

Lucien leapt into the air beneath Jae. He slowed her freefall by altering her trajectory with his body. They crashed together, Lucien slamming hard into the ground, breaking Jae's fall as she landed on him.

The shadow beast landed a short distance away, sending out a shock wave of dirt and dust. Dare scrambled across the grass to them, and as Verity turned toward Corvin, she registered somewhere in the back of her mind that Jae was barely moving.

And Lucien wasn't moving at all.

Verity reached into her wellspring of power, reciting the familiar incantation. She'd done it a hundred times. But she augmented the middle portion of the spell to increase the rate of transference, changing what should have been a single blast into a channeled beam. With her soul open and empty, the periapt clutched in her hand, Verity unleashed herself upon Corvin Crosse.

The beam of force slammed his shield, sending him staggering. She let the magic flow through her, knowing it would take her strength along with it. She didn't care. She was going to end this. Now.

Corvin struggled to maintain the shield as Verity poured more and more magic—more and more of herself—into the spell. The shield shattered. Verity's magic—more magic than she had ever channeled at once—barreled into Corvin with a sickening *crack*, hurling him through the air. He landed near the wall in a crumpled heap. He didn't move.

Verity lowered her hands, her breath trembling as she inhaled. The soft glow from the periapt was completely dark as she let it fall from her fingers. The shield was heavy on her arm. She swayed as she forced back the exhaustion and tried to shove the sorrow and darkness away again, willing herself to feel something. Anything.

Fire and wind hurtled through the gardens as Solace's magic flared indiscriminately, uprooting shrubs and launching stones and mulch in every direction.

Dare hauled Jae to cover behind the sacred tree. She crouched with him, holding one arm against her side, her face tight with pain. Gregor appeared on the path coming from the palace and joined them.

Dare left Jae with him and made a run for Lucien. He was in his human form now, but still lay unmoving in the grass. But Dare's sprint drew Solace's attention. A wall of fire burst from the ground to block his way. Dare stopped short, throwing up his hands to guard against the searing heat.

And where was Finn? Verity scanned the walls around the garden, but she was nowhere to be found. Verity hoped that she was some place safe.

Warmth slowly trickled into her chest. She focused on the images of her friends. Finn and Jae comforting her in the woods outside Brookshire. Dare singing raunchy songs as they traveled through Aethir. Lucien and Gregor riding across the plains to save Solace.

Solace. The kindest, gentlest soul she'd ever known. Solace, who didn't deserve any of what was happening to him.

She held those thoughts in her mind, forcing out the emptiness that had taken over.

Her legs shook, and her shield hung by her side, but Verity started toward Solace. Rain began to fall, hissing where it struck the flames burning in the grass.

As Solace thrust his hand at Dare again, shards of ice erupted from his fingertips. Verity threw her magic into a wall in front of Dare. It was one of the first spells she'd mastered at the College. She could do it in her sleep. But she'd drained herself smashing Corvin's shield, even with the periapt. She barely got the wall up before the ice shattered against it. Her leg buckled, dropping her to one knee.

Dare swung back behind Taerna's tree, putting the massive trunk between him and Solace. He met Verity's eyes through the storm of mist and smoke. He opened his mouth but closed it again without a word. Verity nodded all the same.

Nothing needed to be said.

Solace stalked toward Verity, his face empty, blank. Only the weapon remained. She willed the gears in her arms to move, dragging her shield up to block another volley of ice.

Exhaustion crept through her body, taking root in her legs and the shoulder of her sword arm. She forced herself to her feet. The chill wind whipped through the courtyard as though in a hurricane. Verity sidestepped away from the tree, putting more distance between her and the others. Up ahead, beyond Solace, Lucien stirred.

"Solace!" she cried over the roar of the wind. "Solace, listen to me. You're not a weapon. You're human. You're a *person.*"

His face tensed. Just for an instant, he gritted his teeth. The wind picked up, and a gout of flame shot from his hand, burning the grass at her feet.

He was fighting it.

On the other side of the tree, Gregor and Jae darted to Lucien's side, but Solace didn't try to stop them. His attention was on Verity. Good. Let him focus on her. Let her buy them time to get out.

The five of them were all connected through their shared histories, their shared experiences—Finn and Dare; Dare and Gregor and Jae; Jae and Lucien. She was the outlier. They were her friends, and she knew they cared about her, but what they had with each other was different. Special.

She would be the tower that guarded them. Her body would be the wall that shielded them from harm. Just as *he* had done so many years ago. Just as Drystan had done. They had shielded her so that she would live. So she could get to *this* moment. So she could save her friends.

The gale was so strong against the broad side of her shield that she slid back a couple of inches in the mud, her knees shaking.

A presence appeared at her back, bracing her against the wind. "I'm here," Dare said.

Her jaw clenched. "Get them out of here!" she shouted.

"We're not leaving." He tucked his shoulder in behind her, keeping her from sliding back any farther. "We're in this together. All of us."

The warmth of his presence and the strength of his resolve solidified within her, joining the images of her friends that she'd been holding onto, bolstering her.

With Dare steadying her, Verity called out again, "Solace! I know you can hear me. I know you're still in there."

He prowled closer, something like pain or rage twisting his features. Verity stepped toward him, and Dare moved with her.

"Please, Solace." Another step closer. "You're *not* a weapon." Another step. He was only a few feet away. "You're our friend."

The vortex of wind around them burst into flames, hissing in the cold rain. The ground split and cracked. Fire and smoke and bits of stone encircled the three of them. She couldn't see the others anymore. She couldn't see the palace or even the tree. It was only Solace in front of her and Dare behind her, as though the rest of the world had exploded into fire, and they were all that was left.

"You're our friend, Solace!" Verity shouted. Her voice broke like the earth at her feet. She pressed forward, desperate to keep her and Dare from sliding back into the flames. She didn't know how much longer she could remain standing against the storm. "*Please.* Come back to us."

Solace took another step forward, and something inside him shattered. A shock wave rippled from him. Dare threw his arm around Verity's waist, as though he might be knocked away by the impact. Solace roared and fell to his knees, clutching his head in his hands.

The vortex of fire and smoke remained. The rain still fell. But when he lifted his face, it was no longer the weapon staring blankly back at her.

It was Solace.

"Verity . . ." His voice was so small and tired. He looked down at his hands, like he wasn't sure if they were truly his.

She stumbled the short distance to him, sliding onto her knees in the mud. The ground heaved and split again, rain and mud sloshing into the fissure that opened around them. Dare jumped across the gap that had formed and skidded to a stop beside Solace.

"You're alright," Verity breathed. She threw her arms around his shoulders. He sank into her, shaking. She eyed the wall of flames still swirling violently. "The fire," she said. "Can you stop it?"

Solace pulled back and surveyed the bubble the three of them were trapped in. "I can't. I'm not—"

Dare grasped Solace's hand. "You have to try."

"I can't," he said again. "You . . . You have to end it."

Verity's breath caught in her throat. No, not after everything. Not after they just got him back. "No," she choked out. "No, there has to be—"

"Verity, there is nothing left of me to save." His eyes were filled with tears.

Her heart cracked.

"This is all I have left. Just this. This moment." Solace took a deep, ragged breath. "Corvin smashed the wall." He set a hand over his heart. "The wall that let me stay . . . it's gone. I felt it crumble, and I started to melt away." He met her gaze and held it as he said, "But I heard you." He squeezed Dare's hand, bringing it to his chest. "I felt you. I fought my way back. But I . . . can't stay."

"Solace, we can fix it," she said, taking his face in her hands.

A tear rolled down his cheek, joining the rivulets that fell from his rain-soaked hair. "There's nothing left to fix." His jaw clenched, and his eyes shut tight as he grimaced. "I can't . . . I can't . . . Please, I don't want to hurt anyone. I don't want to hurt you."

"But the tree," Dare said, a tightness in his voice. He looked over his shoulder to where the tree stood somewhere beyond the maelstrom. "If we could get to the tree, we could—"

"I can't control it," Solace forced out. His breathing was coming in shallow gasps. "Dare, I'm already gone." He doubled over with an anguished sob. His grip tightened on Dare's hand, as though that might be enough to hold him here just a little longer. "Please," he begged. "End it."

If he was right . . . if this last piece of Solace slipped away, they wouldn't survive. Not here, on their knees in front of a living weapon of the gods. And if Corvin was the only one who knew how to control it . . .

Solace's back arched sharply as he cried out. The firestorm surrounding them flared with the spasm and drew closer. He slumped forward, his shoulders shaking.

Verity drew her sword and set the broken point against Solace's chest. *Pyrannis, please, give me the strength . . .*

Solace opened his eyes. "Please . . ." It was scarcely a whisper.

"I can't," she breathed. "Gods, I can't."

Dare wiped the rain from his eyes, tears falling in its wake. He set his hand on hers where she clutched the hilt. He still held onto Solace with his other hand, his knuckles white.

Solace looked to each of them. "I am so grateful," he gasped, "to have known you both."

Verity tightened her grip, Dare's fingers mirroring hers. "I'm sorry," she whispered.

And together, they drove the point of her sword—of her knight's sword—through Solace's heart.

CHAPTER 65

ONE OF DARE'S HANDS still held Solace's. The other was wrapped around Verity's where she gripped her sword. He held his breath as she flung her other arm around Solace's unmoving shoulders.

"I'm sorry," she whispered again. "I'm sorry. I'm sorry."

The rain still fell, and the wind and flames that spiraled around them began to slow but didn't stop. How long would the power last without . . .

He nudged her fingers with his. She withdrew the blade and let it fall into the mud. Dare put his arm around her back, holding her, holding them both, letting the rain wash the blood away. He wanted to say something. He wanted to comfort her, but the pain in his own shattered heart weighed down his thoughts and his words, and he could find nothing within himself but sorrow and grief.

And so Dare did the only thing he could. He held them both, and he let his tears mix with the rain and the river of blood that flowed onto the ground and into it, through the fissures all around their own small island of mud.

He watched it fall and disappear into the cracks where there was nothing below but darkness and dirt and roots—

The roots.

Dare tensed as he shook Verity gently by the shoulder. "Verity, the roots of the tree . . ."

She lifted her head, a question on her lips, but she didn't have a chance to ask it. The rain and wind, the flames and the stone that swirled around them crashed inward in a flare of light that imploded, snuffing itself out. The power of it tore through Dare with all the force of a volcano exploding in the depths of the ocean.

He felt that armor of night and stars slam down around him, shielding him. He tried to hold onto Verity and Solace, but their hands slipped from his fingers as the world spiraled into silence and darkness.

462

CHAPTER 66

THE WORLD HAD GONE still. In the vortex around Verity, only the fire still raged, burning bright, no longer a danger but a beacon. A flare of power. Verity knelt alone in the center of it. She watched the flames whirl even as the smoke and stone were still, as the rain hung unmoving in the air. Her heart thundered in her chest as the flames danced and pulsed.

Pulsed. Like a heartbeat.

Her heartbeat. The fire thrummed in time with her heart. At the realization, the fire flared again, stronger and brighter than before.

She took in the empty space around her. *Dare . . . Where's Dare?*

The flames crackled like a log in a hearth. *Safe,* it said.

Verity turned toward the sound, but there was only fire. "And Solace?"

Tongues of flame sparked. *His essence has returned to the stars.*

Verity blinked back tears. Her legs were still weak, but she forced herself to stand. "Was there no other way?" she asked the flames.

No. The fire drifted closer, the circle constricting. *You have rekindled us.*

She swallowed hard. "Rekindled?"

Awakened.

"You're . . ." Verity licked her lips. The flames mirrored her movement. "You're Pyrannis?"

A pop of fire. *That is one name humans have called me.*

Her mind was reeling. "Why are you here?" She could hardly believe she was demanding answers of a god, but she needed to know.

There was a hiss of laughter as the fire swirled closer until its fingers could brush against her arms. *Your spirit. Your sacrifices. They called me.*

She clenched her fist, the metal plates grinding against each other. "My sacrifices . . ." she repeated.

Your strength in the face of them. Much has changed while we have slumbered, the fire crackled. *Will you be my hand in the world?*

How was this possible? How was any of this possible? Verity peered into the flames. The words stuck in her throat, so she thought them instead. *Your hand? As in—*

Will you be my champion, Verity Corallan? The flames popped. *My Chosen?*

Little tendrils licked up her arms, caressed her face, sending up a quiet hiss as they evaporated the tears on her cheeks, though the flames didn't burn her.

She cleared her throat, finding her voice again. "I haven't had the best experiences with fire," she said quietly.

There was another spark of laughter. *I know. And yet you face your fear despite it.* There was a pause as the fire gently stroked her cheek. *You have more to offer the world. More sacrifices to be made, but more good to be done. Balance to be protected.*

Hope blossomed in her chest as she pictured Drystan, his hand on her shoulder, that small comfort he always offered. He was still with her and always would be. Would he be proud of her? For the work she had done? For the work she could still do?

Do you accept?

She closed her eyes.

"Yes."

✹

Verity looked up into a clear, twilit sky.

"Thank the fucking gods." Dare appeared over her. His eyes were red, but the tension in his face relaxed as he looked her over. "Are you alright?"

Before she could answer there was a groan from nearby. Dare's head jerked toward the sound and he vanished from view, muttering another curse.

Verity pushed herself up onto her elbows. "What happened?"

Jae, Lucien, and Gregor were scattered in the muddy grass. Dare darted from one to the next as they stirred, a new wave of relief washing over his face each time. He knelt beside Gregor, the last to move, his blond hair now filthy and caked in mud.

But Solace . . .

Verity sat up, searching around her. He was here. She'd been holding him when he . . . He'd been right here.

Where is he?

An echo of Pyrannis's voice stirred in her mind. *His essence has returned to the stars.*

"Dare, what happened?" Verity repeated.

He rubbed at his face with both hands, the backs of them smeared with dried blood. "Solace . . ." When he lowered his hands, his face was pained. "When his blood touched the roots of the tree, there was . . ." He shook his head. "I don't even know how to describe it."

"An awakening," Gregor said softly.

Dare nodded. "I passed out. When I woke up, the maelstrom was gone, Solace was gone . . ."

Gone. *Only ichor freely given to the channel of the gods would unmake the weapon.* And so it was. The weapon had been unmade, along with Solace. Not even a body to bury.

Dare took a slow breath before adding, "And Crosse—"

"What about Crosse?" Verity struggled to her feet and staggered toward where she'd last seen his body.

"He's gone," Dare called after her.

No, no, he couldn't be gone. "Where is he?"

"Verity, he was gone when I woke, and you all were . . ."

Something in his voice made her stop. When she looked back, Dare was still kneeling beside Gregor. He moved as though to touch Gregor's hand, but stopped himself. "I didn't know if any of you would wake up."

Verity turned her focus inward, to the broken pieces of her heart. Where before there had only been the emptiness of all the losses she had suffered, she found now a little flame glowing among the shards, pulsing in time with the beat of her heart.

Hello, she said in her mind.

The little flame danced at her thought. *Hello, Verity Corallan*, it answered.

She searched the faces of the others and thought for a moment that she felt little sparks of power flickering in response. Too faint to pinpoint them, but they were there, like a star you can only see when you start to look away.

"Did you . . . ?" She let the question trail off. She wasn't even sure of the words she needed. Yet somehow, the others knew.

"I did," Jae said, a quaver in her voice.

Lucien nodded slowly.

Beside Dare, Gregor lowered his head. "And me."

With Verity, that made four of them.

Four elemental gods.

Dare started to speak, but a shout from the courtyard gates cut him off. A few guards ran in, followed by King Dominic, who moved with long strides toward the palace, something cradled in his arms. Another guard was at his side, holding what looked like a bundle of dark cloth against whatever Dominic carried. Verity couldn't get a good look.

"Find Epione," the king commanded, his voice like the crack of a whip. "Have her meet me in the southern hall." One of his soldiers sprinted across the courtyard.

Dare inhaled sharply, his hands opening and closing at his sides. "Finn . . ."

Her golden hair fell across her face, sweat-streaked and bloody, and her arm hung limp at her side as Dominic cradled her. Verity ran to the king, who didn't slow as he crossed the gardens. Blood, black dust, and sweat stained Dominic's shirt, though he appeared unharmed.

Verity's head swam. It was so much blood. "What happened?" she choked out. She followed after him, though she could barely keep up. The exhaustion in her muscles dragged at her as she forced herself forward.

The king's pace didn't falter. "She took down a dozen of those creatures, at least," he said. He took the palace stairs two at a time. "When I found her, three had circled her. One of them caught her leg before I could get to her."

Inside the main hall of the palace, Dominic used his elbow to shove a large crystal vase off the table in the center of the foyer. It shattered on the tile, sending water and flower petals splattering across the floor. He laid Finn down on the table gently, almost reverently. The soldier who had been at the king's side all along was pressing a tabard to Finn's leg.

"She's lost a lot of blood," Dominic said as Verity came to Finn's side. "But we have the best healer in Drahkonia."

Finn lay unmoving. A leather belt was tied tightly above where the soldier still held the tabard, slowing the flow of blood.

A voice called from the grand staircase in the hall, "I can't find her, Sire."

"Check her rooms," Dominic snapped. "Now!" He turned to one of the other guards that had followed. "Go to the infirmary. Bring bandages, disinfectant, whatever you can carry. Go."

The soldier ran off without a moment's hesitation, dropping something he'd been holding. Wood clattered against the tile. It was Finn's bow, broken in two, lying discarded on the floor.

Another broken bow.

Verity took Finn's pale hand and cursed at not being able to feel the touch of her skin. She pressed Finn's hand to her cheek. She was so cold.

Ever since Drystan's death, Finn had been the one helping her through. Finn had been the one looking after her.

If you're not going to take care of yourself, we will.

But what about you? How are you?

It's only over if you give up.

"Finn," she said, pressure building in her throat. She couldn't lose anyone else. She couldn't lose *her.* "Finn," she whispered again. "Hold on . . . please. I . . ." Hot tears slid down her cheeks as she smoothed Finn's hair away from her face.

Even with the belt and the soldier holding the cloth tight against her leg, blood trickled from the open wound, pooling on the table and dripping steadily onto the floor.

"I need you to hold on, alright? We're going to go to Embercliff. Remember? You're going to love it there. We'll sit on the edge of the cliffs and watch the boats glittering across the sea." She squeezed Finn's hand, holding it to her cheek. "Alright? We'll go. I promise. But you have to hold on."

The fire in Verity's chest roared to life. Pyrannis's fire. It stretched within her, reaching for Finn.

It was the same power Solace had had. The power he'd used to heal Dare, pulling him back from Death's Gates. The power that could have saved Drystan.

That *could* save Finn.

I can save her.

"Move back," Verity ordered. With a glance at the king, the soldier stepped back and released the pressure he'd been keeping on the wound. Verity pushed the cloth aside, revealing a jagged, bloody gash on Finn's thigh. The white of bone shone through the mass of torn flesh and muscle.

Verity set her hands on the wound. Even with both hands side by side, it barely covered the length of it. She had no idea what to do, but if there was a chance . . . She had to try.

She closed her eyes and found that fire within her. The raging, cleansing, purifying fire. She could see the wound behind her eyelids, and she directed the fire to flow into Finn, willing it where to go, what to cauterize.

When the flare of power subsided, Verity let out her breath and checked beneath her hands. The bleeding had stopped. Thick white scar tissue encompassed the entire area where the wound had been.

"Pyrannis's flames," Dare swore behind her. She hadn't realized he'd followed. "Verity . . ."

She glanced over her shoulder.

Dare's finger lightly brushed the scar on his chest. "It's like . . ."

"I know," she said.

"How did—" He stopped before he finished the question.

"Verity?" The quiet voice was barely audible.

Dare choked on a laugh as tears filled his eyes. Verity spun back to the table to see Finn smiling weakly up at her.

Seeing her alive, awake, Verity let out her own laughing sob. Finn was still so very pale. Verity took her hand again and didn't let go until the old healer, Epione, arrived and shooed everyone off. Verity allowed Dare to lead her away from the table with his arm wrapped around her shoulders.

After the healer fussed over Finn for several long minutes, two more guards arrived with a litter and gently transferred Finn onto it at Epione's instruction. They bore her away without another word.

Verity wanted to follow, but Dare still held onto her. The touch, the weight of his arm around her shoulders, grounded her. She guessed it might be doing the same for him. She wasn't sure which of them needed it more.

The old healer, white haired and stooped with age, lingered for a moment with the king, who had to nearly bend in half so she could speak in his ear. He nodded and said something quietly in return. After, she turned toward Verity, and Dare stepped back to give them space. Her lined face was stern, but there was a kindness in her bright eyes.

"I don't know what you did," Epione said, "but from what I can tell, and what Dominic just told me, I don't think that young girl would have survived until I got here. You saved her life." She touched Verity lightly on the arm. "I will tend to her. And if you or your friends need aid, come to the infirmary. I'll take care of your injuries personally."

Not a single thought passed through Verity's mind as the old healer walked away. But Dare jostled her out of her mindlessness when he threw his arms around her in a tight hug.

"You did it," he said, holding her close.

Verity wrapped her arms around him. "We did," she said. "It hardly seems possible."

King Dominic crossed the room to them. With one last squeeze, Verity stepped away from Dare. "Taerna and the other gods are awake," she said to the king.

He nodded, moving past the both of them, toward the open doorway. Her friends had gathered just inside the foyer. They were exhausted and hurt. Jae clutched one arm to her chest, and Lucien leaned against Gregor. Each one of them, Verity and Dare included, were covered in cuts and bruises and mud.

But they were alive.

"Incredible," King Dominic said, peering out across the ruined gardens. The tree in the center still stood as tall and proud as ever, but the amber and sepia tones in the leaves had been replaced by healthy, vibrant greens. In fact, it seemed as though the whole tree stretched even higher toward the evening sky.

"The six of you will stay in the palace as my personal guests for as long as you'd like," Dominic continued. "I shall have to think of a fitting reward, though I don't know what could possibly suffice, so for the moment I will simply say, *thank you*."

And King Dominic Drahkon bowed his head and knelt before them.

CHAPTER 67

DARE STOOD ON THE battlements overlooking the courtyard. He stared through the darkness at the cracks and up-heaved ground around the sacred tree. He could mark without a second thought the exact spot where Solace had died hours earlier. He focused on it, remembering how Solace's blood had run into the earth where the three of them knelt together.

Was it fate or just luck?

"I thought I might find you here." Gregor stepped onto the stone battlements, arms wrapped around himself in the chill autumn night.

"You did?"

Gregor smiled. "No. Honestly, I almost gave up." He leaned his elbows against the top of the parapet and looked out across the gardens. "You know, you're hard to find when you don't want to be found."

"A useful skill in my line of work." Dare set his hands on the top of the wall, his arm brushing Gregor's. There was a gentle thrumming to the touch that hadn't been there before—soft and light, like leaves dancing on the wind. That would take some getting used to.

Gregor pulled his arm away, putting space between them.

"It's alright," Dare said, inching closer to him again.

"But you can feel it, can't you?" Gregor knew how magic felt to Dare. He was one of the very few who had always known.

"I can," Dare said. "But it's different. It's not like regular magic. And it's not like Crosse or Tanithe either."

Gregor pulled his arms tighter around himself, but Dare brushed the back of his hand against Gregor's cheek.

There was a soft tingle against his skin, like a gentle puff of wind. "This feels . . . nice."

Gregor eyed him sidelong, as though he wasn't sure he believed him. "Really?"

Dare leaned one elbow against the top of the battlement as he angled to face him. "In all the time we've known each other, when have I ever lied to you, Gregor?"

He smiled. "You mean besides when you and Jae were trying to convince me we weren't going to get in trouble?"

Dare snorted a laugh. "*Besides* that."

Gregor sidestepped into him, leaning his shoulder against Dare's chest.

Dare wrapped his arm around Gregor and pulled him in. "How does it feel to you?" he asked. "I have to admit, I'm curious."

Gregor was silent for a long while. "I don't know," he said at last. "It's strange. It doesn't *feel* strange, I mean . . . it . . . it feels right, and I find that I can't quite recall what I felt like before. Like . . . it's just always been here. And yet I have no idea what any of it means." He sighed and leaned into Dare a little more. "Does that make sense?"

Dare kissed the top of his head. "Perfectly."

"Why the four of us?" Gregor whispered the question into the night.

"Maybe it was fate?"

Gregor set his head against Dare's shoulder. "Then why not you?"

"Maybe that was fate too," he said.

After another long moment, Gregor sighed. "Where do you think she went? Tanithe."

Dare gave half a shrug. "Hopefully she found some hole to crawl into and died. From what you told me, that was a hell of a stab wound you gave her." When Gregor tensed in his arms, he added, "Honestly, I don't know. Maybe back to Valda. I'm sure she'll want to spin a story for the Council before Drahkonia's emissaries get there."

"Do you think she'll come back?"

"I don't know," he said truthfully. "I don't think it's likely. I suspect she'll want to wait and see how things play out."

"I'm sorry about your dagger," Gregor said.

Dare's arms tightened around him. "I don't care about the dagger."

Gregor relaxed into him again, and they stood out on the battlements for a long while. Finally, Gregor looked up at him. "How are you not tired?"

"Oh, I'm exhausted," Dare said, almost before he'd finished the question.

Gregor laughed. "I'm falling asleep on my feet." He gave Dare's arm a gentle squeeze before turning back to the palace. "Are you coming in?"

"Not just yet," Dare said.

"Don't stay out here too late."

"I won't."

With a sleepy wave of his hand, Gregor disappeared inside.

Dare turned back toward the courtyard and leaned his arms on the parapet again. "You never answered my question."

A voice echoed through the back of his mind. It sounded a little like his own, but he knew it wasn't—not now that he knew what to listen for. There was a duality to it, like two voices speaking at once. *You seemed occupied.*

"So . . . ? Was it fate or luck?"

A soft, if somewhat sly smile flashed in his mind. *There is often only a faint line between the two.*

"And you?" he asked, looking up at the stars. "Who are you, exactly?"

I've had many names, most long forgotten. The easiest name for you to comprehend is Tykaras.

Dare stiffened slightly, his fingers curling around the edge of the parapet. Verity had asked him about that word on the plains of Southreach. She'd said it appeared in the text from the library with the strange, beautifully painted eyes filled with galaxies. Those eyes—*that* was what he'd seen when Verity had channeled magic through him. And again during the battle, when Tanithe was in his head.

When the voice had offered to help him.

He swallowed. "So, you're another god?"

There was a strange pause before the voice answered, *What did you think I was?*

"Honestly? I was getting a little concerned that I was losing my mind."

The god in his head made a noise—was that a laugh? *The one does not preclude the other.*

Dare chuckled. "That's fair," he said. "Am I allowed to ask . . . what kind of god are you? I'm embarrassed to say, I've never heard of you before."

You may ask me anything you wish, Child, though I may not always choose to answer. I have been forgotten in most of the mortal lands, as my influence is a subtle one, not conducive to vivid displays of power. My realm is that of fate. The voice paused, and Dare swore he could hear a smirk in the tone when it continued. *Or luck. There is often only a faint line between the two.*

Dare had another question but didn't dare speak it aloud. And so, within the quiet of his own mind, he asked, *I've heard you before, haven't I? Before today?*

Yes, Tykaras said. *I've followed you for some time. Since you approached the weapon's location in the area you call Westhold.*

"His name was Solace," Dare said aloud.

It was not, but that is how you knew him.

Dare's hands tensed against the stone.

This bothers you?

"He was my friend, and we just killed him."

His words were met with silence.

"Yes, it bothers me."

I see.

Dare ran his fingers through his hair. "Why weren't you slumbering with the other gods?"

Because I wasn't there when they poured their power into the weapon and fought back against the interlopers.

"The interlopers?" *Ainam and Vire?* He didn't want to speak their names aloud.

Yes.

They don't belong here?

No.

But why weren't you there? Why didn't you fight with the others?

A long sigh tickled the back of his mind. *I was otherwise occupied,* Tykaras said.

Dare wasn't sure what he'd expected, but it wasn't that. He clenched his fists as he leaned against the battlements, taking in the courtyard and the rest of Taernfane beyond. Somewhere across the river lay Brookshire and, still further, Valda. "So you've been here this whole time? While the other gods slept and the world went to shit, you've been here?"

It is not as simple as that.

"Then explain it to me," Dare snapped.

I will, the god said. *But not tonight.*

Dare deflated, the gentle tone quieting his frustration.

Humans are such beautiful, fragile things. Sleep for now, my child.

He found it difficult to argue with that. He'd barely stayed awake while he bathed earlier, the warm water soothing his aching muscles as it washed away the caked-on mud and dried blood from the battle.

Dare turned toward the palace, but stopped just before stepping inside. "Earlier today," he said, "when you helped me . . . When Tanithe was in my head . . ." He sighed, unable to bring himself to speak the words aloud. *Am I your Chosen?*

The voice was quiet, but a gentle caress trailed along the inside of his mind and down into his chest. It was expansive, as if all the world could be wrapped up within that one touch, and yet it soothed all the worries and fears that stretched into the deepest parts of him.

I will explain, Child. But not tonight.

Dare remembered neither finding his room, nor falling into bed. But he slept more soundly than he ever had.

Epilogue

I SIT IN THE shade of the tree with Verity. Everything's returned to normal now—as normal as things are going to be, in any case. People walk through the gardens, enjoying the sun or admiring the beauty of Taerna's tree, evergreen in the late autumn light.

One family is having a small picnic nearby, taking advantage of the warm day. I can see the pain in Verity's eyes as she stands. She tells me she's going to check on Finn in the infirmary, but I know that's only a half truth. I know that it hurts too much to see the rest of the world move on.

I can still see Gregor and Jae lying in that same spot, unmoving in the grass after we killed you. That was when the power from your death tore through us all, and I thought for sure they were all dead and that, somehow, I was the only one left. I was convinced I'd lost everyone I'd ever cared about on that very spot, and here's this kid eating a fucking pastry like everything's fine.

And as far as they're concerned, I guess everything *is* fine now.

The earth has been smoothed, but the grass hasn't grown back yet. It won't until the spring, so for now I can still see the worn patches of dirt where the three of us knelt together.

And that's where I sit. When I think back on it, I can still feel the cold metal of Verity's hand in mine as she holds her sword.

She can't do it, not alone. I hold her hand, letting her know I'm here. We'll do it together.

Your blood flows warm over my hand and hers. She can't feel it, but I can. It runs along my fingers and down my arm. My other hand holds yours. You're gripping it so tightly, trying to hold on long enough to see it through. I'm holding onto you just as hard, willing you to stay. And then you stop breathing, your hand going slack in mine. And I realize in this moment, as I'm covered in your blood, that I don't know your name.

Even now, the thought jars me awake sometimes. And on those nights, when I can't get back to sleep for all the thoughts swirling in my head, I come to the courtyard, and I sit here.

It's strange to think that now that the gods are awake, my friends carry a kernel of their power. I can feel it in each one of them.

Of course I can. How could I not?

There's the hearth-like warmth in Verity, the sturdy solidity in Lucien, the eddying tides in Jae, and Gregor, a breath of fresh air.

And then there's me . . .

The family finishes their picnic and folds their blanket. The child waves at me as they move past. I smile, though it doesn't reach my eyes.

The difference between Verity and me is that she always carries her knight's memory with her because she thinks she failed him. But I will always carry your memory with me because, while I wish with all my heart that I could have saved you, I know that you—your death—led us to where we are.

Fate or luck . . . however you look at it . . . they can only set the pieces on the board. You still have to make the move. The path is before you, but you can choose to walk it or not.

And it is because of the path you walked, that I can now walk mine.

What's your name? But I catch myself before I fixate on the question. It doesn't matter who you were, or what you did before I knew you. Only the actions you took matter. Only the path you chose. And in the end, the name I know you by is the greatest gift you've given me—given all of us.

Solace.

ACKNOWLEDGEMENTS

Although I'd often dreamt of writing a book, it never seemed attainable. It was always that "wouldn't it be cool if" thing that hung out somewhere in the back of my consciousness. Until November 2021. In the middle of a global pandemic, with a child who was turning four that month, I participated in a novel-writing challenge that I hadn't done since college (far too many years ago) and had never successfully completed. The goal was to write 50,000 words in 30 days. I told myself I would just go as far as I could, and anything would be better than nothing. I had an idea I'd been kicking around off and on since 2019 and had a few scenes drafted, so I decided to work on that project. By the end of November I'd written 75,000 words, and suddenly the idea of writing a *whole book* was well within reach. The first draft of *Fire's Hand, Fate's Heart* was completed less than a month later.

There are many people to thank when it comes to the genesis of *FHFH*, and if I miss anyone in the list below, please know that I'm truly sorry and that I appreciate you even if I blanked on your name while drafting these acknowledgements. I love you and feel free to never let me live it down.

First and foremost, this book wouldn't exist in anything resembling this form without my husband. His ongoing support has been nothing short of herculean. He would talk me down when I worried the whole story was terrible, he was a font of inspiration whenever I got stuck with a plot point, and he helped me create the gods and a few of the places. He also created the original versions of several characters, including Lucien and King Dominic. And he was the one who handed me a character sheet for a thief with no backstory or personality, with only one word written at the top: *Dare.*

I want to thank my parents, who have supported my creative ~~obsessions~~ endeavors my whole life. I wouldn't be who I am without their support and unconditional love. They always encouraged my creative spark, whether it was writing, theater, arts and crafts, or just using my imagination. My dad was the first one to introduce me to some of the great fantasy movies, like "Willow." My mom often bought me blank notebooks, even when she knew I was on a notebook-buying-ban until I filled some of the ones that I already had. Both of them devoured the beta copy of *FHFH* in less than a week and have been asking when book two is coming out pretty much since that day. Thank you for literally everything. I love you both.

Thank you to Sammy, my first writing buddy, whose unhinged comments, keyboard-smash responses, and relentless shipping of Dare and Gregor kept me going in the early days of that first draft.

Thank you to Gina, who's been my best friend, cheerleader, and fangirl all rolled into one. Her encouragement, prolific emoji use, and on-point gif reactions have helped keep me going when I wondered if anyone would care about my silly little weirdos. If at any point during this book you felt like there was too much angst, you should probably blame her.

Thank you to Xander, Justin, Jillian, Kitty, Ryan, Kyle, Veronica, Joe, and Will, who were part of the games where Dare and Verity first came about. Special thanks go to Xander and Justin, whose characters combined to help inspire Drystan, and extra special thanks to Xander for being with me for Dare's original journey to the Black Gates. And thank you to Matt V. who provided inspiration years and years ago for Ainam.

Thank you to my OPAAT friends, Sarah, Hannah, Becca, Lauren, Birgit, Serria, Chera, and Vivian. Your ongoing support and friendship have made a lonely journey a lot less lonely.

Thank you to my editor, Hannah, for her thoughtful suggestions throughout the revision process that absolutely made *FHFH* a stronger book. Thank you for encouraging my "knife-twisting" tendencies.

I want to also thank fellow indie author Ryann Fletcher, whose own journey with publishing the Cricket Chronicles inspired me to pursue indie publication for Five Fates. Sometimes we don't see the impact we have on other people, but it's appreciated all the same.

Thank you to my beta readers who helped polish the story so that it shone. Alyssa, Becca, Brook, Cara, Chera, Gina, Jon, Lauren, Lindsey, Mary, Nancy, Paul, and Sam. Thank you for taking the time and effort to provide feedback.

Lastly, I want to thank my son, who reminds me to stop and see the beauty and wonder in everyday life, even during the darkest times. Your light shines the brightest of all.

ABOUT THE AUTHOR

Lindsey Brounstein worked in the publishing industry for fifteen years and now spends her days as a freelance editor and author in New Hampshire. For as long as she can remember, Lindsey has had a crazy cast of characters kicking around inside her head. Sometimes, she likes to put two of them in the same room to see what happens — which is how Verity and Dare ended up on this adventure. When Lindsey's not writing, she loves immersing herself in both board and video games, knitting and — of course — reading.

You can follow Lindsey on Instagram or Threads as @writerlindsey or you can email her at lins@lindseybrounstein.com. You can also sign up for her newsletter at www.lindseybrounstein.com.

THANK YOU FOR READING

Thank you for reading *Fire's Hand, Fate's Heart.*
If you enjoyed it, please consider leaving a review. Your ratings and comments help indie authors like me reach wider audiences, and they help other readers find books they might love.
Scan the QR code below to connect to various reviewing platforms.

www.ingramcontent.com/pod-product-compliance
Lightning Source LLC
Chambersburg PA
CBHW030332010826
48973CB00004B/968